Praise for *New York Times* bestselling author Lori Foster

"Foster brings her signature blend of heat and sweet to her addictive third Ultimate martial arts contemporary."
—*Publishers Weekly* on *Tough Love* (starred review)

"Readers will be thrilled with Foster's new sexy batch of fight club heroes and the women who love them."
—*Kirkus Reviews* on *No Limits*

"Storytelling at its best! Lori Foster should be on everyone's auto-buy list."
—#1 *New York Times* bestselling author Sherrilyn Kenyon on *No Limits*

"Foster's writing satisfies all appetites with plenty of searing sexual tension and page-turning action in this steamy, edgy, and surprisingly tender novel."
—*Publishers Weekly* on *Getting Rowdy*

"Foster hits every note (or power chord) of the true alpha male hero."
—*Publishers Weekly* on *Bare It All*

"A sexy, believable roller coaster of action and romance."
—*Kirkus Reviews* on *Run the Risk*

"Bestseller Foster...has an amazing ability to capture a man's emotions and lust with sizzling sex scenes and meld it with a strong woman's point of view."
—*Publishers Weekly* on *A Perfect Storm*

"Foster rounds out her searing trilogy with a story that tilts toward the sizzling and sexy side of the genre."
—*RT Book Reviews* on *Savor the Danger*

"Steamy, edgy, and taut."
—*Library Journal* on *When You Dare*

LORI FOSTER

FIGHTING DIRTY

AN ULTIMATE NOVEL

HQN™

ISBN-13: 978-0-373-78917-7

Recycling programs for this product may not exist in your area.

Fighting Dirty

This edition published by arrangement with Harlequin Books S.A.

For questions and comments about the quality of this book, please contact us at CustomerService@Harlequin.com.

® and TM are trademarks of Harlequin Enterprises Limited or its corporate affiliates. Trademarks indicated with ® are registered in the United States Patent and Trademark Office, the Canadian Intellectual Property Office and in other countries.

www.HQNBooks.com

Printed in U.S.A.

Dear Reader,

I'm so excited to finally bring you Armie's book!

Every ongoing series I've written seems to have had that one fan-favorite secondary character—the hero readers can't wait to see finally get a happy-ever-after. In the case of my Ultimate series, about mixed martial arts (MMA) fighters and the women they fall for, it's safe to say that Armie Jacobson stole the show. With his cocky charm, strict code of honor, dedication to his friends, and boundless appreciation for the female population (not to mention his awesome T-shirt collection), Armie definitely leaves his mark.

But Armie is more than just a good-time guy. Those of you who've read the previous books in the Ultimate series—*Hard Knocks*, *No Limits*, *Holding Strong* and *Tough Love*—have seen Armie privately begin to grapple with both demons from the past and his fierce attraction to Merissa Colter, the one woman he believes is forever out of his reach. In *Fighting Dirty*, those internal battles take center ring as Armie is forced to contend with old scars...and come to terms with his love for Merissa once and for all.

His road hasn't been an easy one, but I hope you'll find his story was worth the wait.

Fingers and toes crossed that you enjoy Armie and Merissa's romance. And of course, you're always welcome to reach out to me. I'm active on most social media forums including Facebook, Twitter, Pinterest and Goodreads, and my email address is listed on my website at lorifoster.com.

Happy reading to all,

Lori Foster

PS: Some of you will recognize Jude Jamison from his own book, *Jude's Law*. He was the first MMA fighter I wrote, so it seemed appropriate to let him pop in for a few cameos!

Here's to awesome reader Kizzie Brown,
who allowed me to "borrow" her name so that
she could be one of the more persistent,
outrageous ladies from Armie's past. Kizzie,
I hope you enjoy your small role in the book. And
please accept my thanks for all the terrific reviews.
I hope my stories never disappoint you!

CHAPTER ONE

"Jesus, Quick. You're a freak of nature. You know that, right?"

Armie Jacobson, known as Quick to his fighter friends, ignored the complaint and threw a few more jabs, then a solid body shot, making Justice, a six-foot-five heavyweight, double over. Stepping back, Armie flexed his hands, bounced on the balls of his feet and waited.

Unfortunately, Justice only put his hands on his knees and sucked air.

Frowning, Armie removed his mouthpiece. "Seriously? Come on, dude. Let's go."

"Screw you." Schlepping back to his corner, Justice grabbed up a water bottle. He doused his head and chest and then started chugging.

Aware of others watching, Armie said nothing. Everyone worked out, trained and sparred in the rec center, but lately, whenever he did, a dozen or more people stopped to watch. He didn't mind an audience. Hell, he couldn't be a competitor if he did. For the most part he paid no attention. Once he got in the cage, he went into a zone and the world receded.

But this insane ogling shit, as if he was a damned sideshow, bugged him big-time.

A trickle of sweat tracked down his temple from

his headgear, and he swiped a forearm over his face. His muscles burned and more sweat soaked his chest, abs and rolled down his spine. He was figuring out what to say to Justice to get him back in action when he picked up *her* scent. The faint perfume cut through the rec center air, thick with the smells of sweaty men working hard.

Trying to look casual, Armie stared at Justice but in his peripheral vision he saw her striding across the room. No mistaking that long-legged gait, or that longer dark hair. He swallowed, frozen.

"What?" Justice asked, sounding both suspicious and ridiculously alarmed with the way Armie had locked onto him.

Armie shook his head—and thankfully Merissa disappeared into the hallway leading to the offices.

Releasing a breath, he looked toward the clock and frowned. Yeah, they'd been at it for a while, maybe longer than he'd intended. His cardio was better than most, definitely better than Justice's, the big lug.

Armie walked over to him. "You need to get more gas in the tank."

"Go fuck yourself."

When Armie grinned, Justice eyed him warily. "Stop it."

That switched his grin to a frown. "Bitchy much?"

Justice slouched against the wall and glared back. "You shouldn't be able to grin, you prick. You should be as tired as me."

A natural trainer, Armie took pity on him. "You're a lot bigger." As a six-foot-tall middleweight, Armie stood five inches shorter and weighed a lot less than Justice.

"Lotta good it does me."

Squatting down in front of him, Armie said low, "People are watching, so stop whining."

Justice's gaze slipped past him and he groaned.

"Yeah, the big dogs are here again." Damned nosy bastards. Ever since he'd signed with the SBC, the powers-that-be had been scoping him out like their newest lab rat. "Stand up, go another two minutes with me, then we'll call it quits."

Huffing out a breath, Justice lumbered to his feet. "Freak of nature," he muttered again, but he followed Armie out to the center of the ring, and he did his best.

His best was nowhere near good enough against Armie.

But then, they fought for very different reasons.

Twenty minutes later, fresh from the showers, Armie was ready to head out. The mid-February weather left frost on every surface, so he tugged on a stocking hat over his still-wet hair and pulled a thick hooded sweatshirt on over his clothes. Carrying his gym bag, he entered the main area cautiously. This late in the day, the mats were now cleared. Miles and Brand took their turn mopping with sanitizer. Many of the lights were turned down and only the core group of friends remained, clustered together in conversation.

The SBC heads were gone, and better still, he didn't see Merissa anywhere. She'd probably just been dropping off paperwork for her brother, Cannon, who owned the rec center.

Relieved, Armie started for the door. With any luck, he'd manage it before someone stopped him—

"Hey, Armie."

Damn. After a slight hesitation, he turned to where

Denver, Stack and Cannon all stood together. "What's this? The three Married Musketeers?"

Stack, who'd only married a month ago, reeked of satisfaction. "Aw, he's jealous."

Yup. But since he'd die before admitting it, Armie said, "Nope."

Denver, still a newlywed himself, grinned. "Probably lonely, too, poor guy."

Very. Groupies, orgies and random one-night stands could only take a guy so far. He had a rep for sexual excess, and that's what the ladies wanted from him. That, and nothing more.

Checking the time, Armie said, "I could be lonely with three very nice ladies if you yahoos would let me leave."

Unlike the others, Cannon didn't laugh. "Seriously? Again?"

Why the hell did his best friend have to sound so disapproving? And if he knew why Armie had made those plans, he'd probably be pissed as well as disapproving, because it was thoughts of Cannon's little sis that he worked so hard to obliterate. Not that a foursome would accomplish much beyond taking the edge off. His obsession with Merissa seemed to amplify by the day.

Copping an attitude, Armie shrugged. "Yeah, really. Unless you have something—" *or someon*e "—better for me to do?"

"As a matter of fact, that's why I wanted to talk to you."

Well hell. He hadn't figured on that. Armie ran a hand over his hair. "Then let's hear it."

"Yvette wanted everyone to come over tonight to hang out and visit."

Armie adored Yvette. She was perfect for Cannon and a real sweetheart. But damn... "Who all will be there?"

With a very knowing smile, Cannon said, "Everyone important to us. So don't miss it."

Double damn. Merissa definitely counted as important.

Armie didn't want to, but with all the guys eyeballing him, how could he refuse? "What time?"

"Now."

Armie scowled. "What do you mean, now?"

"Now, as in you don't have time to do anything else, so forget it."

Justice came dragging out, his faux-hawk hair still wet, his goatee in need of a trim, and his cauliflower ears worse than ever. He shoulder-bumped Armie as he passed. "If you hadn't been determined to cripple me, maybe you'd have had more time for playing."

"Wuss," Armie accused with a grin.

"He has a point," Brand said as he pushed a mop bucket toward them.

Miles, giving one last swipe of the mat, followed him. "Keep pushing that hard and you're liable to hurt something before the competition."

"I still have two months." Two months of freedom and he'd spend it however he wanted. Sure, Armie knew there were established training methods, but they weren't for him. Never had been, never would be—no matter who he fought for.

"This isn't local fighting anymore," Denver reminded him.

As if he'd forget.

"Carter Fletcher isn't a slouch," Miles added. "You might not walk through him like you do the local guys."

"They call him Chaos for a reason." Brand frowned. "I've seen him fight and he's unpredictable."

Yeah, so his first opponent was supposed to be a stud. Big deal. Armie shrugged to show he didn't really care. Not that long ago the SBC, the most widely known MMA organization, had run him to ground and all but coerced him into signing on with them. Cannon had helped with that, pushing him to take the next step since he'd already demolished all the records in local venues.

It was a big step, too, something all the other guys had worked for. The SBC paid a lot more and offered incredible name recognition. Their fighters traveled the world to compete.

But Armie liked being low-key; it was a hell of a lot safer for multiple reasons. If it wasn't for Cannon—

"He'll do fine against Carter," Cannon said. "And don't worry about his training. Armie motivates differently, that's all."

Always, no matter what, Cannon had his back. As the only other person to know why he'd avoided fame and fortune, Cannon understood. They weren't related, but they were brothers all the same.

Which was the second biggest reason he couldn't, shouldn't, crave Merissa the way he did. Cannon protected those he loved.

And he loved his sister a lot.

"It's getting late," Cannon added. "Don't want to keep Yvette waiting."

Glad for the switch in topic, Armie pulled out his phone. "Guess I better make some calls and let the ladies know I won't make it after all."

Stack looked at Denver. "If it was anyone but Armie, I'd think he was making it up."

"Lonely," Denver confirmed.

Armie walked away knowing they were right.

MERISSA COLTER LEANED against the counter in the kitchen, sipping a wine cooler and watching as Yvette prepared a platter of lunch meat and cheeses. "You sure you don't want my help?"

Yvette flashed her a happy smile. "There's not that much to do. Besides, you're dressed so cute tonight, I don't want to risk you getting messy."

Looking down at herself, Merissa said, "I just felt like a change, you know?"

Smile sly, Yvette nodded, then wiped her hands on the apron she wore. "It's nice for a lady to switch things up every now and then. And with your long legs, that's a good look for you."

"Vanity shopped with me." Vanity was Yvette's best friend, now Stack's wife, and a regular fashion plate without trying. "She insisted on the boots."

"With heels," Yvette enthused, since Merissa almost always wore flats. "I approve."

"It's just that I'm so blasted tall—"

"Like a model."

"I don't know." More often than not, she felt gangly, not model-worthy.

"Trust me," Yvette said as she laid out the last pieces of cheese on her lunch-meat display. "You'd be terrific. Everything you wear looks amazing on you. You're slim but still shapely."

Merissa choked over that. "I'm barely in a B cup. Nothing shapely about that."

From the kitchen doorway came a sound and Merissa looked up to see Brand, Miles and Leese all standing there grinning at her. They were all three gorgeous, all three buff, all three talented.

But none of them were Armie.

How she felt about them, and vice versa, wasn't anything close to romantic. But still, heat rushed into her face. After all, they'd just heard her discussing her boobs.

Looking around for a weapon, Merissa grabbed up the dishcloth and threw it at them. "Pretend you didn't hear that!"

"Too late." Leese caught the towel, then carried it over to the sink. "Whatever you think you're missing, let me tell you, it's all there." He looked back at the other two fighters. "Am I right?"

"Hell, yeah."

"Definitely."

Humiliated, but appreciating their input, Merissa laughed. "You guys are my friends. You have to say that."

Crossing his heart, Leese insisted, "Honest truth." He snagged three beers from the fridge, then tossed one to Brand and the other to Miles.

With his sinfully dark gaze moving over her, Brand stepped farther into the kitchen. "And that getup?" He cocked a brow. "Smokin' hot."

She suddenly felt very conspicuous in her V-necked tunic sweater, tights and ankle boots.

"There, you see?" Yvette said. "You're gorgeous. Who cares if you're not top-heavy?"

She cared.

"It's the whole package," Miles insisted. He and

Brand both had dark hair, but Miles's eyes were bright green, his smile crooked, and he flirted with every woman alive. "Trust me."

Leese ran a hand over his inky-black hair, his pale blue eyes playful. "I'm an ass man, myself." He winked, letting her know she fit the bill.

It was a wonder she could think at all when surrounded by so many certified hunks. Maybe if she felt about one of them the way she felt about Armie, her life would be easier.

Yvette started forcing them all from the kitchen. "Stop embarrassing her."

"We were reassuring her," Brand protested.

The guys dragged their feet, making Yvette work at getting them clear of the door. After they'd gone, Yvette's smile lingered and her eyes were warm with happiness.

Merissa knew something was going on. Both her brother and Yvette *glowed*. Setting aside her wine cooler, she asked, "So, what's up with you and Cannon?"

Humming, Yvette got down a bowl and filled it with chips. "I don't know what you mean."

"Uh-huh."

Just then Armie stuck his head in the kitchen. "Hey, Yvette..." His voice trailed off when he spotted Merissa.

Expression arrested, Armie's attention crawled down her body, taking in every detail. His chest expanded on a slow breath. Merissa didn't move. Seeing him had an entirely different effect on her than she'd had with the other men. Just about everyone had commented on her new duds. But this was Armie. She didn't want his opinion to matter—yet it did.

Belatedly, his gaze came back up to her face and locked with hers. His jaw flexed. His dark eyes consumed her and just when she thought she'd pass out from lack of oxygen, he started to turn away.

Clearly Armie hadn't expected to see her and hadn't wanted to see her. It hurt.

Yvette stopped him. "Armie! Come on in. What would you like to drink?"

With his back to them, he stalled. Muscles shifted in his shoulders, his upper arms—then he very deliberately relaxed and faced them again. The heat in his eyes had cooled to indifference and his cocky smile almost made her believe she'd imagined the tension. "I'm good."

Merissa snorted. She didn't mean to. It just came out.

His dark sinner's gaze zeroed back in on her. "Something funny, Stretch?"

God, how she hated that nickname! It emphasized her height, but worse, it proved that Armie didn't see her as a desirable woman. "You? Being good?" She snorted again. "I hope I'm not standing close when lightning strikes you."

Stepping the rest of the way into the kitchen, he said to Yvette, "I'll take a beer."

"Sure." Yvette poured an unsweetened tea. She handed it to Armie, kissed his cheek, then picked up the platter and carried it to the dining room.

Nonplussed, Armie looked at the glass.

Merissa looked at Armie.

Until recently he'd kept his hair bleached almost white, but lately he'd left it alone and now it was back to a more natural dark blond. Still a little spiky, but not such a dramatic contrast to his chocolate-brown eyes.

Tattoos lined his forearms, and though she couldn't see it right now, not with him wearing a shirt, she knew he had another, more understated tat between his shoulder blades.

Faded jeans sat low on his lean hips, hanging a little long over running shoes. Boldly displayed across the front of his snug-fitting black T-shirt were the words FREE ORGASMS.

Merissa cleared her throat. "Don't like tea?"

"Not particularly." He set the tea aside and went to the fridge.

With his head stuck inside, Merissa felt free to look over his body. Her gaze went to those colorful tribal tattoos decorating his thick forearms up to his elbows. She didn't mind them, but she loved the smooth, taut skin over his biceps more. For one startling second his shirt pulled up and she saw a strip of flesh above the waistband of his boxers. Muscles shifted everywhere, sending liquid heat to burn through her system.

She fanned her face. "Yvette is trying to save you from yourself."

"Lost cause," Armie muttered as he stepped away with a beer and closed the refrigerator. Leaning back on the table, he popped the tab, lifted the beer to his mouth—and Yvette snatched it away as she reentered the kitchen.

Very sweetly, she said, "Cannon told me you're on a strict diet for your upcoming fight."

"It's two months away!"

"Cannon said you'd say that."

"Yeah?" His eyes narrowed as he looked around. "Where is your husband?"

Ignoring his implied threat, Yvette laughed.

Armie gave up the hard act. "One beer won't hurt anything, honey." He took it back from her. "Promise."

Yvette didn't look convinced, but she gave in. "All right. *One*." She slanted her gaze to Merissa. "Do me a favor, Rissy, and make sure he behaves."

Merissa sputtered, but Yvette had already walked off with the chips, again leaving her alone in the kitchen with Armie.

His expression carefully blank, his muscles tensed, Armie looked at her.

She let out a long, dramatic sigh. "One Mississippi. Two Mississippi. Three Mis—"

He frowned. "What are you doing?"

"Seeing how long it takes you to panic and run."

He took a step back. "I don't *panic*."

"Bull." She pushed away from the counter and saw his eyes flare. "Ever since that ill-fated kiss a few months ago, you see me and hightail it in the opposite direction. But don't worry, Armie. You're safe from my evil clutches. I got the message loud and clear." Leaving her drink on the counter, she started off.

Armie caught her arm.

Just that. His big hand wrapped around her upper arm, warm, strong. Gentle but firm.

Her back to him, her heartbeat thundering, Merissa waited. He said nothing, but after a few seconds his thumb moved over her skin. It almost stopped her heart, and how pathetic was that? He didn't want her. He'd made it as plain as he could. Back in November he'd kissed her, and then immediately told her it was a mistake. Now it was February and in all that time he'd barely even looked at her.

"I don't mean to run you off." He stepped closer. Close enough that she felt the warmth of his body.

Shoring up her resistance, forcing herself to remember her new resolve, Merissa turned to face him. Her height and the small heels on her boots put her on a level with him.

He stared into her eyes, and then down at her mouth.

Desperate yearning stole her breath and turned her denial into a whisper. "No."

"No?" he asked, just as softly.

Flattening both hands to the front of that ridiculous shirt, her palms over his solid chest, she stepped him back. "You kissed me once. Felt like you meant it at the time—until you got all disgusted."

His chin hitched. "Disgusted? Not even."

Undeterred, Merissa pressed a fist to her heart. "You leveled me, Armie. You made me feel terrible. Over a *single kiss.* So yeah, I get it. You don't want me. Understood. Believe me, I don't want to put myself through that again."

Before she could move he caught her arm once more.

She stared at him, waiting, some small part still hopeful that he'd say something to change it all.

He didn't. His gaze shuttered, his jaw working, he fought himself. And then, as if by force of will, he opened his fingers and turned her loose.

Almost choking on her hurt, Merissa turned to leave—and nearly crashed into her brother. His muscular little mutt, Muggles, yapped at her.

Cannon took one look at her and drew her into his side. "Hey, you okay?"

Armie made to move past them, but without accusation, Cannon blocked him.

Merissa muttered, "I'm taking off. It was a long day and I'm beat."

He kissed her forehead. "All right." Turning to Armie, he included them both when he said, "Yvette has an announcement to make first."

Keeping his arm around her, Cannon led her to the living room. Muggles ran up to Yvette, who stood at the front of the room with that giddy smile back on her face. All around her were their friends Denver and Cherry, Stack and Vanity, Gage and Harper. The single guys— Leese, Justice, Brand and Miles—had all arrived solo, so maybe they'd known this would be a party with an intimate announcement.

Guessing their news, Merissa found another smile, too. "Go on," she told Cannon. "I'm fine."

He hugged her, then joined Yvette up front. He scooped up the dog in one arm and put his other around his wife.

Feeling a little giddy herself, Merissa ignored Armie at her side and just concentrated on her brother's happiness.

Leaning her head on Cannon's shoulder, Yvette said, "I'm pregnant!"

And Cannon, so much in love, added with satisfaction, "We're having a baby."

The cheers were nearly deafening, and that set Muggles to howling in excitement, his pudgy legs pumping as he tried to run. Everyone started hugging everyone else and somehow… Yeah. Merissa ended up against Armie.

He looked as stunned as she felt, but only for a second. Then he grinned, hugged her off her feet and whirled her. When he set her back down, his grin tapered off to a fond smile. "You're going to be an aunt."

"A baby." Tears pricked her eyes and her own smile kept twitching. "I can't wait."

When Cannon regained everyone's attention, they faced forward again. But this time, Armie slipped his arm over her shoulders. It was so much like the old days when she'd been younger and Armie was always around, teasing her and looking out for her. Just being there. Emotions swelled.

"I've known for a little while now," Yvette said.

That got everyone playfully complaining.

"We had Denver's fight, and then he and Cherry got married," Cannon explained. "Then Stack and Vanity turned Vegas into a wedding, and we figured that was all good news enough."

"Ours could wait," Yvette said. "But now I'm so glad to share."

"Must be something in the air," Vanity said. "Stack's sister is expecting, too."

Denver cocked a brow at Cherry, but she hurriedly said, "No. Not me. I'm enjoying being a wife for a while."

Vanity saluted her. "Hear, hear."

For the next hour everyone chatted and laughed, discussing everything from names to nursery furniture to a baby shower. The food Yvette had set out got devoured in record time and overall, the mood remained jovial. After she'd put in enough time for Cannon and Yvette to know she was thrilled with their news, Merissa decided to slip away. Or at least, she tried to. Armie followed her without being obvious to others. She, of course, was acutely aware of his nearness. If he looked at her, she felt it like a warm touch. Whenever he brushed against her, it hit her like a jolt. Maybe he could take it, but she couldn't.

For the sake of her own pride, she needed away from him. Right now.

Yet when she hugged her brother and Yvette good-bye, Armie was there. She pulled on her coat and bumped into him. Without bothering to button up, intent only on escape, Merissa darted outside.

Finally alone, she paused a moment and concentrated on regrouping. The brisk evening air stung her nose and a chilling wind cut through her. She closed her coat and turned up the collar.

She'd just taken a deep breath when the door opened again and Armie stepped out.

The porch light illuminated them and part of the yard with its yellow glow. In nothing but his T-shirt, shoulders up against the cold, Armie watched her.

"What," Merissa demanded, "are you doing?"

He shoved his hands into the pockets of his jeans. "I wanted to talk a second."

No and no. She didn't want to talk. She already knew what he'd say anyway. "Not necessary." She turned and headed to her car, and damn him, he stayed right on her heels. At the curb she spun to face him. "Armie!"

One side of his mouth curled. "Rissy."

She threw up her hands in an expression of frustration.

He rubbed one eye, the back of his neck. Dropping his hands, he stared at her. "That kiss?"

Shocked, all the air dragged from her lungs, she went still.

"From a few months ago," he clarified, as if she

didn't remember, as if it didn't replay in her mind almost nonstop, every single day. "In Rowdy's bar?"

"Right. I remember." Although she often wished she could forget.

She'd tried hitting on Leese, just to shake off her melancholy over Armie. But Leese was a pretty awesome guy and he'd let her down easy, while making it clear he'd be on board except he knew her heart was elsewhere. Since then, she and Leese had become even closer friends.

"What about that kiss?"

For the longest time Armie stared at her, then he stepped closer and breathed, "Hottest fucking thing I've ever felt."

Oh God. She couldn't hear this. She couldn't feed the hope.

"I'm going to be straight with you."

Her heart punched. "Okay."

"There's not a thing in this universe I'd enjoy more than having you."

Having her? Just hearing him say it made her body react.

He touched her hair, smoothed it back over her shoulder. "Not winning the lottery. Not a title belt. Nothing."

His thumb moved over her neck and her pulse leaped.

"I've thought about it," he whispered. "A lot."

"Me, too."

"Shh." He touched a fingertip to her lips to quiet her. "I seriously doubt we're thinking the same things."

She badly wanted to know what he thought. Armie was known for his sexual excesses and the variety of his experience. Far too often she tortured herself wondering what things Armie might want to do with her.

"And that's the problem," he added.

She wanted to cry that there was no problem, but she could already see he wouldn't listen.

"I want you, Rissy. That should never be in question." He held her chin, searched her face, and repeated, *"Never."*

And there it was: unrelenting hope. Unsure what to say, she nodded.

"But more than that, I want you to have better than me."

Wait... *"What?"* He couldn't be serious. Better than him? Did he not know what an amazing man he was? How could that be? He had friends who cared about him. He had Cannon, and damn it, her brother was the finest man she knew. Cannon wouldn't be best friends with a man who wasn't every bit as awesome.

"I know you're leaving your brother's house because of me, and that's the last thing that should ever happen. I don't want to chase you away from your family. I don't want to make you feel bad."

"Too late."

His face tightened. He dropped his hands and took a step back. "This is where you have to help me." Looking far too serious, he said, "I don't ever want to hurt you—you have to know that. So you need to get your priorities straight."

She shook her head—but he said it anyway.

"Move on. Find yourself a good guy. Hell..." He choked a little, then whispered, "Settle down, get married, have kids of your own."

Without him.

That's what he meant. Do all of that—*without him.*

A refreshing wave of anger helped to smother some of the awful pain. "You think I can't?"

"I know you can." He swallowed. "Any man would be lucky to have you."

That made her laugh. Any man—other than him. "Did you notice my new look? I mean, all the other guys did."

Very quietly, he confirmed, "I noticed."

"Well, that's me, moving on." She flipped her hair. "New look, new attitude. I might even take a new position at the bank." A different managerial position that would give her some distance from Armie. Sucked that she'd also be farther away from her brother—especially since she'd soon be an aunt—but she didn't know any other way. "I've decided to take a page from your book, Armie."

"Jesus."

"What? You think you're the only one to play the field, to get a little wild? I want experiences, too." She'd wanted those experiences with him, but never would she beg him. "Go on about your life with a clear conscience—because I'll be going on with mine."

Jerking away, she got in her car and fumbled for her keys. Armie stood there, rigid, his gaze unreadable. And somehow, despite being a real badass, he looked wounded.

Finally, when she got the car started, Armie walked off, across the street in front of her to the other curb, where he got in his truck. Breathing hard, Merissa stared at him until he gunned the engine and pulled away.

Going the opposite direction of her. Always.

And damn it, it cut so deep she couldn't stop the tears. Because this time she knew it was over—when it had never really begun.

CHAPTER TWO

MID-FEBRUARY TURNED INTO early March and Armie didn't see Rissy at all. Not at the rec center, not at Rowdy's bar where everyone usually hung out on Friday and Saturday night, and not at her brother's house. He wanted to ask about her but knew he didn't have the right.

Sitting alone at the bar, drinking a freaking lemon water, he only half listened as Miles and Brand talked about upcoming fights at the table opposite him. Women tried to get his attention but he didn't have any interest. He'd put up a good front, given it a shot several times, and he'd probably convinced everyone with his bullshit, but the truth was that he hadn't had any real interest in a good long while.

Not since that day he'd finally tasted Rissy.

His gaze went to the small hallway in Rowdy's bar. Dim and narrow, it led to an office and the johns. Months ago he'd caught Rissy there and for a few minutes he'd lost the fight. Mouth on mouth, tongues playing, damp heat and a firestorm of sensation. Remembering, he closed his eyes and gave in to the surge of molten lust. God Almighty, she'd tasted good. Felt good. Fit against him perfectly.

An elbow to his ribs got his eyes open again. Instead

of one of the guys, it was Vanity, Stack's wife, who slid onto a stool beside him. "What?" he asked.

"You tell me," she said, her gaze unwavering, her nails tapping on the bar counter.

Gorgeous beyond words with long blond hair, a killer body and an angel's face, Vanity was still one of the most down-to-earth, kindhearted people he knew. "Is that supposed to make sense to me, Vee?"

"Yes. You're moping and I want to know why."

Stack stood behind his wife and braced an arm on the bar. "It's the upcoming fight," Stack predicted. "He's getting cold feet."

"No way," Justice said, taking a seat behind Armie.

Armie looked back and forth between them. "Sure, join me. Make yourselves comfortable."

Vanity patted his arm in a pitying way. "We don't stand on formality, not when we see a friend moping."

"I'm not moping," he denied. God, he was *so* moping.

Justice laughed. "I've watched five different women hit on you. All fuckable—excuse me, Vanity—and you made excuses to all of them."

"No offense taken," Vanity said, and then to Armie, "Seriously? Are you off the market?"

She looked way too pleased by that notion.

Stack laughed. "That's even more ridiculous than my gibe about him having cold feet."

A brunette approached the bar and Armie swallowed a groan. Of course he remembered her, but he pretended he didn't.

Because he was a dick like that.

"Armie?" Ignoring the others, she trailed a finger up his arm and over his shoulder. "I'm free tonight."

"Yeah?" Armie looked at Justice. "So is he. You two should hook up."

Justice straightened. "Gospel truth, ma'am."

The brunette's eyes narrowed. "I was talking to you, Armie."

"And I handed you off. Take it or leave it."

Vanity slugged him.

Stack coughed.

Justice just looked hopeful.

The brunette asked expectantly, "Will you join us?"

"No!" Justice said quickly. "He won't."

Armie looked at the lady's pout, Vanity's disapproving expression, Justice's appalled frown, and he had to laugh. "If you'll all excuse me?"

Paying no attention to questions, he threw some bills on the bar and took off. Halfway toward the door, Miles called out to him.

Armie kept going.

Two women tried to waylay him, but he pretended not to notice. Once outside, he sucked in the cold evening air, but it did nothing to clear his head. And suddenly, without looking behind him, he knew Cannon was there. "Shit."

Cannon laughed. "You're okay to drive?"

Working to clear all emotion from his face, Armie turned to his friend. "Can't get drunk on nasty lemon water, now can I?"

"Is that what you wanted to do? Get drunk?"

No, he wanted to drag Merissa to bed and keep her there until his blood no longer burned and lurid thoughts of her cleared out of his brain. He popped his neck, shook his head and said, "I don't know."

"It's not the fight." Folding his arms, Cannon leaned

back on the outside wall of Rowdy's bar. "I know you too well to think you're concerned about Carter."

"I'll either win the fight or not. I'm prepared." Armie shrugged, showing his indifference. He never thought in terms of winning or losing. Just winning. And to that end he did what he needed to do to ensure success.

"Everyone assumes there's added pressure because you'll be in the SBC now. But again," Cannon stated, "I know you better than that."

"A fight is a fight," Armie confirmed. "The size of the crowd—"

"Or the size of the paycheck?"

"—doesn't matter to me."

"I know." Cannon lifted a brow. "So you want to tell me what's eating at you?"

A bad case of desperate lust for your little sister. Not something he'd ever share. Rather than deny the problem, Armie shook his head. "I'll deal with it."

"By avoiding sex?"

He jutted his chin. "Who says I am?"

Cannon didn't blink. "Man, I know you. Better than anyone. You thought I wouldn't notice when you went cold turkey?"

That so shocked Armie that he took a step back. He couldn't think of a single thing to say. If he tried to blame it on fight preparation, Cannon would just laugh at him again. "I don't suppose you'd butt out?"

"Sure. If that's what you really want." Cannon straightened away from the wall. "But if you want to talk, if you need anything—"

"I know." Once, a lifetime ago, Cannon had been the only person to back him. Against all odds and ugly accusations, he'd stood with Armie and never, not once, showed a single shadow of doubt. Uncomfortable with the idea of ever again being that needy, Armie flexed his shoulders and said, "Thanks, but it's fine."

"I know that." Cannon squeezed his shoulder. "You just need to start believing it."

Armie glared at his friend as he went back into the bar. He didn't need that melodramatic crap heaped on him. Breathing hard, he looked around at the moon-washed blacktop, the frost-covered bus bench, then up at the inky, star-studded sky.

What was Merissa doing right now? Was she with another man—as he'd suggested?

It's what he wanted, what would be best—for her—but at the same time... Jesus, it tortured him.

After the life he'd led, the background he'd overcome and the physical ability he'd gained, he wasn't afraid of anything or anyone, except Merissa Colter's effect on him. That scared him all right. Bone-deep, heart-sucking fear.

He glanced back, and through the big front window of the bar he saw his friends. *Merissa's friends.* Only she wasn't there—because of him.

It was past time he stopped being a coward so instead he'd face the fear. Tomorrow morning, he'd face *her*.

And somehow he'd make it all right.

MOST PEOPLE THOUGHT bank managers worked a perfect nine-to-five job. Ha! As Merissa looked from the impatient customers still in line to her harassed tellers and the clock, she knew it'd be another late day. What should have been five minutes more would likely turn into at least half an hour.

The phone rang, and as she went to answer it the

front door opened again. Along with a gust of cold air, two male customers stepped in, bundled up in heavy winter coats and stocking hats, with thick knit scarves around their throats.

Right behind them was…Armie.

Unlike the other men, he wore only an open flannel over his thermal shirt. His cheeks were ruddy from the cold, his blond hair disheveled as usual, and he looked so good her heart skipped a beat, then went into double time.

For weeks now she'd been telling herself she was okay—better, in fact—without him. She'd almost convinced herself, too. But one look at him and she was right back to sick-in-love with him all over again.

"Hello? Are you there?"

Realizing she hadn't said anything after lifting the phone receiver, Merissa pulled her gaze away from Armie and went into professional mode. Or at least she tried to.

The second Armie looked at her, her skin prickled and butterflies took flight in her stomach. She sank back in her padded chair, glad for the support.

The annoyed customer had overdrawn his account and wanted the bank to waive the fees. Merissa only listened with half an ear and finally, unable to concentrate anyway, she agreed and transferred the call over to one of her tellers.

Since it was now time to close she needed to lock the door, but that would mean she'd have to go past Armie. She waffled, deciding what to do, but then he took the decision from her and approached.

Jumping to her feet, she met him at the door to her office. As casually as she could, she said, "Hey, Armie."

His gaze dipped over her. This time, being at work, she wore a button-front sweater, long skirt and flat boots, but his attention sizzled all the same. He flexed a shoulder, shifted. "Could we talk?"

Again? Hadn't he said enough? For someone who wanted nothing to do with her, he sure liked to chat.

"Armie," she whispered, feeling conspicuous, because seriously, no one in the bank would overlook him. He had that type of presence: big, badass, capable. And sexy.

So damned sexy.

He continued to watch her in that sharply focused way, his gaze warm and steady, and she caved. "Okay, fine. But I have to lock the front door, and then it's going to take me some more time before I'm done here."

"Because you're closing, I know. No problem." He released a breath. "I'll wait."

As Armie headed to the couch in the corner of the bank, one of the men who'd come in ahead of him strode toward her. Standing at her office door, ready to politely redirect him back to the teller line, Merissa smiled—and he literally pushed his way in.

Incredulous, she took an automatic step away from him. "What do you think you're doing?"

He shut the door. Hat pulled low, the scarf hiding most of his face, he withdrew a gun and said with silky menace, "Shh."

Her mouth went dry—especially when those narrowed eyes coasted over her body.

"But—"

"You and me," he said, shushing her again, "are going to play in here while my buddy takes care of business out there. And, honey, you better play nice."

Fear and shock immobilized Merissa as she realized she was in the middle of a robbery—and oh dear God, Armie was on the other side of the door.

THE SECOND HER office door snapped shut, Armie knew something was wrong. He felt it in his guts. He took one step—and the dude in front of him withdrew a gun.

Son of a bitch.

"Everyone be cool," the man shouted, stepping back to encompass all the customers and tellers in one sweep of that weapon. "Arms up, tellers. *Now!* My partner has your manager. Anyone hits a panic button and she's the first to go."

Until that last statement, Armie might have let it play out. But at the mention of Merissa being held against her will, dread and rage swirled together in a combustible mix. He went rigid, his heartbeat slowing, his focus narrowing.

"No one overreacts. Tellers, unlock your drawers, and remember, make a wrong move and you lose one of your own."

White-faced, the tellers did as told.

"Great. Now everyone, get to this side of the room."

Perfect, Armie thought. It put him closer to Merissa's office. He went along with the small group, using his body to block the elderly couple in front of him and another woman clutching a five-year-old. The last customer, a college-aged guy, watched the robber with sharp-eyed wariness. Two of the tellers were forty-something women. The other was probably in her twenties.

The robber aimed his gun at the younger guy. "You."

College boy froze.

"Go collect the money. Empty the drawers of bills and rolled quarters. Make it fast."

The young man said nothing, just took the bag the robber handed him and jogged to the teller line. As he filled the bag, Armie saw that he also kept an eye on things, looking up often.

A noise, like someone landing up against the door, sounded in Merissa's office. Armie's senses sharpened further, but otherwise he didn't move.

The idiot robber laughed, as if amused by whatever he thought might be going down in that small office.

The five-year-old started to cry, drawing the robber's attention. Armie stepped in front of him, blocking his view of the boy. Surprised, the robber looked into his eyes, and whatever he saw there clearly alarmed him.

"Don't try it," the robber warned.

Armie held up his hands—but he didn't look away.

"Give me the damn money," the thug shouted, and the college guy came back, holding the bag out to him.

"Set it there," he said, indicating a kiosk filled with deposit and withdrawal slips. "Then get your ass over there with the others."

"Okay, sure."

Impressed, Armie watched the young man set the bag down slowly and back away. College boy looked to be nineteen or twenty at the most, but he was smart, taking his time—giving Armie an opportunity to evaluate things.

The gunman looked skittish. Above the scarf, faded blue eyes repeatedly flinched left and right. The hand holding the gun trembled ever so slightly. He kept shifting his feet as if resisting the urge to run.

Rolling a shoulder, Armie loosened up. Should be a piece of cake.

Another thump sounded in the office and Merissa cried out, sending a stab of fear straight through Armie's heart and stealing what little patience he had left. Taking a step away from the others, Armie regained the robber's attention. The college kid, pitching in, went in the opposite direction.

"What are you doing?" Panicked, the thug swung the gun left, then right. "Stop moving. Both of you."

Making sure the idiot focused on him and only him, Armie inched toward him. "Or what?"

"I'll fucking shoot you, that's what!"

Ice-cold with fury, desperate to see Merissa safe, Armie smirked. "Yeah? With the safety on?" Closer and closer.

The guy breathed fast. Even beneath the thick coat, Armie could see the bellowing of his chest. "Glocks don't have safeties."

"That's not a Glock, asshole."

The second the guy glanced down, Armie kicked out and the gun went flying. It skidded across the floor and under the kiosk. The college kid slid down to his knees, trying to retrieve the gun.

"Help!" the gunman got out a mere second before Armie's fist met his face, sending him wheeling backward, tumbling over his own feet to wipe out on the floor. His head smacked with a thump, dazing him, keeping him from rebounding to his feet.

More noises sounded from the office.

Already charging toward it, Armie whispered, "Get down!" to the other customers, who, except for the college guy, immediately hunkered on the floor together.

That put them to the side of the office door. Armie reached it just as the door flew open. He had only a split second to see Merissa locked in front of the gunman, secured with a meaty arm tight around her throat. Her makeup was smeared, her hair a mess, but her gaze was incendiary. Rage, more than fear, consumed her.

A large bruise already showed on her jaw and she clutched at the restraining arm as if struggling to get air.

The gun, thankfully, wasn't aimed at her.

The man held it outward on a stiffened arm, giving Armie the perfect opportunity to grab the trigger well with his left hand, and strike the man's wrist with his right. The bastard didn't have a chance to get a shot off before Armie had control of the gun.

Cursing, the thug shoved Merissa into Armie, unbalancing them both. He caught her, and as she scrambled to regain her balance, she inadvertently knocked the gun from his hand.

Seeing a ham-sized fist aimed his way, Armie gave her yet another quick push to put her out of harm's way and took the punch to the chin. It snapped his head back, but hell, he could take a punch. He shook it off— then went about demolishing the bastard who'd dared to touch Merissa.

Armie had always been a fast, adaptable fighter. He moved by rote, adjusting as he needed to, dodging blows while landing his own with added force. The robber was big and muscular. Armie felt the bastard's nose crunch, saw blood spray from his mouth.

Women screamed and the five-year-old cried.

The college guy yelled something, and a second later the other gunman, who'd finally regained his wits, hefted a fifteen-pound post from a rope barrier used to keep customers in line. He brought it down across Armie's back.

And mother-fuck, that hurt.

It knocked him to the ground, but it didn't stop him. Hell, his ground game was as good as his stand-up.

Two to one made it a little trickier. Normally he'd consider that a piece of cake, but not with so many possible victims in the way.

The man who'd hurt Merissa tried to kick him in the ribs while he was down. Armie caught his leg and jerked him to his back. He landed awkwardly, cursed and immediately rolled to a less defenseless position.

The man wasn't a slouch. As a fighter, Armie recognized right off that the guy had some training.

Merissa tried to assist him, but Armie barked for her to stay back. College boy tried to edge in, but with fists and legs churning fast, it wasn't easy.

Or necessary.

Both men together were still no match for Armie. He bounced back, regaining his feet just as the second man again swung the heavy post. Armie ducked, but the post clipped him on the forehead, stunning him and sending a trickle of blood into his eyes. He swiped at it, and heard Merissa gasp.

The man who'd followed her into her office had retrieved one of the guns and had it aimed at her, point-blank.

Armie barely remembered moving, but a split second later he stood in front of her, spreading his arms and using his body to shield her.

"Armie," she pleaded.

Blocking out her shaking voice, he kept her tucked behind him, his gaze locked on the gunman. The robber's hat was now gone, his scarf askew. But with his face so mangled from Armie's punches, he didn't need a disguise.

Odds were his own mother wouldn't recognize him right now.

His nose, crooked and covered in blood, had turned a sick shade of purple, matching the shiner on his right eye. His lips were swollen, also bloody. Part of a torn nylon stocking drooped around his neck.

Armie focused on his eyes. They were a clearer blue than his pal's, without an ounce of conscience.

"Armie, *please*." Merissa struggled. "Don't do this!"

With one hand Armie kept her locked behind him. He said nothing. What was there to say?

He'd die before he let her be shot.

The second man pulled at his friend's coat, urging him to flee while they still could. "I hear sirens! We have to *go*."

And still the bastard kept that gun aimed, his indecision thick in the air.

Holding his ground, never breaking eye contact, Armie calmed his breathing and waited to see the verdict.

Those icy-blue eyes smiled at him—and a second later both men bolted.

Armie started to follow, but Merissa fisted both hands in his shirt. "Damn you, no!"

He heard the awful fear in her voice, and reluctantly obeyed her order. When the men disappeared out of sight, Merissa went limp against his back. Soft, warm, *safe*. Armie swallowed, closed his eyes for only a moment, then turned to her.

She could have died.

He clasped her shoulders. "You're okay?"

Mouth firmed, she nodded. Then she thwacked his shoulder. "Are you insane?"

He touched her cheek, and her expression softened. "Oh God, Armie, you're bleeding."

The bastard had hurt her. "It's nothing." Using his shoulder, Armie cleared the blood from his eye, then lightly touched a bruise on her jaw. "Rissy...what happened?"

She crushed herself closer to him, her face in his neck. "Just...give me a second."

Hands shaking, Armie stroked up and down her back. He didn't want his blood on her. He didn't want her tainted in any way. "It's over now." Knowing he could have lost her, his eyes burned as he kissed her temple. "It's over."

"Yes." He felt the deep breath she took and the way she stiffened her shoulders. Suddenly stepping away, she swiped her face and, visibly gathering her thoughts, looked around the bank.

Armie did the same.

The college guy finally retrieved the gun from under the kiosk, but he didn't look keen on using it, thank God. Gingerly, he set it on a stack of deposit slips and was quickly backing away when his eyes widened. "They left the money."

There, on the floor, was the bag with the money still in it. "Unbelievable." Armie grabbed it up, put it in Rissy's office and shut the door.

The tellers were plenty shaken. The little kid clung to his mother, whimpering.

"Everyone okay?"

Pale faces blinked at him. Yeah, unlike Merissa, they

probably weren't used to seeing bloody fights. He lifted the hem of his shirt to clear away more of the mess.

"Thank you, Armie." All business now, Merissa hurried to the front door and locked it. "I'm sorry," she said to one and all. "In case those sirens aren't for us I have to call this in. We all need to stay put until the police get here." Brisk, she strode toward her office. "Armie, the bathroom is through there." She pointed. "Valerie, could you show him, please? He needs to…" She swallowed hard. "To clean up the blood. Could someone find a first-aid kit, please?"

Armie stood there, staring after her. He watched her use the phone, saw her nod and replace the receiver. She went to a cabinet and a few seconds later returned with papers in her shaking hands. "The authorities are on their way." Hastily, she handed out the papers to the other bank employees.

Impressed by her, Armie asked, "What do you have there?"

"Post robbery packets," she answered, and then to her employees, "Read these again and follow procedure."

It amazed Armie to see her like this, so take-charge, so in control despite what had just happened. She got a lollipop for the little boy, cans of Coke for the other customers.

With that handled, she turned back to Armie and blew out a breath while looking him over. Neither he nor Valerie had moved. "Oh, Armie." She took his arm and, treating him like an invalid, started urging him forward.

"Uh…where are you taking me?"

"The bathroom."

"Why?"

"You're hurt and bleeding and just standing there." She stripped his flannel off him and liberally doused the hem under running water in the sink.

Expression far too grave, she gingerly dabbed at the blood from the right side of his face, over his eye and up to his temple. "It looks terrible."

Valerie silently set a first-aid kit on the sink for her.

When she reached for it, he caught her wrists. "Honey, I'm fine."

Her throat worked and she shook her head, her gaze going just past his shoulder.

"Rissy, talk to me."

"I can't believe you did that." Her brows pinched together and her lashes lowered. "You almost dared him—"

"Shh." That small, broken voice squeezed like a vise around his heart. He stepped closer, letting her feel his strength, proving he was unharmed. Because he needed to know, and she maybe needed to talk, he said, "The bastard hit you?"

She nodded.

Glancing at the popped button on her sweater, he strangled on fury but kept his tone soft. "He attacked you?"

Her face tightened and she swallowed convulsively. "He… He said he wanted to—"

"Cops are here!"

"College boy," Armie said, hoping to lighten her mood. "I like him."

Her tensed shoulders loosened with the interruption, and she turned brisk again. "Yes. He was helpful." She rinsed her hands in the sink. "I have to go."

"I know. We'll talk later?"

At that she half laughed.

"What?"

"You always want to talk." Shaking her head, she left the small room and hurried to the front to unlock the door. Two uniformed cops came in, guns drawn, but after a few questions and a quick look around, they holstered their weapons and began separating everyone. One of them tried to insist on calling an ambulance, but Armie shut them down on that. Merissa refused, and nooo way in hell was he leaving her. Besides, he knew his own body well enough to know the thump on his head wasn't anything serious. He might need stitches, but he'd try taping it first.

Shortly after that an FBI agent came in with Detectives Logan Riske and Reese Bareden. Luckily, Armie knew them both through Cannon.

Cannon. Shit. He had to call him. Armie got his phone out, only to find the screen busted. Shit again. Like all the guys from his inner circle, he carried two phones, the second one for emergencies. Because they'd formed a neighborhood watch, the separate phones were set for a distinctive ring so they'd know when one of the others had something urgent going on. But the second phone wasn't in his pocket any longer. He could only assume he'd lost it during the skirmish.

He was looking around for it when Logan approached. "Damn, Armie."

"It's nothing." And he was getting tired of telling that to people.

Logan frowned. "I'll take your word for it." He nodded at the cell phone. "That got broke in the fight?"

"Yeah." His muscles remained too tense and his temples throbbed. "I need to let Cannon know. If he hears about this, he'll die three times before he knows she's okay."

"I'll take care of it. Do me a favor and sit, will you?"

"I want to talk to Merissa—"

Logan stopped him. "Sorry. Protocol. You all have to stay separate until we've gotten your stories. We can't risk anyone's memory being influenced by something someone else says."

Yeah, that made sense. He didn't like it, but he wanted the bastards caught.

He looked around, saw that from the couch he'd be able to see into Merissa's office, where she was currently speaking with the FBI guy. "All right." He worked his jaw, then sat. Using his flannel, he continued to clean off his face, but yeah, that wasn't quite cutting it.

He was a mess and he knew it.

"Stay put." Logan headed to the bathroom but he had his cell to his ear. Returning, he set a stack of paper towels, some wet, some dry, on the small coffee table littered with magazines. "Cannon wants to talk to you."

"Sure." Armie took the phone, saying immediately, "I swear she's okay."

"Logan told me."

Armie recognized that deadly tone from his friend. "You're on your way?"

"Yeah. Logan said all I can do is wait in the car but I want to be there when she's done. Let me know when it's clear to see her, okay?"

"Sure."

Cannon hesitated. "How about you? Logan said your head is busted?"

"Superficial." He didn't mention the strike he'd taken to his back. "I'm fine." Neither of them said it, but a real injury could've screwed him on his SBC debut. Not that missing a fight mattered with Rissy's safety on the line. "Logan's waiting to grill me. She really is okay, so drive careful."

Three hours and a million questions later, with dusting powder everywhere from forensics taking fingerprints, they were finally free to leave. Armie had found his emergency cell kicked under the couch, so he let Cannon know they were coming out.

Meeting his sister at the door, Cannon checked her face and cursed over the darkening bruise there.

Before Cannon could ask any questions, she said, "I'm okay."

He cupped her face, kissed her forehead, then carefully hugged her. "Thank God."

Next he turned to Armie, and blew out a breath. "Damn, man."

"What?"

Eyes narrowed, Cannon checked over Armie much as he had Merissa.

"If you kiss me," Armie said, "we're going to have a problem."

Instead, Cannon gave him a bear hug. Low, he whispered, "Thank you for looking out for her."

"I was there." And they both knew that meant he'd do whatever necessary to protect her.

Cannon turned back to his sister. "I heard the basics from Logan, but I want you to tell me what happened."

She nodded. "I will, but later please. Like…maybe tomorrow? Right now, I just want to get home and shower."

"I guess we can talk in the morning over coffee."

She angled up her chin. "I have to be at work by nine."

Both of them stared at her.

She continued in a brisk tone. "Maybe lunch, if you really want. But honestly, I'd rather wait until after I'm done for the day."

Cannon spoke first, saying, "You can't go in to work tomorrow."

Testy, she asked, "Why not?"

They both verbally stumbled, then Cannon said, "It's Saturday."

"So? The bank is open." She slanted an accusing gaze at Armie. "Do you plan to skip the gym?"

He frowned. "No." At the moment, nothing appealed more than pounding the hell out of a heavy bag.

"So why would the two of you assume I'd miss work?"

Armie half turned his head. "They expect you to come in?"

"They offered me the day off. I said no thank you."

Wow. Okay, so it could be that, like him, she needed to stay busy. A day off would only give her time to dwell on the violence.

Firmer now, Cannon said, "Come home with me and we'll talk it over."

"It's my decision," she said, sparing her brother the heat she'd thrown Armie's way.

"Yvette is making up the guest room for you."

"Cannon." She smiled at him. "I love you so much. Yvette, too. Thank you for offering. But really, I don't want company tonight, and I don't want to miss work tomorrow. I just... I want to deal with it, you know?"

He touched her chin. "You don't have to deal with it alone."

Her bottom lip quivered, and damn it, Armie couldn't take it. Like her brother, she had an amazing inner strength. Few strong people wanted to advertise their moments of weakness. "Let up, Cannon. She knows she can count on you, but maybe right now she just wants some privacy." God knew she'd been through hell and probably felt like crumpling. She needed to let go, but she'd never do that with an audience.

"That's it exactly," she said quickly, and then with an appealing pout, "Please understand."

Cannon studied her face, glanced at Armie and finally relented enough to say, "As long as you check in a few times, tonight before bed and tomorrow before work—"

Her laugh sounded of tears and heartache and gratitude. "I bet you drive Yvette insane."

Cannon softened. "Grant me the right to worry about the people I love." He pulled her coat lapels closer under her chin. "It can be one of your usual messages if that makes it easier."

"Yes, okay."

Rissy's usual messages consisted of *Rissy was here*. She left those three small words in texts whenever someone missed her call. She sometimes left notes, or in his case, wrote in the dust on a truck window. Armie knew her philosophy was that she wanted folks to know she'd stopped by or called, but didn't want them bothered if they were busy.

Knowing she'd be in touch, Armie felt as much relief as Cannon did.

"I'll drive you home," Cannon offered.

She bent another stern look on him. "I want my car. I don't want to be home without it."

"Tell you what," Armie said, seeing her start to shiver in the cold. "Ride with Cannon and I'll bring your car."

"But you're hurt. You need—"

"A shower," Armie said. "And some sleep." And he wouldn't mind getting his hands on those two creeps again. "That's all."

She looked at the cut on his head, which had thankfully stopped bleeding due to the butterfly bandage, and then the other bruises on his face.

"You've seen me looking worse after fights."

"Not really." She searched his face. "Armie, I—"

Softly, he said, "I know. We'll talk later, okay?"

She turned to her brother. "You know what he did?"

"Logan told me."

Armie scoffed. "It was nothing. Now let's go. I'm freezing my ass off."

He had her walking through the parking lot when she said, "What about your truck?"

"I'll get one of the guys to pick it up for me, or Cannon can swing back by here and drop me off. It'll be fine."

"All right." After a long look she handed him her keys—and then took him by surprise with a hug.

Stunned stupid, Armie inhaled, hesitated, but he couldn't resist returning her embrace. Never, not for a million years, would he ever forget the fear of losing her. Unable to stop himself, he cupped a hand to the back of her head and pressed his jaw to hers.

She smelled of warm skin, flowery shampoo and

pure sensual appeal, a scent guaranteed to keep him in turmoil for the rest of the night.

"Armie?" she whispered. "Thank you. For everything."

With no words to suffice, he nodded, stepped back and watched as she got into the passenger side of the car.

Cannon narrowed his eyes on Armie. "You sure you're okay to drive?"

"Yeah, I am." He started away. "See you over there." He planned to drop off her keys, and then stay out of the way, giving her and Cannon plenty of time to talk.

He needed some privacy—to do his own crumpling.

CHAPTER THREE

MERISSA LOVED HER BROTHER. She'd always seen him as Superman, larger than life, a rock whenever she'd needed one. He was only a couple of years older than her, but for as long as she could remember he'd seemed grown-up.

Right now, Superman was in her kitchen, insisting on getting her a drink when all she really wanted was the time alone to let go. She knew if she fell apart in front of him, Cannon would never leave her.

He didn't need to be a savior, not right now.

"Here." He returned with a cola over ice, urging her to the couch. He smoothed back her hair, his gaze drawn to the bruise. Yes, it hurt. But the physical discomfort was nothing compared to the fear.

And here she'd promised herself, long ago, that she'd never again let herself be that type of victim.

But this fear—it was more about Armie standing in front of her, using himself as a shield. Risking his own life.

Willing to die.

"Take these." Cannon handed her two aspirin.

She tried a teasing smile. "This feels so familiar."

He stalled, then shook his head. "Don't think about that."

She couldn't help herself. They'd lost their dad when

she was only sixteen. As the owner of a neighborhood bar he'd resisted the extortion of local thugs, refusing to pay their demanded fees for "protection." Late one night when he'd been closing, men had come in and beaten him to death.

Devastated but determined, their mom had nearly worked herself into her own grave trying to keep them afloat. Merissa could remember it all like yesterday. The goons wanted her mother to sell but she'd refused.

Until some of those goons had cornered Merissa on her way home from school.

"It's all the same. You coddling me, being the strong one for both of us."

"You were a kid then."

"You're only two years older than me," she reminded him with a shoulder bump. "You were a kid then, too."

"Maybe. I remember feeling so damned helpless."

"Like you feel now?" She knew her brother, knew he wanted to make things right for her when that wasn't his responsibility. "I'm not a kid anymore, Cannon. I can handle it."

"You don't have to."

"Yes, I do," she told him gently. "Because I don't want my big brother stuck taking care of me again."

He folded her hand into his own. "You know I enjoy it, right?"

Her laugh sounded pitiful. But she still remembered how her mother had given in because of her. Cannon had found those men, and even at eighteen he'd made them pay with his fists—because of her.

She'd influenced him into becoming a fighter.

And it was because of her that he'd formed the neighborhood watch. Everyone loved Cannon, but no one could love him more than she did.

"Superman," she teased. "This time, I promise I can take care of myself."

A slight knock on the door made her jump.

"It's just Armie," Cannon said with a squeeze to her shoulder. "I'll let him in."

Nodding, she again thought of the way Armie had stood in front of her, willing to block bullets if necessary.

Emotion welled up, choking her, *killing her*.

She quickly took the aspirin and tried to get herself together.

Armie peeked in cautiously, saw her on the couch and came in farther. "She okay?"

"Yes," Merissa and Cannon said at the same time.

Armie gave a slight, tilted smile. "Hey, Stretch." He came over to her, laid her keys on the coffee table, then winced at the darkening discoloration on her jaw.

"I bruise easily," she explained. "By tomorrow it's going to look worse, believe me. But it was just a slap. I doubt you guys would have even noticed."

Armie crouched down in front of her. "Hey, you're not a fighter, hon."

She liked it when he called her something other than Stretch. Something affectionate. "No kidding." She hadn't fought at all; fear and the furious beating of her heart had kept her malleable and weak. It infuriated her. "I may be big, but I lack muscle." And guts.

"Tall," Armie corrected. "You're tall, but far from big. More like..."

"What?"

He thought about it. "Delicate."

A genuine smile took her by surprise. So Armie Jacobson saw her as delicate? Huh.

Knowing she needed to get this over with, Merissa took another drink, then set her glass aside and stood.

Armie slowly did the same, his cautious gaze never leaving her. Cannon stood near him, strangely quiet. They both watched her as if expecting her to lose it at any second.

And maybe she would—if she didn't have an audience.

She moved a few feet away, needing the distance to get it said. "I think that man just wanted to toy with me. I mean, no matter what he said, there wasn't time to…to…"

Armie and Cannon both went so still, they seemed frozen. She wasn't helping by dragging it out.

Pasting on a smirk, she said, "He claimed he wanted to rape me, but we all know he wouldn't have. Not in the middle of a robbery, right? Instead he tried to grope me a little." The words strangled in her throat; she touched the front of her sweater with the missing button and made herself continue. "He slapped me when I pushed away from him. That's the mark on my jaw. I stumbled and some stuff fell off my desk. He was coming after me again but then Armie… Armie saved me." Hands locked together, she looked at the two people who were most important to her. She loved them both but in very, very different ways. "That's it, guys. I promise. I got hit once, felt up a little, but nothing worse than that."

"Rissy."

That single whispered word from Armie almost made gelatin of her knees.

"Now you need to go," she insisted urgently. "Both of you." An invisible clamp tightened around her lungs. *"Please."*

Looking tortured, Cannon said, "You'll call me if you need anything?"

She nodded fast. "Yes."

"And you'll check in just so I know—"

"I'll text you a couple of times tonight and tomorrow morning before work, too, I promise." *Please, please just go before I come undone.*

Armie jammed a hand through his hair, then cursed low.

"Problem?" Cannon asked.

"No."

Merissa looked at the dried blood in his hair, on his shirt. In her mind, over and over, she kept seeing how he'd shielded her. "Cannon should be fussing over you because you're in far worse shape than I am. Go home and do whatever it is you do to make yourself feel better."

Which probably meant he'd find a willing woman— or three—and lose himself in an orgy of pleasure. *Damn it, she couldn't let that bother her.*

His nostrils flared, but Armie nodded. As if he'd just lost an internal battle, he flexed his hands. "If you want to talk…" He did more flexing, almost agonized. "Just let me know."

She whispered, "You might be busy."

He gave one shake of his head. "No." He pulled her in for another hug that was so gentle it nearly demolished her resolve.

After the soft, warm press of his mouth to her forehead, he headed for the door. "I'll wait outside."

Merissa watched him walk away, his stride long, his step hurried.

It almost looked like he was running away.

Even after the door closed quietly behind him, she stared. Concern for Armie made her forget her own uneasiness.

"Rissy."

She jumped, and her gaze shifted to her brother.

"You know I love you—"

"Yes." Never in her entire life had she ever doubted that.

"I also love Armie. In a lot of ways, he's like a brother to me."

Despite everything, her lips shifted into a smile. "I know."

Cannon let out a big breath, then took her hands. "He's not a brother to you. Not even close. I would never betray either of you, but…"

When he trailed off, Merissa got alarmed. "What?" She squeezed his hands. "What's the matter?"

"He'd deny it till hell freezes over, but Armie's hurting. Not physically. I don't mean that."

She couldn't breathe, couldn't swallow, so she just waited.

"Maybe you should give him comfort, and it would give you comfort in return."

Her jaw loosened. She didn't know how to comfort Armie. He'd rejected her. Though they hadn't discussed it, Cannon had to know that she had a thing for Armie. Their circle was small and everyone seemed to share everything that happened.

She shook her head, but Cannon smiled at her.

"There's something about Armie you should probably know."

Oh wow. Her own situation faded as a million sce-
narios ran through her mind. Would she learn the reason Armie had avoided the SBC for so long? Would she
find out why he refused to commit to a woman, why
he avoided "nice" girls? Heart thrumming furiously,
she whispered, "What?"

"Armie won't be busy tonight."

She narrowed her eyes. "How do you know?"

"Because for weeks now, he's been celibate." She was
stunned stupid as Cannon bent and kissed her forehead.
"Something to think about, okay?"

He didn't wait for an answer; he just headed to the
stairs to the door. On his way, he said, "I've locked the
door, but reset the alarm, and don't forget to check in."
And then he was gone.

And Merissa, still reeling, dropped to sit on the
couch.

Armie Jacobson, hedonist extraordinaire—celibate.
For *weeks*?

Yep, that certainly gave her a lot to think about.

AFTER A LONG, steamy shower, where he lingered for
far too long, Armie pulled on boxers, fixed a drink and
crashed on the couch. He turned on the TV but didn't
really focus on anything. His internal battle kept him
too wired.

A few drinks later, more than a little tipsy, he still
couldn't stop thinking about Merissa home alone,
maybe upset. She hadn't wanted to call him. That had
been as plain as the bruise on her jaw.

She might anyway.

She probably wouldn't.

She had Cannon to comfort her.

But did she want *Armie*?

On and on it went, circling in his brain, making him nuts, and no amount of liquor would blunt the torment. For the tenth time he checked his cell. Had he reminded her to use the emergency cell? He couldn't remember. Maybe he should text her and let her know...

No.

What he should do is leave her alone, stop lusting after her.

Stop *needing* her.

He dropped his head back and closed his eyes. His temples throbbed and his back ached. He couldn't believe he'd let that putz catch him twice. Luckily no one wielded metal posts in cage fights.

Also, he didn't have an innocent audience, guns or Merissa Colter in danger during cage fights.

He flexed a shoulder and looked toward the dark window. It was—what? Nine-thirty? Still early. Maybe he needed to get back in the saddle and ride. He wanted to snicker at his own wit, but even for a drunk guy that was a shitty analogy.

If only he had even the smallest interest—

The knock on his door had him bolting upright. He stared toward it as his heartbeat ratcheted up and desire kick-started a slow burn in his gut.

Standing, he set aside his drink and, still wearing only boxers, went to the door and opened it. Disappointment hurt worse than that metal post had. "Shit."

"Well, hello to you, too." She winced at the damage to his face. "What happened to you?"

Armie stared at the brunette he'd brushed off at the

bar the other night. "Just a misunderstanding." To discourage her from trying to come in, he stepped out and pulled the door partially closed behind him. "C'mon, Cass. You know better than to show up without an invite."

"I called your cell but you didn't answer." Her hungry gaze went over him, caught on his crotch and stayed there. He recognized that particular smile curling her lush lips.

"My cell got broken," he explained. "But seriously, hon, you didn't get the message at Rowdy's?"

"No one treats me like you do, Armie."

"I'm an asshole and I know it. You should steer clear."

She put a hand to his abs and started teasing her fingers downward. "I didn't mean that weird rudeness at the bar. I meant in bed."

He caught her wrist. "Not happening."

She seemed to puff up with determination. "I'm getting married in a month."

"Yeah?" He put her hand back at her side. "Congrats."

"I love him."

"Glad to hear it."

This time her smile looked genuine. "He's a great guy, Armie. Smart, sweet, but macho enough that even you'd like him."

With no idea where she was going with that, Armie just cocked a brow.

"But in bed..." She sighed. "He's not you."

Armie laughed, turned it into a groan and rubbed his face. "Let me guess. You haven't told him what you like?"

Now sounding desperate, she asked, "How can I? He's so nice and he's not like you and me."

He stepped away from the door and, feeling indulgent, said, "Hon, *I'm* not like you. But between what you told me and how you reacted to stuff, I figured it out. Most guys like hot sex. It's hotter when the chick is into it. So just tell him what you want. Trust me on this, he'll be into it."

"But what if he's not?" Uncertainty shadowed her eyes. "What if he thinks I'm…weird or something?"

"You're healthy, not weird. And if he doesn't dig it, then do you really want to be married to him for the long haul?"

"I don't know."

"A lifetime of mediocre sex? I'd vote no."

Her heavily made-up eyes studied him. "You don't like the stuff we do?"

She looked vulnerable, and because of that, Armie kept his tone gentle and reassuring. "If you have to ask that, then you weren't paying attention."

"But you just said—"

"It's your thing, honey, not mine. But I'm always happy to oblige."

She leaned closer, and her voice went lower. "Now?"

Half smiling, he said, "Except for now." Her pout was cute, but had no real effect on him. "If you're getting married, you should be saving all those looks for him."

"Like *you'd* ever be faithful."

"If I got married, damn right I would. Now go." He turned her, swatted her on the ass and said, "All things considered, you shouldn't contact me again."

Face flushed and eyes dreamy, she rubbed her tush. "I guess."

"And you'll talk to the fiancé?"

"Yes." She bit her lip. "I'll tell him. But if you're wrong, I *will* come back here just to smack you."

Armie grinned. "You can try."

As soon as she headed down the steps, he went in and shut the door, strode to the couch and fell facedown onto the cushions.

Did Merissa have any fetishes?

God, he'd love to find out.

Turning his head to the side, he checked his cell phone one more time, and there it was. A text message that read, Rissy was here.

SITTING ON THE STEP, smothering in indecision, Merissa avoided looking at the brunette who went past her with a polite nod. The woman was smiling, happy and on her way out.

Merissa wasn't a natural-born eavesdropper, but when she'd gotten to the top of the stairs and heard Armie speaking to the woman, she'd frozen.

Once she caught the conversation she couldn't have moved even if she'd wanted to. Her feet had turned to lead blocks and her ears had been attuned to every single word they shared.

Sure enough, Armie had turned the woman down.

But the things they'd discussed… What did the woman like?

Merissa held her phone, waiting, hoping, and the text message dinged an alert.

Licking her lips, she read: You okay? Need to talk?

Yup. Yup, she did. She texted back, Busy?

No.

Wow, that was fast. She twisted to look up at the landing, saw the still-closed door, and turned back to her phone. He was so close. In person?

Seconds ticked by. She compressed her mouth, held her breath, tapped her foot rapidly on the step.

Finally the message appeared: You shouldn't drive.

Merissa thumbed in the reply, hesitated, hesitated some more, then hit Send. Already have.

ARMIE STARED AT the message. Already have. What did that mean? Was she out tooling around?

Bad idea.

He typed in: Where are you? If he needed to, he'd go get her. Somehow. But hell, he was drunk and he knew it.

A cab. He'd take a cab—

Here.

His eyes went wide. Here? Stupidly, he looked around his apartment, then sent another text. Here?

Yes.

Here-where?

A very soft, single knock sounded on his door.

He went still, then everything accelerated. His heartbeat, his breathing.

The rush of blood through his system.

Coming to his feet, Armie crossed the room and jerked the door open and—ah, hell. He didn't blink. "Hey, Stretch."

One brow shot up. "Are you drunk?"

"No." Definitely. And because of that, he felt sluggish and pretty damned unsure how to welcome her.

Or should he send her on her way? He knew he wouldn't, wise as it might be, so maybe he should call Cannon—

She came in uninvited.

His back still to her, his thoughts struggling to catch up, Armie stood there.

"You're in your underwear."

Oh shit. He'd forgotten. Leaving the door open, he faced her. Damn, she was close. Like kissing close.

Like *fucking* close.

"They're cute."

"They're absurd," he corrected. The boxers sported two arrows—one that pointed up and said, The Man, and another that pointed to his junk and said, The Legend.

"I like them." She leaned in—nearly stopping his heart—and gave the door a push to close it. Then she stayed right there, letting him breathe her in and feel the heat of her slender body and smell the scent of her skin.

She touched his head as if to check the butterfly bandage. "You showered."

"Yeah." And jerked off while he was in there. Not that his dick seemed to remember it now.

"This isn't as tight as it should be." She prodded gently at the special bandage, securing it again.

Taking her wrist, he pressed her palm to his jaw and closed his eyes.

"Armie?"

Get it together, he warned himself. "Come here."

Slipping an arm around her shoulders, he walked her to the couch and got her to sit. "Want a drink?"

She lifted his glass and sniffed, took a tiny sip and made a face. "Whatever you're drinking would be fine."

He tucked in his chin. "You don't drink whiskey." Except she'd just sipped it straight from his glass.

"Today is a good day to start, don't you think?"

Yeah, probably. "One." He glanced at her slim jeans, flat-heeled boots and the oversize hoodie, but didn't allow himself as long a look as he'd have liked. "Stay put. I'll be right back."

On his way to the kitchen he felt her gaze on his ass. Literally *felt* it. He needed some jeans, only that'd look chicken shit. Or maybe modest.

He wasn't either.

After getting another glass he poured her a shot of whiskey and went back to find her sitting cross-legged, a pillow hugged to her chest, her head down.

Softly, he said, "Hey."

She looked up, those sparkling blue eyes sad but filled with so much pride and strength. "Will you sit with me?"

Armie clenched all over. She might as well have asked, "Will you rub your naked body over mine?" because his body reacted as if she had.

But damn it, he had control and somehow he'd find it. "Sure." He lowered himself to the couch about a foot from her. "Here."

She took the glass, sipped, made another face, then licked her lips.

Blindly he reached for his own glass and downed it.

Merissa studied him. "How much have you had to drink?"

"Not enough." Clearly. Because all he could think about was pulling her close, kissing her, laying her down on the couch.

Under him.

Her lashes lowered. "Are you still thinking about it, too?"

Sex? "Yeah."

"I keep remembering…"

Not sex. Letting out a breath, Armie took her hand. "Maybe you should have spent the night with Cannon." He could still get her there, either by calling a cab, or Cannon himself—

"No." She snuggled in, her arms around his waist, her head on his shoulder. Her long hair teased his skin and the rest of her teased his libido. He wanted to put his hands all over her, but instead kept them on her shoulders.

Until she said, "I'm sorry, Armie, but I'd really rather stay here with you."

He lurched back so fast he almost fell off the couch.

They stared at each other.

Usually, when he balked at her suggestions, Rissy's feelings got hurt, which in turn made her pissy. Not this time.

This time she smiled gently and slid over to sit closer again. "Is that asking too much?"

He croaked, "No." Nothing was too much for her, but how the hell would he handle it?

"Good." Sighing, she hugged him. "Thank you."

Um… "Welcome."

"You really are drunk, aren't you?"

He shook his head—which made the room spin. Lethargy and lust battled. "I'll take the couch."

Instead of arguing, she again snagged her drink, settled back against him and sipped. "What are we watching?"

He glanced at the TV. "I don't know."

She picked up the remote. "Do you mind?"

Against him, away from him, against him, away from him. Her bouncing back and forth made him more than a little nuts.

A hand in his hair, Armie shook his head. "Help yourself." As she flipped through the channels, he wondered what the hell had happened. One minute he'd been sitting alone worrying about her, and now she'd put on an old movie and was tugging off her boots.

Drink in hand, she made herself comfortable—back against him again. After a second, she readjusted, taking his arm and looping it around her shoulders, then wiggling in closer. "Is this okay?"

He had a boner, his heart was trying to pound its way out of his chest, and every muscle on his body contracted, but whatever. "Sure." He dropped a throw pillow over his lap.

"I saw before that you've got a terrible raised welt on your back. Does it hurt?"

Sexual need muddled his brain further. "No." Though tomorrow he'd probably be feeling it.

After a half hour or so of blessed silence, where he'd finally gotten his gonads to calm down, Merissa turned up her face to look at him. He felt even drunker now, but some of that might be overwhelming need blunting his brainpower.

He tried to resist, but finally glanced at her—and got caught.

"How's your head?" she asked.

All his concentration went to her mouth, and he had to fight the urge to give her a long, hot, wet kiss. *Think, Armie.* An idea occurred to him. "You tell Cannon you were coming here?" He already knew she hadn't because if Cannon knew his baby sis was hanging out at his apartment he'd have already come to collect her. No guy in his right mind would want a female relative slumming with Armie, but Cannon was more protective than most. "He needs to know—"

"You're right." She got her phone from her purse, thumbed in a message, then put the phone on the coffee table. "All done."

Armie stared at that phone, willing Cannon to reply, and when it finally dinged he released a tense breath of both relief and disappointment. She needed to leave, true. But damn, it was so nice having her close.

She leaned forward, looked at the screen and smiled.

Smiled?

Suspicious with a vague sense of dread, Armie asked, "He coming to get you?"

She shook her head. "No."

"What'dya mean, no?"

She held the phone for him to see the message.

He read: Good. I'm glad you're not alone. Now I can stop worrying.

Confusion nearly crossed his eyes. "You told him you were with *me*?"

"Yes."

Tunneling a hand into his hair again, Armie wondered what the hell Cannon was thinking.

When the room went quiet his heart stalled. Wide-eyed, he realized that Merissa had turned off the television. He tracked her every move as she replaced the throw pillow in the corner of the couch, then stood and carried her boots over by the door. The finality of the lock clicking into place jump-started his heart again.

He shifted around and watched her remove her socks and peel off the hoodie. Scalding heat washed over him. She tucked the socks into the boots and left the folded sweatshirt on top.

Now wearing only skinny jeans and a big SBC T-shirt, she came back to him and held out a hand. "Come on, Armie. I'm ready for bed."

CHAPTER FOUR

MERISSA HAD NEVER felt so daring in her entire life.
Leading Armie to bed—yup. That topped the list of
daring feats. For some reason she felt powerful tonight,
powerful enough to make some headway with the man
of her dreams.

Maybe it was escaping the violence. Maybe it was
how Armie had so gallantly protected her.

Maybe it was her brother's encouragement—and
tacit permission.

Whatever the reason, she was here, and she was willing to fight dirty to get what she wanted.

Armie had accepted her hand and now their fingers were very loosely laced together. Gaze intense and
big body taut, he came along quietly, perhaps a little
stunned. Sexual tension filled the air, thick enough to
trip on.

She didn't know her way around Armie's place so she
peeked into rooms as she went. He kept things mostly
tidy, but was far from immaculate. His black-and-white
bathroom had a towel on the floor, another over the
shower rod. A laundry hamper overflowed and she saw
his bloody flannel shirt on top.

It leveled her to remember the moment he'd stepped
in front of her, willing to take a bullet. Emotion swelled

until it burned her eyes but she fought it. She wasn't a crier, never had been, and saw no point in it.

These were very different circumstances, so eventually she might break down—but not on Armie.

He'd been through enough today, more than her for sure, given he'd offered up his life to protect her.

She didn't always understand him, what motivated him or why, but she loved him. For tonight, that seemed like enough.

Next to the bathroom was an open bedroom. Biting her lip, anticipation keen, she peeked in. Heavy black furniture dominated the room. The unmade bed was king-size with a directional light overhead. On the wall facing the bed was a gigantic mirror. Otherwise, it looked like the rest of his apartment—comfortably masculine and lived in.

Crowding close to her back, his voice dark and silky with menace, Armie asked, "Having second thoughts?"

She shook her head.

"Looking for my whips and restraints?"

She spun around to see him, which meant they stood very close, eye to eye, mouth to mouth. "Do you have them?"

His firm lips quirked up. "Curiosity killed the cat."

Guessing that he only wanted to scare her off, she taunted him. "I don't think you do."

His eyes narrowed. "I have whatever I need to make a lady happy. And by happy, I mean screaming as she comes."

Wow. He certainly sounded confident as he said that. "So…restraints if she asks for them?"

His expression hardened more. "I'm not having this discussion with you."

"Pretty sure you are." She tried to sound cavalier when really, inside, she was a little appalled. And maybe just the tiniest bit turned on, too. Not by the idea of being physically hurt, but any thoughts of Armie in sexual mode made her tingle. "Besides, I heard you talking to that woman. I'm dying to know what you did with her."

Confusion overshadowed his antagonism. "What woman?"

"The one who came to visit you tonight."

His jaw loosened, then he clenched it tight. "You eavesdropped?"

"Afraid so." It'd be hard to question him without admitting that much. "But not on purpose. I came to see you, and she was already there. I didn't want to intrude, so I waited."

"Within hearing distance?"

"You were both in the hall. Not like I put my ear to the wall."

Annoyance had him breathing harder and his right eye kept twitching. "Shit. I'm too far gone to figure this out."

"Far gone?"

"Drunk." He waved a hand at her. "And you being here isn't helping."

"Don't ask me to go." For good measure, she admitted, "When I'm alone, I can't stop thinking about the robbery and that man and how he—"

"Shh. That's over." There, outside the bedroom, while stepping in against her, Armie caught each of her hands and pinned them to the wall at either side of her head. "You're okay."

The press of his body all along her length caused

her breath to hitch. Especially when his solid erection nudged her belly. He wore only the silly boxers, and she could feel each and every long, firm muscle through her thin T-shirt and low-riding jeans.

His gaze drifted over her face, lingered on her mouth, then down her throat to the tops of her breasts. The side of his nose brushed hers and she could smell the whiskey on his breath. "You don't know what you're asking for, Stretch."

This time the nickname didn't faze her. "Yes, I do."

His lips grazed her bruised jaw, over to her earlobe. "Rissy..." he said, sounding pained.

"I'm asking for you, Armie. Just you."

He hesitated, then thrust himself away from her. "Not that easy and you know it. No one comes to my bed wanting just *me*."

"I would," she whispered. "I *do*."

He groaned. "Jesus, I'm drunk."

If that was true, and she was pretty sure it was, then it wouldn't be ethical of her to take advantage of him. He wanted to resist her and she wanted to wear him down.

But she didn't want to dupe him into doing anything that he'd later regret.

She gave him a long look and went into the bedroom.

He laughed, rubbed his tired eyes and muttered, "I tried."

"Yes, you did." To get him to join her, she asked, "Would it help you to relax if I told you all I want is to sleep? Beside you, I mean, because I honestly don't want to be alone." And she was pretty sure he didn't want to be alone, either.

Full of regret, he shook his head. "Sorry, babe, but I can't. I'll crash on the couch."

Babe? That was a new one, but again, he'd had too much to drink and wasn't firing on all cylinders. "It's going to be crowded with both of us out there."

When he stood there—neither leaving nor making a move to stay—Merissa decided to try to sway him. She reached for the snap on her jeans.

Armie didn't look away from her eyes, but he breathed harder.

She dragged down the zipper, then slipped her hands into the jeans along her hips and slowly pushed down the tight material until she could step free.

His nostrils flared.

She dropped the jeans over a chair, pulled back the comforter on his bed and, full of uncertainty, slipped beneath the covers. To make room for Armie, she scooted over to the middle, looked at him and waited.

"If I wasn't drunk," he whispered, staring at her, "I might be able to do this." He edged closer, caught the comforter and dragged it away from her body. His blistering gaze surveyed every inch of her, leaving her singed. "I don't want to hurt you."

"You won't." He'd been prepared to die for her. She trusted him completely.

A deep, harsh groan tore from his throat, and then he was in the bed, gathering her close, one hand in her hair, the other low on her back, almost to her derriere. Their legs tangled, his hairy and muscular, hers smooth and slim. She felt soft chest hair against her cheek, and the heavy bumping of his heartbeat.

"Armie?"

"Shh. Give me a minute."

"Okay." He smelled so good and felt so nice, she didn't mind just being close with him. But as the time slipped by, she started to wonder if he'd fallen asleep. The bedside lamp was on and the comforter remained at the foot of the bed.

Levering back from his hold, she tipped up her face and found his eyes closed, his brows lightly pinched.

She scooted upward to kiss the injury to his head, and that's when she saw the restraint hanging loosely from his headboard. She couldn't quite look away from it, either, now that she'd spotted it.

"Armie?"

His dark lashes left shadows over his high cheekbones. "Hmm?"

Now she frowned, too. "Are you playing possum?"

"Concentrating."

"On what?"

His hand slid farther down, over one cheek of her behind. He stroked with his thumb, fondled, then returned to the small of her back. Voice raspy, he said, "Not doing more of that."

After that sizzling, sensual caress, it took her a second to regain her voice. "Oh." She cleared her throat. "Can we talk about this tie hanging from your bedpost?"

His eyes opened, dark, compelling. "We could talk about you losing this shirt."

That low, rough voice enticed as much as the suggestion. "Oh, Armie," she whispered. "If you weren't drunk, I would."

"If I wasn't drunk, I wouldn't ask."

Probably true. She sighed.

As if to convince her, he said, "I'm a better cocksman when inebriated."

The laugh almost burst out. "Cocksman?"

He nudged his erection against her. "Like a swords-man, but with my dick."

"Yes." She had to work at keeping the smile at bay. "I understood the reference."

The hand on her back began toying with her shirt. "Want me to show you?"

"I want you to explain the restraint."

His eyes went heavy, sensual. "I use them to tie up frisky ladies so I can do as I please—and they love it."

"Is that one of the things women ask of you? To be tied down?" Being at Armie's mercy—she wouldn't mind that. In fact, her toes curled just talking about it.

"Yeah." He drew her down for a kiss. "They *beg* for it."

Merissa avoided his mouth and instead kissed his forehead, then the bridge of his nose. "The woman who was here tonight, that's what she likes?"

"She likes her bottom hot." Armie turned his head and nuzzled into her neck. "But I shouldn't be telling you that."

On the contrary, she found it fascinating. "So you… spank her?"

"Yeah." He lightly bit her shoulder, then stilled. "You into that?"

Merissa gave an emphatic, *"No."*

Armie relaxed again. "Good. I would never want to hurt you. Not in any way."

Touched by that confession, Merissa hugged his head to her breasts. The way he'd said that though, *not in any way*, had her thoughts churning.

He did a little more nuzzling, getting close to her nipples. She scooted back down so they were again face-to-face.

Armie just looked at her, his gaze probing and aroused, but also slightly off focus.

"I sort of expected your bedroom to be full of sex toys."

"Mmm," he murmured with a smile. "Women bring their own."

That reply took her by surprise. "Really?"

Trailing his fingertips down her arm, he said, "I figure they can handle their own cleanup."

Euewww. "TMI."

He laughed, kissed the top of her head. "How can it be too much information when you're grilling me?"

"I didn't expect..."

"Sex is a messy business." His voice went deeper. "Women get nice and wet when turned on, and men come." He stroked her hair back. "You know that."

She knew plain vanilla sex with men she hadn't loved. No sex toys, no restraints and definitely no spanking. She didn't need kink with Armie, but she wanted him happy. "What you said to that woman..."

"It's really bad form for me to spank and tell."

She scooted closer. "But I'm curious."

"God," he groaned, "don't be."

She loved the sprinkling of chest hair over his solid pecs, and that tantalizing trail that bisected his body. She loved that he respected women enough to care about sharing things private, and that he didn't want to take advantage of her.

She loved his body and his attitude, his capability and his concern—she loved everything about him. "I'll keep it general."

He rocked her a little and asked, "Why don't you sleep?"

"Do you enjoy spanking women?"

He groaned again.

"Armie," she persisted.

He silently stared at her for a good long while, then surprised her again by turning to his stomach, stacking an arm under his cheek, and getting comfortable.

"Armie?"

Time ticked by. Merissa narrowed her eyes. "If you just fall asleep, I swear I'll—"

He didn't move. Didn't open his eyes. She huffed. He'd actually gone to sleep. She watched his back rise and fall with deep, even breaths. Seeing the raised, discolored welt there softened her annoyance.

Then she noticed that when he'd turned over, he'd displaced his boxers. The waistband was tugged down a good three inches on one side, showing a strip of paler flesh over the top of his firm butt. With one fingertip she traced his spine, and still he didn't stir.

Would he remember any of this tomorrow morning? Oh, it was evil of her, but she almost hoped he wouldn't. It'd be fun to give him a hard time, to reveal to him, little by little, everything they'd discussed and how many times he'd kissed her.

As to that, she smiled, thinking wicked, very naughty thoughts as she watched him sleep. Her gaze went to his partially exposed backside.

Well, she did leave her signature note everywhere.

Grinning, she slipped from the bed but returned within a minute. Armie's breathing had turned into a light snore, and he slept through the writing of her note.

With that done she crawled back into the bed, curled up close to him and fell asleep with a happy smile on her face.

ARMIE WOKE SLOWLY, his eyes blurry, his head more so. When he moved, several things hurt. Nothing new in that. He sparred hard, fought hard and often woke with sore muscles or minor injuries. He stretched awake.

And suddenly remembered.

Sitting up with a jolt, he looked to the other side of the bed and found it empty. He was out of the room in a heartbeat, searching until he found the pot of coffee in the kitchen and the note folded against it that read *Rissy was here*. Damn.

Turning to the kitchen sink, he splashed his face and tried to get his bearings. He remembered her coming over, remembered her leading him off to his bedroom.

Remembered her stripping off her jeans.

His gaze shot down, and relief rolled through him when he saw he still wore his boxers. That told him a lot because no way would he have worked around them if they'd gotten busy.

So clearly they hadn't.

Dropping back against the sink, he racked his brain and finally remembered his lame plan. He'd figured on pretending to be asleep to both discourage her from asking sexual questions and encourage him to keep his hands to himself.

Unfortunately, he must have actually passed out on her.

Embarrassing, but also a lifesaver.

Had he held her all night? Turning, he strode back down the hall to his bedroom and stalled at the sight of his bed.

He'd been there with Merissa. Memories of touching her, kissing her, teasing and talking with her all drifted in and out of his thoughts.

He recalled those long, killer legs of hers tangling up with his. Her dark, thick hair trailing through his fingers. Her nipples pushing against the T-shirt. Her warmth and curiosity and openness with him.

No one comes to my bed wanting just me.

I would. I do.

When the cell phone rang, he jumped a foot, then rushed to answer. Glancing at the screen first, he saw it was Cannon, and braced himself. "'Lo."

"How do you feel?"

Armie held the phone out, stared at it, then put it back to his ear. "I'm fine. Why?"

Cannon laughed. "You were in the middle of a bank robbery yesterday. You got clubbed on the head and across the back."

And I slept with your sister. "It's all good." He faked a yawn. "Just woke up."

"Yeah. Rissy texted me a half hour ago. After everything that had happened I wanted to talk to her, too. She sounded fine, like her old self. Said she was running home to shower and change before work, but that you were still snoring."

Armie's heart dropped to his feet. His sexcapades were vast and varied, but had never involved a discussion with anyone's brother.

With humor in his tone, Cannon said, "We have a special guest today, so do you think you can hustle it up?"

In a rasp, he asked, "Special guest?"

"Jude Jamison."

Holy hell. Jude owned mega stock in the SBC organization. He'd once been a champion fighter before he left and became an even more famous actor. Then he got accused of murder, survived a grueling trial where most believed he was guilty but couldn't prove it, fell in love and finally cleared his name. "Why?"

"You already know why. The organization is focused on you."

He grumbled, rubbed his tired eyes and knew there'd be no help for it. "This sucks."

Cannon laughed. "Most fighters would be thrilled to get Jamison's attention."

Yeah, well, he wasn't most fighters. Already heading to his dresser, he pulled out clean socks and sweatpants and sat on the side of the bed to dress. "I was going to grab a cup of coffee and then stop on my way to get my regular cell phone fixed."

"Harper can get it fixed for you."

Harper, who'd started as a volunteer until she'd married Gage, now worked full-time at the rec center and was there almost as often as Armie. Since the cell store was only half a block down, she probably wouldn't mind. "Fine. I'll come right in. Okay if I drain the pipes and clean my teeth first?"

"Sure. And take five minutes to put some fuel in the tank. I have a feeling Jamison will put you through a workout." And with that, Cannon disconnected.

"Pain in the ass," Armie muttered, and finished pulling on his socks. Knowing he'd shower at the rec center, he packed his gym bag, brushed his teeth and ignored the whiskers on his face and his unkempt hair. Since he could smell the coffee, he filled a travel mug to take with him then rinsed out the carafe. He'd have to explain to Rissy that he tried to avoid caffeine.

No, wait. He wouldn't have her over again so he didn't need to explain jack shit to her.

Of course the coffee was perfect. Everything about her was perfect.

He wished she had awakened him before leaving. Now, despite what Cannon had said, he'd be wondering all day whether or not she'd slept, and if she was nervous about returning to work.

Last night she'd wanted to be with him.

Today, how would she feel? He chowed down a protein-rich breakfast bar on the way to the rec center. For most of the ride he stewed and finally gave in. As soon as he parked his truck he called Merissa.

On the third ring she answered with a rushed, "Armie, hey!"

She sounded breathless, which sort of stole his breath, too. "Did I catch you at a bad time?"

"Sorry, just out of the shower and hustling to get dressed so I get to the bank on time."

That put an immediate visual in the forefront of his brain.

"Armie?"

He shook off the image of her wrapped in a small towel, her skin still damp, her face flushed. "How are you?"

"You and Cannon," she teased. "I'm fine. What about you?"

"I'm good." He paused, but couldn't hold back. "You should have woken me up before you left."

"I'm sorry. You looked so peaceful, and I knew I couldn't stay anyway. It seemed a waste for us both to be up rushing." Now she paused, then added, "Thank you for inviting me over again tonight. I appreciate that."

Armie went blank. *He'd invited her back over?*

"I get off work at five, but it'll probably be five-thirty before I get away. Then I'll need to run home and change. I'm thinking six, maybe six-thirty. Does that work for you? I thought I'd cook you dinner."

"Um…" He scrambled for an excuse, came up blank and rubbed the back of his neck. "Should work."

"Great. I'll see you then." She disconnected.

Armie sat there, equal parts confused, concerned and anxious to see her again. "Idiot," he muttered to himself and left the truck.

He saw the crowds right away. Figured a big shot like Jude Jamison would draw in the gawkers. Slinging the strap of his gym bag over his shoulder, he headed in.

Wasn't easy, not with an influx of semiswooning ladies all jockeying for better positions in the crowd. "Excuse me," he said about a dozen times until he finally reached Harper, Gage's wife.

She stood on tiptoe, and she smiled.

Armie said, "Not you, too."

She elbowed him. "It's *Jude Jamison.*"

"Yeah, so?"

Harper turned to blink at him. "He's a movie star!"

"Used to be." But Jude had left that all behind.

"Once a movie star, always a movie star." Harper sighed. "Just look at him. He's gorgeous."

"They're *both* gorgeous," another woman said.

Armie leaned around them to see the mat and realized Jude and Cannon were sparring together. He grinned. "Got your ovaries aching, huh?"

Harper elbowed him again. The other gal sighed, *"Yes."*

Shaking his head, Armie sidled past them until he'd reached a more open area where the other fighters stood. Gage immediately asked him, "Harper still all moony-eyed?"

"'Fraid so."

"I'll get her mind on other things once we're out of here." He bobbed his eyebrows to ensure everyone understood his meaning.

Leese nodded at the mat. "Jude said he hadn't done any actual sparring for a while, but it doesn't show. He's still slick with his moves."

"And those direct shots," Gage added, then slanted a look at Armie. "How he throws a punch, straight and fast, reminds me a little of you."

Folding his arms, Armie watched for a minute and noticed that Cannon was holding back. A smart move, really. No reason for Jamison to get hurt or for Cannon to stroke his own ego when there was a lot more to be gained in a good relationship with someone of Jamison's caliber.

Then to Armie's surprise, the men finished up and Jamison said, "Thanks for going easy on me." He grinned like he'd had the time of his life.

Armie understood the feeling. For a man who liked to use his strength and test his speed, there wasn't anything else like MMA.

Cannon laughed. "You haven't lost it, that's for sure."

"I stay in shape," Jamison said. "But there's *in shape* and then there's *fighting shape*. In this business, speed is the first thing to go and it makes all the difference between a champion and a mediocre contender." He clapped Cannon on the back. "Thanks for indulging me."

"Anytime."

They stopped in front of Armie, and Jamison, after

freeing himself from the fingerless gloves, offered his hand. "Armie, thanks for coming in early."

Cannon snorted. "He's here all the time. Believe me, this is late."

Armie felt his neck go hot. *He was late because he'd been sleeping with Merissa.* Best rest he'd had in forever, too. "Not a problem. So what's on the agenda? Cannon said you wanted to see me?"

"I've got all day. Mind if I just watch your normal routine for a while? After that, we'll all sit down and talk."

Rolling a shoulder, Armie said, "Sure. Suit yourself."

For the next three hours he tuned everyone out and went through his usual workout. Normally he could get into the zone and his brain would be blessedly clear. This time though, even as he went from throwing hard punches and solid kicks, to grappling with other fighters, and then to lifting weights, his thoughts stayed centered on Merissa. True, he'd been hammered last night, but not so far gone that he didn't remember the stirring way she'd removed those formfitting jeans.

When she'd bent to push them down, her long hair had tumbled forward, almost touching the floor. Her dark hair had inspired plenty of fantasies for him. And those beautiful bright blue eyes—they were the same color as her brother's, and both siblings had thick, dark lashes, but on Merissa the look was sexy as hell. So many times he'd imagined anchoring her with his hands fisted in that silky hair, staring into her mesmerizing blue eyes and riding her hard until he watched her quicken, then felt her come.

He could almost feel it now, those long, slim legs

hugged around him, hear the catch in her breathing, feel the wet slickness…

"Ready to spar?"

Drawing a deep breath, he turned to Leese and saw he wore headgear and had his mouthpiece handy.

Leese grinned. "We played paper/scissors/rock and I lost."

Not understanding, Armie shook his head.

"Not sure if it's for Jude's benefit or if you're pissed about something, but you're really pounding out the workout today."

Armie frowned, glanced out at the room and saw a whole lot of people watching. What the hell? He wasn't a Hollywood star like Jamison so they could all just go about their business.

To Leese, he said, "You can take whatever I throw at you."

Leese grunted. "Going to be one of those days, huh?" He followed Armie to the corner where he had his gear. "Truthfully, though, I like it. Better opportunity for me to learn."

Since the improved attitude was still a somewhat new turnaround for Leese, who had, at one point, been something of a dick, Armie always enjoyed working with him. He learned fast, put his heart into it and was proving to be a better fighter than any of them had expected. Armie wasn't sure if Leese had what it took to be a champion, but he could put on one hell of a fight.

After wedging in his mouth guard and fastening on his headgear, Armie said, "Let's go."

For another hour they sparred. Armie alternately put it to Leese, and then instructed him. That was all well and good, but then Jude wanted to see Cannon with him.

"You too tired?" Jamison asked him.

Cannon spoke for him, saying, "Armie has more energy than any fighter I've ever seen. He doesn't gas out, ever."

Rolling his eyes over that effusive praise, Armie said, "If you were a chick I wouldn't mind getting stroked, but from another dude it's getting weird."

Cannon laughed. "So you are tired?"

"I'm fine."

Jamison studied him. "I'd say by those bloodshot eyes you had a night of it."

New heat joined that from exertion. Again he said, "I'm fine."

Jamison looked at Cannon, who smirked, and they both laughed.

"Yuck it up." Armie flexed his shoulders. "We'll see who wears down."

Cannon joined him on the mat. "Challenging me?"

He sent his friend a mean grin. "You won't be any good to Yvette tonight."

"Boys, boys," Jamison said, but Armie could tell he loved this shit. "I don't want anyone mangled. Just spar so I can see the moves, okay?"

Cannon said, "Yeah, Yvette prefers me physically available."

They all laughed over that.

Apparently Jude Jamison didn't realize that he and Cannon were like brothers and one would never hurt the other. Of course, it was possible Cannon might drop down a weight class one day. If he did and the SBC set them up to actually compete against each other, they'd both give it their all. But that was for sport, without an ounce of animosity involved.

Armie and Cannon engaged, and pretty soon everyone stood alongside the mat watching. Most of the ladies had finally cleared out; they didn't really hang at
the rec center all day the way many of the athletes did.

His friends, Gage and Justice, Brand and Miles,
Leese, Denver and Stack, all called out different sub-
missions. Armie went through each one. Of course,
Cannon was resisting but, for the sake of giving Jamison
a demonstration, he didn't really fight back. If he had,
it wouldn't have been so easy.

By the time they finished it was pushing four o'clock
and sweat covered Armie's entire body. He'd had a few
quick breaks and wolfed down the lunch Harper put together for him, but otherwise, he'd been busy.

Stack did him a solid by helping him get his gloves
and headgear off. "You have really sick speed."

"I agree," Jamison said as he joined them. "And you
honestly don't look tired."

"Getting there," Armie said. Sometimes his over-
abundance of energy was a problem. Like the times he
tried to screw himself into exhaustion so he could sleep.
Usually the woman wore out first, and then he had a
hell of a time getting her up and out of his apartment.

"He and my wife are both endless sources of energy,"
Stack said. "Although it pisses her off when I compare
her to Armie, given his rep and all."

"It'd piss me off, too," Justice told him. "That is, if
I was a sweet lady like Vanity."

"You're jealous," Denver accused. And then to Jude,
"Armie racks up conquests left and right."

"Usually," Miles added, "it's the ladies chasing him."

"So I've heard." Jamison clapped Armie on the

shoulder. "Get your shower and change, and then we can talk business."

"Sure. Be back in ten." After drying off his face, Armie slung the towel around his neck and grabbed up his gym bag. Chatting together, Leese and Justice followed him toward the showers. Cannon had paused to talk to some of the newer fighters hanging out.

The tepid water of the shower felt good and helped Armie to clear his thoughts a little. He scrubbed off the sweat, and then just soaked his head for a few minutes under the spray.

Merissa would be over again tonight and he honestly didn't know if he'd be able to keep his hands off her. He wouldn't drink. He'd be crystal clear. But that might not help when put up against the force of her appeal.

For so damned long he'd been hankering for her. When she hankered back… Yeah. He had knockout blows, but he wasn't strong enough to resist that.

Knowing he shouldn't keep Jamison waiting, he turned off the water and quickly dried, then stepped out of the shower.

"Holy shit."

He turned, saw Leese looking stunned and asked, "What's your problem?"

"Whoa!"

He turned again and saw Justice standing there slack-jawed.

Quickly getting irked, Armie scowled. *"What?"*

Cannon strode in, his cell phone to his ear, and suddenly Leese was at his back, way too damn close for two naked dudes. Armie was ready to shove him away when Justice stepped in front of him. Crowded between a lot of naked muscle, Armie said, "What the hell?"

In a low whisper, Justice told him, "Hold up a second."

"Dude, we're a hair from crossing swords."

Justice practically shoved him back into the shower, and Leese, looking a little panicked, helped.

Stumbling, Armie grabbed the shower wall to brace himself. "If this is some new hazing deal, I'm going to kick both your asses!"

Oblivious to the altercation, Cannon turned near the lockers and headed to the back of the room.

Leese let out a breath. "It's your ass, Armie."

Yeah, that cleared up nothing. "I know the ladies like it, but you, Leese?"

Justice shoved him. "*Look* at it, idiot."

"Look at my own butt?"

Grumbling, Leese grabbed up a hand mirror used for shaving and held it down by Armie's backside. "Look."

Baffled, Armie peered over his shoulder at the mirror, and his eyeballs almost fell out.

Written across the top of one glute in what must've been permanent marker were the words *Rissy was here*.

Damn it, she just might get that spanking after all.

CHAPTER FIVE

WITH HIS HEART thumping into overdrive, Armie snatched up a towel and wrapped it tight around his hips before glaring at both men. "Not a word. Not a single. Fucking. Word. To *anyone*."

Mute, Justice used one finger to draw a cross over his hairy chest, right where his heart would be.

Wearing a look of disdain, Leese said, "I wouldn't have helped you hide it if I planned to blab it."

Leaning in, his voice faint, Justice asked, "Want me to see if Harper has anything that'll remove marker?"

"No." Good God. The last thing he wanted was Harper asking questions. He'd take care of removing it at home, alone. And seriously, he *should* give some thought to putting Rissy over his knee.

In a rush, their conversation about spanking came flooding back and he scrubbed a hand over his face. She wasn't into it and he wasn't into hurting her. If he got her pants off her again, he could think of a lot more interesting things to do with that bared tush.

But seriously, one good swat might be in order.

Annoyed at the path of his thoughts, Armie said, "Keep watch while I get dressed."

Both fighters, arms crossed, did as asked. But damn it, Armie could feel their censure while he quickly pulled on boxers and then jeans and then, for good measure, a T-shirt. He tugged the hem of the shirt down to ensure nothing, not a speck of flesh showed.

When he finished, he turned to the guys. They stood there, lips curled, eyes narrowed, biceps bunched.

He glared at them both again. "It's a joke, okay?"

Leese glared back. "If you say so."

"Hell of a joke," Justice added.

God, he hated explaining himself to anyone. And if Rissy wasn't involved, he wouldn't bother. But she was, and Armie couldn't bear the thought of anyone thinking whatever they were thinking.

"You know she was robbed, right? At the bank, I mean."

They both nodded.

"Well, I was there."

"Heard all about it," Justice said. His gaze went to Armie's head. "That's how you got your noggin knocked and that big bruise on your back."

"Yeah. Well, after going through that, Rissy didn't want to be home alone last night. Since Yvette just announced they're expecting, I guess she felt like she'd be intruding to go to her brother's. So she came to my place. I was already in my underwear when she got there, and drunk as shit, and I passed out on her. Must be when she wrote that."

The tension eased out of their stances, and Justice even grinned. "Man, she got you good."

"So until just now," Leese asked, still sounding skeptical, "you didn't know it was there?"

"Had no clue. You think I'd go advertising that?" Especially with Cannon nearby. Hell, Cannon and Rissy were the two most important people in his world. He'd never do anything to embarrass or malign either of them.

But when he got hold of Rissy…

"Lady in the hall," Harper called out.

Armie strode over to the doorway. "Trying to get a peek?"

"Now, Armie. Would I announce myself if that's what I wanted?" She held out his phone with a receipt. "They only had to replace the screen. Good as new."

Armie repaid her. "You're a dream, Harper. You know that, right?"

She stuffed the bills in her pocket, blew him a kiss and took off again.

When he walked back in, Cannon joined them. "Good show today, Armie. You impressed Jude."

"Wasn't my intent to impress anyone." He hadn't altered his workout except to add the extra sparring Jude had requested.

Grinning, Cannon said, "You did anyway."

While he dressed, Justice and Leese said their farewells and took off, leaving Armie and Cannon alone in the showers.

"Rissy called," Cannon said. "I asked her to check in every so often."

"How's she doing?"

"All right, I guess. But she's too stubborn to tell me otherwise." Cannon finger combed back his hair, then let a fist drop against the locker. "I can't get it out of my head."

"I'm there with you." The fact that someone had manhandled Rissy, threatened her, kept an uneasy turbulence churning inside Armie. "Any word from the detectives?"

"Not yet, no." Cannon turned his head to face Armie.

"You were there. You think it's possible it was more than a robbery?"

Over and over, it had played in Armie's mind. "I honestly don't know. I mean, one guy seemed to make a beeline for Rissy. I'd just noticed that he closed the door on her office when the other guy pulled the gun. But I don't see how that setup helped them. I get that she's a manager, but why separate her from the others?"

"I don't know." Cannon sat on the bench and pulled on his shoes. "I have a bad feeling about it."

Cannon had a lot of contacts on the street, but mostly in the neighborhood surrounding the rec center. Whether or not those contacts would be of use for a bank robbery, Armie didn't know. Thanks to their combined efforts, these days there was less crime and more enterprise. But on the outskirts of their small town, the criminal element still thrived. "You have feelers out?"

"Yeah. And I know Reese and Logan are on it. But I'm not going to rest easy until they catch the bastards."

"And until that happens, Rissy's going to keep checking in with you?"

Cannon shrugged. "She's understanding about it."

"She knows you love her."

Cannon went quiet again, then said, "Thanks for keeping an eye on her last night. I appreciate it."

Armie almost choked. "No problem." It amazed him that Cannon wasn't raising holy hell about his sis being alone with someone of his ilk. But then, he probably had no idea that Rissy had peeled off her pants, insisted on sleeping plastered against him, asked about sex games and left her MO emblazoned on his ass.

"It might cramp your style, but if she asks again—"

"I'll look out for her," Armie promised. He'd do

whatever he thought was best to protect her—even if it meant protecting her from him. "You know that."

"Yeah." Cannon watched him. "I do." Putting that discussion aside, Cannon switched gears. "I'm looking forward to hearing what Jude has to say."

Armie eyed his best friend. "You know it's going to be some idiotic promo shit they want me to do." And he hated it. Not the camera—he'd never minded that. But the dog and pony show wasn't his way.

"Maybe," Cannon conceded. "Promo is good. Since we finally got you in the SBC we might as well ensure you make a big splash." But since he knew that wasn't what Armie wanted, Cannon clapped him on the shoulder. "Try having a little faith, okay? You have the organization behind you. That counts for a lot."

"If you say so."

Together they went back into the main gym and met up with Jude, who wanted to take them to a nearby diner to talk "away from everyone else." Sounded ominous to Armie, but what the hell. He had time yet.

The diner surprised him. It was a local family-run place. Armie had been there before, but for a man of Jamison's stature, a freaking movie star, as Harper had pointed out, it seemed pretty humble.

Recognizing the direction of Armie's thoughts, Jude said, "I don't want to be recognized, and I don't want to keep you long. I assume this place is okay with the two of you?"

"I know the owners," Cannon said. "They're good people."

"And they serve killer homemade soups," Armie added. "Just didn't seem like your speed."

"I was a fighter before I hit Hollywood. And believe me, I prefer the fight circuit a hell of a lot more."

Once they were seated in the back corner booth with drinks in front of them, cola for Jude, lemon water for Cannon and Armie, Jude got down to business. Hands folded on the table, leaning in, he addressed Armie. "You know I was once accused of murder."

Whoa. Definitely not what he'd been expecting. With dread, Armie figured he knew now where this was going. "Everyone's heard. You were also cleared."

"Yes, but to much of the world it didn't matter." He looked at his hands. "Everyone thought I'd just gotten away with it. That I'd somehow bought my freedom."

With conviction, Cannon said, "Everyone was wrong."

That made Jude smile. "Yes, they were wrong. But you just reinforced my point." He looked at Armie again. "When all of Hollywood and most of the world continued to accuse me, the SBC stood behind me. They were my family, my friends, there to support me. They knew me and believed in me."

Armie sat back in his seat.

"They'd be there for you, too."

Well, hell. Somehow, Jude Jamison had uncovered his deepest, darkest secrets. "You know, don't you?"

Jamison nodded. "Simon and Havoc told me you were tough to nail down, and that although you'd signed on, you still seemed to be resisting. Throughout my career I've worked with a lot of hard cases, guys teetering on a life of crime, trying to clean up their lives."

"That's not Armie."

Again, always, Cannon was quick to defend him. He turned to Cannon now. "I'm guessing he already knows part of it or we wouldn't be here."

Jude shrugged. "I got curious. After what Simon and Havoc told me, that you had all the right tools to be a champion but no real desire to make it happen...well, it didn't sound plausible."

Armie scoffed. "Believe me, I'll do what I can to win the fight." He didn't know how to fight any other way. "If you're worried about that—"

"I'm not. The thing is, I want you to want it, too."

Enthusiasm? Was that what Jude needed to see?

"I watched a few of your fights," Jude admitted. "I haven't seen many with your raw talent. So I checked into your background. It was easy enough to find out why you're hanging back."

"I'm not." Jesus. He'd signed on. What more did the SBC want?

"You're not full-go," Jude insisted. "Not yet. But we'll get you there."

Talking about it always made Armie edgy with suppressed rage. The urge to walk off clawed at him. But damn it, he'd walked away so many times, from so many opportunities.

"The SBC has resources." Jude gave him a level look. "And I have resources."

Oh, hell no. Armie didn't want Jamison using his own funds to defend him.

Jamison held up a hand before Armie could protest. "False accusations are personal to me."

"And they *were* false," Cannon assured him.

Jamison half smiled. "I drew that conclusion all on my own after I found out all the details, including how you, Cannon, helped to back down the accusers."

"Temporarily," Cannon clarified. "They said they'd dredge it all back up if Armie didn't disappear."

"Let them try. They think money and clout gives them leeway to spread lies. I look forward to proving them wrong."

"Damn." Armie had thought that whole episode of his life was completely buried—and would stay that way as long as he kept out of the limelight. "You must have some great contacts to know so much about it."

"The best money can buy," Jamison stated. "So what do you say? Will you dive in and give it your all?"

He didn't relish the idea of reliving that particular hell.

"Until you do," Cannon told him, "it'll always be there."

"True words," Jamison agreed. "A woman taught me that. Until she came into the picture I was content to ignore the sensationalizing media and the scum-sucking liars. I've never regretted the decision to finally fight back, because now she's my wife."

The claws of uncertainty retracted a bit. "She never believed the lies?"

"Not even for a second."

Cannon clasped Armie's forearm. "You're better than them. I've always known it. Now you need to know it, too."

"And then you can show the world."

Armie had come to expect Cannon's unwavering support. But Jude Jamison's? That left him perplexed. "Some accusations have a way of hanging with a guy."

"Like being called a murderer," Jamison confirmed. "But it's past time to shake it off." He held out his hand. "Agreed?"

Armie hesitated, but damn it, he knew Cannon was right. He'd had enough of that particular shadow hanging over him. "All right, Jamison." He took his hand. "Thank you."

"Call me Jude. You're going to be seeing a lot more of me so we might as well be friends."

Just how involved did Jude plan to be? "You don't say."

"I've invested in the sport, you know that. Well, Armie, now I'm going to invest in you. And as anyone can tell you, I'm good with money."

They spent another half an hour talking about his opponent, Carter Fletcher. According to Jude, Carter had the second-best camp and representation in the business. He was quickly making a name for himself and a lot of behind-the-scenes people were saying he'd soon get a shot at the championship belt.

Armie had never been all that interested in a belt. For the longest time his focus had been on working at the rec center and dominating in every smaller-venue fight in the tristate area. He'd had enough trouble adjusting to the idea of throwing himself into the SBC without leaping ahead to thoughts of a title shot.

Jude, however, had other plans. He expected Armie to win, and win big. Sketched within a short time frame, he'd drawn a path for Armie to go straight to the top.

For the very first time, Armie decided he wanted it. And there was something else he wanted. Something he'd craved for too damn long, something he'd denied himself because he hadn't deserved it.

Merissa. Naked, in his bed.

Merissa—*maybe forever.*

If he could really have a second chance, if he could win the belt, maybe he could have Merissa, too.

Though the old fear still existed, for once he was ready to ignore it and go after what he wanted instead.

But it wouldn't be fair to go there without her first knowing everything. And if they were alone at his apartment, he wasn't sure they'd get around to talking.

As to that, he wasn't sure he wanted to go into it all tonight. He needed some time to come to grips with the changes, to figure how to explain it to her. If she didn't trust him, if she didn't believe in him, it would level him as nothing else could.

One thing at a time, he decided, no matter how it might kill him to wait.

With that decision made he drove toward her house, his intent to put her off at least until tomorrow. Lunch, maybe. Yeah, they could have a conversation over lunch. In a crowded restaurant.

Where he wouldn't be tempted to strip off her clothes.

Unfortunately, when he pulled up to her house, he saw her ex, Steve, standing on the stoop talking to her.

What the hell? She'd dumped that loser months ago, so why was he here now? Standing so close. Smiling at her. *Schmoozing.*

Whatever plans Armie had made disappeared like vapor. Steve was a creep, but Rissy might not know that because he'd never told her.

Another idiotic decision—one he could set straight right away.

AFTER A GRUELING, nerve-racking day at work, Merissa wanted nothing more than to escape her own jitters. It shamed her that every time the front door of the bank had opened, tension had dug into her spine, leaving her heart racing and her palms clammy.

Her tellers, who were all nervous, needed her to lead by example. She didn't want to be a coward so she'd done her best to hide the reactions, especially when talking to her brother. But no matter how she tried, she couldn't stop thinking that the robbers might return. Everything they'd done had felt so personal, as if they'd come specifically for *her*, not just to rob the bank.

Detectives Riske and Bareden had assured her that the police would make frequent drive-bys to check on things. The FBI even had a plainclothes officer keeping watch, occasionally inside the bank.

None of that had mattered to the fear that repeatedly surged to the surface.

By the time she'd left the bank she felt so tightly coiled she wanted to scream. Even at her house, with the security system on, she hadn't been able to regain her calm. Part of that, she knew, was living alone. Her bilevel home was fixed up so that she could live on the upper floor and, until recently, Cherry had lived on the lower level. But once Cherry and Denver married, the space became empty and she hadn't so far rented it out again.

The long, warm shower that should have been relaxing instead left her straining her ears listening for any unfamiliar sounds.

By the time she'd dried her hair and dressed casually in jeans and a fitted T-shirt, stuffed a few necessities into a tote bag, and gotten out the door, all she could think about was seeing Armie again.

Unfortunately, she'd found Steve, a very unwelcome

ex, coming up the walkway. And for the past five minutes she'd been attempting in vain to get rid of him.

"I'm concerned for you, Merissa." He reached out to touch the bruise on her face, but she leaned away. Lips pressed together, he dropped his hand. "After the robbery yesterday you have to be shaken."

"No, I'm fine." *And I'm a good liar*—but it wasn't Steve she wanted to comfort her. They hadn't been together for months so why he thought he could waltz back in now, faking concern, she didn't know. "I'm running late so if you don't mind—"

"Merissa," he said in a tone as thick as honey. "I know you better than that." His gaze went to her house. "And didn't you lose your roommate? You shouldn't be alone."

"I'm not." Another big lie, but no way did she want Steve to think she'd be the only one in the house. "And really, Steve, it's not your concern. We're over."

"But still friends."

"Since when?"

He sighed. "I don't blame you for being bitter. The way I treated you—"

"I'm not bitter," she said from between her teeth. "I'm not anything—except in a hurry."

Just then, she recognized Armie's truck as he pulled up to the curb and her frustration mounted. She didn't need a conflict between the two men and worse, if Armie was here to cancel on her, she'd... Well, she didn't know what she'd do. Maybe try insisting.

But he wouldn't be drunk now and that meant her odds of swaying him to her way of thinking were greatly diminished.

When the sound of his slammed truck door echoed over the street, she urgently wanted Steve to take off.

"I'm sorry," she said, racking up her third lie, because she wasn't sorry at all, "but I'm not interested."

"Not even in a drink?" Steve cajoled. "Just for old times' sake? Friend to friend?"

"Hey," Armie said, looking so awesome in a snug-fitting long-sleeved T-shirt that, for once, didn't have any provoking writing on it. Had he made that concession for her?

She'd have to tell him that she liked the raunchy sayings on his T-shirts.

But maybe later. Right now, his gaze was only on her. He didn't even acknowledge Steve.

"What are you doing here, Armie?" *She* glanced at Steve and found him studying Armie, his expression hostile. "I was just heading to your place."

Armie seemed to fight some internal battle before saying, "I wanted to follow you."

"Why?" She didn't want Steve to know how upset she'd been. "I'm okay."

Pulling her in, Armie brushed a warm kiss over her mouth, rendering her mute. "'Course you are. But it'll make me feel better. Okay?"

Spellbound by that spontaneous, casual kiss, she nodded.

And Steve suddenly exploded. *"You."*

Armie smirked. "Didn't recognize me at first? Yeah, I always figured you to be obtuse. Now beat it."

Wait a minute. Merissa looked from one man to the other. What was she missing? "You two know each other?"

"In a way," Armie told her.

"He," Steve said, "attacked me!"

Merissa looked at Armie, and sighed. "Why?"

He laughed. "That's it, Stretch? You don't even ask if I did it?"

"No need. I can see it on your face."

Armie tweaked her chin. "Well, you're wrong. What I did was defend myself after his boyfriends jumped me." Armie shrugged. "And yeah, after I finished with them I kicked his ass a little, too."

"A little?" Steve demanded. He turned to Merissa. "You saw me! You know how bad it was."

"When you were bedridden? Yes, I remember." She huffed. "If you had your boyfriends—" Shoot, now she sounded like Armie. "Your *friends* jump him, then you all got what you deserved."

"Why thank you, honey."

"He was following me," Steve insisted.

"Not exactly how it happened," Armie told her, sounding bored. "And if you want all the deets I'll give them to you. But if I stay next to this bozo one second more, I'm going to have to deck him. And then you'll have blood all over your porch. You don't want that, do you, honey?"

"No." Merissa hiked her purse strap over her shoulder, lifted the tote bag and took Armie's hand. "Later, Steve."

"It might not be so easy this time, you bastard!" Steve followed them off the porch. "I've been working out!"

"Yeah?" Armie glanced back, his expression hopeful.

"No," Merissa said firmly. "Keep walking."

He didn't.

Turning to look over her ex, Armie said, "You got

some pretty muscles now, Steve-o? You wanna see how we match up?"

"Armie Jacobson, don't you dare!" Merissa put both hands flat to his chest and pushed.

She might as well have been pushing on a brick wall.

A little panicked, she whirled around on Steve. "You've always been an idiot, but for God's sake, use what little sense you have and *leave!*"

"Hey." Armie's hands settled on her shoulders. "Calm down, honey. It's okay."

She pivoted back to blast Armie. "I do *not* want you demolishing him where my neighbors might hear."

He cocked a brow. "So that's your only concern?"

"I live in a nice, quiet neighborhood of elderly people," she growled. *Did he actually think she still cared for Steve?* "Take him apart on your own time, but *not* in my front yard!"

"Okay, okay. Take it easy."

Knowing she'd overreacted and now feeling like a fool, Merissa tried to step around him.

Armie pulled her against his chest. Near her ear, he said, "I'm sorry. I would never deliberately do anything to embarrass you."

That he would be so considerate, that he could pull his anger together so easily, amazed her. She dropped her forehead to his shoulder. "You won't kill him?"

His rough laugh teased along her nape. "Naw. I'll leave him intact—for now." He set her away from him, studied her face and asked, "Okay now?"

They both ignored Steve.

"Yes, thank you."

Steve wasn't ready to let it go. "I looked for you. Did you know that?"

"No, I didn't. But I wish I had."

"Now I know who you are!"

Dark eyes glittering, Armie smiled at him. "I've always known who you are. Keep that in mind."

Okay, wow. That made Merissa shiver. And when she glanced at Steve, he looked far from unaffected.

Armie took the tote bag from her, put an arm around her waist and walked her to her car. She got behind the wheel and set her purse and tote in the passenger seat.

"I'll be right behind you," Armie promised.

"You don't mind that I'm coming over?"

Instead of answering that, he brushed the backs of his knuckles over her cheek. "We need to clear the air anyway." And with that he stepped back and shut her door.

Uh-oh. That didn't sound promising.

In the rearview mirror, Merissa watched Armie go to his truck. Steve still stood on her walkway, glaring and looking like a disgruntled bully. She didn't like leaving him there, but her house was locked up, the security system on, so there really wasn't any damage he could do.

When Armie started his truck, she pulled away from the curb. He followed. With every mile the anticipation ramped up and by the time they reached his apartment she'd worked herself up to a near frenzy of hyperneed and nervousness.

Dinner, she reminded herself, trying to stay on task. Armie wanted to talk, too. She needed to know what had happened between him and Steve. Then, finally, she could try getting him back into bed.

And this time, maybe they'd do more than sleep.

CHAPTER SIX

NEVER BEFORE HAD he been so acutely aware of a woman, but this woman had only to breathe and it turned him on. Having her in his apartment was like foreplay, even though sex wasn't on the agenda.

Torturous.

While trying to stay otherwise busy, Armie heard her in the kitchen, moving around, cooking for him, and damn it, he liked it.

He liked having her here, liked her being involved, liked the elusive daydream that maybe this could be a recurring thing.

Together with Rissy. Playing house.

He pressed the heels of his hands into his eye sockets, drew a breath and, feeling slightly better grounded in reality, joined her in the kitchen.

She wore a soft T-shirt and another pair of jeans that hugged her pert ass and long thighs. She'd left her shoes by his front door and stood at the stove in her socks.

Stirring something in a big pan, she glanced up. "All done?"

He'd thrown in some laundry and done a quick, general pickup of his place. He wasn't a neat freak, but he wasn't a slob, either. After that he'd returned some calls to sponsors, a few to other camps that had invited him to work out and one to Drew Black, the president of the SBC. He'd taken his cell to the bedroom to talk and Rissy had stayed in the kitchen, and still, every second, one part of his brain had dwelled on her nearness. "I'll have to switch to the dryer in twenty minutes."

"I'll remind you," she promised, and her upbeat tone showed that she wasn't suffering the same emotional uproar as him. "Dinner will be done right around then."

"What are you cooking anyway?" Scented steam floated in the kitchen, making his stomach rumble. He made a point of eating something every couple of hours. Usually some type of protein. But Rissy kept him so off-kilter he sometimes forgot to breathe, much less eat.

"It's a chicken dish my mom used to make. Don't worry, Cannon approved it for his diet, so I'm guessing it's okay for you, too."

As she stirred, her hips moved, and that stirred him, too.

Feeling awkward in his own kitchen, Armie asked, "Anything I can do to help?"

"Nope. I've got it covered."

"Okay then." He pulled out a chair and sat. Might as well get the show on the road. The sooner he put it behind him, the sooner he could get his head on straight again. "I guess we can talk now then."

Rissy flashed him a worried look, then went back to the food before her, her shoulders slumped. Seconds ticked by before she said, "Do I need to sit down for this?"

Tension pulled his brows together. "Do you still care about Steve?"

Her gaze shot to his. "No."

"Then it shouldn't bother you to know I did, in fact,

beat the shit out of him, as he accused—but not without good reason."

Her expression eased and she smiled. After stirring the food one more time she turned it on low and wiped her hands on a dish towel. Joining him at the table, she sat and took one of his hands. "Armie."

Alarm skittered up his spine. "Uh...what?"

"I already knew you wouldn't have pulverized Steve, or anyone else for that matter, without a very, *very* good reason. You didn't have to tell me that."

So she thought she knew what motivated him? He almost laughed.

"But if you'd like to tell me, I'll admit I'm awfully curious."

When she looked at him like that, her eyes big and happy and sincere, especially while also touching him, he could barely think.

"About Steve," she prompted.

Shit. "Right." He freed his hand and sat back in the chair, putting a marginal amount of space between them. "I overheard him talking one night about getting his jollies with some other chick while you were in Japan with Cannon."

"Huh. Well, not surprising," she said. "I never could credit him with a lot of integrity."

"Yet you stayed with him."

"Just casual dating." She shrugged. "I'm twenty-three, Armie. Spending my nights at home alone didn't sound all that fun, you know? Steve was a way to pass the time. We both knew it wasn't serious. And honestly, if he'd told me he wanted to date other people, I probably wouldn't have cared all that much." She tipped her head. "But you wouldn't have smashed him for that."

Still reeling over the idea of her being home alone, maybe lonely, Armie shook his head. "No." An awful suspicion flamed to life in his guts, starting a very uncomfortable burn. Had he hurt Rissy by trying to protect her? Had she been home alone because he'd turned her down?

She crossed her arms on the table, a smile dancing over her lips. "My curiosity mounts by the second. Out with it already."

Needing to move, he left his chair and went to the stove on the pretense of stirring the food. "He'd made a few shitty jokes about the lady, saying how he'd gotten her stoned to make her more agreeable. That was bad enough, but then he said he needed to restock his supply before you got home. So I followed him."

Merissa came to stand at the counter beside him. "Steve was planning to *drug* me?"

"I only know what I heard." He avoided her gaze; her nearness was already testing him enough. "Since I didn't make a big secret out of following him, he had some of his friends circle around." Satisfaction gave him a smile. "Guess he thought they'd outnumber me or something."

"Dumb," Rissy said, showing a lot of faith in his ability. "So did you leave them all as beat-up as Steve?"

"Close." Finally he faced her. "If they hadn't jumped me, I'd have let it go." Maybe. "But once that first punch was thrown…"

She patted his chest. "I understand." She stopped patting and just let her hand, small and warm, rest against him. "Why didn't you tell me all this before?"

Beneath her palm, his heart thundered. Absurd that a simple, friendly pat would do that to him. "You dumped him, and good riddance. I figured that was the end of it until I saw him at your house today."

Her fingers curled against him the smallest bit, almost a caress. "You don't have to worry about Steve."

He'd worry if he wanted to. "Stay away from him, okay? He's bad news."

"No problem. I'd already told him there wasn't anything left between us."

Because she wanted him, instead? Armie went around her. "Gotta get my laundry. I'll be right back."

"Okay," she called after him. "Dinner is ready, too."

"I won't be long." And even though it felt like fleeing, he got out of there as fast as he could. In the basement of the building, he switched his laundry into the dryer, then just took a moment to get it together. Tension gripped him the exact same way it did during sex.

And Rissy had only stood there, looking like herself, cooking for him, touching his chest once.

Maybe the celibacy had finally caught up to him.

Maybe the ever-growing need had reached the boiling point.

In the past, he'd managed by steering clear of her. He couldn't do that anymore. He sure as hell couldn't do it tonight.

They still had more talking to do. Maybe after he told her everything, it would cease to be a problem. Rissy could end up avoiding him, and that would be the end of his torment.

Or it could be hell on a whole new scale.

BY THE TIME Armie returned some fifteen minutes later, she had the table set, the food served and drinks poured.

She felt ridiculously nervous, spending the evening

with him this way. As a natural-born hostess who loved to cook for others, she'd been serving dinners since she was fourteen. But never for her and Armie alone. It felt far more intimate than it should have, and that made it more important than it needed to be. She sensed Armie had let her in, just a little, and she didn't want to do anything to change his mind.

She also didn't want to have to walk on eggshells around him. She wanted to be herself—and she badly wanted him to be okay with that.

He came into the kitchen cautiously, every muscle in his chiseled body tensed, his dark gaze unreadable. It wasn't until he looked away at the table that she was able to draw a breath.

"Ready?" Hopefully she'd infused just the right amount of casual ease into her tone. "You better be hungry."

"I am."

The way he said that, how he again looked at her, made her laugh nervously. She clamped her lips together, cleared her throat. "Then I hope you like it."

He held out her chair.

Too warm, a little breathless and very aware of his nearness, she sat down.

He seated himself across from her and waited until she'd taken a bite to do the same.

Waiting, Merissa watched him. "Well?"

"Good. *Really* good." He forked up more, then gave an appreciative hum. "You're an amazing cook."

"Thank you." Relaxing a little, she teased, "I would've loved to make you dessert, too, but I know that's pushing it."

"Once a week," he said. "That's what I allow myself. Keeps me from ransacking the doughnut shop."

"Is that what you like? Doughnuts?"

"And cakes and pies and cookies." He smiled at her. "Seems like every time I'm at your place, you have sweets set out. I've never been able to completely resist."

Not dessert, no, but it seemed he resisted her just fine. Except, maybe he'd finally stopped resisting, at least to a point. "If you don't mind, I'd like to make you something each week. Maybe just two portions? Like two cupcakes? Or two cookies, or—"

"You don't have to twist my arm."

As if she even could. She glanced at his thick wrist, then at his broad hand and long fingers, his hard knuckles. His hands were big and capable and, compared to hers, so much stronger.

Thinking about the differences in their sizes had her tingling in places inappropriate to the dinner table.

While they ate, she continued to silently study him while thinking about the fact he'd defended her against Steve. She remembered Steve's battered state and didn't have a single ounce of pity for him. She also agreed with Armie that it'd be best to totally steer clear of him. It seemed Steve had been an even-worse choice than she'd already realized.

When his cell rang, he glanced at the screen, clicked a button and set it facedown on the table.

Merissa just *knew* it was a woman trying to reach him.

A second later, an incoming text dinged. Again he glanced at it, then disregarded it.

Peeved, Merissa said, "If you want to reply—"

"I don't." He tipped up his glass and finished off his tea. "Perfect meal. Thank you."

Still nettled, but knowing she had no right to be, she followed his lead and let it go. "You're welcome." She started to stand.

"Rissy."

Her gaze lifted to his.

"There was something else I wanted to talk about."

Sensing his seriousness, she sank back into her seat. The dishes could wait. "Okay."

"You're a few years younger than me, so you probably don't remember, if you were even aware at the time, but when I was eighteen, I got into some trouble."

She fiddled with her fork. "I remember there was something going on, but I don't think I ever knew the details. I asked Cannon a few times but he always avoided a straight answer."

Armie stared right at her, into her eyes, almost as if he needed the connection. "He would have protected you from the ugly details."

Ugly details? Merissa didn't look away. "Whatever it is," she told him with certainty, "it couldn't have been that bad."

He gave her a cross look. "Because your brother is still my friend?"

"No." She took in his careful expression, saw the hurt and loved him all the more. "Because I know you're a really good man. *Everyone* knows you are. No, don't shake your head at me, Armie Jacobson. It's true. How you are with the kids at the rec center, how you back up your friends, men and women alike. How you always defend the underdog, how you treat people in general.

If you made a mistake when you were eighteen, well, that was a long time ago. It doesn't matter anymore."

"That's where you're wrong. It matters a lot now that I'm going into the SBC."

"Why does the SBC change anything?"

"Because I'm in the limelight and certain people are likely to notice."

That didn't make any sense to Merissa. "Who will notice? And why will they care?" This was why he'd always avoided advancing? Because he didn't want to be recognized?

Armie continued to watch her, his expression intent and somehow fatalistic, as if he thought she might begin to hate him at any minute.

She pushed back her chair and stood. "Tell me what happened so I can prove you're wrong."

He stood, too, although more slowly. His jaw worked; his face tightened. Merissa wanted to go to him, hold him and assure him that no matter the problem, it didn't matter, not to her. But he looked so deliberately remote, she wasn't sure if he'd welcome her touch or reject her.

"I was accused of rape."

That stark admission was so ugly, so unreal, it landed between them like a thunderclap. Merissa took an involuntary step back. Almost immediately she surged forward again. "That's insane!" She grabbed a fistful of his shirt. "Who accused you?"

Surprise flickered over his features, then settled into a curious, cautious frown. "Does it matter who?"

"Of course it does, because she's a liar!" She leaned into him, eye to eye. *"Who?"*

Looking very uncertain, he scratched his neck. "You're sure she's lying?"

"Don't be stupid." She gave him a push that didn't budge him at all. "You're no more a rapist than I am."

His lips twitched, not so much with a smile as with relief. And maybe some confusion, as if her reaction had thrown him. "No, I'm not."

"Give me a name."

With a halfhearted shrug, he said, "Lea Baley. But you wouldn't know her since she's a few years older than me."

"So why did she accuse you?"

He made a face. "Sorry, Stretch, but she's never really shared her reasons with me."

This time Merissa poked him, both for the nickname and for not giving a straight answer. "You have a guess. What happened?"

Frowning, he rubbed his pec. "That hurt."

Baloney. His chest felt like granite.

Merissa guessed, "You broke things off with her and she had a hissy?" When his eyes flared a little, she said, "That's it, isn't it? You being the man-whore that you are, you're never content with one girl and that particular girl didn't want to share so she spread those lies to…what? Get even with you?"

"I'm not a man-whore."

"Oh *please*." How Armie could deny that with a straight face, she didn't know. "*Total* man-whore. But so what? You're an adult and if you want to sow enough wild oats for a battalion, it's your own business."

"I—"

"But at eighteen, well, how many oats could you have sown?" She couldn't ever remember Armie not being sexual. By the time she was old enough to really take notice of him, he'd already been experienced, or at least it had seemed so to her. Girls chased him, same as they did her brother. She'd grown up with that as a fact of life.

"You were so popular—of course you didn't want to get tied down."

"I—"

"It's ridiculous." She hadn't known the details of his experience, only that he always seemed to be with a different girl and that the way he looked at that girl had been noticeably aware, with the full force of his hungry, blatantly sexual attention.

As he'd grown and matured, his nature had ripened. How he smiled at, listened to and focused on women made them hot and needy and ever-so-willing. She knew, because even when he wasn't trying to seduce her, he managed to anyway.

But when he'd been eighteen—surely no one had expected him to get into a serious relationship at such a young age. Or at least, no one should have.

"Yes, you're out there," she said, because no one could deny his pleasure-seeking lifestyle. "Sometimes *way* out there from what I've heard. I mean, two or three women at a time? Outrageous. But force?" She made a rude sound.

"You saw the ties on my bed."

"Yeah, and we've *all* seen the women *ask* you to… do things to them." Merissa tried to ignore the heat in her face. "Geez, I imagine you have a hundred women who could be character witnesses. Lea should have known—"

Armie kissed her, fast and firm, putting a halt to her rant. It dazed her, that warm press of his lips to hers. When she got her eyes opened again, she saw him grinning.

"You—"

Before she could get too annoyed by his humor, he pulled her in close and laughed.

His body was warm, solid, and his scent surrounded her. Giving in, Rissy savored the moment. "Ridiculous," she couldn't resist grumbling one last time.

"Thank you." He held her back the length of those long muscular arms. "For knowing better."

Did he really think anyone who knew him would believe the lies? "You're welcome." Because it was so nice, she moved back against him again—and Armie let her. "So what happened after you broke Lea's heart?"

His hands opened on her, one on her nape under the fall of her hair, the other low on her spine. "Lea's heart was never involved. She was a nice, sweet girl, who, as she put it, wanted to take a walk on the wild side before she headed back to college at the end of the summer break."

"Having you qualified?"

"Given her pampered life and the rich boys she was usually around, I guess I did. At first I wasn't on board. I didn't want to be some princess's trophy, you know? But she tracked me down everywhere I went, constantly flirting, damn near throwing it at me, until one night at a party I finally gave in."

Merissa tilted back to eye him suspiciously. "Is she homely or something?"

He snorted. "No. Or at least, she wasn't then. I haven't seen her since."

"So you were resistant only because you didn't like

her motives? Hate to say it, Armie, but that doesn't sound like you."

"I know." Armie absently smoothed her hair while thinking about it. "Lea was one of those rich girls, and I couldn't figure out why she was after me. She always had a gaggle of her goofy girlfriends with her and they'd watch her approach, egg her on and then giggle about it. Like it was a joke maybe. Back then, the thought that she was slumming spooked me a little."

Slumming? How sad that he would think that.

"I wish I'd stuck with my instincts because I no sooner banged her than she became a superstalker and I couldn't shake her."

"Guess she liked slumming."

He gave her an absent smile. "A quickie in the upstairs of a friend's house during a crowded party wasn't all that memorable, believe me. But she started claiming she was in love with me and trying to buy me stuff. Like she offered me a car. How crazy is that?"

"A little crazy," Merissa admitted.

"I got these anonymous naked pics, some of them pretty raunchy. They didn't show a face but I knew they were from her."

"Because any other girl would have claimed them?"

"Right. How else could I show my appreciation?" He shook his head. "She stuck one under the wiper on my car, mailed a few to my house, even managed to stick one in my locker at work."

"Wow." Very stalkerish.

"Finally I just flat out told her I wasn't interested. I gave her the whole bit about it was me, not her, and that she was super sweet and all, but Cannon and I were both interested in MMA and anything serious with a girl just didn't factor in."

"Clearly your rejection didn't go over too well."

"A few weeks later the accusations started. It blind-sided me. I didn't hear them from her. It was her old man who confronted me, and he was nothing like his daughter."

When Armie went quiet, Merissa crowded in closer in silent support. For a full minute, he just held her, and she waited, not about to press him.

Finally, he said, "Mr. Baley showed up at our house with a couple of cops. He…"

Merissa stroked his chest, pressed a quick kiss to his neck.

Like steel bands, Armie's arms tightened around her. "I didn't know what the hell was going on, but Baley was quick to tell me. He said I'd raped his daughter and left her devastated. But the real kicker was that Dad didn't back me up. He was just coming off a bender, and I swear he was…I dunno, gleeful to see me under attack. He told them I was a violent punk and said I was out of control, that I'd attacked him."

Oh my God. Heartbroken for him, Merissa pushed back to see his face. "Armie, no."

"Yeah. And it was a partial truth, I guess." He shifted, seeming uncomfortable in his own skin. "You know my mom took off when I was fourteen, right?"

"I knew she was gone, but I don't recall any details." She'd been a kid back then, very uninvolved with her brother's friends.

"The details suck. Basically she just decided she'd had enough of Dad drinking and cheating, so she booked. Left me with him and never looked back."

Merissa couldn't imagine such a thing. What a devastating blow that had to have been to a teenage boy.

"I guess Dad hated being alone because over the years he moved in one woman after another. Maybe a dozen or more."

He hadn't been alone, Merissa wanted to say. *He'd had a son.*

"The last woman," Armie explained, "stuck around longer than the others, which didn't make sense because Dad didn't even seem to like her most of the time. They argued constantly and when he drank, he'd get too rough with her. One night he backhanded her and busted her lip. She crashed up against the wall, knocked over a lamp, then cut her foot on the glass." He shook his head. "Dad was enraged, standing over her and shaking his fist, threatening to throw her out while she sobbed that she didn't have anywhere to go." Armie's hands gently tangled in her hair. "I usually ignored him when he got that way, but this time it bothered me and I stupidly got between them. I told him he wouldn't touch her again."

That didn't surprise her. Armie wasn't the type to see any woman bullied. Stroking a hand down his back, she asked, "How did he react?"

"He slugged me, we tussled and I pinned him down on the couch. I never hit him, but I didn't let him go, either, not until he'd stopped raging. His lady friend was frantically cleaning up the mess and telling Dad it was okay, that she was fine, and begging him to calm down. And finally he did." Armie laughed, a humorless sound of remorse, and stepped away from her. "She should have been pissed. She should have left him. Instead, she got him another drink and apologized. Made no fucking sense to me."

Merissa whispered, "You did the right thing."

"Apparently she didn't mind the rough handling as much as I'd assumed, because when my dad bad-mouthed me to the cops, she chimed in, too. The way they told it, I had anger issues and they both acted like me forcing a girl wasn't that far-fetched."

Merissa hurt for him. She remembered her dad being very much like Cannon; a caregiver, a protector, always there whenever she needed him. He'd made her laugh when she was sad, encouraged her when she felt like giving up and loved her without restriction. Never, ever, had he laid a hand on her in anger.

Even after her father's death, her mother and Cannon had given her everything she ever needed. There hadn't been a single day where she'd ever felt unloved. She couldn't imagine her own parent turning against her the way Armie's father had turned on him. "I'm so sorry."

He shrugged that off. "I haven't seen either of them since that day."

So he'd lost first his mother, and then four years later, his father, too. Her heart tried to break, but Armie didn't need her to be wimpy. He needed her strength—and her understanding. "Good for you."

"I'd just finished school and I had a job, so as soon as the cops left, I gathered up my shit and walked out."

And went where? She recalled him spending a week or so at their house. But that was shortly after her father's death and she'd been grieving, paying less attention to her brother's hunky friends.

"I had no idea if I should get a lawyer, or how I'd even do that on minimum-wage pay." As he talked, Armie began to gather up the dishes, so she helped.

"Did you get arrested?"

"That's what Mr. Baley wanted." Armie stacked plates in the dishwasher with the ease of long practice. "He was shouting that his daughter had been abused, calling me a savage and saying I should be locked away so I didn't hurt any other girl."

Merissa tried to find some understanding for the father, knowing he'd only heard one side of a story. But the image of Armie so young, hurt but proud, made it impossible.

"Didn't work out quite the way Baley wanted, though, because the officers, a guy and a woman, said they had to investigate the concern before they started arresting anyone." His posture defensive, face averted, Armie paced away to wipe off the table. "Unfortunately, that meant talking to everyone who'd been at that party, which included most of my friends. I'd walk by and people would stare, then whisper."

"They're idiots. If they knew you then they should have known better."

"They probably did—at first. But you know how it is with nasty rumors."

"They spread like wildfire," she acknowledged, cringing for him.

"That damn story circulated so many times, hell, I almost started to believe it." He came back to the sink, braced his hands along the counter and stared out the window. "Overnight, everything changed. I don't mind admitting, I was pretty scared. It was my word against Lea's, and her father seemed not only influential, but hell-bent on seeing me crucified."

Even though it was in the past, it crushed Merissa to hear what he'd gone through—so how must it have been for him to live it, and forever remember it?

"My options seemed hopeless…" Armie turned his head toward her. "Then your brother stepped in. He worked a few miracles…and gave me the advantage."

CHAPTER SEVEN

SOUNDED LIKE HER superhero brother. "Cannon to the rescue?"

"Pretty much." A slight smile chased the grim memories from Armie's eyes. "I figured it was going to come down to my word against hers, and with her daddy's money, I wouldn't stand a chance. But Cannon had other ideas. The night Lea's dad claimed I raped her, the party was at this nice house with security cameras at each door. Cannon was friends with the family, so they didn't mind giving him the different video feeds."

"The police hadn't asked for them?"

"They probably didn't know about them." He shrugged. "I didn't. The cameras were hidden, and since there weren't any in the rooms where she claimed I raped her, the home owners might not have thought about it, either."

"But Cannon did."

"Yeah, and good thing. See, there was one in particular from the front porch that showed Lea kissing me goodbye, grabbing for my junk, riding my leg and basically hanging on me until I finally had to pry her away."

Merissa felt like her eyes might fall out. "Wow." She cleared her throat. "And that would have been after you'd supposedly forced her?"

"Yeah. It was pretty clear that I was trying to get

away and she was doing what she could to get me to stay." Armie's gaze held her. "After I drove off, she was twirling in the yard, all happy and shit."

Picturing that, Merissa almost felt sorry for the foolish girl—except that she'd put Armie through hell. "That sounds like powerful evidence."

"Embarrassing, too, especially for her." Next to Merissa, he leaned on the counter, his arms folded over his chest. "Cannon and I talked about it and decided it'd be best to see Mr. Baley before we took that video to the cops."

So even then, he'd been a gentleman. "Amazing."

"Don't saint me, Stretch. I knew if we took it to the cops it might've prolonged things while they sorted it out. So we took it to Baley. I wanted to go alone, but you know your brother."

"Yes, I do." And she could guess his argument. "You were already under the microscope. Cannon didn't want anyone to be able to pin more trouble to you."

Armie nodded. "So I stood back while Cannon showed the video to Lea's father. The man almost blew a gasket, threatening us both, lunging for Cannon, getting in his face."

Merissa didn't know Baley, but she'd still put her money on Cannon. At eighteen, her brother had been incredibly fast, strong and capable.

"I couldn't stay apart from that. But Cannon was right—I didn't want assault charges on my back, too. So I told Baley I was calling the cops." Armie drew a breath. "That, and the fact that Cannon didn't back down, that he didn't even flinch, forced Baley to calm down."

"I almost wish Cannon could have hit him a few times."

Armie gave a rusty laugh. "Yeah, me, too. But Cannon kept his cool. He told Baley he could round up more evidence from cell phones, that he could find a dozen of our friends to explain how Lea had chased me. How she'd chased me even after the supposed rape. Put that way, Baley had no choice but to let it go."

"To spare his precious daughter's rep?"

"And his own, I assume. But he was still furious, claiming I'd somehow drawn in his baby girl, that I was the one who'd corrupted her. He gave me a choice— fade away so there'd never be any chance of Lea seeing or hearing my name again, or he'd destroy me. He made it clear that he had enough money to do it, that not only could he buy witnesses and judges alike, he'd drop enough cash on my own father to get him to testify to whatever he wanted. He said regardless of any truths, the entire world would believe what he wanted them to believe if I didn't keep a very low profile."

"The nerve!"

"At the time, I just wanted to let it go."

"Why?"

Armie met her gaze. "Because he threatened Cannon, too. He said we'd both go down. And I couldn't take that chance."

Merissa already knew exactly how her brother would have reacted to that. "Cannon wanted you to fight back."

Armie cut a hand through the air. "Cannon wants to defend everyone he cares about. But this wasn't his fight! Hell, you guys had just lost your dad and he was trying to make things better for your mother, and for you." He worked his neck, as if trying to ease the tightness. "Your brother didn't need to take on my bullshit, too. Besides, I never thought it'd be an issue. Until Cannon got into the SBC, I figured I'd be a fry cook or something most of my life, just doing MMA for the fun of it. Nothing public about that."

"No reason for Lea to ever encounter you again—unless she came looking." But now he was in the SBC, already making headlines. There would be endorsements, interviews… Did Armie honestly think, after all this time, Mr. Baley was still willing to go after him? The man would have to be insane.

He crossed his arms. "Lea did try to get hold of me again."

"That bitch!" Merissa gasped.

Armie's smile twitched.

"What," she demanded, "is funny about her trying to stir up more trouble?"

"Not a damn thing, and believe me, I wasn't as nice when I told her to get lost." He touched one fingertip to the corner of her lips, and his voice went deeper. "But curse words sound funny coming from this soft mouth."

A rush of heat dipped into her belly and scattered her thoughts. "I…um…don't curse often."

"I know." He dropped his hand and took a step away. "Don't hate Lea. She was just a pampered kid who wanted to spread those wild oats you mentioned. Unfortunately, her dad is a ruthless prick and he's never let it go. Over the years he's sent me subtle reminders that he's still aware of me, and still waiting for an excuse to shred me."

"But you have proof!"

"You've seen the news, Stretch. Lead stories are all about sensational possibilities, not necessarily facts.

Once rape is mentioned, it sticks in people's minds. They think where there's smoke, there's fire. Even if I fought the lies, some would still believe them."

"But…" He couldn't be serious. "There's no 'if' to it. You *will* fight them."

Appearing curious over her reaction, he said softly, "I shouldn't have to."

Suspicions stirred, making her uneasy. "Armie?"

His gaze, suddenly heated, moved over her, head to toes and back again. "Hmm?"

"I'm glad you trusted me enough to tell me all this, but…why now?" There had to be a reason that he'd brought it up now.

He smiled at her, his dark eyes scrutinizing her expression. "Because I expected you to be furious."

The gentleness of his voice stirred the tension coiling inside her. "I am."

"You misunderstand, Stretch. I expected you to be furious *at* me, not for me."

She shook her head. She wanted to comfort him, to reassure him. She wanted to be with him.

His acute interest moved to her chest. "I thought you'd leave—"

"No." The air between them thickened, and her knees trembled.

"—and be done…"

She snapped out of the daze. "Wanting you?" Suspicions confirmed! "That's what you mean, isn't it? You wanted to scare me off."

He let his silence say it all.

And *that* made her furious. She got in his space, sharing her anger. "Is that what you want? For me to go?"

Both hands cupped her face, his thumbs brushing her cheeks. "No." He stared at her mouth. "Not anymore."

His ever-shifting moods kept her on a dizzying roller-coaster ride of emotion. But this mood, all dark and dreamy, she liked. She leaned in for a kiss.

And he said, "God, how you tempt me. But there's one more thing we need to talk about first."

"What?"

He brushed one very light kiss over her lips, then whispered, "The ink on my ass."

Oh.

Demeanor stern, Armie said, "You want to explain about that?"

Merissa bit her lip and, despite the blush she felt flooding her face, fought a grin.

His brow went up. "You think it's funny?"

Wow, he sounded so serious. "No?"

"I was in the locker room," he said with emphasis. "So were Leese and Justice."

More heat burst into her cheeks. "You didn't wash it off before you went to the rec center?"

"No, because I left here unaware that you'd played word games on my ass."

Was he really mad, or playing? She couldn't tell, and now she was starting to feel guilty. "I thought you'd see it."

"I don't make a habit of checking out my own butt." His touch, oh so tender, tucked back her hair. "Cannon called and I had to rush out of here. Imagine my surprise when I *did* finally see it—thanks to Leese holding a mirror for me in the shower."

Picturing that caused a bubble of hilarity that she tried to suppress. This was a new mood for Armie and it left her very confused, too warm, and uncertain. Laughter, she was pretty sure, wouldn't help the situation. "The, um, the guys pointed it out to you?"

"With a lot of mean mugging, yeah. Being they always have sex on the brain, they made the logical leap into some pretty big assumptions."

The nervous snicker took her by surprise before she could stop it. She slapped a hand over her mouth, but too late; his eyes had already narrowed. "Sorry," she whispered with her lips still twitching.

"You know what, Stretch? I don't think you are."

Her breath hitched when he traveled his hand down her back, past her waist, to her bottom where he clasped one cheek.

Oh Lord. He didn't do anything else, just held her. His hand was big enough that he completely enclosed half her behind.

His dark eyes stared into hers. "You put me in an uncomfortable position—and for that, I think you deserve a spanking. Don't you?"

Seriously, did she still have knees? Didn't feel like it. Armie was being all macho sexy dominant seducer, and she almost couldn't take it.

She gulped, snickered again and shook her head. "No?"

"You aren't sure?"

He looked so incredibly hot in sensual mode; his body angled toward her, his expression warm and intimate, his voice husky. And finally, for the first time, it was all aimed at her.

Unable to speak, Merissa shook her head again.

Slowly leaning in, Armie caught her bottom lip in his teeth, gently teased, nuzzled against her mouth, slicked his tongue past her lips just once, and retreated. "Maybe you need to think about it while I go get my laundry. But make up your mind fast. I'll only be five minutes."

DAMN, SHE LOOKED HOT. Turned on and uncertain but willing. Despite her denials, was this her thing? Armie knew he'd find out. He'd played this game many times with many women, always successfully. Merissa had asked an awful lot of questions about spanking, so secretly, shyly, she might love the idea.

Keeping his smile at bay, he gently squeezed one soft, round cheek. She had a killer body, long and lean, with just the right amount of curves. Now that he'd made up his mind to have her, lust kept his blood singing. If he waited any longer, he'd never be able to keep control.

With that one hand on her ass he brought her into full-body contact, kissed the corner of her mouth and murmured, "Be right back."

"O...okay."

Soon as he walked away, the grin came. He knew women, and that small, quavering voice was the sound of excitement. Already he had lethal wood, so hopefully he wouldn't run into anyone he knew.

Feeling more anticipation than he had in years, he jogged down the steps to the basement, folded the laundry into a basket and was back up to the apartment in the allotted five minutes. Silence greeted him when he stepped inside, but he sensed she hadn't run off. He locked the door, peeked into the empty kitchen, then headed to the bedroom.

With her socks gone, wearing only her jeans and the cute T-shirt that showed off her small waist and modest boobs, she sat on the side of his bed. Their gazes locked as soon as he stepped in and kicked the door shut.

He set the laundry on the floor and came to stand in front of her. Before he could say anything, she blurted, "I thought you weren't particularly into spanking."

He was into whatever pushed her buttons. Sitting beside her, their hips and shoulders touching, he took her hand and asked, "You don't think you deserve a few swats?"

Embarrassed heat kept her face flushed, making her blue eyes even brighter. She giggled again, swallowed it down and blinked fast.

Gently, his heart pounding, Armie urged her to her feet and guided her to stand between his knees. Through her shirt and bra, he could see her tightened nipples—an irresistible lure. He cupped her breasts, let his thumbs play over her nipples, and relished her quick breaths.

"Armie?" She nervously licked her lips. "I like you like this."

Ready to put her over his knee? To be sure, he asked, "This how?"

"All intent and sexy and focused on me."

"Yeah?" He'd been focused on her for a very long time. Sliding his hands under her shirt, over her silky flesh, then up, he lifted the material. "Raise your arms, honey."

She did, and he whisked the shirt away, then stared. The ice-blue lace of her bra almost exactly matched the color of her eyes. Breathing deeper, Armie said, "Pretty." He wondered if the panties were the same and brought his hands around to the snap of her very low-riding jeans. *No rush*, he told himself, and took the time to look at her flat belly, the noticeable hip bones, the slight indent of her navel. Unable to resist, he leaned forward and took a soft love bite of her flesh.

Her hands sank into his hair, and she said, "Oh."

He raised his face. "What?"

"I thought your hair would be gelled or something."

Snorting, he went back to kissing her body. "You think I mess with hair products?"

"It…" Her breath caught when he dipped his tongue into her belly button. "It stands up, all crazy, so I assumed—"

"Grows that way, I guess." Without her realizing it, he'd opened her jeans and now he teased the zipper down.

"I…um…"

Armie looked into her beautiful eyes. "What?"

"Are we going to have sex?"

Absolutely. But he said, "Let's talk about that after."

"After what?"

Without warning he shoved the jeans midway down her thighs, then guided her over his lap.

"Armie!"

Keeping one hand on the small of her back he held her steady and traced his fingers over the matching lace of her itty-bitty panties. He rested his palm flat against her.

And she started snickering again.

Hearing her made him smile, too. "You ready?"

"I thought you didn't want to hurt me!"

He gave her one firm swat, waited for her gasp and giggles to end, then asked, "Did that hurt?"

She could barely get it said around her jittery laughter, but she nodded hard. "Yes!"

"Fibber." He gave her another one, slightly harder, on the other cheek.

"Ow!" she said, then started cracking up while trying to scamper away.

Armie kept his hand against her so she couldn't lurch free, and locked one leg around hers. "We're not done, so settle down."

She went still—and kept laughing.

"You think it's funny?"

She nodded. "Yes, sorry."

When he lifted his hand, she struggled. "No!" Putting both her hands over her bottom, she gave in to more laughter. "No, it's not funny. I swear."

"But you're still laughing." He caught both wrists in one hand and exposed her ass again.

"Can't help it," she quickly explained. She drew three breaths, blowing each one out slowly, and managed to muffle some of her glee. "I'm sorry I wrote on your butt, Armie. I swear." Then she burst into another round of insane hilarity.

Armie started to chuckle, too. Clearly, while the idea tantalized her, she wasn't getting into it. He pushed her jeans the rest of the way off, then pulled her up and flat to her back on the bed. Liking the sight of her there in that sexy underwear, he stood and stripped off his shirt, then shucked off his jeans, leaving his clothes in a heap on the floor.

Her grin fading, Merissa watched him with big fascinated eyes. He didn't remove his boxers. It'd be safer, for now, to leave them on.

"You're hard," she pointed out needlessly.

"That surprises you?" He stretched out over her. Her

long hair was now tangled and residual amusement left her eyes sparkling.

"Does it mean you liked swatting me?"

He liked knowing she'd be his tonight. "Did it make you contrite?"

"Yes." She kept smiling while trying not to and, damn, it charmed him.

"You don't sound all that sorry, Stretch."

She bit her lips and blinked those mesmerizing eyes at him. "Was I supposed to moan?"

"Mmm." He bent to kiss her. "And get wet."

Her eyes widened. "Well…"

"Yeah?" Interesting. "So maybe I should check." Watching her, he flattened a hand to her belly and slowly moved it down, over her panties and between her legs. "What do you think? You're hot." So damn hot. His voice went rough. "Bet you're wet, too."

Her eyes turned all smoky and heavy and her lips parted.

He loved seeing her this way. "You like that?"

"I like *you*."

Armie wouldn't let himself get too pumped over that. Aroused women said all kinds of stuff in bed, some of it true, some of it bullshit. Merissa had wanted this, sex with him, for a while. Now that she was getting her way, she might say anything to keep on track. "What else do you like?"

"Not spanking."

He grinned with her. "You had that coming."

"I really am sorry." She cupped a hand to his jaw. "I honestly thought you'd shower and see it and just… maybe think of me."

He thought of her all the time, even when he

shouldn't. "It's permanent marker. How am I supposed to get it off there?"

"Do you have any rubbing alcohol?"

"Should."

"Then I could use that to remove it."

Which meant she'd be fiddling around on his ass again—and he'd have to have his pants off. "Only if we're both naked."

"Okay."

That immediate answer shouldn't have surprised him. Merissa had made her interest more than clear. But for a girl with the giggles, she'd gotten serious real quick.

So many times she'd come on to him, but he'd always had to put her off. No more. "You want to have sex with me, Rissy?"

"Yes."

Another fast reply. He felt compelled to ask again. "You're sure?" He didn't want her to have any regrets.

She pushed against his shoulders and he willingly went to his back. Now she loomed over him, her long hair spilling across his chest and shoulders. "I want you, Armie. You can't have any doubts at all."

His dick rejoiced.

His heart tried to join in, too, but he ignored it. One step at a time, he told himself. "We need to come to a few understandings."

"If you mean more spanking—"

God love the girl, she turned him on. "No. Not unless you want me to."

She shook her head fast. "Nope."

He couldn't hide his smile. "You have a very sweet ass, Rissy."

"Really?"

"And gorgeous legs." He put his hands on her waist and eyed her cleavage. "Everything about you is sexy as hell."

"I'm so glad you think so." Fretting, she touched the bandage on his head. "You're okay?"

"You're almost naked, talking about sex, stretched out on top of me. I'm better than okay." He tangled a hand in her hair, drew her down so he could kiss her bruised jaw. "You?"

"I'm fine."

"How was work today?" Hard to believe he'd just asked that. With any other woman, he'd be zeroed in on getting fucked. But this was Rissy, and she'd been important to him for a very long time.

She shrugged one narrow shoulder and didn't meet his gaze. "I was antsy at the bank. Dumb as it is, I couldn't stop thinking that the guys might return." She released a big sigh. "Thank you for letting me be here with you."

He needed her to know that she'd be spending the night. "Tomorrow," he said, "if you wake before me, no more sneaking off. Understand?"

"I'm off tomorrow, so that should be okay. Anything else?"

"Yes." He moved her to the side of him and came up on one elbow. "I've thought about this, about you, a million times. But the reasons I held off so long are still there." With a hand at the back of her neck, he held her still for a gentle kiss. It was something he savored, being free to kiss Rissy whenever, however, he pleased. He wanted other, deeper, hotter kisses, but he didn't mind building up to it. "I can take it if anyone attacks my character. I'm braced for it and I'll deal with it. But I won't let you get caught up in it."

She narrowed her eyes, studied him, then said, "You don't want Cannon to know."

"I have a feeling your brother already does, but he's being cagey about it." Armie had no idea what Cannon was up to, but he wasn't a mental slacker. He knew Armie better than anyone else, so no way would he think Rissy spent the night, twice, and nothing happened.

She looked momentarily nonplussed, then resigned. "You're probably right. I never could keep anything from him."

And *everyone* knew she had a thing for Armie. Maybe an infatuation, maybe curiosity because of his rep. At the moment Armie didn't know and didn't care.

He'd savor her nearness and take the rest day by day.

"What about the other guys? Their wives?" She rubbed her fingers over his bristly jaw. "I'm supposed to lie to them?"

Armie knew he had to be firm on this. "They know you stayed with me because of the bank robbery, but they respect you too much to outright ask you. Let them suppose whatever they want, just don't confirm anything publicly."

She snorted. "The guys might not ask, but believe me, Cherry is going to grill me until she hears every detail."

Armie grinned. Cherry was a superstacked doll, and so in love with Denver it was fun to watch. "I still remember telling her how hung Denver is."

Rissy's face went red.

"Yeah, you should blush, because I remember how nosy you were about it, too."

Her smile twitched and she whispered, "I'd heard so many rumors..."

Whispering, too, Armie said, "He's not here, Stretch. He can't hear you."

Laughing, she turned into him, her face tucked near his throat, one of her legs between his. He wanted her bad, but he didn't feel rushed because it all felt so special.

It was nice, indulging in presex laughter with Rissy. Probably the nicest thing he'd ever experienced.

They'd have all night, so he didn't need to miss a thing.

He hooked an arm around her, keeping her close. "Denver's a damn stallion."

"I know," she admitted. She tipped her face up to see him. "Cherry brags."

Enjoying her embarrassment, Armie teased, "Want me to take a picture for you?"

She gasped, Armie laughed, and for a second or two they wrestled.

When they stopped, Armie had her bra undone. "Well, look at that," he said. "Your bra unhooked." He tugged the material away.

"Armie!" She crisscrossed her arms and closed her hands over herself.

With one finger, he traced the pale flesh plumped up above her concealing hands. "I love watching a woman touch herself."

Her eyes went wide. "I'm not!"

"Then move your hands." He kissed her knuckles. "Let me look."

Seeming momentarily shy, then determined, her gaze locked with his and she slowly rested her hands at either side of her pillow, palms up.

Armie inhaled deeply. "Beautiful." Her breasts were round and firm, her nipples a dusky brown, drawn tight, and he wanted her in his mouth. "Tell me you can keep this, what's between us, private."

Her eyes went heavy, sexy. "An illicit affair with the notorious Armie Jacobson? Sure, I can do that."

He started to lean down and she added, "There's something you need to understand."

By the second, his need ratcheted up. "Let's hear it."

"It can't be just once."

"Guaranteed."

She flattened a hand to his chest, holding him off. "I don't mean just once tonight. I mean I want tomorrow, too."

"Count me in."

Again she held him off, this time with both hands. "I don't mean to pressure you. I know you have a fight soon—"

"Wouldn't matter if the fight was tomorrow. I'm done denying myself."

"Well then, as long as we're having this illicit affair, it's just me, no other woman."

She was so adorable. Like he'd want any other woman with her near? Hell, it felt like he'd been waiting forever for this. "You're saying you don't want a threesome?"

"Not unless you're talking another guy."

He went blank, then hot with a rush of anger, then... he saw her grin. His damn palms were damp, his heart galloping. Jesus.

"That," he growled, "might earn you another swat."

"So we agree that's out."

He pretended to think about it. "So no spanking, no threesomes. Tell me then, what are you into?"

"You." She hooked her arms around his neck. "I'm into you, Armie."

For some reason, that spooked him a little. He was known for outrageous sex. Wicked, kinky, sometimes taboo sex. Women chased him down for it. For the *sex*, not necessarily for him.

Didn't bother him; he always aimed to please.

More than any other, he wanted to please Merissa.

"You can have me." He kissed her again, this time not so sweetly. She opened for his tongue, teased her own against his, pressed closer and gave a soft moan. Against her lips, he whispered, "Don't be shy, honey. Tell me what you like."

Eyes heavy-lidded, lips swollen, she nodded, then looked around the bedroom. Tipping her head back, she let her gaze zero in on the Velcro tie at the headboard post. "I guess, if you really want, you could tie me up?"

He frowned over how she'd put that, like a question instead of a statement. "You'd like that?" He sure as hell didn't want to do anything to her she didn't like.

She nodded at the post where the tie was fastened. "I'm guessing you do, right? You use that to fasten around a woman's wrist?"

Smiling, he pressed closer to her. "These," he said, reaching up to the middle post to flip the double-hanging Velcro cuffs, "are for her hands."

Confusion beetled her brows. She studied the soft ties in the middle of the headboard, then the other ties at the outside posts. "So then those…?"

"Are for her ankles."

Her eyes went comically wide. She rounded on him. "No," she whispered.

Armie took great pleasure in saying, "Yeah. It leaves her vulnerable, as you can imagine, and has the added bonus of giving me a lot to look at."

"I'm not into that, either!"

She was so damn funny, he couldn't resist teasing her. "Oh, I dunno, Stretch." He gathered both her wrists into one hand and held them over her head, then stroked down her side to her hip, and into the back of those tiny lace panties. "You'd look awfully sweet spread-eagle—"

She squirmed, then gasped when his fingers brushed along her cleft. "Ain't happening, Armie!"

"Why not? You brought it up." He held her secure when she tried to twist away. Kissing her jaw, her ear, he whispered, "I love your ass."

"You can love it untied!"

He laughed. "Okay, don't get riled. We'll put that on the back burner for now."

She settled down with a few deep breaths. After searching his face, she said, "I have an idea."

"Yeah?" He looked at her breasts and was amazed at his own restraint. "Let's hear it."

"I think it's pretty different, at least for you."

His cock swelled more. "Okay."

She tugged at her hands so he released her, then she again pushed him to his back. Crawling half over him, her hands at either side of his face, she smiled. "Tonight, how about you tell me what *you* like, and I'll take it from there."

CHAPTER EIGHT

MERISSA LIKED THE stunned look on Armie's face. Wasn't often she could take him off guard.

She watched him gather his wits, saw his eyes narrow, and then he reached for her breasts. "I'll like making you come."

"I'm sure I'll like that, too." She didn't dissuade him from touching her. Heck no. She'd craved his touch for so long she couldn't deny him now even if she wanted to. "But do you like this? Touching me?"

Voice gravelly and deep, he said, "I *love* touching you."

"I think you'd like me touching you, also. Right?"

He went still. "Yeah."

"Could we get naked first?"

His chest expanded. His gaze burned over her. "Yeah. Naked is good."

Merissa usually felt a little insecure about her figure. She was long and lean, lacking lush curves, especially on top. But the way Armie looked at her, with so much palpable lust, she knew he liked what he saw and that made her feel sexy. She moved off the bed, smiled at him and skimmed her panties down.

Slowly, he sat up, his gaze consuming her. In a near growl, he murmured, "Come here."

She walked over to him—but when he reached for her, she took his hands and urged him to his feet.

"I want to see you, too, Armie." She didn't wait for him to remove the boxers. She did it for him, stepping close and coasting her hands over his broad chest and his hard back, and then down until she had both hands over his muscled tush.

Sinking to her knees, she took the boxers down.

Armie breathed harder.

Could a man be more stunning? His messy hair, beard scruff and tattoos added an edge to his gorgeously honed body. Everywhere she looked, everywhere she touched, he was rock solid. Sleek, taut skin on his shoulders and biceps led to sparse chest hair over his chiseled pecs, then down to dance over the ridges of his carved abdomen. With his feet stationed apart, she admired his strong, hairy calves and his thick thighs.

Finally she looked at his erection; heat expanded, spreading out to her limbs and making her tingle all over.

"I love your body, Armie. I love looking at you and feeling free to touch you." She lightly dragged her hands up the front of his thighs, then asked again, "What do *you* like most?"

"You, naked and on your knees in front of me, has to be pretty damned close."

"Good." She brought her hands up the insides of his thighs. "I can work with that."

"You don't have to work, honey." He sucked in air when she curled her hand around his straining erection. "Believe me, I want you enough already."

She stroked him slowly and reveled in his harsh groan. "For so long, you've rejected me."

"You know why." His hand petted over her head until his fingers tangled in her hair. "Truth is, I've wanted you since you were sixteen years old."

Shocked, Merissa looked up at him.

"That surprises you?" His face looked hard, his eyes dark as he struggled for composure. "I was twenty— too old to be perving on you like I did. But you were so damned sweet, so hot. You'd smile at me and all I could think about was getting under your skirt."

"You hid it well." She went back to stroking, but brought up her other hand to fondle his testicles.

"Fuck," he groaned, his eyes momentarily closing before he opened them again to stare at her with blatant hunger. "You're my best friend's lil sister. Your family was always special, to the neighborhood and to everyone who knew the Colters. I was just the guy with the drunk for a dad and the mom who ran off and—"

Merissa pressed a kiss to the underside of his erection, stopping his awful speech. She didn't want to hear him run himself down. To her, he was…everything. Protective and brave and funny. Armie was honor, reliability and the best of friends whenever someone needed him.

"You smell so good," she whispered, brushing her nose along his length, then licking back to the head, over the tip where she stole a drop of precum.

Armie said nothing, but he now had both hands in her hair, and she felt him shaking. She looked up and found him watching the mirror. She'd forgotten all about it, but as she glanced that way, too, she saw what he saw; their bodies in profile, his big and strong, his muscles clenched in arousal while she knelt before him, her hair held in his fisted hands like reins.

Still he said nothing, but in his face she saw naked emotion. In his stance—feet apart and hips forward, shoulders braced—she saw pure, piercing lust.

She loved having him like this. She loved his pleasure.

She'd loved *him*—since she was sixteen years old.

Opening her mouth, she drew him in, taking him as deep as she could.

"Rissy," he whispered, agonized.

She felt him growing taut, tasted more of him, and knew he was close—so fast. She'd expected him to last longer, but the fact that he didn't, that maybe he couldn't, thrilled her.

Each time she took his length, she sucked, and as she withdrew, she worked her tongue over him.

His powerful legs stiffened. He murmured low words, encouraging, cursing, praying a little…

Cupping one hand at the back of her neck, he drew her closer, and gave a harsh groan as he released.

Merissa stayed with him, her own heart racing, her body buzzing in excited awareness. When at last he relaxed again, his hands stroking her head, she eased back and looked up at him.

He breathed heavily, his shoulders loose, his expression both quizzical and poignant, somehow shaken and maybe even pained. He released one more big breath, then whispered, "Now you."

With ridiculous ease he caught her under her arms and lifted her up and onto the bed, parting her legs as he came down over her.

His weight pressing her into the bed was a special delight, also the way he put hot, damp kisses on her shoulder, her neck, along her jaw. His mouth touched hers as he whispered, "When you start the night like that, it's tough to beat."

She smiled, pleased that he was pleased.

Then he added, "But let me try."

SURROUNDED IN SENSATION, Armie struggled to find his usual finesse during sex. You'd think something he'd done so often, so many different ways, should be routine.

Not so, not with Rissy. The subtle scent of her hair and skin, the feel of her tight body beneath his, the touch of her small hands and, most of all, the emotion she gave him, all conspired to leave him nearly sick with need. The moment was fresh and new, incredibly hot, but also indescribably sweet, and it shook him.

I want you.

An invisible fist squeezed his heart, making him desperate to ease the restriction with her touch. With her taste. With the sounds of her release.

He kissed her, meaning for it to be sensual, an act of foreplay.

Damn if that didn't turn near desperate, too. It seemed he'd been craving her for a lifetime, with familiar fantasies that played and replayed in his mind.

But the reality was far different from anything he'd expected. She was different.

Better, when he hadn't known that was possible.

He moved down to her breasts, molding the small mounds in his hands, loving her delicate curves, and loving even more her faint gasps and whimpers as he licked her nipples, then drew one in, sucking gently. He could have done that for an hour, just relishing the intimacy as he learned her body, the feel of her, the taste of her, touching her in ways he found she liked, and ways she shied away from.

He always paid close attention to a woman's reactions, but now it wasn't a deliberate move to enhance the sex. It was because this was Rissy, and what she liked fascinated him.

He loved witnessing her building need.

"Armie," she whispered, her back arching, one leg wrapping over his.

He switched to the other breast, this time not as gently. Her hips rocked against him; he was hard again, throbbing, hurting for relief.

Leaving each nipple ripe and wet, he put open-mouthed love bites down her body, occasionally sucking to mark her, licking in certain spots, nuzzling in others.

Coming up to his knees between her long legs, he opened her thighs. He hadn't lied about enjoying the sight of a woman, most especially this woman. Her sex looked very pink and slick against the dark curls of her pubic hair. "God, you're beautiful."

She choked. "Armie."

His fingers sank into her pale inner thighs and he used his thumbs to part her lips. She was wet, glistening, her clitoris swollen with need. On a groan, he leaned down and licked over her, then in her, gathering her sweetness, inhaling the heated aroma of her arousal. He loved eating Rissy, feeling the tension grow in her lithe body, how she shifted and moaned and whispered words of entreaty.

Her cries went higher, thinner, mixing with short moans and gasps. One hand locked tight into his hair, the other fisted in the sheets. "Armie..." she breathed, then more frantically, *"Armie."*

He stayed with her, knowing she was close, pushing her, and she came with a trembling sob that went on and on. Even after she sank boneless back to the bed, he continued to lazily lick and taste her. She flinched. He knew he should stop, but this was Rissy, a fantasy come to life. He pressed his face to her, locked his arms around her thighs.

He didn't want to let the moment go.

"Armie," she whispered. "Please. Come up here to me."

His heavy heart beat like a bass drum. Sentiment tried to well up, but Rissy tugged at his ear.

"Armie," she pleaded. "I want to feel you inside me."

God, he wanted that, too. To be a part of her, to take everything from her, at least everything physical.

Taking his time, he nibbled his way back up her body. Her skin was now dewy, her scent intensified and twice as rousing.

When he reached her mouth, she smiled and said, "That was pretty amazing."

"Yeah." He kissed her neck to keep from letting her blue eyes consume him.

"I see you're not surprised," she teased. "But it was a revelation for me."

"I love eating you, Rissy."

She hugged him tight. "I liked going down on you."

His arms constricted around her. He wanted her to be his, but he had no right to expect that. Hadn't he already told her that no one could know about them?

Hating that thought, he levered up and reached to the nightstand to snag a condom. Once he had it, he fell to his back and tore it open with his teeth.

"Already?" she asked, sounding a little worried.

"Yeah." He seemed to be the master of one-word answers tonight. With haste, he rolled it on and braced himself over her again. *Beautiful.* Her feathery lashes lowered and she bit her bottom lip. Aroused color clung to her cheekbones. Armie kissed her, at first barely there, then pressing firmer, touching his tongue to her soft lips, slowly licking in until they were involved in a hot, wet mating of the mouths.

When her arms crept up around his neck, he kneed her legs farther apart and wedged one hand down between their bodies.

So slippery, soft and ready. He slicked his fingertips over her, parting her, spreading her wetness, then pushed two fingers into her.

She freed her mouth from his and put her head back. "Ah… God."

Pleasure pulsated, expanding and withdrawing, until all he could see, all he could feel and taste and smell was Rissy. He took her mouth again, drunk on kissing her, raw with need. He worked her with his fingers until she was again ready, then shifted, nudged against her with his cock and slowly sank in.

They groaned roughly together.

Rissy immediately moved against him, lifting into him with a frantic rhythm.

He gentled her with a hand to her hip. "Slow down, babe. Nice and easy." He didn't want to come too quickly, not with her.

Her nails sank into his shoulders. "I don't know if I can."

Pulling her hands down and lacing her fingers with his, he pressed her hands to the pillow and nuzzled her throat while slowly, heavily thrusting. He watched her, how her eyes went dazed and the wild tripping of the pulse in her throat.

That damned emotion ripped at him again, making it hard for him to inhale, to swallow. Putting his forehead to hers, he shared her breath as he ground against her, feeling her tighten, squeeze him, milk him.

To keep his release at bay, he concentrated on her. Deliberately he brushed his hairy chest to her sensitized nipples, thrust shallow and slow, then deep and fast, teasing her, keeping her on the very edge.

Heat built between them. Their skin melded together. She tossed her head, straining, wanting to come but controlled by him. Releasing her hands, he came up on stiffened arms to watch the shimmying of her breasts. Thinking of how she'd gone down on him so naturally, how she'd seemed to enjoy it, he pumped faster, pressed deeper.

"Come with me," she gasped, her hands clutching at him. "Armie, *come with me*." Her slender body bowed and she cried out, the sound first high and thin, before going low in a deep guttural moan as she climaxed.

Overwhelmed by the potent mix of emotional and physical pleasure, a first for him, Armie put his head back and let himself go. The release was so intense, so shattering, that he lost himself, only to realize a short time later that Rissy was stroking the back of his neck and putting an occasional affectionate kiss to his shoulder.

Ah, hell. Still sucking air, he sluggishly lifted up to see her.

All gentle and sweet and satisfied, she smiled at him. Her silky hair was everywhere, her lips reddened from his kisses, her eyes smoky.

"You're dangerous," he told her.

Her laugh was happy, carefree, and proved she didn't believe him.

Keeping her close, Armie rolled to his back and released a big breath. Rissy curled against him, her fingers playing with his chest hair.

"Armie?" She sighed and kissed him again, this time on his chest. "That was pretty wonderful."

He hugged her, kissed the top of her head and concentrated on finding the right words.

He didn't have to bother, because Rissy had plenty to say.

"The other night, when you were drunk?"

Dreading her answer, he asked, "What about it?"

He heard the grin in her voice when she said, "You talked about your cocksmanship."

God. "You should never pay attention to the ramblings of a drunk."

"You said you were a better cocksman when drunk."

Wishing she'd quit saying it, he bit back the groan of humiliation. "Sounds like me."

"Something about—" she snickered "—using your cock like a *sword*."

"Enough." He turned so she was under him again. "I think someone liked her spanking and is looking for another."

Now she laughed outright. "Maybe I want to try spanking *your* sexy butt."

What an appalling thought. "Never happening, Stretch, so forget it." He dipped down to take her mouth, then liked that enough that he kept on kissing her, until kissing wasn't enough, until they were both primed again.

He'd just come twice. That should make him good for some extended foreplay. Rissy deserved that, and more.

For now, at least, he was the lucky man ready and willing to give it to her.

STEVE PACED THE private room at the club, his anger simmering just below the surface. He would never forget the feeling of broken fingers, busted ribs.

And that damn nut shot. His balls hurt just thinking about it.

Armie Jacobson—*now he had the bastard's name*—had really put it to him. *After* he'd taken apart Steve's friends. He'd walked through each of them as if he fought women. Or kids.

Steve wasn't a slouch, damn it. He knew how to fight, was strong and fast. But clearly not strong enough or fast enough to go up against a trained MMA fighter.

"You know where he is," Keno said with a shrug. "I'll go there and put a bullet in him. End of story."

First thing he'd done after leaving Merissa's house was a quick internet search of Armie Jacobson. Since he frequented the same rec center as Merissa's brother, it had been easy enough. Jacobson lived in the area, worked at the gym and apparently would be competing on a professional level.

It was no wonder he hadn't stood a chance against him.

"I don't want to murder him," Steve growled. Jesus. That was the problem with hiring lowlifes. They were always pushing to cross the line. "I just want to destroy him."

Boyd said, "Death would destroy him."

Steve ignored them both, still pacing. He'd found out what he could locally; Jacobson's address, his Facebook profile, his work schedule and when his next fight would be. Then he'd hired a professional PI to find out everything else. He'd used the PI before and knew he could be counted on for discretion.

Bored, Keno said, "You realize I have better shit to do than watch you fret like an old lady."

Eyes narrowed, Steve turned to him. Keno looked like shit—more of Jacobson's doing. "If you hadn't fucked up the robbery, she'd be with me now. But he handed your ass to you." He slanted his attention to Boyd. "To *both* of you. And you were armed!"

"Didn't know a fucking MMA fighter would be there."

Keno took it one further, standing to face off with Steve. "*You* fucked up, not us. You said to spook the woman. Period. You didn't say anything about a professional ass kicker playing her personal bodyguard."

"I didn't know he'd be there, either." Steve ran a hand over his head, leaving his hair mussed and not giving a shit. All he'd wanted was for Rissy to be robbed. Everyone would know about it, of course, and that'd give him a viable reason to check on her. He'd already learned that her roommate was gone, so she'd be in her house, alone, vulnerable, shaken from being robbed at gunpoint. And he'd have played her hero.

For months he kept thinking she'd come back to him. But she didn't and it still infuriated him whenever he thought of how she'd walked away. He hadn't loved her, but more than any other woman, he'd cared for her. They'd been good in bed, and out of bed she wasn't too demanding. She was independent rather than needy.

She could carry on an intelligent conversation. And her brother was a local hero. He'd figured on marrying the bitch eventually. But when he'd been at his worst, beaten and hurting, she'd given him the boot.

No one treated him that way.

It had taken him months of stewing to finally decide he couldn't just let it go. He had to get even—so he'd instigated a simple robbery. He knew enough about her branch that it was easy to plan. Boyd and Keno were capable, but perhaps too ruthless.

Though not ruthless enough to finish the job properly.

Right now, Merissa should be welcoming him back into her life, full of apology, needing him—and then the outcome of their relationship would be in *his* hands.

Instead she was with Jacobson and it enraged him.

"We were supposed to keep the cash," Boyd complained.

Of course they were. But they'd fucked that up, too.

Boyd shrugged. "Now we got jack shit."

With enough sense to know he didn't want to get on Boyd or Keno's bad side, Steve shook his head. "I'll pay you a grand each." He needed their silence and co-operation. Especially now that shit had gone sideways.

The thugs shared a look, and Keno turned cagey. "Make it fifteen hundred apiece and we might be agreeable."

Through his teeth, Steve said, "You're the ones who left the money behind."

"So?" Keno narrowed his cold blue eyes. "We put it

on the line for you and things did not go as you claimed they would."

Shit. "I don't know if I can scrape up that much, but give me a few days to see." Steve had that and more, piece of cake. But he wasn't in the mood to be hustled by two clowns. "Now—"

The ringing of his cell phone interrupted him.

A glance at the screen told him it was the PI. Did he have news on Jacobson already? Maybe the prick was married, or even engaged. That'd get him tossed out of Merissa's life real quick.

After he answered the call, Steve realized the PI had something even better than a romantic commitment.

He had the big score.

It'd be the perfect way to drive the fighter away from Merissa—and in the process he'd get to destroy him.

For good.

LEESE LEANED HIS elbows back on the counter at Rowdy's bar. It was crowded, as always on a Saturday night. He saw most of the guys from the rec center, but Armie and Merissa were notably absent. Smiling, he sipped his drink and took in the different ladies glancing his way.

Cannon joined him, his arm around Yvette. "Solo tonight?" Cannon asked.

"So far." He tipped his head at Yvette. "How're you feeling?"

"Just fine." She put a hand over her belly. "Excited."

Funny, because she didn't look preggers, but she already glowed. He figured that was happiness more than the baby.

Just then his phone beeped and he took it out of his pocket to see a message.

Rissy was here—but she won't be there. Sorry!

Standing next to him, Cannon saw and lifted a brow. "She's texting you?"

He sent a No problem text back to her and returned the cell to his jeans pocket. "She'd said she might be in tonight, depending on how things went with…" The words fell off, and he exchanged Armie's name with "…her day."

Cannon gave him a funny look, but then Yvette spoke to him, indicating that she was going to join Stack and Vanity at a table. He kissed his wife, put a hand to her flat belly and kissed her again.

Leese felt like a damned voyeur, so he looked away and thought again about that message scrawled on Armie's ass. Despite the explanations he'd been given, he knew Rissy was nuts for Armie. He assumed Cannon knew it, too, but things might be viewed differently by a brother.

"So she's not coming in?" Cannon asked after his wife had walked away.

Leese shook his head. "Guess she has other plans." Plans that probably involved private time with Armie.

"You two had a date?"

Quick to shake his head, Leese said, "Negative." Jesus, he didn't need Cannon thinking things like that. "She'd asked if I was going to be around, that's all. In case nothing better came up." He was pretty sure Armie was finally "up" with Rissy. And he was happy for her, as long as Armie didn't break her heart. "We're just friends."

"So you don't mind that she's probably with Armie?"

"No." Cautiously, Leese asked, "You assume she is?"

Cannon's grin came slowly, then turned into a short laugh. "I like that you're trying to protect her, but you don't ever need to do that, not with me." He ordered a beer, then took the bar stool beside Leese. "You know Armie was there with her at the bank when the robbery happened."

"Everyone knows." And Leese also knew that since then, Armie had been different with Rissy, less like a friend and more like a man guarding what was his.

"I think it shook up both of them, and it's nice that they can work that out together."

"If you say so." He watched a woman walk by, appreciating the smile she sent in his direction. "Look, I know Armie's a really good guy."

Cannon nodded. "The best."

"He has a great rapport with the kids, especially the little toughies." Kids from bad homes, some of them neglected, came in with bad attitudes and a lot of hurt. "Armie has a way of getting them to settle down and take part."

"He gives them a positive focus. For some reason, they relate to him."

Leese laughed. "One toughie to another?"

"Probably," Cannon agreed with his own grin. "They're in awe of his tats. Plus he never looks riled. He just reins in tempers and keeps kids in line so that the quieter kids and the potential punks can all get along. It's always impressed me. That's one reason why he runs most everything at the rec center. He has a knack for it."

Leese set his drink on the bar and shifted to face Cannon. "He has this way of acting like he's known everyone forever. You know what I mean?"

"I do." Cannon, too, set aside his drink. "Armie isn't easily impressed or intimidated, so to him, no one is a big deal or a problem. He isn't shy or modest and no one scares him."

"Oh, I dunno." This is where Leese felt he had to tiptoe. But Cannon seemed in the mood for a heart-to-heart, so why not? "I think your sister scares him plenty."

Cannon studied him, then clapped him on the shoulder with a grin. "That's pretty damned observant. And yeah, I've always thought the same. It's because she matters to him. Armie is like a brother to me, but it's different with Rissy. Not like the significant others with his friends, and not like the women who helped to build his rep."

"His rep would scare most brothers."

"Rissy is a really strong person. Independent, too. She knows I'd like to spoil her, but she insists my success is my own and she can take care of herself. But the robbery, being held at gunpoint…" His jaw worked. "Regardless of how she tries, having some bastard maul her and put a gun in her face, that's not something she's going to push past. And if I can't be with her, then I'm glad Armie is."

Nice that Rissy's brother was okay with the setup. For her sake, Leese hoped Armie felt the same. But given what he'd witnessed so far, he wasn't convinced.

Seemed everyone was on board with them being together—except for Armie himself.

When Yvette called him over, Cannon stood. "I'm glad you're keeping an eye out for her."

"No problem." Hell, all the ladies, especially Vanity and Rissy, considered him a confidant. For whatever reason, they trusted him with their secrets, and their worries. Leese wasn't sure if that was a compliment to his character, or an insult to his masculinity.

"You might not see it," Cannon continued, "and Armie would deny needing it, but do me a favor and keep an eye out for him, too, will you?"

"You're serious?"

Cannon nodded. "Everyone is so used to Armie being outrageous, it's tough to notice when he's struggling. It's not the workload, and it's not the SBC debut. But seeing Rissy threatened—that put him in a tail-spin."

"What do you expect me to do?" Leese just naturally looked after kids or women or whatever. Old people or stray dogs. But Armie was a phenomenon. A natural fighter that everyone assumed would carve a straight line to the title belt. How the hell would Leese be of any help?

"You're single. If you see him out and about and he has a problem, any problem, whether you think he'd want your interference or not, let me know."

"Sure." But it felt weird as shit to babysit Armie "Quick" Jacobson.

"Thanks. And Leese? Keep it to yourself."

"What?"

"All of it. Anything to do with my sister or Armie."

Yeah, that was the big brother speaking, what he'd expected all along. "For the record," Leese said evenly, "I would have done that without the warning."

"I figured. Thanks."

Cannon no sooner left than Justice and Brand joined him. A few minutes after that, several ladies invited them to their table. Leese soon had his mind on other things—like the cute brunette who invited him back to her place.

Right before they left, he heard two of her friends ask about Armie, and he smiled. Since he knew Rissy wasn't the type to share, he figured Armie was off the market, at least for now.

And if Rissy got her way, Armie would never have another three-way. He almost felt sorry for him—except that Rissy was a catch, and if the lucky SOB didn't screw it up, Leese was pretty sure she was the one woman who could make Armie a very satisfied man.

CHAPTER NINE

THE NEXT MORNING, Armie woke when Rissy left the bed. He cracked open an eye and watched her pull on a sweatshirt. Shame to cover that sweet body. When she peeked back at him, he closed his eyes and feigned sleep.

Being with her like this was incredible, but also left him reeling. How long could he keep her?

He sensed her moving closer to the bed, and then the mattress dipped.

He turned to face her, saw her startled expression and said with stern warning, "You weren't planning to write on my ass again, were you?" It had taken her a damn hour scrubbing with rubbing alcohol to finally get the marker removed.

Part of the problem was her distraction. She kept pausing to fondle his balls, or kiss the back of his thigh...

"Rissy?"

Holding up both hands to show she didn't have a marker, she bit back a grin. "I was just looking to see if it was all gone."

"You damn near scrubbed my skin off."

"Want me to kiss it?"

That did it. Full-blown boner. "C'mere." He caught

her and dragged her into the bed atop him, then wrestled off the sweatshirt she'd just put on.

Unfortunately, when he started to kiss her, she stiff-armed him. "Wait!"

"Okay." Releasing her and scooting up in the bed to sit against the headboard, he asked, "What's up?"

Fussing, she pulled up the sheet to partially cover her body, then smoothed back her hair. But her longer than long legs were right there, her feet tucked under her, and she looked like a wet dream come to life. "I need to brush my teeth."

First time a woman ever said that to him. But then again, he didn't have many morning-after conversations with women. "Seriously?"

She nodded. "And I need…makeup. And a shower. We *both* need a shower."

Her modesty softened his heart. "You saying I stink?"

"No!" Immediately she was against him, her nose in his neck, brushing against him and making his dick harder. "You smell *so* good."

Armie laughed—and subtly tried to lead her hand south. "I was teasing, Stretch."

Not so subtly, she tucked her hand under the sheet and wrapped her warm, slender fingers around him. "Mmm. You want me again?"

God, he wanted her always. "Yeah."

"I'd like to shower with you."

"Okay, sure." Hard to talk now with her stroking him.

Hesitant, she tipped her face back to see him. "The thing is, I'm not sure what we're doing."

Easy enough. "You're jerking me off and I'm close to losing it."

Laughing, her hand going idle on his junk, she whispered, "You are so bad."

"I'm not the one with a dick in my hand."

"Armie." Surprising him, she crawled up and over him to sit on his abdomen.

He felt the heat of her on his stomach, how her silken inner thighs hugged his ribs. Looking beyond her, he caught the reflection of her back and small bottom in the big mirror on the wall. *Slender and sexy and, for now, all his.*

"Damn, Stretch, I like this even better." Fingers spread, he coasted his hands from her knees up the outside of her thighs to her bottom cheeks. Watching her intently, he traced her cleft—and saw her face go pink as he let his fingers play.

That turned him on more, so he urged her forward a little until she balanced on her knees over him. Putting one hand under her, he found her heated vulva with his fingertips—and saw everything reflected in the mirror.

Knowing he could see her, she whispered brokenly, "Armie…"

"You're beautiful."

A wave of flushed heat stained her breasts, throat and face—but she didn't deny him.

Nice. She wanted to satisfy him. Not as much as he wanted to satisfy her, but that'd be impossible anyway. With one fingertip, he parted her lips, barely entered her, and teased along already slick, sensitized flesh. "If you grab a condom," he told her in a growl, "you can ride me."

Biting her lip and closing her eyes, she nodded. Then

she inhaled and stared down at him. "I need to know what we're doing today. And no, don't go into more sex jokes. I'm off—"

"Well I'm still *trying* to get off."

"—and I know you don't usually hang at the rec center on Sunday. At least, not all day." She cupped his face. "So what are we doing? Should I get dressed and leave?"

"No." Hell no. He was on the ragged edge and she talked about booking?

"Or we could have sex, and then I could head home to shower."

"I have a damn shower." And he'd already imagined being in it with her.

"Or," she said, visibly bracing herself, "we could spend the whole day together. Sometimes having sex, maybe watching a movie. I could cook for you and we could talk more. Whatever you want."

Why the idea of spending the day with her panicked him, Armie couldn't say. Other than indulging in a sexual marathon, he'd never spent that much time with a woman. Sure, he wanted to talk with her. And he'd help her cook.

The idea of the two of them, all cozy on his couch, soaking up a movie—the image played out like a daydream, surreal but awesome. And that left him unsettled, too, but he hoped he hid it well. As quick cover, he teased, "Whatever I want, huh?"

She surprised him again with a very serious, somber nod. "I trust you, remember? I know you wouldn't ask me to do anything I didn't want to do."

What did she want to do? His heart started pounding, only partly because of the carnality of her offer.

The rest was straight-up uncertainty of the future, of wanting what his conscience told him he couldn't have. She taunted him with near impossibilities. As exposed as he felt, he couldn't bear the idea of ever hurting her again—and yet, letting her in might cause her the most pain.

Still, it was possible that she'd get her jollies, and then move on. His guts cramped at that thought, but it'd be best for her. She wanted this, with him, and he was more than happy to oblige her. But anything more?

The future, *her* future, would be up to her and Rissy was a smart woman. She always made good choices.

Odds were she wouldn't choose him.

"All that?" she asked, touching her fingers to his brow, easing his frown. "I'm sorry. I didn't mean to put you on the spot."

The vulnerability on her face decided him. "Stay." He took her shoulders and pulled her down so he could hug her to his heart. "I need to jog, then we can shower. And a movie sounds great." He turned to put her under him. "But first, I need you." He kissed her, his lips brushing over hers, nudging hers to open so he could slip his tongue in, gradually going deeper, hotter, until they were full-on making out.

She'd clearly forgotten about morning primping.

When he took his attention to her delicate throat, she gasped, "Okay."

"This is going to be fast." Waking up with Rissy had him ready to explode. "But during the shower I'll need you again."

She laughed as he put damp nibbles down to her breasts. "Sounds like a plan."

"And maybe during the movie…"

"Bad," she whispered, when he latched onto her nipple and sucked softly. "You are so bad and, oh God, Armie, so incredibly good."

ON WEDNESDAY, AFTER a crazy day at the bank, Merissa was more than thrilled to be heading home. She hadn't been at her house much, mostly just to grab clothes and check on things. So far with Armie, the more time they spent together, the more he seemed to want her around.

She loved every second with him, so she'd never complain, but she wished she knew what it meant. There were times when he looked like he wanted to devour her. Granted, she was usually naked while receiving those hungry stares.

But there'd been a few other times, like when she woke up on Monday and found him propped on an elbow, just looking at her all superserious and intense. For a second, she'd thought she saw love in his eyes. But then he kissed her and she couldn't concentrate enough to analyze anything, much less Armie's moods.

So far, the way they worked it was that she'd spend the night with him, then run home early enough in the morning to change into her work clothes. But each day before she left, he'd give her one of those probing stares, almost as if he fought with himself, or couldn't figure her out, then he'd say, "See you back here later?" As if it didn't matter, but in his dark eyes, she saw the uncertainty.

She wasn't a fool. She knew she wouldn't change Armie. But she now knew the facts, knew of his childhood and everything he'd gone through. It didn't explain his sexual overdrive, but it did make sense when she considered his apparent lack of interest in a lasting relationship.

She respected her brother for keeping Armie's secrets, but if she'd known sooner, it might have made a difference.

Never would she pressure him; she had too much pride for that. But she couldn't help hoping that he'd enjoyed their time together as much as she did and that maybe, just maybe, he'd fall in love with her.

March had rolled in with unusual springlike weather, and as Merissa left the bank, she didn't bother buttoning up her coat. The sun felt heavenly. Soon the days would be getting longer; a blessing, given it was usually dark when she went into work, and dark still when she got off.

She'd almost reached her car when her phone rang. Thinking it'd be Armie, she paused to snatch it out of her purse and swiped the screen without even seeing the number. "Hello?"

"You hussy."

Oh. Not Armie, but her closest friend, Cherry. "Hey." Continuing on to her car, now smiling, she asked, "What's up?"

"Armie, apparently nonstop. I mean, that's all I can assume since you've been MIA and so has he. I'm right, aren't I? Please tell me I'm right!"

Laughing, Merissa unlocked her car and got in. "I told him you would demand I tell you everything."

"Great. So let's do dinner. I want to hear every juicy detail."

"Umm…" Much as she loved Cherry, she really looked forward to heading over to Armie's.

"No hedging," Cherry told her. "Armie's held up at

the rec center so you may as well kill some time with me. I'm not taking no for an answer."

"Okay, but only if you promise not to tell anyone."

"Ohmigod." Cherry's voice lowered to a scandalized whisper. "It's all kinky, isn't it? I *knew* it would be."

She laughed. "No, and where do you want to meet?"

"Rowdy's will do. I love their soup on Wednesdays. How soon can you be there?"

"I just need to run home to change. So…forty minutes?"

"I'll be there." Cherry hesitated, then added, "I'm so happy for you, Rissy."

Merissa thought she might burst. Grinning, she admitted, "Me, too." It'd be great to share with a friend. Keeping all the wonderfulness bottled up hadn't been easy. She made a kissing sound through the phone, disconnected, put her phone on the dash—then jumped when someone tapped on her driver's-side window.

Hand to her heart, she turned and found Steve standing there. The setting sun gilded his brown hair and reflected off his mirrored sunglasses. A little unnerved, Merissa rolled down her window. "Steve. What are you doing here?"

"Checking on you." He folded his arms over the base of the window frame and leaned in, smiling at her. "Should I be jealous?"

"Um…" She leaned as far away in her seat as she could. "About what?"

"Whoever you were just kissing on the phone."

"Oh." Laughing, she shook her head. "That was my friend, Cherry."

"Really?" He took off his sunglasses. "Now there's a visual that'll keep me intrigued for a while."

Perv. "I love her like a sister, Steve."

"I know. I remember Cherry." His gaze moved over her face, and his voice softened. "I was just teasing." Before Merissa could ask him to leave, he said, "She moved out, didn't she? Married some big hulk?"

"Denver Lewis, and yes, they're married now." Very happily. Denver was something of a caveman, overly protective and very possessive, but in the gentlest way possible. And he adored Cherry. In contrast, Vanity's husband, Stack Hannigan, was deceptively laid-back. It took a lot to get him riled, but once there, look out. It was pretty awesome that they'd gotten married around the same time. "Now, why are you here?"

"I was in the neighborhood, having lunch with a client." Voice going smooth as velvet, he said, "I think about you a lot. How are you holding up?"

"Because of the robbery, you mean?" It was conceivable that he'd had lunch. There was a nice Italian restaurant only a block away from the bank, and as the CEO of a marketing firm, he often had business lunches.

"Yes." Before she could stop him, he reached for her chin, tipping her face to see her jaw. "That awful bruise is almost gone."

Most of the time Merissa forgot about it. Lifting away from him, she said, "I'm fine."

"I'd still like to see you."

"No."

"Because you're involved with Jacobson?"

Oh, how she wanted to say, *Yes, we're an item*. But she'd promised Armie to keep it quiet, so she just sighed. "He has nothing to do with it. I told you we're over, and I meant it. A few months hasn't changed anything."

"It's changed me." Dropping his head forward as if dejected, he said, "I screwed up and I know it."

"Wasn't you," she told him honestly. "It just wasn't there."

"Maybe it was for me."

Then he'd hidden it well. "If that's so, I'm sorry." Making a point of checking the time, Merissa said, "I need to go."

"Right. I didn't mean to keep you. But will you promise me something?"

Doubtful. "What?"

"If anything happens, if you just need a friend to listen, give me a call. I promise I won't let you down."

Damn it, now she was starting to feel sorry for him. "Sure, thanks." She smiled. "Now I really do need to go or I'm going to be late."

Nodding, he stepped back.

Merissa quickly put the window back up and started the car. She didn't want to hit the locks with Steve standing there, listening, but his nearness bothered her on multiple levels. She didn't breathe easy until she'd pulled away and put him in her rearview mirror.

Anticipating lunch with Cherry, and then the evening with Armie, she shook off her misgivings about Steve. He was in her past, and now she only wanted to concentrate on the future—with Armie.

HEADING INTO ROWDY'S bar with the heavy hitters, Armie felt like a fraud. He despised the fanfare.

Why couldn't he just fight, like he'd always done? Wasn't his performance in the cage enough?

As they entered, Jude turned heads. Though he hadn't been in a movie for a while, everyone recognized him. He stayed visible by actively supporting the troops, heading up numerous charities and promoting the SBC.

The fact that he had fight legends Simon Evans and Dean Connors with him only added to the stares. Even though he'd been married awhile now, women claimed that Simon was so gorgeous, panties just automatically dropped. And Dean, better known as Havoc and also married, got his own fair share of admiring stares.

He might as well have walked in with a king, the pope and the president for all the attention they got.

Rowdy met them halfway across the floor. "Bringing in the big guns, Armie?"

"They insisted."

That made Rowdy grin. "Sorry I don't have a private room, but Avery is clearing a back booth right now if that'll do."

Jude held out his hand, thanked him and agreed to let Rowdy take a photo for the wall.

Shaking his head, Armie looked at Dean. "How do you stand it?"

"He's too nice to despise."

"I tried," Simon said, then studiously avoided looking at a woman who whistled.

Jude took it in stride, grinning at them and following Rowdy to the booth.

That was one thing Armie truly admired about the men—they were dedicated to their wives. Many men with their clout would use the popularity to carouse, but from what he could tell these guys were each faithful, showing only polite manners to the outrageously flirting women.

Because he despised cheats, Armie knew if he ever married, he'd be the same.

"I'll apologize in advance," Rowdy said, "but there are a lot of fight fans here and they can only be held off for so long. In a town this size, word is going to spread fast."

Armie looked around the room and saw at least two dozen people frantically sending texts. "Shit." He shrugged at the men who would be his company for the next hour. "You guys want to do an impromptu gig? Rowdy'll be better able to hold them off if you agree to some fan photos in say…" He checked his watch, realized Rissy was off work and wanted to groan. "How about an hour?"

Jude said, "Why not?"

"Fine by me," Havoc said. "Simon?"

"Sure. And if any new fighters are around, gather them up. We'll give them some exposure."

Brows lifted, Rowdy said, "That'd be great if you're sure it's not a problem."

"No problem at all."

"All right, I'll spread the word and buy you some privacy until then." After taking drink orders, he left them.

Simon watched him go, then eyed the others at the table. "Is it just me, or does Rowdy seem like he has a whole hell of a lot more going on than bar owner?"

Armie grinned. He wasn't about to go into Rowdy's history with everyone, but he did say, "He's only the latest owner of the bar. Before that, yeah, he had a lot going on."

"He's got an edge to him," Jude agreed.

"Cannon told me some of it." Havoc sat back. "I don't think he'd mind if I shared."

"You do that," Armie said as he took out his phone and quickly texted Rissy to let her know he was held up. Just as he was about to send the message, he heard her laugh.

What the hell? Midstory he made Havoc move to let him out, stepped from the booth and scanned the room. Merissa had just walked in with Cherry and already guys were eyeballing them. Together the ladies made an interesting contrast; Rissy was tall, slender, with long dark hair, while Cherry was much shorter with a generous rack and curly blond hair.

Damn it. Where the hell was Denver? He'd keep the knuckleheads away.

When Rissy pulled off her coat, the sight of her squeezed all the oxygen out of Armie's chest. She wore a stretchy, black lace top that hugged her upper body enough to make his mouth water. Her jeans, superlow and long, emphasized the length of her killer legs. She'd added extra makeup and even curled the ends of her long hair.

For who?

"Problem?" Havoc asked.

Hell, he'd almost forgotten he had an audience and definitely hadn't realized they'd stopped talking about Rowdy. Without looking at any of his companions, Armie said, "No." Not one that he could acknowledge anyway, definitely not one he'd share with another guy.

He sent the text, saw Rissy immediately grab her phone, smile and quickly thumb in a reply. Soon as it hit his phone, Armie read, Cherry told me. Visiting w/ her @ Rowdy's. Let me know when ur done & I'll head over. Miss you!

So it wasn't that she'd accepted Cherry's offer over

seeing him, and it wasn't to get with another guy. She'd dolled up extra sweet for him.

Tension uncoiled from his neck and shoulders, when damn it, tension shouldn't have been there anyway. He missed her, too, but only texted back, Will do. Have fun. Then took his seat again.

Havoc looked at him, then toward Rissy and back again. "Should I ask?"

"No."

Frowning in confusion, he slid into the booth seat. "Isn't that—"

"Thought you weren't going to ask." Armie stared at him, hard.

Jude and Simon both looked quizzical.

With a slow grin, Havoc shrugged. "Long as it doesn't interfere with your debut—"

"Don't worry about it."

"Ah," Simon said, nodding his shaved head with sage wisdom. "A woman."

"That's usually the only interference mentioned," Jude agreed.

They both started to scan the room, presumably to find the woman in question, but with perfect timing, Rowdy returned with their drinks. "On the house," he said as he served them. "It's the least I can do, so feel free to order whatever you want."

"Burger and fries?" Simon asked.

"I've had the cheeseburger," Havoc said. "Really good."

"My cook, who's also a fight fan, will own eternal bragging rights," Rowdy told them. "How about I bring a platter and some plates?"

The offer was met with enthusiastic agreement.

So they planned to do dinner? Shit. Armie stewed over that, wishing he could be elsewhere.

Like with a certain tall, adorable lady, who also happened to be scalding hot—

Just then, Cherry and Merissa took a table across the room from them. It was distracting enough thinking about her, but now he could see her, too—her every smile, how she gestured while speaking enthusiastically with Cherry, the way the ladies laughed together.

Watching Cherry go wide-eyed, a hand over her mouth, Armie wondered if they were gossiping about sex.

When Cherry fanned her face, he knew they were.

Merissa nodded, then crossed her heart, and Armie outright laughed, making the other men wonder.

"Sorry." Clearing his throat, he folded his arms on the booth top and asked, "So, what do you need me to do?" Maybe once he gave agreement and assurances, he could get on his way.

Not so.

For the next hour they talked promo and appearances. No problem. He never minded talking with spectators.

"Usually," Havoc said, "we ask the guys to dress it up a bit."

"Suit and tie," Simon said. "Take it serious. Be sincere."

"I can do that," Armie told them, but he already dreaded it. He was much better at just winging it, at listening to the fans and laughing with them, mugging for photos and all in all, having a good time. But he had given his word that he'd dive in, so—

Jude shook his head. "We discussed it before coming here, and part of your appeal—"

Lip curled, Armie asked, "My *appeal*?"

"—is you."

They all waited, putting him on edge. "What the hell does that mean?"

Deliberately provoking, Simon said in an aside to Havoc, "Touchy." Then he grinned at Armie and overly articulated, "Your fans like you 'as-is.' They don't want you prettied up."

Prettied up? Armie scratched his chin. "So no suit?"

"You might have to tone down the suggestive tees," Havoc explained, "but otherwise, just be yourself."

"You've already built this enormous fan base," Jude said. "And they don't want you to change."

"Whatever you say."

"They like your rebel attitude."

Armie snorted. "I'm not a rebel." That sounded insecure and annoying.

"Nonconformist then." Jude disregarded the wording as if it didn't matter. "The fact you've avoided the SBC, that you fight without the fame—"

"Or the bumped-up paycheck," Havoc added.

"—has impressed a hell of a lot of people."

Armie frowned. "It's not about impressing anyone. I just like to compete."

"And win?" Havoc asked.

He shrugged. "Prefer it to losing, sure."

The three men grinned as if he'd just given the right answer.

"Without near the exposure most fighters in the SBC get, you've made a name for yourself."

"Wasn't trying to."

Simon nudged Havoc. "He wasn't even trying."

"It's like this organic movement, growing bigger every day." Jude pushed aside his empty plate and leaned forward. "Talk to just about anyone competing in the sport and they've heard of you. Spectators who follow the sport know your name."

"No shit?" Well hell. His intent had always been a low profile.

"They whisper about you," Havoc said, "like you're an urban legend."

"Or," Simon added, "the average man's hero. You're more like them, but doing what they can't do."

Jude gestured. "It's as if you represent all of them."

Frustrated, Armie rubbed both hands over his face. "Look, you want me to fight, so I'll fight. And I'll do my damnedest to win. But I'm not trying to represent anyone."

"Tough," Simon told him. "That's how it is with hometown heroes. People admire you."

"Now wait a damn minute." Intent on correcting them, Armie straightened in his seat. "Cannon's the hometown hero, not me."

"That's not how Cannon tells it." Havoc indicated the crowd at the bar, including many of his friends. "Or any of the other fighters in your camp."

Armie thought about pounding all of them. Well, except maybe Cannon. He was long used to Cannon's never-ending backup. "Why the hell would anyone tell you that bullshit?" It was irritating and ridiculous and he was *not* a fucking hero.

Misunderstanding, Jude said, "You're humble. That's good."

It felt like his temples tried to compress his brain.

"No," Armie growled out, "I'm not." He was the outrageous one. The one who bragged. He had no modesty, and he sure as hell wasn't *humble*.

"Just take a breath," Simon encouraged. "It's all good."

Sure, if by "all good" he meant seriously fucked. "This is why I avoided the SBC. It's not me. It's not—"

"Anonymous enough?" Jude shook his head. "Forget it, Armie. Anonymity is over. We already covered that and I got your word that you were all in."

"All in on the fighting, not this other nutty psychobabble stuff."

Havoc ordered him another unsweetened tea. "You'll be good for the sport, Armie. And believe it or not, the sport will be good for you."

He didn't need—what? Anything *good*? His gaze automatically sought out Rissy. She was as good as it got. A good girl. A good sister, good employee and a good cook. *Really* good in bed...

Brand and Miles had joined the ladies, so at least Armie knew other men wouldn't be hitting on her. Calmed by the sight of her and her nearness, he gave his attention back to Jude, Simon and Havoc.

A trio of true badasses. Three of the most elite fighters in the sport. Men who had retired as champions. They had their shit together, and he saw respect in their eyes.

Respect for *him*.

They wanted him to join in. It wasn't just Cannon anymore. It wasn't just his friends at the rec center.

He didn't know what the fuck to do, so he said, "Fine." Ignoring all the hero BS, Armie agreed. "I'll dial down the raunchiness on my tees. Anything else?"

As if they knew they'd won, they each loosened their posture, got comfortable, smiled.

Jude said, "You need a manager—"

"No thanks. I can manage myself. Is that it, then?"

Havoc shook his head. "Cannon will be in your corner?"

"Probably, unless something comes up."

"So if not him, then who?" Simon asked.

"One of the other guys. Does it matter?"

Jude rubbed his face. "This is the SBC, Armie. As professional as it gets. You need a manager, and you need a dedicated coach, so quit arguing every point, will you?"

Before he could dispute that, Simon said, "You probably know I was Havoc's manager. Now I'd like to be yours."

Other fighters would wet themselves for that honor, so how the hell could he refuse it?

"And I'd like to coach you," Havoc told him.

Armie's head spun. They were investing more than money in him, and really piling on the trust—because they assumed he'd be worth it. "You know," he told them softly, "some guys might be intimidated by all these expectations."

"But not you." Havoc held his gaze. "I'll consistently be in your corner, Armie, but I don't mind if Cannon joins us when he can."

From one earnest face to the next, Armie sent a forced smile. "Great, thanks. Problem solved."

Droll, Simon asked, "Why do I get the feeling he's still not taking this seriously?"

Seeing them exasperated made Armie feel better, so

he didn't mind annoying them a little more with a reminder. "You just told me you like my methods."

"No," Jude said. "Spectators like it."

"I'm thinking about coming out of retirement,"
Simon said with menace.

Armie laughed. "Anxious to kick my ass, huh?"

Cocking a brow, Simon asked, "Could I?"

Armie shrugged and said, "No one is invincible."
He'd let Simon wonder if he meant him, or himself.

Simon laughed. "Tell you what. Come to my camp
for your last two weeks of prep. We'll have you sparring
more, doing drills, and we can work on cage strategy.
I have some guys who've already fought Carter. They
can give you some pointers."

"I've seen him fight." Carter "Chaos" Fletcher liked
to constantly switch gears, going from boxing to kicking to takedowns and submission attempts. Armie
knew how Carter worked, had seen his strengths and
his weaknesses. Carter was good at a lot of things, but
not great at any of them. He was fast, but not precise.
Armie had seen plenty of holes in his game, so he wasn't
worried.

Besides, the possibility of picking up and relocat-
ing didn't thrill him, and he knew why. It was beyond
idiotic, but he dreaded leaving Merissa for two weeks.
Not only would he worry about her because of what
she'd gone through at the bank, but their relationship
was very new, and he had no idea how long it'd last.

What was he? A snotty-nosed mama's boy?

Proving himself to be astute, Havoc eyed him, then
suggested, "Or maybe since Cannon swears you're his
right hand, Simon and I could bring a few guys here to
work with you."

"Yeah." Armie jumped on it. "If it's not too much trouble, let's do that."

Simon laughed. "Know who he reminds me of?"

"Handleman?" Havoc guessed.

"Yeah. Same chip on his shoulder, same dislike of promo."

Fuck, Armie hated comparisons. "Harley retired as a champ." As had each of the men at the table with him.

"That he did." Jude lifted his drink in a toast. "To talented assholes who give new meaning to stubbornness."

Havoc and Simon said, "Hear, hear."

Armie couldn't help it. A genuine smile cracked, and once it did, they all laughed. He'd gotten through his first round of SBC planning, and although he'd lost a few, he'd also won a few.

Best of all, he'd be sticking close to Merissa, so he could chalk up the rest as no big deal.

CHAPTER TEN

"THE BAR SURE is crowded tonight," Cherry complained when two women rushed by and one bumped her elbow, almost spilling her drink.

Brand smiled at them both, his sinfully dark eyes teasing. "You ladies haven't noticed that we have celebrities among us?"

"Who?" Merissa looked around but couldn't see past the crowd.

"Armie's with them. Opposite side of the room."

"Armie is here?" Just knowing he was near made her heart race. "You're sure?"

"Positive. He came in with Jude Jamison, Simon and Dean."

"Why?"

Brand rolled one bulky shoulder. As a heavyweight, he was a big guy with plenty of thick muscle. "Everyone is really pumped about him signing on with the SBC."

Miles leaned in. "Word is, they're courting him."

Understanding some parts of mixed martial arts competition, but not all of it, Merissa tipped her head. "They'll expect him to switch camps?"

"It's possible. But Cannon's got the rec center so fine-tuned, most other camps are trying to get their guys here to train."

Brand chimed in, saying, "You look at the fact Cannon is a champ, and Denver is kicking ass left and right, and now Armie is stepping up. They see a lot of talent coming from here."

"Speaking of talent," Miles murmured, smiling at a small crowd of women dressed as if they were in a nightclub instead of Rowdy's local bar. "Excuse me."

Cherry laughed. "And he's off."

"Can't say as I blame him." Brand pushed back his chair. "You ladies are hot, but taken."

Both Merissa and Cherry laughed over that.

Giving them a crooked smile, Brand asked, "You two going to get in on the photo op?"

Merissa tilted back to see him. "What do you mean?"

Nodding toward Armie and the visiting fighters, Brand explained, "They agreed to do some fan photos. Rowdy didn't tell you? That's why the place is packed. Everyone is flocking in for the impromptu meet and greet." He walked off after that, joining the group of welcoming women.

Soon as they were alone, Cherry leaned in to be heard over the drone of conversations and laughter. "Does Armie know you're here?"

"I told him in a text."

"So maybe he'll join us."

Merissa was pretty sure he wouldn't. She hated the idea of secrecy, but she had agreed to Armie's request, and she wouldn't start regretting it now.

When Leese came in, she saw him as a welcome interruption and waved him over.

Looking very fine in faded jeans and a denim jacket, his inky-black hair mussed, beard shadow on his lean face, Leese got a lot of looks on his way to their table.

Anxious to see him, barely able to keep her smile

suppressed, Merissa stood. More than the other guys, Leese knew how she felt about Armie and now she couldn't wait to give him the details.

When he got close, he surprised her by grinning and offering a high five.

She laughed and smacked her hand to his.

Light blue eyes teasing, Leese spoke close so others wouldn't hear. "I take it things went well?"

"Things went *amazingly*."

"Glad to hear it." His gaze cut to Cherry. "She knows?"

"Yup." Linking her arm through his, Merissa said, "You guys are my two best friends."

"I'm honored."

"Do you have plans? Miles and Brand just left so we have an empty chair. Want to join us?"

"Be glad to." But once she'd scooted in her chair, Leese put two hands to the table and stretched down to say, "In case you didn't notice, Armie is mean mugging me."

Merissa popped her head up, looked across the room and got caught in Armie's forceful gaze.

"Wow," Cherry whispered.

"Yeah." Leese laughed. "At least you're the recipient now instead of me."

"Is he jealous of you?" Cherry asked.

"Naw. He's just coming to grips with things."

Merissa remembered Leese once telling her that Armie was fighting too many battles at one time. She didn't want to be another battle.

She just wanted to love him.

Apparently, so did a whole bunch of other women. One by one, and occasionally in groups, they visited his table. Armie declined their company each time. Couldn't the pushy women see he was involved in a meeting? That didn't stop them from hanging on him, offering hugs and sometimes kisses and, given the many whispers in his ear, more.

Merissa distracted herself by spending the next twenty minutes chatting up Leese and Cherry. She'd already had a glass of wine, so when Leese bought a new round of drinks, including a beer for himself, both she and Cherry ordered Cokes.

Leese told her what to expect in the coming weeks for Armie, including the possibility that he'd go to a different camp.

"He hasn't told you any of this himself?"

"We haven't really talked much about his fight career." They'd been too busy covering everything else, including his past. "And I guess I haven't paid enough attention to Cannon's routine. At least the fight is close. Cincinnati's totally drivable."

"They probably want his debut fight to be for his hometown. I'm sure they're expecting big things from him."

Cherry nodded. "Denver told me Armie will be the middleweight champ in no time."

Merissa looked at him again. "I knew he was good…" Good enough that he was now surrounded by people.

Leese huffed a short laugh. "He's a whole lot better than good. They're calling him a phenomenon." He cocked a brow. "Luckily Armie doesn't suffer from performance anxiety."

Cherry bobbed her eyebrows. "Yeah, from what I heard, he doesn't have that problem."

Casting Merissa a knowing look, Leese teased, "And now you're blushing."

"Because she's a straight-up hussy," Cherry told him, then sighed. "I hope Armie appreciates how good he's got it."

"Armie's not a dummy. I think he knows." Leese patted her hand. "I need to go. They're getting ready to do photos." He looked at each of them. "You two going to take part?"

Cherry wrinkled her nose. "I'll leave Denver to his adoring fans."

Shaking her head, Merissa said, "I'll keep Cherry company." That would be a lot more comfortable than waiting in a line full of fawning women, all anxious to get a picture with Armie when he was the only one she cared about.

It was another hour before the crowd finally began to disperse. Merissa saw Leese head off with a cute blonde, and Brand and Miles returned to the tableful of ladies, this time with Justice joining them.

"Do you ever wonder," Cherry asked, "what they're into?"

Confused, Merissa turned to her. "What do you mean?"

Moving to a closer seat, Cherry hunkered in and said low, "You know, the other guys." She bobbed her eyebrows. "I know what Denver likes."

Matching the quiet tone, Merissa asked, "What?"

"He's very controlling and protective."

Expecting something more titillating, Merissa scoffed. "*Everyone* knows that."

"He's really good, Rissy."

Hearing her friend sigh, Merissa laughed. "I'm glad you're so happy."

"So…you said Armie's good, too?"

"Oh yeah. He's so…attentive. You know, paying a lot of attention to…details." Even as she said it, she blushed.

Cherry grinned at her. "So don't you wonder about the other guys?" She flapped a hand. "Not with like… personal interest or anything. You know I'm crazy in love with Denver. But aren't you curious?"

Merissa frowned. "I never really thought about it."

"Well, look at them. Brand is all cocky smiles, a little distanced, and that lady with him is all about getting him alone. But Miles keeps joking and every time that woman laughs, she inches closer."

Yes, she did see it now. "They're both on the make, but in very different ways."

"Justice just bulldozes forward. He scooped that woman into his lap and she hasn't budged since."

Merissa turned her head to see Leese at a small table with the blonde. He sat very near her, staring into her eyes, listening intently to whatever she said. And he kept touching her in small ways, like brushing his fingers over the back of her hand, or tucking her hair behind her ear. "Interesting."

"So what does Armie like?"

Merissa lifted her brows in a "Really?" expression. From what she could tell, Armie liked sex—just about any way he could get it.

"Denver loves it when I nibble on him. His ear, or his neck, or…you know." Cherry sighed again. "And he loves it when I touch him and he's not expecting it. Like the other morning, he'd just gotten out of bed and was stretching. Denver stretching is *incredibly* hot, so I reached around him and copped a feel. Let's just say it was a good thing we'd gotten up early because he spent an hour showing how I'd fired him up."

Even though it embarrassed her a little, Merissa whispered, "I wrote on Armie's butt."

Cherry's eyes went wide, then she insisted, "Details!"

It was during the retelling that Merissa glanced up and again caught Armie watching her.

His look was so knowing, it was as if he'd overheard her talking. Which, of course, was impossible, given the distance between them and the noise level in the room.

When Armie shook hands with the men and pulled his jacket back on, Merissa rushed to tell Cherry, "I need to get going."

"So early?"

"I have work tomorrow."

"So do I," Cherry said, "but it's only eight-thirty."

"Armie's done."

Cherry glanced at him, then back. "So tell him to join us."

"Cherry," she remonstrated. "I told you—he doesn't want everyone to know we're seeing each other."

Cherry tucked in her chin. "I thought you meant the sex. But it *all* has to be secret?"

Unconcerned, Merissa shrugged. "We're being discreet."

Cherry's narrowed gaze shifted to Armie again. "So you have to…what? Wait for him to leave then follow ten steps behind?"

That gave her pause. "You're making it sound really bad."

Rushing to reassure her, Cherry said, "No, not bad at all. I'm happy for you, you know that. It's just—" she shrugged "—dumb. Our friends are all going to know—not that I'll go blabbing or anything. But do you really think you can keep it secret, even from Cannon?"

Merissa bit her lip. "I don't know." But for now, she didn't want to do anything that might drive Armie away. "For now, being with him is enough. You know?"

"I do." Eyes full of concern, Cherry took her hand. "Maybe if you keep having awesome sex, the rest will fall into place?"

"I hope so."

"It worked wonderfully for Denver and me."

"What," Armie asked from the side of the table, "worked for you two?"

Taken by surprise, Cherry blurted, "Great sex," and then she realized Denver stood with Armie, looking even more shocked than she had. She covered her face. "Oh God."

Armie grinned, Denver sighed and Merissa lost it.

She started laughing, and almost couldn't stop.

"GET IT TOGETHER, STRETCH." Seeing Rissy's hilarity kept the smile on Armie's face. He turned to Denver. "Apparently your skills have left her hysterical."

"Armie." With her face bright pink, Cherry looked up at her stern husband. "You're wonderful in bed. You know that."

Rissy broke out into new guffaws, making Armie shake his head.

"Rissy," Cherry hissed while giving Denver an apologetic smile. *"Stop it."*

Hand over her mouth, shoulders shaking, Rissy tried.

"Sorry," she snickered between her fingers. "It's just with what she was saying—"

"Cherry Pie," Armie teased, using his pet name for her. "Were you gossiping about sex?" He shifted his gaze to Rissy. She, too, went red. "Comparing notes, maybe?"

"Um…" Cherry choked, glanced at Denver's scowl and started her own nervous giggle. "Mostly I was bragging."

Denver shook his head. "I think Armie is rubbing off on you."

"There's a visual," Armie said. "But no, I haven't. Swear."

"You—" Denver reached for him.

Armie ducked away, laughing. "You said it, not me."

When Cherry chuckled, Denver took her by her upper arms, lifted her from her chair and kissed her.

Brows up, Rissy watched the public display.

Armie nudged her. "No longer taking notes?"

She shook her head.

"Denver is a possessive ape." Armie said it loud enough for Denver to hear.

When his friend finally let up, Cherry was limp in his arms, so Denver gave him a triumphant smile. "Whatever works."

Still looking sappy, Cherry sent her elbow into his gut, making Denver grunt.

"Yeah," Armie said. "Clearly a good boning has turned her into a pacifist."

Laughing, Denver pulled Cherry in for a hug and said with humor, "Now, let's don't get carried away."

Watching them with admiration, Rissy sighed. Armie saw the wistful, almost-sad smile on her face.

Is that what she wanted? The same comfortable, easy, funny relationship that Denver and Cherry had? He had to admit they were great together.

Could he ever make Rissy that happy?

Pulling on her coat, trying, and failing, to sound blasé, Rissy announced, "I need to get going."

Since Denver and Cherry both watched him, Armie couldn't say any of the things he wanted to. Like, *I'll be right behind you.*

Or, *Go to my place and get naked.*

And, *Wait for me in bed.*

Resisting the urge to clear his throat of guilt, Armie said, "I'll walk her out."

"Uh-huh." A beefy arm over Cherry's shoulders, Denver eyed Armie. "That's a euphemism, right? What the cool kids are calling it these days?"

"Fuck you."

Cherry laughed at him.

Denver just shook his head in a pitying way. "Go on."

Okay, so he wasn't fooling anyone. It was about more than their close friends. The bar was crowded, people snapping pics left and right, and he didn't want rumors started about him being with Rissy. Given his rep, and his background, she'd get shredded.

It was part of why he'd always steered clear.

Rissy suddenly looked undecided and uncomfortable.

Unfortunately, just then, Havoc called him over. When Armie looked, he saw some adoring fans—a guy and his girlfriend, apparently. They looked hopeful for yet another photo. They were supposed to be done now, but yeah, he hated to disappoint anyone. Pasting on a false smile, Armie sent Havoc a thumbs-up to let him know he'd be right there.

He grumbled under his breath until Rissy gave a push to his shoulder. "Go. Please the masses."

Warring with himself, Armie hedged—and then Leese was there.

"I'll see that she makes it to her car."

A red haze clouded Armie's vision, but what could he say? If it was anyone other than Rissy, he wouldn't think a thing of it.

"Seriously." Hands on her hips, Rissy huffed at one and all. "I can walk out on my own steam."

Leese shifted impatiently. "Where are you parked?"

Her umbrage lost its edge. "Um…across the street in the lot—"

"Right." He turned back to Armie. "Say your good-byes, already. I have a date tonight and I don't want to keep her waiting."

"I do *not* need you to walk me out." Then in quick succession, she said, "This is ridiculous. If it'll make you feel better, just watch until I get to my car. You can see me from the front door."

Looking beyond Leese, Armie saw the stacked blonde seated at a small table, watching them.

Knowing Leese wasn't making moves on Rissy made it easier. "Thanks. Wait until she pulls away." He glanced at Rissy and kept it casual. "Drive safe." Then he headed over to Havoc. The sooner he got done, the sooner he could join Rissy at his apartment.

Why the hell hadn't he given her a key already? He'd take care of that as soon as he got home.

He tried to greet the rabid fans while also keeping an eye on Rissy as she headed to the door with Leese. He smiled toward the camera but his gaze slanted to Leese, leaning against the door frame and keeping watch as Rissy headed out across the busy street and into the dark lot.

They finished taking a corny picture of Armie and the other dude, fists up and mean mugging. Thinking he could head out, that he'd only be a minute behind her, Armie was thanking the fans when suddenly Leese went rigid, then took off in a dead run into the night.

Fear cut into Armie.

Something had happened.

Blindly he pushed free of the small crowd and shoved his way across the room and out the door—where he saw Rissy knocked to the opposite curb, one shoe in the street, her purse dumped.

Rage blocked out everything and everyone but her. With no thought for the traffic, he charged across the street. Leese was already helping her to sit up and she said, fast and breathless, "I'm okay!"

Kneeling in front of her, Armie smoothed her hair away and saw blood on her bottom lip. "What the hell happened?" Gently, he gathered her into his lap.

"She was damn near hit," Leese said. "Some idiot…"

Armie looked at him. It surprised him to see Leese was also infuriated, even shaking with it. Their gazes met—and Armie knew.

Standing, Leese looked up and down the street, then crouched down again and in an enraged whisper, said, "Swear to God, Armie, it looked like the lunatic tried to run her over."

THEY BOTH PULLED into his apartment parking lot half an hour later. Armie hadn't wanted her to drive, had in fact wanted to call the police. But Merissa insisted it was her fault, that she'd been daydreaming and not paying enough attention to traffic and she'd already been embarrassed over drawing so much notice.

Half of the damned bar had emptied to gawk at her. Denver, Miles, Brand, Justice had all stood together, creating a solid wall that offered her some privacy as she straightened her clothes and smoothed her hair. Leese had fetched her shoe from the road. Cherry had gathered up the belongings of her dumped purse.

Knowing how their inner circle worked, Leese had quietly told him, "I'll ask around, but I doubt anyone saw anything."

Since Rissy had insisted on driving, Armie had helped her to her car, then taken a moment to talk with Denver, who would in turn get in touch with Cannon and together with Leese they'd decide if something more was going on. One of them would be in touch with him.

And of course, this meant Cannon would know Rissy was staying with him again. Armie wasn't sure how he felt about that—or how Cannon would feel about it.

But he did know Rissy shouldn't be alone. Not tonight, not tomorrow.

Not until they knew what the hell was happening.

A robbery and then a near miss—that was too much coincidence for any intelligent man to swallow.

Leaving his truck, he hustled over to Rissy's car and opened the door. "Here, let me help you."

"You're being ridiculous." Surly, she hitched her purse strap over her shoulder with more force than necessary and stepped out. "I keep telling you, I'm *fine*."

Emphasis on the *fine*, and Armie well knew when

women started using that word, there was a problem. "Oookay."

She took a step, and limped.

Son of a bitch. He felt so damned helpless, he wanted to howl. "Okay, screw it."

She arched a brow, her look lethal.

"I am who I am, Rissy." He pointed at her. "You know that. You pushed your way in—"

Both brows now snapped down. "I—"

"—and now it's too late to back out on me. You're here, so you'll just have to suffer me."

"I have no idea what that— *Armie!*"

"Shush." Lifting her into his arms, he started for the apartment entry door. "You have road rash on your cheek—the same cheek that still shows a faint bruise from the robbery. Plus I saw you limp, and you know me well enough to know I'm not going to ignore that."

"I told you I'm—"

"Yeah, I know. You're fine." He shouldered the door open and started up the steps with her. "But I'm not." Hoping she'd understand, he admitted softly, "I need to hold you, okay?"

Gradually her frown smoothed out and now she just studied him, her expression enigmatic. When they reached the upper landing, she said calmly, "Put me down so you can unlock your door."

"You won't budge?"

"I'll stand here like a good little victim."

He rolled his eyes, but took her at her word and put her back on her feet. It took him only seconds to unlock the door, then he scooped her up again.

This time she looped one arm around his neck and with the other she closed and locked the door.

Armie started down the hall.

Resting her head on his shoulder, she asked, "Where are we going?"

"To the bed."

"Ah, okay." She brushed her lips to his throat, up his neck to his ear. "Now you're being more reasonable." Sharp little teeth nipped his earlobe.

The muscles in his thighs tensed. "Behave." As he lowered her to the bed, he got a text on his phone. After he had her situated against the pillows, he pulled the phone out of his pocket, checked the text, then put it facedown on the nightstand. "Just relax."

When he started to remove her shoes, she said, "Stop."

Wrapping a hand around her ankle, he looked up. "What?"

"Who texted you?"

Not about to touch that one, he shook his head. "It's nothing. Now—"

She snatched her foot back and in a near-demonic tone, repeated, *"Who?"*

Armie tilted his head, took in her antagonistic posture and smiled. She was in quite the mood tonight. "You wanna do this now, Stretch?" Maybe she needed a diversion to get past the fact that someone had tried to run her down. "All right. It was a chick I used to bang."

Her jaw clenched. Sneering, she asked, "You're not *banging* her now?"

"Nope." He hadn't been with another woman for some time. To him, a man used to frequent satisfaction, it felt like an eon. Until Rissy, he just couldn't work up any enthusiasm. "Right now, I'm trying to check your swollen ankle. And yeah, it is swollen."

Begrudging, she admitted, "I twisted it when I jumped out of the way of the car."

Fresh rage burned through him. "A car you insist wasn't trying to hit you." He peeled away her sock, put his warm hand around her arch and studied her slim ankle.

"Why would anyone *want* to hit me?"

His gaze lifted to hers. Yeah, that was fear he heard—which maybe explained her antagonism because a woman like Rissy would rather give in to bluster than show anxiety. "No idea," he lied. He had plenty of ideas. "But maybe it was just some drunken prick who decided to watch you dive for cover. People are twisted."

Her shoulders relaxed a near-infinitesimal amount. "You think?"

"It's possible." He quickly removed her other shoe and sock, then opened the snap and lowered the zipper to her jeans.

"Armie Jacobson, are you trying to get me out of my pants?"

"Yeah." From angry, to vulnerable, to teasing. He eyed her anew. "How much did you drink?"

"Not much. And come to think of it, I'm starving."

She hadn't eaten at Rowdy's. As preoccupied as he'd been watching her, he'd have noticed. "Lift your hips."

She did, and he stripped off the jeans. She wore black lacy panties that looked supersexy with the lace top. On stiffened arms, Armie loomed over her. "When you walked into the bar, I damn near got hard." He lowered down to kiss her brow, her cheek above the road rash, then the corner of her mouth. "You're always pretty, but I like how you dolled up."

"For you," she whispered.

Yeah, he'd figured that out. Armie treated them both to a deep, soft kiss, and though it wasn't easy, he kept it to just that, no more. "I'm going to get you some ice for your ankle."

"Okay." Her hand knotted in his shirt. "Soon as you tell me why women keep texting you and why you haven't made it clear you're off the market, for however long we last."

CHAPTER ELEVEN

MERISSA KNEW SHE was deflecting. She was shaken, her cheek burned and more than her ankle throbbed. When she'd landed against the curb, it had felt like she'd rattled her entire body. She had a tight grip on Armie's shirt, keeping him close, not to blame him or start an argument with him. Just to ground herself.

Having sex with him, right now, would go a long way toward making everything else disappear.

Had someone tried to run her over? Maybe.

But she had been daydreaming—about Armie, of course—and not paying attention, and what Armie said made sense; it could have just been a drunken prank.

Although, Rowdy's was the closest bar and there weren't many who'd be able to leave his establishment that drunk, not if they intended to drive. Somehow Rowdy always seemed to know and he'd insist people call a cab.

Plus, crazy as it seemed, she thought she might have heard someone laugh as the car zipped past her.

When she shuddered, Armie pulled the blanket from the end of the bed. "You're chilled? Would you like a warm bath? You could prop your ankle on the tub ledge and ice it—"

"I want a shower, not a bath. And I want something to eat."

"Okay—"

"And I want an answer."

He freed her fist from his shirt and sat back, then rubbed both hands over his face. "If I start telling women I'm off-limits, that's going to give rise to questions. We're trying to keep this quiet, remember?"

"Ohmigod." Her aches and pains forgotten, she jerked upright. "You're keeping all your options open."

"Damn it, don't put words in my mouth." He put a hand around the back of her neck. "You're the only option I want and I'm *trying* to protect you."

Her heart expanded. "Then tell the women you're off-limits for your fight."

"That's a myth, Stretch, and they'll only feel challenged."

"Do something, damn it!" She shoved him aside and went to stand. "How would you feel if I was constantly being contacted by—"

As if she'd willed it, her phone began ringing.

Armie narrowed his eyes at her.

"It's probably Cannon." Grabbing for her purse at the side of the bed, she dug out the phone, read the screen, and— Oh damn.

"Who is it?" Armie asked silkily, already looking over her shoulder.

"You know it's Steve."

"Want me to answer for you?"

"No." She brushed her thumb over the screen, then said, "Hello?"

"Merissa. How are you?"

Ignoring the heat of Armie's stare beside her, she cleared her throat. "I'm fine. What do you want?"

"You," he said immediately. "A second chance."

"We already covered this." It didn't make sense. Steve was not the persistent sort—unless his ego demanded he get her back, since she was the one to walk away from him. "I've moved on, and I'm sure you have, too. Please don't call again."

"Wait—"

Disconnecting without hearing what he had to say, she tucked the phone back in her purse, then faced Armie. "And that," she told him, being snippy, "is how it's done. Maybe you should have taken notes."

Armie grinned at her. "You're hot when you're pissed." He stood, took her hands and gingerly pulled her to her feet. "If I promise to deter any interested ladies, will you stop giving me the stink eye?"

She blinked. "I'm not." That sounded so awful. And appropriate.

"So is it a deal?"

She sighed. "You'll let them know, for whatever reason, that they don't need to keep checking in?"

He crossed his heart. "Now, why don't you get your shower while I pull together dinner?"

"I could cook."

"Let me, okay?" One hand to the back of her head, the other on her waist, he took her mouth in a sweet kiss that lingered, went deeper, turned scorching. His tongue leisurely explored her mouth, and his breathing deepened.

When he slid his hand from her waist, under her shirt and then up, she made a small sound of compliance.

Until he got to her ribs.

Inadvertently flinching away from pain, she said, "Ouch."

Concerned, Armie said softly, "Let me see." He peeled up her stretchy top, then muttered, "Ah, hell."

Rissy peered down at the expanding bruise. "I think that's where I hit the curb." Now that she saw it, it hurt even worse, as did her hip. She lifted the waistband of her panties and found another, smaller bruise that had been hidden. "Looks like I landed on a rock, too, maybe."

"Why didn't you say something, Stretch?" Showing incredible gentleness, he took her shirt off over her head, unhooked her bra and stripped off her panties.

"Armie..."

"Let me look, okay?" Far too intently, he examined every inch of her, lifting each arm, brushing her hair forward as he trailed his rough fingertips over her shoulders and down her spine, then lifting her hair back again as he gently cuddled each breast and circled both nipples, before going to his knees.

Finding a few smaller bruises and another scrape, he kissed each and every one, fanning her desire and making the insubstantial injuries forgettable.

"You have the cutest ass," he teased, nibbling on one of her cheeks.

Merissa held her breath.

His hand reached around in front of her first, touching between her legs and surely finding her ready. He growled, then shifted around so he knelt before her.

She tunneled her fingers into his cool hair. "Armie?"

His damp lips lingered over her hip. "Mmm?"

"I need my shower now—and then I need you."

He looked up at her, his dark eyes full of heat. "I need to feed you."

"I've lost my appetite."

His smile was one of the sexiest things she'd ever seen. He kissed his way up her body, making her gasp a few times before he finally stood before her again. He lightly kissed her lips, then lifted her again.

"I can walk, you know."

"Yeah, I do know." He carried her into the bathroom and slowly lowered her back to her feet. After he started the shower and set out a few towels for her, he said, "Do whatever you need to do while I fix us some food. You can ice your ankle while we eat."

"What about sex?"

He bunched his hands in her hair, kissed her again and whispered, "As long as we're together, I promise you won't ever go to bed wanting."

Merissa was swaying on her feet when he walked out. Getting enough air into her lungs wasn't easy. The thought of dinner didn't appeal.

But being pampered by Armie—now that was an experience she didn't want to miss.

WITH HIS CELL PHONE held between his shoulder and ear, Armie turned the chicken in the cast-iron skillet. "No, it's not like that. No, not personal at all. I'm just out of commission for the foreseeable future. Yeah, at least that long. Sure, when things work out I'll give you a call. But until then…right. Glad you understand. Thanks."

"When things work out?"

Armie set aside the phone and turned to see Rissy in the doorway. She had her hair tied up and wound around in a sloppy bun or something, but plenty of long pieces had come loose, clinging to her damp shoulders and upper chest. She looked great barefoot, wearing only one of his shirts that said: I am the man from Nantucket.

"That was my way of saying, 'Don't call me, I'll call you.'" His gaze repeatedly went over her body. "You know, since the texts offend you."

"Uh-huh." She ran a hand over the shirt, from upper chest to waist. "You don't mind that I borrowed it, do you?"

"No." He glazed over there a little, seeing her hand coast over her breast. The shirt looked better on her than it ever had on him. After tamping down the surge of lust, he turned off the chicken and pulled out a chair for her. "C'mon. Take a seat."

No way could he miss her careful gait as she tried not to limp. Folding his arms, he said, "You're not a fighter, you know."

"Is that supposed to mean something?" As she sat, she held the shirt down.

"It means you don't have to man up." He pulled another chair out for her to prop up her foot, then was startled when he lifted her leg and realized the shirt was literally all she wore. Standing there, her foot held aloft, he froze as his eyes glued to her body.

"I don't have any panties here," she murmured, her tone low and husky, her gaze expectant.

So this was her idea of teasing? A come-on?

He liked it.

After pulling himself together, Armie nodded. "I was thinking about that." It seemed easier to cover this while busy, so he placed the folded towel under her foot, then carefully placed the ice pack on her ankle.

She hissed in a breath, as much from the cold, he knew, as from any pain.

"It'll help, I promise." He also handed her two tablets. "Just OTC pain meds."

She swallowed them down with the tea he'd poured for her. "What were you thinking about? My panties?"

"Well, that, too." Mainly about how much he liked her without them. "But I meant clothes for when you're over. And maybe…" He served her food and avoided her gaze. "A key. To my place, I mean."

No reply. No anything.

The silence became deafening. He'd never given a woman a key. Never worried about her having a change of clothes. Hell, he'd never wanted a woman to stay over.

Feeling like an insecure juvenile, he returned the skillet to the stove and took his own seat and then, bracing himself, he glanced at her.

Her eyes were huge, her mouth trembling with a smile. Ah, hell. "Rissy?"

She nodded fast, blinked faster and failed miserably at sounding casual when she croaked, "Sure. That'd work."

"Rissy," he said again, this time with affection. He took her hand; she squeezed his. "Tell me what's wrong."

"Nothing. I just…" She blew out a breath, laughed a little. "You surprised me, that's all." More blinking, and a big sigh. "But yes, I'd love a key. For convenience. For when…when we've made plans to get together and things like tonight happen."

He didn't understand her. She sounded both thrilled and devastated. "That's what I was thinking." Brushing her knuckles with his thumb, he explained. "I wanted to see you tonight, but I didn't want you sitting in my parking lot alone, waiting for me."

"Right. Perfect example."

Never had he meant to make her ill at ease or so jittery. "Maybe," he teased, "on the nights when we're getting together, you could wait for me in bed naked?"

"Maybe. Sure."

Her immediate agreement surprised him—and yeah, turned him on. Of course, everything she did pushed his buttons. From the time she was an awkward teen and full of curiosity, Rissy had done it for him. But as she'd matured, as he'd witnessed her generous nature and experienced her sweet outlook on life, her stiff independence and unbending pride, he'd fallen hard.

And every time he saw her, it got worse.

Quickly she snatched back her hand and forked up a bite of chicken. "Mmm. Good."

Damn, he'd muddled this, but he didn't know how to fix it without possibly making her more uncomfortable. So instead he changed the subject. "You think you're up for sex tonight?"

She choked, nodded hard again, swallowed, grabbed a drink and nodded some more. "Yes. Definitely."

He had to laugh. "We'll see how it goes." No way in hell would he hurt her. He wanted her, but with those bruises—

"No." She pointed her fork at him. "There's no *seeing*. We're having sex. Period."

From flirting to demanding? Rolling with it, he sat back and said, "You're hurt."

She huffed rudely. "Bruised is not *hurt*."

He started to debate that with her, but she cut him off.

"If you were bruised, would it keep you from having sex? No, of course it wouldn't. Heck, half the time you have bruises and sometimes worse than that. You still have a lingering bruise on your back from the bank robbery and your head is only just now healing up. But it didn't slow you down, did it?"

"No."

"See? That's my point. And before you say it, yes, I know I'm not a big old macho fighter. But I'm not a wuss, either."

It felt like his heart smiled. "No." Not a wuss at all.

"And I want you."

He'd never tire of hearing that. "It's getting late. Why don't you finish up, then do whatever else you have to do before bed, and we can turn in?"

Her lungs expanded. "For sex, right?"

Happiness spread from his heart to every corner of his universe. "Sex first, sure." Reaching out, he fingered one of those long, silky hanks of hair that had fallen from her messy and somehow sexy bun. "Then I want to enjoy sleeping with you again."

"I like that plan." She finished up her meal, eating most of the chicken and all of the asparagus, plus some cherry tomatoes. "You're a good cook."

"I get by."

"Do you really?"

"Get by? Yeah."

She shook her head. "No, I mean…do you really enjoy sleeping with me?"

He started to tease, but the look in her eyes told him this wasn't the time. She needed the truth. And hell, so did he. "Yeah, Stretch. I like sleeping with you." Accepting it, he grinned and let the reality of it encompass him. "When you're curled up with me, I sleep better than I have in a very long time."

She put a hand to her heart and in the softest voice he'd ever heard from her, she admitted, "Me, too."

Armie knew he was in deep, but at the moment he flat out didn't care. "Is your ankle feeling better?"

She nodded.

"Sit tight a minute." Aware of her watching him, he cleared the table with practiced ease. "You're not used to letting someone else do for you, are you?"

"Are you kidding?" She licked her lips. "Cannon insists on doing things for me *all* the time."

"He helps you, yeah. But I mean personally." He rinsed out the dishrag, took the ice pack from her and put it back in the freezer, then carefully lifted her from the chair. "You're like this natural-born caretaker. You like to cook and keep your house spotless and you play hostess to everyone."

"My mom was like that." She traced the neckline of his shirt, over his collarbone. "I loved cooking with her, learning from her."

"I remember your mom being pretty terrific."

Rissy nodded. "Dad, too."

"Yeah." She came from an amazing family, and that brought with it certain expectations. Her brother's fight name was "Saint" for good reason.

Which always made Armie wonder—could he ever measure up?

When they reached the bedroom, he carefully lowered her to the bed and stripped off her shirt, leaving her beautifully naked.

Rising up to her elbows, she smiled at him.

Armie knew he needed a distraction and fast, before he forgot she was special, and hurt, and his best friend's little sister. She didn't deserve for him to lose it; she deserved every wonderful sexual experience he could give her.

Stepping back, he started removing his own clothes, starting with his shirt. "Did I ever tell you how I got my fight name?"

"Quick?" Her hungry interest moved over his chest and shoulders. "I assumed because you throw such fast jabs."

Armie shook his head and toed off his shoes.

"Then is it because you end fights so quickly?" Her breathing deepened. "Most of the time it seems like the fight barely gets started before you're finishing it with a knockout or a submission."

"Nope." Appreciating how she focused on his hands, he opened his jeans—and saw her lick her lips.

So suggestive.

Glancing at the mirror, he caught her pose in profile. He loved Rissy's body, and he especially loved her body in his bed.

He bent to drag off his socks, straightened again and carefully stepped out of his jeans. He had an erection—no hiding that—but he'd spent so much time denying himself, and denying her, too, that now he wanted her to know how badly he wanted her.

Always.

Buck-ass, he tossed his clothes over the dresser and his shoes into the closet. "Do you want to know?"

"What?"

Contentment settled into his soul. "How I got the name."

"Yes." She held her arms out to him.

Armie enjoyed stretching out with her crossways in the bed, facing her propped on one elbow, the mirror beyond her. "Are you paying attention?"

With her snaking a hand down to his junk, she nodded.

He caught her wrist, kissed her palm, and put her hand on his shoulder. "Back in high school, even before Lea, this superhot cheerleader decided she wanted to get me off behind the bleachers."

Rissy made a face. "I bet you put up a real fight, didn't you?"

"Not really, no." Grinning, he bent to her neck, taking a few soft love bites of her fragrant skin and leaving damp kisses along her throat. "At not quite seventeen, I was all about sex."

"That young?" she asked, before adding with a frown, "And you're still all about sex."

"You want to hear this or not, smart-ass?"

Dropping flat, Rissy turned those smiling blue eyes on him. "Go."

Her hair was a distinctive turn-on for him. Using one hand, he eased out the cloth-covered band and sifted his fingers through the long, heavy length, spreading it out around her. "She got me off, all right. Gave me my first blow job."

"So...you were a *quick* conquest?"

He arched a brow. "Actually, about one minute in, I reached my breaking point." It still made his ears hot to think about it. "Of course, that wasn't what she had planned."

Rissy didn't laugh, but he saw the humor in her eyes. "Oops."

"Yeah. Her grand plan had been to tease, then get laid. Instead, I unloaded early...thus the nickname Quick."

Turning toward him, Rissy lifted a leg over his. "You're not quick anymore," she assured him.

"Never was again after that, not unless a quickie

was on the agenda from the get-go." He worried for her ankle, but she seemed to pay no mind to it, behaving much as he would. "I made it up to the girl later. First time I'd ever—" he looked at her curious but sweet expression and censored the crude description "—given oral sex."

"I'm not sure I want to hear this."

Since he didn't plan to go into details with her, she didn't have to worry. "But by then your brother and a few others had already heard and as soon as I started MMA, I got dubbed with that handle and it stuck."

"Poor Armie." She put the softest of kisses to his throat. "Most think it's because of your fighting skill."

"Trust me, the guys correct anyone who has misconceptions on the genesis of the meaning."

Her tongue took a damp path up his neck to his ear. In a seductive whisper, she said, "That's so mean of them."

Wrapping a hand in her hair, he tugged her head back, then kissed the grin on her mouth. "I can tell you're heartbroken for me." Another kiss, and then another. It was so easy to lose himself with her. "Rissy…"

"Mmm?" She didn't want to leave his mouth and kept getting him off track. Her lips were full and soft, her tongue damp and warm.

"I've never talked about that with another woman."

For a second she went utterly still, then he found himself flat on his back with Rissy stiff-armed over him. At first she just stared into his eyes, as if gauging the truth. But she must have liked what she saw because she gradually sank against him. "Thank you for telling me."

For some reason, he'd needed her to know. She might

not realize the significance of him sharing in ways he never had with any other woman—but he understood, and for now that was enough.

"Will you tell me something else?"

Her hair fell around them, shielding her face and moving over his shoulders like an intimate caress. He used both hands to tuck it back. "What do you want to know?"

She turned her head to kiss each of his forearms. "Why did you get these? Do the tattoos mean anything?"

The laugh took him by surprise. He brought her down to his chest, hugging her. "They mean about as much as my goofy shirts or my ever-changing hair color."

When she struggled to lift up again, he restrained her until she settled against him. He liked her right there, her heart beating with his.

"They mean I'm a little different." He thought about it, and shrugged. "Also, if I see something I like, I go with it."

"Not me." Her fingers played over his fevered skin. "You liked me, right? But you always kept me away."

His arms tightened. He'd liked her most of all and denying himself had been hell. "We're here now, right?"

Ignoring that, she asked, "And the tattoo on your back? The winged heart wrapped in thorns?"

Breathing became a little more difficult.

"It's not colorful," she said, gliding her fingertips up and down his forearm. "Not like these."

He wouldn't lie and tell her it meant nothing, so instead he said, "It's just different, that's all." And it was far too freaking personal to discuss with anyone, but especially Rissy. To keep her from digging, he abruptly turned, tucking her under him. He nudged her legs open and, damn, his dick aligned with her sex. They both went still, except that he felt Rissy's nails on his shoulders, digging in.

He liked that.

"Your ankle is okay?" he asked.

Eyes vague, she nodded.

Seeing that particular lost look on her face pushed him past common sense. Though he badly wanted to, he didn't enter her. Instead he slowly rocked his hips and with each pass his cock spread her wetness, gliding between her lips, making her pant with the friction to her clit.

Fuck, it felt good moving against Rissy without any barriers between them. He watched her face, loving the slippery heat of her, how she squirmed and lifted into him.

Yeah, she was already on the ragged edge and he wanted to push her over. Framing her delicate breasts with his hard hands, he lowered his head and licked at her nipples, nipped carefully with his teeth, alternately drew each nipple in for a soft, leisurely suck, then tugged carefully with his teeth.

Her breath caught. She strained away before curling closer. Soft, desperate whimpers told him she was almost there. While drawing on one nipple, he scooped a hand under her ass and angled her up, tighter against him.

A few more strokes and she came with a short, stifled cry, her willowy body bowing hard.

Raising his head to catch every nuance of her release, Armie watched her, absorbed while also worried for her ankle—and his own sanity.

Taking short, panting breaths and moving sinuously

beneath him, she began to calm. "Mmm," she purred. "That was...surprising."

She was surprising, in a million different ways. "Don't move."

At Mach speed he rolled on a condom, settled back over her and slowly went deep. Urgency throbbed in his veins, but he made himself take it easy, giving her time to catch up again.

And she did.

Thirty minutes later, one of her hands fisting the hair on the back of his head, she groaned, "Enough, *Quick*," mocking his name since he'd just dragged out the pleasure for her in an excruciating way.

"Funny," he whispered, watching her face contort with raw pleasure. "It doesn't sound bad at all when you say it." She broke again, and this time he joined her.

Nothing seemed bad with Rissy.

But in his heart he knew it couldn't be this easy. Not for him.

CHAPTER TWELVE

SEVERAL DAYS LATER, Armie wrapped up a stint of working on cage strategy with some of the guys Havoc and Simon had sent up. It had been a good deal for all; the guys new to the rec center had enjoyed mixing it up as much as Armie had.

He only had four weeks left before the fight, and he knew he was in better shape than he'd ever been.

There'd been nonstop promo to do, with radio interviews running into online chats and too damn many photo shoots and fan meet and greets for him to keep count. He understood the necessity, but that didn't mean he liked all the fuss.

There were plenty of fighters who loved the attention, getting off on all the praise. Since he wasn't one of them, he was thrilled that the majority of the fuss was now behind him.

Only a few people were left at the gym this late and already Armie looked forward to getting home to Rissy.

Ever since he'd given her the key, she'd all but moved in.

'Course, her house was still there, comfortable, cozy. A real home.

Waiting.

At any minute she could walk, and for her it'd be

seamless. It made him antsy to think about it. He didn't want to jump the gun, but once he got past this fight—

"Hey." Denver, who'd still been around working with some high school boys, joined him now that he'd seen the last guy out the door. "Harper said you wanted to see me?"

"Yeah." That had been a couple of hours ago, before Harper and Gage left. "You've been busy today."

Denver winced as he stretched, flexing his shoulders and popping his neck—which usually came from frustration-based discomfort, not a workout. "You know that kid, Bray Huggins?"

"Fifteen, shit attitude, shittier home life." The kid was usually tired, and his clothes looked like they came from the laundry basket. "I've been working with him. What's up? He piss you off?"

"I wish that was it." Denver folded his arms and leaned a shoulder against the concrete wall. "He had some bruises."

Armie paused in the middle of putting weights back on the rack. "Where?"

"Here." Denver ran a hand over his own massive biceps. "Little bruises, like fingertips. And he has a cut on his nose and a scrape on his neck."

Ah, hell. Armie forgot all about the weights. "I don't suppose he was in a fight?"

"He told me to mind my own business when I asked, but I don't think that was it." Disgusted, Denver told him, "I think someone in his family is roughing him up."

"Damn." He hated it, but Armie nodded. "I've had a few doubts myself. I asked Cannon about it, but he doesn't know the family, either." Which was unusual, because Cannon knew pretty much everyone in their small town.

"I considered talking to Logan or Reese—"

Detectives. Armie cut him off. "Bringing in the police should be a last resort. If the parents skate by, it could just make them defensive and they might stop Bray from coming around." Then they'd have no idea what was going on, and Armie knew that'd eat him up.

As if he'd already come to that conclusion himself, Denver cursed. "He asked about you."

"Bray? Yeah, I've been working with him."

"He knows you're prepping for a fight so he hated to get in your way—his words, not mine."

"You should have told me earlier."

"I tried. He was pretty adamant and if I'd pushed it, he might've booked."

"So instead you spent extra time with him?"

"Yeah. Not sure if it helped or not, though. Bray's not real talkative."

No kidding. "His specialty seems to be sullen disgust."

Denver grinned. "Pretty much."

To give himself a second to think, Armie went back to cleanup, putting the weights where they belonged.

"You know you don't need to do that now."

He glanced at Denver, who'd fallen into step beside him, doing his own fair share of end-of-the-day arranging. "I don't recall you, Cannon or Stack dodging chores just because you had an upcoming fight, especially not a month out."

Miles, pushing a mop bucket, said, "You can both call it a night if you want. I've got this."

"Thanks," Armie said. "But I don't mind." He checked

the time. Rissy would be off work shortly, probably
headed straight to his place now that she had some of
her stuff there.

She tended to peel out of the business clothes the
second she hit the door. Around the apartment she
favored pajama pants, big sweatshirts and bare feet.
Rissy's idea of sloppy comfort never failed to fire his
libido in a big way.

It wouldn't kill him to be an hour late. Mind made
up, he told Denver, "I think I'll go by Bray's house. Get
a lay of the land, you know?"

"I already checked." Disgusted, Denver explained,
"He's in the worst part of town."

"Yeah, I know." A lot of the kids that straggled in did
so out of boredom, anger or need. Armie had a feeling
Bray hit all three categories.

It was a hell of a setup Cannon had created, a real
way to help the neighborhood.

And to help Cannon, Armie stayed up on everyone who came or went, especially the kids in need. "I
wanted to ask you about something else, if you don't
mind."

"Sure." Denver did his own check of the time.
"Cherry will wait another thirty minutes before she
gets too impatient." He said it with a big sappy grin.

"Cherry Pie," Armie said, knowing it'd irk Denver.
"Did you give her hell for comparing bedtime stories
the other night?"

"Naw." Denver sent him a man-to-man look. "Gave
her some better stories to tell, though."

Armie grinned. Not that long ago, Denver had been
denying himself, and although she'd put up a good front,
Cherry was miserable about it. He was glad they'd fi-

nally worked out their differences. They both deserved the best.

"So what's up?" Denver asked.

It was an awkward conversation and Armie wasn't quite sure how to get started. "You've had first fights."

"Nervous?"

Armie snorted. "You know I'm not."

"No, you probably aren't." Grinning, Denver said, "So spit it out."

"Fine. They're paying me a shitload." And he wasn't at all sure how he felt about that. Until now, he'd mostly just ignored the fact. But that was the stupid way to deal with it and Armie tried not to be stupid—even about money.

"I'd heard." He clapped Armie on the back. "After you win, you'll get a bonus. And I'm betting you get the fight of the night bonus, too."

Damn. The financial aspect of fighting for the SBC sometimes boggled his mind. He'd spent his life being frugal, but he'd never wanted for much, had always been able to afford what he needed, and he was comfortable. But now...

It'd be a lot easier to just concentrate on Rissy than finances. But since he was here with Denver... "You're still an accountant, right?"

"I've kept a few established clients. Why? You need advice?"

From behind them, Miles said, "When doesn't he?"

Armie flipped him the bird. "I've never really done the whole investment thing. I mean, I keep cash in the bank. And my finances are currently...fine. I can't say I'm swimming in it, but I don't have debt, either."

"I'd be glad to help out," Denver said. "We can get together after the fight and figure out a plan."

"Great. I was also thinking about a house. You know, instead of paying rent?"

Denver stared at him.

"What?" Was the idea of him as a home owner so ludicrous?

Miles sidled up, dragging the mop bucket with him. "Why would you want a house?"

Scowling, Armie asked, "Why wouldn't I want a house?"

"Rissy already has one," Denver pointed out. "That's why."

"Since it's her family home," Miles added, "I doubt she'd want to sell it."

Well shit.

Slowly, Denver grinned, then elbowed Miles. "Look at him. He's caught, but not sure how caught, so he's keeping mum."

"Seriously?" Miles scratched his chin. "You thought no one knew?"

"He thought he was being all covert," Denver said in a ludicrous stage whisper. "Real hush-hush."

"With the way Rissy looks at him now?"

"And," Denver added, "how he looks at her."

"Yeah. Almost made me blush a few times."

Armie reached for him, and Miles ducked away, laughing. "Take a breath, man. Relax. If we didn't know you both so well, we might not have noticed. But we do."

"We do," Denver agreed. "And you really do burn the girl up with how you stare."

Armie scowled. "Shut the fuck up." But of course they didn't.

"Why all the secrecy anyway?" Miles asked. "It's not like she's still in high school."

"Or a virgin," Denver said, pushing him. He turned to Miles. "You remember that other douche she dated?"

"Steve," Miles said with a curled lip. "No way was that guy hands-off." He shuddered as if repulsed.

"Hell, I'm guessing everyone will be glad you're in the picture. It keeps creeps like Steve from crawling back in."

"So c'mon, buddy," Miles said, placating. "Tell us all about your worries."

Armie had no idea how to explain, so he decided not to. "Fuck you both." He was just glad that, according to them, most wouldn't have noticed. Because it was definitely the outsiders that concerned him.

Denver was gearing up to rib him more when a knock sounded on the front door. They all three turned to see a hulk of a guy, brown haired with three days of beard scruff, a crooked nose and a neck tattoo, staring through the glass door toward them.

Miles was the first to speak. "Huh. It's the guy you're fighting."

"Carter Fletcher," Armie said, recognizing him right off.

"Chaos," Denver said at almost the same time.

Wondering at the visit, they all three walked to the door. Denver had the keys, Armie assumed Carter wanted to see him, and Miles was probably just nosy.

Carter stepped in, hand extended. "Denver. Good to see you."

Looking more than a little bemused, Denver accepted the greeting. "Carter."

He nodded next to Miles. "Miles Dartman, right? The Legend?"

"Trying to live up to that." Laughing, Miles also took Carter's hand in greeting.

"All right," Armie said, "if you ladies are done with the pleasantries, maybe Carter can tell me why he's here."

Carter rubbed at the bridge of his nose, glanced at each man, then settled on Armie. "Jacobson. I was hoping to talk. In private, I mean."

What now? Seeing no alternative, Armie shrugged. "Sure." He didn't want to stay at the rec center. Closing time had come and gone. And Rissy might be at his place, so he couldn't invite Carter there. "I was on my way out, but we can talk in my truck if you want."

"That's fine. I won't keep you long."

Armie shared a look with his friends. "Looks like you guys are going to finish up without me after all." He pulled his cell from his pocket. "Give me two minutes, and I'll be right with you."

RISSY HAD ALMOST reached Armie's apartment when he called to tell her he'd be pretty late. He didn't say why, and she hesitated to question him. She wanted to be one of those "no pressure" girlfriends who didn't smother him with lack of trust or clinging need.

Girlfriend. Oh, how she loved the thought. Armie had never designated her as such, but she was all the same. She knew it. And despite how he tried to keep things private, all their friends knew she was staying with him at his apartment.

Warfield, Ohio, was small, their neighborhood smaller, and their group of friends tight.

Since all the women knew, that meant their significant others also knew. No one seemed to think anything of it. Heck, she'd even caught her brother smiling at her every so often. Whenever she'd ask Cannon why, he'd just shake his head—and go on smiling.

She was pretty sure those smiles were about her and Armie. Her brother had never liked Steve, but of course he loved Armie. Everyone did.

Her, most especially.

It thrilled her to know they were exclusive.

Armie had a very busy life as a fighter, but he always checked in with her to let her know if he'd be late or away from the rec center. He put in grueling hours on his career, and now, with the upcoming fight closing in, it seemed various promotions also sucked up a lot of his time. And still, he somehow managed to be there for anyone and everyone whenever they needed him. He ran nonstop and yet never tired.

His energy level astounded her, especially in bed.

She knew Yvette, Cherry, Harper and Vanity loved him as a friend. And the guys—well, they could only be described as family.

The family Armie had never had.

Since he'd given her a key, Merissa had done her utmost to show him how important he was to her. She *loved* having sex with him. Armie wasn't crude, but he was up-front and very plainspoken about what he wanted, what he liked, how he liked it.

How often he wanted it.

She also loved sleeping with him, being held against his solid body, carved with muscle and always so warm. Thinking about snuggling up to his chest, how his chest hair felt on her cheek, how indescribably delicious he always smelled, sent a curl of sizzling sensation from her heart downward, until she shifted on the car seat.

Most of all, she loved Armie's playful nature. Around her he'd always been so cautious that she hadn't realized exactly how the other women had seen him. He had a wicked sense of humor, an intimate way of teasing and a genuine caring about him that melted her bones, turned her on and softened her heart.

Now that he'd opened up, now that she experienced his warmth every day, she couldn't imagine ever giving that up.

Despite all he'd endured, despite how his mother had abandoned him and how his father had turned on him, Armie was beyond special.

It amazed her that the other women hadn't fallen madly in love with him. Denver, Stack, Gage—they were all awesome. Really terrific guys. And sure, as ripped fighters, they were total eye candy.

But they weren't Armie.

Pulling into a shopping lot and turning around, Merissa decided to go to her house to grab a few more things. Little by little, she'd set herself up at Armie's apartment—which, okay, didn't make sense.

If anything, he should move in with her. Her house was a lot more spacious than his apartment, and far more private.

Except that when she'd been at home, everyone had forever dropped in. She'd loved that.

She *missed* that.

Maybe Armie would soon stop keeping their relationship secret and instead would let her shout it to the world. She'd give him a little more time before bringing it up.

The sun sank in the sky, turning the horizon shades of gold, mauve and purple by the time she pulled into her driveway. With the weather so mild, the air fresh, she breathed deeply as she left her car and started up the walkway to the front door.

A lazy breeze stirred the air—and suddenly she felt edgy.

Ridiculous. Her house was totally secure; Cannon had seen to that. Looking around, Merissa tried to find the source of her disquiet, but she saw only the usual porch lights on her neighbors' houses and a few cars parked at the curb. Nothing out of the ordinary. Somewhere in the distance, kids laughed. A few doors down, headlights cut through the dusk as a neighbor pulled into his driveway.

For reasons she didn't understand, the unease amplified. Retrieving her key and, feeling ridiculously jumpy, Merissa unlocked the door and stepped in.

Damn, why hadn't she left a few lights on? She hit the wall switch, blinked at the sudden blinding glare and quickly hit the keypad to keep her alarms from going off.

New alertness made her pulse race.

Standing in the foyer of her bi-level home, she looked up the short stairs to the kitchen, then down to the living area below. Cherry used to be there, and now more than ever she missed her best friend.

"Stop being a goof." Going up the steps she hit more light switches until her house glowed. With the bathroom door locked she showered, changed into jeggings and a roomy sweatshirt, then braided her hair. She'd see Armie soon, but she didn't bother putting on more makeup. He'd now seen her fresh from her shower, heck, *in* the shower, as well as when she'd first awakened.

It hadn't run him off yet, and honestly, she didn't want to linger in the empty house. Never before had that bothered her, but she'd gone from the robbery to mostly staying with Armie. Now every shadow looked sinister and every creak sounded ominous.

After gathering up a fresh change of clothes for to-morrow, along with a few food items from her cabinets, Merissa turned to start down the stairs.

She froze at a particularly loud noise in the down-stairs living area.

A second later, the alarm went off, indicating an intruder.

Her heart shot into her throat.

IMPATIENT, ARMIE RESTED his wrist over the steering wheel and looked toward Carter. It was stuffy in the truck, but when he'd started to put the window down, Carter had asked that he not.

"Okay, I give. What are we doing?" Armie asked.

Carter hedged, looking around the area, ensuring they were alone.

Huh. "You planning to murder me, Chaos? Ponder-ing how to get my dead body from here to wherever you hope to dump me?"

Not amused, Carter said, "No."

"Then how about you tell me what you want? I have better things I could be doing right now." Like check-ing on an unhappy, possibly mistreated kid, followed by sexing up the sweet sister to his best friend.

Shit. Armie concentrated on Carter. "Say it or get out."

"You know I've got a big interview with a sports channel?"

"No. Why would I?" For some reason, his mood deteriorated by the moment. "I don't follow your schedule."

Chaos glared at him. "Look, you're being a prick for no reason. I'm not here to cause problems. Just the opposite."

Yeah, Armie knew he was antagonistic and he didn't know why. "Fine. Just get to it, will you?"

"I have a big interview. Really big. More high profile than I've ever had before. That's because of you, by the way."

"Not my doing."

"I realize that. And I honestly think I'll beat you."

"Okay." Armie didn't give a damn what he thought. "So?"

"Soon as the big interview was announced, I got this anonymous tip that while I'm doing the usual trash talk, I should also mention...something else."

Dread stirred in his guts. To hide that reaction, Armie crossed his arms and waited.

Uncomfortable, Carter rubbed the back of his neck. "Fuck it." He lifted a hip to dig a note from his back pocket. With only a slight hesitation, he handed it to Armie.

Armie knew. He didn't have to read the note, but he did anyway. Unfolding the wrinkled paper and holding it up to an interior lamp, he read aloud,

"You want to win even before you get in the cage? Then tell the media about Jacobson's past—as a rapist."

One hand braced on the dash, Carter leaned forward. "I don't know who wrote it. But I hate fucking cowards who skulk around—"

"I'm not a coward," Armie said with a low, lethal edge.

"Not you, you ass." Carter nodded at the note. "The anonymous fuck who left that on my windshield."

On his windshield—*where anyone might have seen it.*

There was a day when Armie would have told Carter to fuck off, to believe whatever he wanted, and then he would have walked away. But damn it, those days were in the past. He wouldn't run from this.

He was sick to death of running, of dodging trouble.

Of letting the cowards win.

So he looked Carter in the eyes and said, "It's not true."

"I figured if it was, you'd be in jail, right?" With it out in the open now, Carter sat back and relaxed. "Besides, I asked around about you as soon as I knew we were fighting. I heard a lot of stuff, including admiration and respect from the men, and a lot of sick swooning from the women."

The side of Armie's mouth kicked up, but mostly with irony and no real humor behind it.

"I haven't shown it to anyone else," Carter assured him. "But if you want some advice—"

"I don't."

"—I think you should show it to the powers-that-be in the SBC. They won't want to be blindsided by this."

So Carter planned to mention it in his interview?

Armie no sooner thought that than Carter clarified. "When I don't bite, they're going to reach out again."

Solemn, he shook his head in regret. "Eventually some knucklehead is going to take that garbage and run with it."

Eyeing the opponent he knew only by his record, Armie felt indebted. "You're not going to say anything?"

"I want a clean fight, not one clouded by idiotic accusations that can't be proved. The thing is, if I thought it had any merit, if I'd gotten even a clue that you'd ever mistreated a woman, I'd take a lot of pleasure in trashing you. Hell, I'd enjoy taking you apart."

Easier said than done, but Armie knew when to keep his ego to himself. "I'd feel exactly the same." He held out a hand. "Thanks for…" He searched for the right words.

"For not being easily duped?" Carter took his hand. "My pleasure." Then he smiled. "And I'm still going to beat you in the cage."

It was a hell of a situation, but Armie laughed anyway. Carter was such a fair guy, he almost hated to disappoint him.

But when they fought, he'd be the winner—no doubts at all.

CHAPTER THIRTEEN

Trying not to be too obvious, Merissa stuck close to the very nice officer who'd shown up to look things over for her.

For the tenth time, Officer Mead asked, "You're sure you're okay now?"

Given she continued to play his shadow, she could understand his uncertainty.

She forced a smile. "Yes. Thank you again. I'm so sorry I overreacted like that."

"You didn't," he assured her. "It's always better to be safe."

Safe—but not hysterical.

Her face burned anew even as her imagination stayed in hyperdrive. First the robbery, then that near miss with a speeding car and now this.

She was sure of the sound she'd heard—and maybe she'd even seen a shadow. That could have been fear playing tricks with her eyes… But what if it wasn't?

Something had triggered the alarm.

Had she become a target, or was she just being paranoid?

She'd never been paranoid before.

The shrill alarm had so badly startled her that a vague darkness had crept in around her. She'd come very close to fainting.

Luckily, at the last second the fog had receded, but then she'd gone straight into panic mode. After ungluing her feet from the stairs, she'd raced like a lunatic into her bedroom where she'd locked the door, grabbed the phone and crouched on the other side of her bed.

The second the monitoring station called, she'd replied that yes, she absolutely needed help, and she was pretty sure she'd sounded out of control.

The security tech promised to send a cop and had put the call through for her. Minutes later the very nice officer had arrived, and it had taken all her willpower to stop cowering in her bedroom and to go to the front door and let him in.

He certainly hadn't been spooked. After she'd shut off the alarm system, he'd gone downstairs—with her trailing close because no way in hell was she waiting behind—and he'd found all the windows and the door to the walkout closed and locked.

Next she'd followed him upstairs, where he'd not only inspected every room, he'd even looked in closets and under the beds.

Still he'd found nothing.

That had led him outside to poke around, again, with her dogging his heels, and finally he'd deduced it could only have been a critter that got in through the attic because every door and window remained secure.

"That could set off the alarm?"

He shrugged. "I don't know. Maybe talk to your security company about it." Going sympathetic, he asked, "Do you have someone you can invite over tonight? You probably shouldn't be alone."

No kidding. "I was just heading out," she promised him. But the way he watched her made her lift her chin.

"I'm not usually this jumpy. I've lived on my own for a while, actually. Sure, I used to have a roommate, but…" Drawing to a halt, she sighed. "You know about the recent bank robbery, right?"

"A month or so ago?"

"Yes. That was me."

His mouth quirked. "A confession? You're saying you robbed the place?"

"No!" She realized he was teasing and relaxed again. "I'm the manager there."

"Well then, no wonder you're a little nervous."

"Right?" She didn't tell him about her near miss in the roadway. Until now, she'd assumed her own negligence had almost caused the accident because she hadn't been paying attention. But now… She'd had one near miss too many for her to entirely dismiss the idea that someone was after her.

Relieved that she hadn't called her brother—or worse, Armie—Merissa walked with Officer Mead out to her car. "So…you won't tell anyone how I totally lost it, will you?"

"You did all the right things," he promised her. "And yeah, I'll probably need to share the incident with Detective Riske since he's working the bank robbery. But I'll only give him details, same as I'll write in my report."

"Thank you." By the time Logan Riske asked her questions, she'd be composed enough not to embarrass herself. And of course, she'd tell Cannon and Armie. If she was in danger, they needed to know.

Realistically she knew neither of them would judge her, but that didn't seem to matter to her pride. Sometimes having a certified badass as a brother, and now being intimately involved with one, had its drawbacks. Comparisons could suck.

"How about I wait until you're out of the driveway," Officer Mead offered. "Once you're on your way, then I'll take off."

Such a kind man. Gratitude engulfed her. "I would very much appreciate that."

"Protect and serve, ma'am." His smile warmed to an intimate degree.

Was he flirting? It certainly seemed so.

If she wasn't already madly in love with Armie, she'd have gladly flirted back, but instead she said, "I've held you up long enough. Really, you've been wonderful. I don't know what I would have done without you, so again, thank you." And with that, she got in her car and secured the doors. Finally she was able to take a deep breath.

With the handsome young officer watching her, she waved, then backed out and drove away. Thinking it'd be better to get it out of the way, she tried to decide who to call first—her brother or Armie. She'd just decided on calling Armie when her phone rang, startling her. With a glance at the screen she saw it was Cherry.

As soon as she answered, she heard a lot of boisterous laughter and knew the ladies had gotten together. "Having a party without me?" she asked her best friend.

"Rissy! Where are you?"

Wondering at that, Merissa explained, "I just left my house and I'm heading to Armie's."

"Scrap that. Come join us instead."

Vanity chimed in, saying, "We're all here and just waiting on you."

"All who?" Merissa asked.

"Me," Yvette sang out, followed by Harper's, "Me, too!"

"Guess what we're doing," Cherry whispered, followed by gales of laughter from the others.

"Drinking?" she guessed.

"Not a drop." Then in a rush, Cherry said, "We're at the porn store. You know, that seedy little place in town that sells DVDs and God-only-knows what else."

No way. *"Why?"*

"We're going shopping," Vanity told her.

Shopping for porn? Merissa laughed nervously. "You're making that up."

"Nope," Yvette said. "And just so you know, I busted Armie shopping here once. I thought it was still just a place that rented DVDs."

The other women started heckling Yvette, and Merissa heard Vanity say, "Yeah, uh-huh, sure you did."

"Hey, I'd just returned to the area!" Yvette insisted. "I didn't have cable set up yet, so I figured to get an old movie. I had no way of knowing things had changed so much."

"The fun part," Vanity interrupted her to say, "is that she ran into Armie, and he admitted he shops there *often*."

Often? Merissa hadn't seen any porn around his apartment, but then, she hadn't snooped. There were a lot of drawers that remained a mystery to her. "What did he buy?" she asked in a whisper of her own.

Cracking up, Vanity said, "Meet us at the shop and we'll all go inside to see."

Oh, she wanted to. Curiosity killed her, but she'd never had the nerve to do more than glance toward the shop whenever she went past.

"You have time," Cherry said, reclaiming her phone while the buzz of conversation drifted in. "Denver called me to say he'd be late because Armie would be late. Something about that guy Armie is supposed to fight—"

"Carter Fletcher."

"Right. He dropped in the rec center so Denver is hanging around to hear what it was about. And then Armie wants to check on a boy who's having a rough time of it, and Denver wanted to go along. They'll be a minimum of an hour late, but probably longer."

"Where are the other guys?"

"Stack's busy setting up some gym equipment in Vanity's basement—"

"It's *our* basement now," Vanity sang out, "because Stack is all mine, so what's mine is his."

Cherry laughed and added, "Gage and Cannon were heading over there to help out."

"So we're all free, then." Did she dare join them? Merissa gave it quick thought, and nodded. "I'm ten minutes away."

"Yay! This is going to be so fun."

Merissa had her doubts about that, but she couldn't let the other ladies go in without her. Besides, after the scare she'd had at her house, she didn't want to be alone in Armie's apartment. "You'll wait for me outside?"

"We're sitting in Harper's car. Drive safe, but hurry!"

Merissa disconnected, and instead of going straight, took the first left. No reason now to call Armie or her brother, since she knew they were both busy.

Later would be a better time to clue them in.

Much, much later.

Soon as Carter took off, Denver joined him, getting into the passenger seat of his truck without fanfare, then strapping on his seat belt.

Surprised, Armie cocked a brow. "Am I playing chauffeur?"

"To Bray's house, yeah. I decided to go along. You can drop me off here on your way home."

What the hell? He didn't need a babysitter. "You want to tell me why?"

With a roll of one shoulder, Denver said, "I'm worried about the kid, too."

That was acceptable, but then Denver went on.

"And you have a fight soon. If shit goes sideways, no reason for you to chance getting hurt."

"Get out of my truck."

Denver grinned at him. "Nope."

"Asshole."

Unperturbed, Denver nodded. "You're welcome."

Sighing, Armie put the truck in gear and pulled away. As he drove, he waited, but Denver didn't ask him about Carter's visit, a fact he couldn't ignore. "Denver?"

"Yeah?"

"Thanks."

As if he'd expected it, Denver said, "There ya go."

Just to lighten the mood, Armie asked, "Will Cherry be at home pining for you while you act as my escort tonight?"

"Maybe." He slanted Armie a look of complete satisfaction. "The way that girl pines is enough to make me rip my jeans."

Armie laughed. "She loves you. That's a good thing."

"Very good."

"And vice versa."

"She's mine," Denver said in agreement. "As it turns out, though, she's out with Yvette, Vanity and Harper. The guys are helping Stack get some equipment set up."

Armie wondered if he could ever claim Merissa as his. In his heart, he'd done so long ago—but his brain had always insisted it wasn't meant to be.

And now, with creeps skulking around and leaving anonymous notes on windshields...

His thoughts came to a screeching halt when he pulled up to the small clapboard house that matched Bray's address. Through the open windows, rank curses echoed around the neighborhood. As Armie sat there—only seconds really—the warped screen door flew open and Bray shot out, tripping over his own feet.

A big bastard lumbered out after him. Dressed in his boxers and a wife-beater undershirt, he stumbled and cursed as he gave chase, fists bunched, face florid—and unfortunately, he caught Bray by the back of the shirt, literally yanking the boy off his feet so that he hit the ground hard.

Behind them a woman cried, feebly tugging at the man's arm.

Both truck doors slammed as Armie and Denver moved at the same time. When Bray tried to get up, the man slung him back to the ground, and to Armie's disbelief, the miserable fuck lifted his boot to kick. The woman sobbed, begging...

"That's enough!"

Armie's command drew everything to a halt. Hell, even the birds in the trees stopped chirping. Stiff necked, Bray rolled away, the man quickly redirected his anger at Armie and the woman slumped down to sit on a broken porch step, her gaze darting everywhere.

Denver's heavy stride kept pace, but he allowed Armie to speak. "Bray, come here."

White with shock, Bray looked up—and no one could miss the wet, red eyes, or the suppressed rage and shame.

Jesus, Armie wanted to kill someone, preferably the man manhandling a fifteen-year-old kid.

Bray stood, shouldering a sleeve over each cheek to remove dirt and, probably, tears. He didn't come to Armie, so with Denver at his side, Armie went to him.

As they neared, the guy eyed him and Denver with loathing, then hauled Bray close, keeping him caught in his grip. "This isn't your business."

"You couldn't be more wrong about that." Without slowing, Armie strode right up to the man until he met him, chest to chest. It'd be so easy, so fucking easy, to give the bastard a taste of his own abuse. Instead, Armie glanced at the hand on Bray's arm, and whispered, "Turn him loose."

Narrowing his eyes and smiling slowly, the man did just that, giving Bray a shove that sent him back to his ass again.

Armie crowded closer. "That was a miserable, chicken-shit move. You any better at pushing around grown men, or do you specialize in boys?"

"Bray," the woman said, her voice high and shrill and fearful. "What's going on? Who are these people?"

Leaving the man to Armie, Denver approached the woman, hand extended. "I'm Denver Lewis, ma'am. And that's my friend, Armie Jacobson. We're Bray's friends."

"What grown men hang with boys?" the man asked.

"We're from the rec center," Denver explained.

"Fighters," she breathed, horrified. "Russell, they're trained fighters!"

Huh. That changed Russell's attitude real quick.

The unholy smile disappeared under a cautious frown. He shifted his heavy gaze away and glared at Bray. "Get your ass back in the house."

"I don't think so," Armie said before Bray could reply one way or the other.

"This ain't got nothing to do with you!" Russell reached for Bray.

Armie stepped into his path. Keeping his tone calm but firm, he asked, "You're his father?"

Bray snorted. "No."

The man snapped, again reaching for Bray. "You better watch that smart mouth, boy!"

Armie stepped him back, all the way to his porch. That must've been pushing the big bully too far, because he threw a wild haymaker, swinging a lunch box–sized fist toward Armie's face.

With practiced ease Armie lifted his forearm to block the blow, then delivered one short jab to the man's bloated gut.

Retching, Russell bent double.

The woman, who only moments before had been crying for her son, immediately fell to her knees, frantically caring for the bully.

"Russell? Oh my God, are you okay? Russell?" She pet on him, hugged him, all the while crying.

Russell gave her a shove, but she scrambled right back.

It was like déjà vu for Armie. The hairs on the back of his neck lifted. Every muscle in his body twitched.

The woman had her own bruises, but she fawned over the man as if he was some innocent victim.

Disgusted, Armie turned to Bray and found the boy walking away.

Damn. "You got this?" he asked Denver.

Denver blinked. "Uh, sure."

In a jog, Armie went after Bray. When he caught up, he didn't touch him, just kept pace. "Where ya going?"

Bray rolled a shoulder, kept his head down and dogged on.

"He's your stepfather?"

"He's nothing." Then, reluctantly, Bray added, "Her boyfriend, I guess. I don't know."

"She's your mother?"

Nothing.

"Can we stop to talk a minute?"

Bray hunched his shoulders more. "No point."

Shit. Armie stepped around in front of the boy. "Please."

With a mammoth chip on his shoulder, Bray met his gaze and waited.

Deciding to just get through it, Armie asked, "Has he been around long?"

"Couple of months."

"He's hit you? Before today?"

Bray's lips trembled, his eyes narrowed and he tried to do more walking.

"Never mind." Before Bray could leave him, Armie thought to ask, "What about before him?"

"Before him there was another guy, and another before that. What of it?"

So his mother routinely brought in abusive asses? A deep breath didn't help much. Mothers should protect their sons. The whole scenario felt far too familiar and personal. Hands on his hips, Armie asked, "Do you have anywhere to go?"

"Sure."

Frustrated with that short answer, Armie asked, "Where?"

"It's called none-of-your-business."

The smart-ass reply so surprised him that Armie laughed. He didn't mean to. Seriously, there was nothing funny about the situation. But he liked Bray, and he especially liked that the boy hadn't lost his backbone. "You know what?"

Bray narrowed his eyes.

"You remind me of me—and just so we're clear, that's not a compliment."

This time Bray's mouth twitched before he firmed it again, quickly reclaiming his "fuck off" attitude.

Growing somber, Armie said softly, "You know I have to call the cops."

"No," Bray growled, "you don't have to do anything."

He wished it otherwise. In fact, Armie wished he could just put the kid in his truck and take him home with him. But Bray wasn't a stray pet, and there were legalities involved, not to mention a whole lot of emotional baggage that Armie might not be equipped to deal with. The last thing he wanted was to screw this up and make things worse for Bray. "I'm afraid I do."

They heard a sudden commotion behind them and turned together to see Russell proving himself to be ten times an idiot as he tried to tackle Denver. Surprised, Denver quickly adjusted and caught Russell in a sleeper hold. The woman wailed and screamed and slapped ineffectually at Denver's bowling-ball biceps.

Again in unison, Armie and Bray sighed.

They eyed each other.

"Damn it." Bray snatched up a rock and threw it hard, narrowly missing Armie's truck, although he hadn't been aiming at anything in particular. "I hate foster care."

Armie's heart wrenched. "You've had some bad ones?"

"No." His nostrils flaring with the fast, uneven breaths, Bray swallowed convulsively. The way he put his shoulders back made him look far too stoic for a fifteen-year-old. "Foster care's been fine."

"Then—"

"I always end up back here." Resigned, the kid looked toward his mother. "Just as well. She needs me."

Armie watched him head toward the woman now frantically calling his name, alternately blaming and pleading for his help.

No way could Armie leave this alone. He wouldn't make promises yet; first he had to figure out the system and see what options he had.

But Bray wasn't alone, and he needed to know that.

The traffic lights cooperated and Merissa made it there in eight minutes. As soon as she got close she spotted Harper and Vanity sitting on the trunk of the car, with Cherry and Yvette both still inside the vehicle. As the sunlight faded a streetlamp flickered on, adding ambience to their adventure.

Grinning, Merissa parked right behind them. Soon as she did, the other ladies emerged.

"You're really going to do this?" she asked Cherry. In many ways, her best friend came off as the life of the party. But deep down Merissa knew she was really reserved about certain things.

"Denver tried to lecture me about sex," Cherry told her, as if that explained her daring. "Do you believe that?"

Vanity said, "I believe it. Denver's awesome, but he's also domineering."

Sighing, Cherry said, "He is," as if that made him more perfect.

Merissa laughed, then asked Vanity, "Does Stack know you're here?"

"Shoot, no."

"He and Cannon would have come along for sure," Yvette told them.

"Stack would gladly tour me through the place," Vanity said with a grin. "But no way would he want me here without him."

"So." Harper lifted her brows. "We going to stand here talking tough, or are we going in?"

Fist in the air, Vanity said, "We go in."

Everyone agreed, and then they all crowded together.

In a tight cluster they stepped through the door and into the well-lit video section of the shop. The cashier, a younger guy with a shaved and tattooed head, glanced up from a magazine, snickered, and then ignored them.

Moving like a gaggle of ducks, they looked around. "It's regular movies," Harper whispered.

Yvette pointed toward a lighted door on the far wall. "The good stuff is back there."

"We're pathetic," Merissa said. Giving Vanity a nudge, she got them moving again. There were a few men in the place, and they tracked the women with interest.

"This is supercreepy." Cherry gave a nervous giggle. "And I feel like an idiot."

When they reached the door, Vanity used the hem of her shirt to protect her hand from the probable germs on the knob. After a beat of expectation, she swung open the door with great fanfare, and together they stepped into the dimly lit room.

Wide-eyed, Merissa looked around. Dildos and vibrators hung from the ceiling in many shapes and sizes and colors. She choked as she took in the elaborate variety.

Her cohorts were equally impressed.

Next Merissa scanned the shelves and saw some… Fake lady parts? She leaned in to look closer. Yup. Lady parts.

In boxes.

A giggle started up her throat.

Then she saw the movies—and *Oh my God*—the movie titles. They were so absurdly bad.

Maybe everything just added up. Maybe she was already strung too tight. For whatever reason she started making these awful, chortling, snorting noises, and even as everyone else turned to watch her warily, she couldn't stop.

Very shortly the rest of the ladies joined her, and within a minute they were all roaring with hilarity.

Cops were just pulling up when Armie got a call. He glanced at the screen, saw it was Leese and answered with, "If it's not important—"

"Rissy's at the porn shop."

Armie almost fell over. *"Say what?"*

In a rush, Leese said, "Not just her, but Vanity,

Cherry, Yvette and Harper, too. Justice and I were driving by and saw them. I was going to beep and wave, but then I realized what they were doing."

Stock-still, Armie asked, "What?"

"Going in."

Couldn't be true. Armie snorted.

"I know, right? But that's what they did," Leese insisted. "They marched in like they owned the place."

"You're positive it was them?"

"I'm not an idiot." Impatience sounded in Leese's tone. "Vanity led the way, Yvette and Rissy were in the middle and Harper sort of dragged Cherry along."

"Un-fucking-believable."

"I just thought you should know."

Armie chewed his upper lip, but he couldn't walk off on Bray. "I'm going to be held up for a bit—"

"Want me to stick around and keep an eye on things?"

"Yeah." He popped his neck, feeling evil. "But if possible, don't let any of them see you. Denver and I will be there as soon as we can."

"Should I call the other guys?"

"Sure." Armie liked that idea. Anticipating their reactions, he said, "Let's make a party of it."

Leese laughed. "Damn, as a single man, I'm almost jealous."

Officially, Armie was still single himself. But he went right past that fact to tell Leese, "You should be. Now keep an eye on things and I'll be there as soon as I can."

CHAPTER FOURTEEN

WHAT A DAY. After explaining everything to the police, who'd apparently been to the house many times, Armie tried talking to Bray alone.

The kid wasn't real receptive. Armie remembered what it was like to be fifteen, feeling so adult, wanting to control his own destiny while others were actually in charge. He gave Bray his number and told him to call anytime. He also promised him that he'd be in touch, that he wasn't going to disappear on him.

Bray hadn't looked convinced. Never one to hold back, and having no skill at prettying up his words, Armie told him, "You're not a problem I'm trying to dump, okay? I just have to follow the law, that's all."

That had startled Bray.

"When I say I'm not disappearing, I mean it. And damn it, I want you to know that."

Reluctantly Bray had nodded. "Yeah, sure. Whatever."

It was a start. Armie held out his hand and that confused Bray, too. But finally he accepted, and when he did Armie pulled him in for a bear hug. He felt awkward as hell, but he liked it all the same.

To cover the emotional moment for both of them, he mussed Bray's hair and grinned. "I'll see what's what and be in touch, okay?"

Bray nodded. "Yeah." His skinny chest expanded. "Thanks."

A social worker approached, her careful smile in place, and Armie wondered how she did it. He'd rather fight in the cage naked every day than deal with the emotional devastation of shitty parenting. At least the woman was familiar to Bray and by the time Armie left, some of the suffocating worry had loosened. It seemed the last foster parents who'd had Bray adored him. It was only the mother's insistence that she get him back that kept his life in turmoil.

The foster parents would be taking him in again. Armie heard the social worker tell the kid that they still had his room all set up.

I always end up back here.

Maybe this time would be different—but Armie doubted it.

After talking to Carter earlier, his mood had soured. Now, after this, he was literally spoiling for a fight. He needed to expend some energy in a bad way, and violence would suit him just fine.

Not the good sportsman competition of the SBC. No, he wanted a street brawl.

For that reason, he'd have preferred to steer clear of Merissa tonight. Maybe Cannon could just—

"You ready to go?" Denver asked. "Bray looks to be in good hands, at least for now."

He'd clued Denver in earlier and naturally he wanted to get to his wife.

"I was thinking—"

"Don't," Denver told him, shouldering him to get him headed to the truck. "You'd break her heart."

Denver's tendency to act like a damn relationship

specialist just because he'd gotten married was starting to rub him the wrong way. "What the hell do you
know about it?"

"I know all the other guys will be there, in on the
joke, and if you're a no-show it's going to devastate
Rissy."

Bullshit. Armie got in his truck and slammed the
door shut. Stewing, he started the truck, then gripped
the steering wheel.

Denver slid in on the passenger side. "You're looking at this all wrong, you know."

"You don't know shit about how I'm looking at
things."

Whistling, Denver eyed him. "You don't want to take
your bad mood out on Rissy."

"No, I don't." And in a dozen different ways, his past
was catching up. His entry into the SBC, notes left by
cowards and now memories stirred up by a boy in need.
He didn't want to see himself as Bray, but damn it, how
could he not? And since he wasn't a boy anymore, why
the fuck did it have to make him feel so hollow?

"She's not fine china," Denver said quietly. "Women
have a nice way of blunting the bad shit."

Armie jerked the truck into gear and pulled out. "You
don't need to lecture me on the joys of sex. Trust me,
I know."

"I'm not talking about getting laid, dumbass, but
yeah, that helps, too."

Don't ask, don't ask—

"I'm talking about a woman you care for."

So he didn't even need to ask? Denver would just
continue to regale him with a married man's wisdom?
"Can you be quiet? I'm trying to think."

"No, you're looking for a way out. Big difference."

"You—" Denver's phone rang, cutting off Armie's venom and making him grind his teeth in frustration.

But then, as Denver said, "It's Cannon," Armie decided it was just as well that he take a breather on the animosity.

After all, he wasn't really pissed at Denver. But this was a perfect example of why he shouldn't be around Merissa tonight. He might say or do something that would—

"Cannon wants to talk to you." Denver put the phone on speaker. "I already told him we can head straight to the shop and Cherry can take me back for my ride."

After giving Denver the evil eye, Armie said, "Cannon, what's up?"

"We're already here, just waiting on you two, so thanks for making it a straight shot. The ladies might head out any minute."

"They're still inside shopping, huh?" *What the hell was Merissa buying?*

"Lots to see," Cannon joked. "While we wait, I figured I might as well get an update on Bray. How'd it go?"

Armie spent the next few minutes telling Cannon everything he knew, as well as his plans.

"I know the foster parents. They're good people. And since Bray will still be in the area, I'm betting they'll let him continue coming to the rec center."

That was a relief.

"See you in a few," Cannon said. "And Armie?"

Dread had him mentally cringing. "Yeah?"

"I'm glad Merissa doesn't have to go home alone tonight."

The call ended and Armie could only stare at the road and concentrate on his driving. *What the hell?* Cannon knew his little sister was buying porn, for God's sake. And he was *glad* that she'd be going home with him?

Laughing, Denver gave a light shove to Armie's shoulder. "Guess Cannon knows she's not made of fine china, huh?"

At the moment he didn't understand Cannon at all, so no way would he weigh in on that.

As they pulled up to the shop, Armie shook his head. "This is probably the most traffic that joint has ever gotten." He knew the ladies were inside, while Cannon, Gage, Stack, Leese and Justice waited outside. If it weren't for his visit with Carter and then Bray's fucked-up situation, Armie would be enjoying this a hell of a lot more.

Together he and Denver approached the others.

"So far," Cannon told him, "there hasn't been much foot traffic. Other than a couple of regulars, they're in there alone."

He looked in through the big front window. "I don't see them."

"Back room," Stack told him, his tone dry.

The notorious "back room" was where all kinds of kinky paraphernalia could be found. *Oh, to have been a fly on the wall...*

Or to have been an escort. He was pretty sure the rest of the guys felt the same.

"While they're in there," Gage muttered, his gaze on the shop, "one of us should slip inside and make sure the cashier knows what's what."

"Dirk's at the desk," Leese told them. "Armie, you know him, right?"

Armie scowled. "We all know him."

"Yeah, but you're friendly with him."

Denver elbowed him. "I hear tell you're his best customer."

Cannon laughed.

Screw it. "Yeah, all right. I'll do it." It'd be better than being needled by the rest of them.

Keeping an eye on the door to the special room, Armie went to the cashier desk, then put a finger to his mouth in the universal "Shh…" sign so that Dirk didn't call out a greeting. Keeping it low, he said, "You have some ladies shopping tonight."

"Yeah, dude," Dirk replied with a smarmy laugh. "Not like I could miss them, right? Pretty clear they were in uncharted territory. You know them?"

"I do." One of them more intimately than the others. "Make sure no one bothers them, okay?" Armie leaned closer. "My friends and I are going to be right outside—which isn't something you need to share with any of them."

Brows up, Dirk leaned to see out the front window, spotted the fighters lounging around, and gave Armie a bug-eyed look of uncertainty. "I don't want any trouble."

"No trouble." Armie slipped him fifty bucks. "We're going to surprise them—like a joke—that's all. And to ensure they don't see us as easily as you just did, we're going to move down the road a little. But we'll be there as soon as they come out. Got it?"

"They'll be fine. Only Gary and Frank are around, and they're not into chicks anyway."

Armie looked. Old Gary and Frank stared through the open door into the room, but yeah, they looked more bemused, maybe even fascinated, but not interested.

His duty done, Armie said, "Thanks, man. I owe you." Then he headed out before he got caught. They all walked down to wait in front of a closed furniture rental building, away from the entrance to the porn shop but with it in clear view.

Everyone seemed to be enjoying the diversion, telling ribald jokes and sharing suggestions. Armie wished he were elsewhere. He wished he were alone with his foul mood.

He had much to think about it, and details chipped away at his concentration. For her own good, the best option might still be to send Merissa home for the night.

He could play it off that he was tired; most men would be. He could say he needed time to think; the utter truth. Whatever Rissy bought tonight, she'd just have to enjoy it by herself.

Aw hell. That particular thought brought with it an explicit image, and of course his dick reacted. Shifting, Armie willed away the rising boner.

What he really wanted, what he really needed tonight, was a hard, mindless fuck to obliterate everything else.

But Rissy deserved so much more than that. Unfortunately, she was his greatest temptation, the one he most wanted to lose himself in.

He would never use her that way, so yeah, he'd definitely have to find a way to send her home. And the worst part? He was already missing her.

WITH CHERRY STICKING close to her side, Merissa perused the aisle of very realistic penises. At a particularly large one, she slanted Cherry a look.

Brows lifted, Cherry whispered, "Close."

It was no secret that Denver was well-endowed—which had been a constant source of curiosity and teasing from all the other ladies. Voice equally quiet and somewhat enthralled, Merissa asked, "Bigger or smaller?"

"Actually—"

"Here you go." Vanity tossed a book at Merissa. "You need this."

Barely catching it against her chest, Merissa turned it to see the title.

Beside her, Cherry read aloud, *"New Ways to Please the Man Who's Done It All."*

Merissa rolled her eyes. "Very funny."

While everyone laughed, Vanity said, "I glanced at it and I think there's good advice inside. Check it out."

She did—and had to agree. "Okay, so I've got my purchase. Now how about the rest of you?"

"A book?" Cherry complained. "Unfair."

Vanity held up a package of edible body paints. "I'm going to create a masterpiece."

Grinning, Harper asked, "Where? On Stack's abs?"

"Most definitely."

Yvette hesitated, then grabbed some massage oil. When she started to speak, Merissa said in a rush, "Little sister in the room!"

Amused, Yvette told her, "Fine. Just know that I'm going to put it to good use."

Striding past all the supersize sex toys, Harper said, "I can't even look at those for fear Cherry will think I'm daydreaming of Denver."

Cherry covered her face, but nodded. Through her fingers, she said, "It's true."

"This." Harper chose a customizable coupon book that included some pretty risqué promises. "Hopefully I can talk Gage into offering me a few coupons, too." She winked theatrically.

And they all turned to Cherry, who gulped. That's when the outrageous suggestions started, and Merissa had a great time ribbing her friend. Finally Cherry chose a really raunchy movie that left the rest of them agog.

Getting checked out was its own unique embarrassment. Two men stood off to the side of the main room, tracking their every move, and the cashier seemed jumpier than he had earlier.

Vanity saved the day by saying, "The gifts are on me." And since she was so well-to-do after different inheritances, no one argued—especially since that meant they could wait off to the side while Vanity handled the transaction.

A minute later, each carrying a different bag, they stepped outside and right into loud applause—from all their significant others, as well as male friends.

The guys were laughing, amused, all except Armie, who appeared far too forbidding. Merissa had a very bad feeling about the long look he gave her. Something had happened, something that had Armie brooding.

Well, too bad.

Right then and there, she made up her mind.

After the earlier scare at her house, she needed

Armie. Regardless of his dark expression, he could damn well comfort her—even if she had to force the issue.

HOLDING BACK, ARMS CROSSED, Armie leaned against his truck and watched the scene before him. Vanity, as energetic and in some ways as outrageous as him, jumped against Stack, planted a big kiss on him, then whispered in his ear.

That got Stack smiling before he took his wife's hand and told the rest of them, "Later." Since Stack had ridden over with Cannon, they left in Vanity's car.

Gage snatched Harper's bag away from her and then, holding it out of her reach, withdrew a small coupon-type book. As he flipped through the pages his eyes widened. Cocking a brow, he showed a particular page to Harper. She gave her husband a sly smile, nodded agreement and just like that, they, too, departed.

Trying not to focus on Rissy, Armie transferred his attention to Yvette. She willingly shared the contents of her bag with Cannon, who had one arm around her shoulders and a protective hand over her belly, while repeatedly kissing her temple. When he whispered to Yvette, she looked equal parts interested and flushed.

Armie shook his head. "Dare I ask?"

"None of your business," Cannon told him. "I'm taking Yvette home. Everyone have a good night."

"Cherry knows," Denver said, as they all watched Cannon and Yvette leave. "I'll get her to talk."

Cherry slugged Denver in the stomach, then shook her hand. "Ouch."

Making a big production of it, Denver lifted her hand

to his mouth, teased his lips over her knuckles, and whispered, "What'd you get?"

Going three shades of red, Cherry opened the bag for him to see.

His smile was slow and suggestive. "That's my girl."

Laughing, Leese said, "If anyone's going to need a ride—"

Denver opened his mouth, but Leese cut him off.

"No, scratch that. I meant a lift home. If you need a lift home, let's get to it before I start blushing at all these demonstrative displays of lust."

"He's jealous," Denver said to Armie. "But since you look like someone broke your funny bone, I think we'll ride with Leese."

"Let's go, then," Justice told them. "I'm thinking there are a few lady friends I need to call tonight and I don't want to wait until it's too late."

Cherry waved to Rissy. "We'll talk tomorrow."

As Armie watched them all walk off, chatting amicably, he heard no reply from Rissy.

His time was up and he knew it.

Then he felt her approach. "Armie?" Her voice was hesitant, hurt. She touched his shoulder. "What's wrong?"

He rubbed his face with both hands, stepped out of reach and tried to summon up a smile. "Nothing. It was just a rotten day, that's all." The evening breeze toyed with her hair, compelling him to tuck one side back. And once he was there, his hand so close to her face, he couldn't resist brushing his thumb over her soft, warm cheek. "I'm sorry, Stretch, but I'm lousy company tonight."

"That's okay," she rushed to say.

Armie was already shaking his head. "No, trust me, it's not. I'm going to head home to jog off some steam. You should sleep at your house and tomorrow we can—"

"No."

He stalled. Had she just told him no? He met her stormy gaze and tried again. "I've got a lot on my mind," he said. "It'll be better—"

"Forget it."

Her scowl surprised him. "Rissy."

She stiffened up. "Don't you *Rissy* me." Bag in hand, she stomped to her car and pretty much snarled, "I'm going to your place!"

He'd never seen her like this before, insistent but also on edge. "I just told you—"

"I heard exactly what you said! But you're not brushing me off, and that's that."

She refused to leave? He stalked up to her car. "Damn it, Stretch, if you'd just listen—"

Instead, she slammed her car door, started the engine and without giving him another glance, drove away.

Heading toward his apartment.

Son of a bitch!

Armie hurried to his truck and followed right behind her, his thoughts churning with every mile they drove. By the time he'd parked in the lot, she'd already jumped out and was literally jogging to his door.

What did she think? That he'd physically bar her?

Feeling like an idiot, his blood pumping hot, he chased after her.

She raced up the steps, and he thundered up behind her, getting to his apartment door just in time for her to slam it in his face. *His* door. Of all the...

He jerked it open, stepped inside and slammed it again. Nostrils flared, he looked around but didn't see her. *"Rissy?"*

"Don't bellow," she bellowed back from the bedroom.

Some anomalous emotion surged through him, tensing his muscles and narrowing his vision. He was furious, but for insane reasons, equally turned on. His nerves sang. His blood burned.

Urged forward by his own carnal imagination, he reached the closed door of the bedroom. More than a little lost, he sorted through a dozen different things to tell her and without settling on a single one he threw open the bedroom door.

It bounced off the wall, but didn't distract Rissy, who stood there topless, hurriedly undoing her painted-on jeans. It fried his eyes, seeing her like this, almost frenzied, her body bare down to her hips. Gorgeous.

Her top was on the opposite side of the room, as if she'd thrown it. Her shopping bag had been dropped on the floor, but at the moment he didn't care what she'd bought.

"I'm not leaving," she snapped, and almost fell over when she struggled to tug the tight jeans off her ankles. She ended up plopping onto the bed, bounced a little, kicked furiously and finally got the jeans off.

She now wore only low, boy-short panties the same color as her soft skin.

Heartbeat hammering, Armie took a step toward her, and she threw up a hand.

"Wait!"

He halted midstep.

Eyeing him warily, Rissy scooted farther into the middle of the bed, skimmed off her panties and flung them at him.

They hit him in the face and fell to the floor. Still he didn't move.

After shaking back her hair, she came up to her elbows, one leg straight, the other bent at the knee, and she smiled at him. "Okay. Now you can join me if you want."

Raw from the inside out, Armie edged cautiously closer. Tonight had been too much, first with Carter telling him his worst fears had surfaced into reality, then seeing a kid abused and having that same kid now distrust him.

Then to know he'd brought Rissy down to his level, that she'd been slumming in some low-class porno dive...

"Yeah," he whispered through his teeth, his eyes burning and his cock throbbing. "I'll join you."

Instead of looking threatened, she breathed a sigh of relief, and this time her voice was gentle when she said, "I'm not leaving."

At the side of the bed, Armie stared down at her long, toned, sexy body, and damn it, he needed her.

More than he needed his next breath.

More than he needed anything or anyone else. She'd given him a few tastes and now he craved her, like an addict.

Casual as you please, her blue eyes intent on his face, watching his reaction, Rissy parted her thighs.

Hotly provoked, Armie worked his jaw, then smiled at her in warning as he covered each of her knees with a hand and opened her wide.

Her breath caught, but she didn't fight him.

Damn, she was beautiful, her slim thighs straining, her sex pink and damp. And his.

"I told you to leave me be tonight."

"And I refused."

"I told you I wasn't fit company." He didn't entirely understand his purpose, but he felt determined on it all the same. "You wouldn't listen." He watched her gaze go heavy and her lips part. Turned on? How long would that last?

Switching gears, he scooped her up and put her properly in the bed, her head on a pillow. Looking her over, he said, "You know what I wanted tonight?"

"Not me," she whispered, bitterness filtering in. "But I wanted to be here all the same."

"You're wrong." Slowly, giving her time, he lifted one wrist toward the center of the headboard and the Velcro cuffs hanging there.

She jerked her head around to watch as he took his time closing the soft cuff around her very narrow wrist.

"I want you most of all," he told her, and then clarified, "But I want to fuck you hard."

She lifted a brow, tested her hand in the cuff, then looked at him. "Okay."

For only a second he closed his eyes, divided over whether or not he liked her easy compliance. Rissy wasn't like other women, not in the most important ways. She never had been. He understood that, and now it was past time for her to understand.

He took her other wrist and fastened the second cuff around it. "Right now you have plenty of slack, but I'd like to tighten that some."

She tugged experimentally, then gave a timid nod of agreement.

Armie straddled her naked body, staying on his knees as he reached for the center of the headboard and the slide loop that pulled her arms up tighter, and tighter still.

He liked this too much, having Rissy stretched out, contained, helpless beneath him.

His to do with as he pleased.

This particular position robbed her breasts of fullness and made her stomach even flatter. He scooted back so that he rested over her long thighs—and could see all of her.

"Armie…?"

"Hush." Very lightly, he trailed his fingertips from her elbows, paused over her breasts to toy with her now-tight nipples, then down her sides, making her squirm. He continued over her belly until both thumbs moved over her sex.

"Armie," she said again.

"I have a gag, you know." Idly he stroked her, parted her to look at her, admired her growing dampness.

"I wouldn't suggest you try it."

At her mean tone, his gaze lifted to hers. "Why not?" Calm, quiet and in control, he continued to touch her. "You don't like the idea of silence? You plan on giving me hell, telling me how you'll do as you please regardless of what I want?"

Her eyes narrowed. "Maybe."

The side of his mouth curled. "I'd like to put you in the ankle cuffs."

"No." With her face beet red, she insisted, "Not happening."

"You don't like for me to look at you?" He cupped his palm over her. "You're pretty here, Rissy. All soft and, yeah…" He watched her as he moved one finger inside her. "Wet."

Catching her bottom lip in her teeth, she lifted her hips against him. "Mmm…"

"You like that." Of course she did. She was getting her way and it excited her.

Hell, it excited him, too.

After two breaths, she said, "I don't care if you look at me, but you're not going to—"

He added another finger, making her trail off with a gasp. "I wasn't asking permission, honey." He pressed deeper, curled his fingers a little and found just the right spot that arched her body and wrenched a moan from her. "I like this, being fully dressed with you naked and restrained."

"Get…get naked."

"Not yet. Not for a while."

Her heavy eyes focused on him. "What do you mean?"

"I want to watch you come a few times first. And, Stretch? No faking. I'll know if you do and I won't like it."

"I wouldn't." She shifted against his hand, then squeezed his fingers. "With you, I don't have—" she panted, twisted and squeaked out "—to."

Satisfaction unfurled. "Getting close, huh? Maybe this'll help." With his other hand, he touched her breasts, lightly stroking, circling around her nipples without touching them. She turned her head from one side to the other, then pressed it back with a frustrated moan.

Taking her by surprise, Armie closed his fingers

around her nipple. Watching her face, seeing every hint of response, he rolled, gently squeezed, then tugged until she started making those stirring, sexy sounds of excitement.

"Armie."

"Hmm?" New moisture bathed his fingers as he continued the slow, measured glide against her, in her. "You ready to come for me, Rissy?"

She didn't answer. He wasn't sure she could. Her body drew taut, heated, then bowed as she ground out a harsh climax, gradually going limp afterward, now with a light sheen glowing on her chest and cheekbones.

Slowly he withdrew his fingers and put them to his mouth.

Rissy lifted her lashes to watch him, her eyes midnight blue and hazy.

"I like how you taste." Moving to the side of her, Armie pulled off his shirt and dropped it over the side of the bed. Next he pulled off his shoes and socks and tossed them toward the closet. Leaving on his jeans he turned back to her.

"Are you sorry I forced my way in?" she asked.

"I'm sorry for a lot of things." Not that particularly, but yeah, he regretted how much she affected him— and he regretted that he hadn't been strong enough to leave her alone.

"Then unhook me." Expression hurt, she tugged at her arms. "I'll leave now."

"Naked?" Again he cupped his hand over her sex. She still throbbed gently. "Soaking wet?"

Twisting her hips away, she said, "You want me to leave, so I'll leave!"

"Now that you got off? I don't think so. I'm still on the edge here."

"So get naked and—"

"Not yet."

She growled, and again tugged at her arms.

Deciding he'd talked about it enough, Armie shifted around between her knees, lifted her legs over his shoulders and said, "Give me two minutes and you'll be moaning again."

She inhaled sharply. "Armie, wait. I'm still—"

"Sensitive? I know." Gently, he drew his tongue over her and felt her flinch. "Christ, you smell good." He nuzzled closer, breathing her in while ignoring her small gasps and futile efforts to shy away. He teased with his tongue, lightly at first, laving softly until her breathing changed and she no longer resisted. Cupping her hips in his hands he lifted her, then closed his mouth around her clitoris.

She gave a guttural moan broken by sexy whimpers that grew into sharp cries, and far too quickly she broke again.

Armie was so hard he hurt, and in record time he'd stripped off his jeans and rolled on a condom. He was back over her before she'd even gotten her eyes open. Pressing her knees back, seeing her how she would have looked in the ankle cuffs, he watched as his erection slowly pressed into her. Other than a faint, vibrating moan, she didn't stir.

"So wet," he growled. "So soft and slick." He pressed deep, ground himself against her and knew he wouldn't last. Not after witnessing her pleasure twice. Maybe with a different woman—but not with her, not with

Rissy. "God," he whispered, because that was better than making admissions he shouldn't make. *"God."*

Amazingly enough, as he came, so did she—a third time.

Luckily, long minutes later when he freed her arms and pulled her against him, she said only, "I'm staying."

Troubles faded away and Armie smiled. "I know."

With him holding her close, she snuggled in comfortably and faded off to sleep. Armie, however, stayed awake much of the night.

CHAPTER FIFTEEN

IT WAS STILL dark when the ringing of Armie's phone caused Merissa to stir. She lifted her head and found Armie looking at her.

A blush immediately burned her cheeks. She'd refused to be put off, had forced her way into his house, and then allowed him to cuff her to his bed.

Giving her a knowing smile, Armie lifted her hand from his chest and kissed her wrist. "Next time," he rumbled in a sleep-heavy voice, "we'll use the ankle cuffs, too."

"No—" she shook her head to emphasize that denial "—we won't."

"Little by little, Rissy. You'll come around." Releasing her, he stretched, then picked up the phone to see who had called. "Your brother," he told her, already pushing up to sit against the headboard.

While he called Cannon back, Merissa made her getaway to the restroom. Scenes from the night before kept playing through her head. *Armie hadn't wanted her there.*

If it hadn't been for the noises she'd heard in her house, pride would have kept her from pushing the issue. As she had in the past, she would have walked away from him.

But the idea of going home alone spooked her, no way

would she have imposed on her brother and Yvette—not after Yvette had just bought massage oil—and she wasn't about to rent a room in her own small town.

So she'd swallowed her pride, forced herself on Armie and gotten phenomenal sex in return.

Not a bad trade-off.

Today, however, she needed to tell her brother what she suspected. Armie, too, in fact. Because she honestly believed someone had been in her house, they both needed to know. She wasn't a dummy and didn't take unnecessary risks. Never mind that the nice officer hadn't found anything; she wasn't an alarmist, and that meant someone might have intruded.

Better safe than sorry.

She finished up and was about to leave the bathroom until she saw her wrecked hair in the mirror. She quickly brushed it, then went ahead and gargled and splashed her face. Still naked, she dried her hands—and Armie pounded on the bathroom door, making her nearly jump out of her skin. "Good grief, Armie!"

"Open up, Stretch."

What in the world? She unlocked the door and Armie stepped in. He, too, was naked, and looking fairly pissed off.

Hands on her hips, Merissa asked, "What's your problem?"

"You had the cops at your house last night and didn't tell me."

Oh. That. "How did you—"

"That's why Cannon called. Damn it, Stretch, you should have told me last night." He loomed closer, crowding her with testosterone and an angry vibe. "If

I'd known that was why you wanted to stay over so badly, I wouldn't have—"

"What?" she asked, her own temper sparking. And then leaning into his space even more, asked succinctly, "Cuffed me to your bed?"

Scowling, Armie opened his mouth, but nothing came out.

With a hand on his chest she shoved her way past him. "And for your information, I'd planned to tell both you and Cannon this morning." How her brother had found out already, she wasn't sure. Maybe Detective Riske had talked with him or something.

Behind her, Armie said nothing. After a long pause she heard the quiet closing of the bathroom door.

She headed into the bedroom to pull on clothes. The tight jeans, turned inside out and tangled on the floor, didn't appeal, so instead she snatched up the T-shirt Armie had removed the night before. She and Armie were of a similar height but given the breadth of his chest and shoulders, the shirt drooped enough to cover her completely like a very baggy dress.

It was still early so she went to the kitchen to make some much-needed coffee. She'd just finished when Armie walked in carrying the book she'd bought and wearing only loose boxers that read: This is where my monster hides.

Fighting a grin, Merissa turned away to stare out the kitchen window. The view wasn't great: just more buildings and a part of the street. But she could see the moon fading into the horizon as dawn lent a purplish hue to the skies.

She heard the book drop to the table and a second later, warm arms closed around her, pulling her back into a warmer chest. Her hands naturally settled over his taut forearms, and she stroked the soft hair covering his colorful tats.

Armie's whisker-rough cheek brushed her throat. "I'm sorry."

Because she hadn't expected that, she asked cautiously, "For what?"

"Being a dick, mostly." He gave a toe-curling love bite to her shoulder. "But not for the sex, because the sex was a milestone for me."

She doubted that, but said, "For me, too." The sex was always amazing with Armie.

"I like your book."

She snorted. "You would."

His smile teased against her skin. "You planning to try some of the stuff in it?"

"I don't know." She wasn't entirely sure what the book included. "Maybe it depends on whether or not you continue being a dick."

Sighing, he let her go and stepped back, leaning on the table and crossing his powerful arms. "We both know I probably will, even when I don't mean to."

That gave Merissa pause. "You know I don't expect you to be perfect, right?" The coffee finished and she poured two cups.

When he only watched her, she handed him the cup and smiled. "Since I'm not perfect myself, I don't expect you to be. We'll both screw up sometimes. No big deal."

He rubbed at a shoulder. "Last night sucked."

Her heart clutched.

"Before you, I mean."

Thankful for the clarification, Merissa took a seat and asked, "Will you tell me about it?"

He eyed the coffee, took a sip and made a sound of bliss. "All right. But right after, we're talking about you."

She could handle that. Gesturing at the chair opposite her, she said, "We have time this morning, right?"

"It's early still." He sat, sipped again, and then being far too brief, told her about the fighter, Carter Fletcher, and the boy, Bray Huggins.

"Someone is trying to sabotage your debut in the SBC?"

"I assume that's what the note is about."

He seemed less concerned with that than he was for Bray. "What will you do?"

His lean jaw bunched and he looked away. "No idea yet, but it's probably going to get ugly."

And he expected her to run scared?

His eyes narrowed. "It could also get dangerous."

Maybe it already had. Maybe that had something to do with her break-in? *If* there'd been a break-in. She still didn't know.

Refusing to look intimidated, Merissa asked, "And the boy? Were you able to resolve anything?"

Armie shook his head. "He's back in protective custody. He'll probably go to a familiar foster family— a family who cares for him. But…" He squeezed the bridge of his nose. "It all sucks for him. A kid should be safe at home. He should have parents who protect him."

With a heavy heart, Merissa reached out and touched his wrist. She knew Armie genuinely cared for Bray, but the situation was similar enough to his own as a youth, it had to be an awful reminder. "I'm sorry."

"That's why I needed some time last night." His big

hand curled into a fist on the tabletop. "I was feeling seriously…"

"Violent?" she offered, imagining how a man with Armie's heart and sense of honor would react to threats both against himself and a boy.

"Good word for it, yeah." He stared at his coffee. "I didn't want to bring that to you."

So he'd tried to brush her off to protect her—at a time when he'd probably needed her most. "It's understandable that you'd be furious. But, Armie, no matter what, I know you'd never hurt me." Deciding there was too much space between them, Merissa left her seat and instead crawled into Armie's lap. "Can I ask you something?"

He gave a rueful half smile. "Pretty sure I couldn't stop you, even if I wanted to."

True enough. Worried for the answer, she put her cheek to his shoulder and avoided his gaze. "You didn't want me over last night, but you did want sex. Does that mean you planned to call another woman?"

He was quiet so long, Merissa got annoyed and sat up to glare at him.

Unfortunately, he glared right back. "Now you're doubting my word?"

"What?"

"I told you I wouldn't see any other women, but you just—"

"No I didn't." Okay, she had, but denial seemed like a good way to go. Merissa hugged him tight again for good measure. "I believe you… I really do."

As if he couldn't resist, Armie tucked her closer. He sounded pained when he admitted, "I don't want anyone but you."

Then she was doubly glad she'd forced her way in last night. "So." Hoping to lighten his mood, she asked, "What were you planning to do before you cuffed me to the bed?"

She felt his body tense, then deliberately relax. "Truthfully? I'd planned to jog and maybe look for trouble."

"What kind of trouble?"

"The kind where I could expend some energy."

"Armie!" *He couldn't be that cavalier about risking his career.* "You have an upcoming fight."

"I haven't forgotten."

His dry tone didn't sit well with her. She frowned. "Then you should know that you can't go brawling in the streets, risking injury or—"

"Right." Cutting off further remonstrations, he tipped her back, looked at her mouth and kissed her. "Now you. What happened last night?"

This would require more coffee. She was reaching for her cup when a knock sounded on Armie's front door.

He blew out a breath and stood her on her feet. "He got here quick."

"Who?"

"Your brother."

"What?"

"Just as well," Armie said, as if she wasn't standing there wearing nothing more than one of his shirts. "You can explain to both of us at once, instead of retelling it to him later."

"You could have told me he was coming over!" *Men.* Dashing away, Merissa headed for the bedroom and more clothes.

Behind her, Armie laughed.

She was still untangling her jeans when she heard antagonistic voices—and neither of them belonged to Cannon.

LIKE A PUNCH to the chest, the sight of his father at the front door stole Armie's air. For damn near a decade he'd imagined the day when he'd see his dad again. He'd planned out what he'd say, how he'd react. Over and over in his head, he'd rehearsed the whole damn thing.

Now, in this particular moment, none of that mattered.

All he felt was crushing resentment.

He started to slam the door, but Mac Jacobson got his size-twelve foot in first.

"Is that any way to greet your dad?" his father asked.

Jaw muscles ticking, Armie said, "We disowned each other years ago, so get lost."

Since his father didn't remove his foot, Armie couldn't slam the door in his face. But that didn't mean he'd let the man in. Bluffing, he said, "Move it or lose it."

"You always were a complete bitch."

Okay, so breaking his foot didn't seem like such a bad idea anymore. Armie was considering it when from behind him, he heard a small sound.

He looked back over his shoulder and there stood Merissa, a million questions and just as many emotions on her face. Barefoot, still wearing his shirt but now with jeans, she watched him.

Mac took advantage of his momentary lack of attention and shoved his way in.

"Shit," Armie muttered.

Nearly as tall as him, with the same bulky shoulders, Mac Jacobson could intimidate a lot of people. But Armie had gone toe-to-toe with him as a kid. Now, as a man, nothing about his father impressed him, not his size, his strength, and sure as hell not his blood connection.

"I'm telling you for the last time—"

Mac pulled a worn cap off his head, showing dirty hair in need of a cut. He nodded toward Merissa. "Didn't realize you had company."

Stepping in front of him, Armie blocked his view. *"Out."*

That made Mac laugh. "Shit, boy. You afraid of me seeing your girlfriend?" His mouth tweaked into a nasty smile. "Or am I interruptin'?"

"She's not my—"

"Armie?"

Jesus, no. He wished her anywhere but here with his estranged father in the room. No good would come of Mac knowing Merissa was important to him. His father would use her like a pawn, uncaring if she got hurt in the bargain.

Without looking at her, Armie asked, "Will you wait for me in the other room?"

At almost the same time, Mac pushed past him, hand extended. "I'm Armie's pops. And you are?"

Armie jerked him back around. *"She's none of your goddamned business."*

Unimpressed with his rage, Mac said approvingly, "She's a tall drink, isn't she?"

Armie didn't want to maim his father in front of Rissy. He didn't want his father to see him losing his shit, either.

And he absolutely didn't want Mac Jacobson to get any info on Rissy at all.

"She," Rissy said, "respects Armie's wishes. So I'll be in the other room."

God love the girl. Feeling empowered by her faith, Armie turned to the man who'd tried to bury him with lies. "You're going to get out now, or I promise I'll throw you out—and I won't be gentle."

"How about we hold up on that." Choosing that inauspicious moment to arrive, Cannon stepped in and clicked the door shut behind everyone. He stared down at Mac. "Armie might not care, but I'm curious why you're here."

"You're right," Armie told everyone. "I don't care."

Cannon smiled at him. "Because you're not yet thinking about connections—but I am. So how about you let me handle this?"

Armie almost laughed, it was so screwed up. He'd never deny Cannon, not if he could help it. And Cannon, damn him, knew it.

Gesturing grandly, Armie said, "Sure. Let the inquisition begin."

Cannon nodded to Rissy, who still hovered near the hallway. "Rissy, you might as well hang around. This could take a while."

Armie met his friend's gaze, and knew Cannon was up to something. Fine, whatever.

But why did it have to involve Rissy?

He didn't want her anywhere near his sad excuse for a parent. But again, if that's what Cannon wanted...

Relenting, he turned to her and held out a hand. "Looks like the party is in here, Stretch, and apparently you're invited."

"I REMEMBER YOU," Mac said. "You and Armie were thick as thieves back in the day. You liked to play his guardian angel, didn't you? Always digging him out of trouble."

"You're as wrong now as you were back then. Not that I expected you to change." Cannon wished he could somehow make this easier on Armie, but with a father like his, that wasn't possible.

"Yeah," Mac murmured, "that's how you always told it."

It all had to be connected: threats against Armie, against his sister, and now, after so many years, Armie's degenerate dad suddenly knocked on his door.

"Let's go to the kitchen," Cannon said, doing what he could to keep things civil. "Rissy, is that coffee I smell?"

"Yes, and there's some left."

Cannon held back and let Rissy go first, then Armie, then Mac. No way in hell would he trust Armie's dad at his back.

Unfortunately, Mac made a beeline for a book on the table, picking it up and then laughing. "Yours?" he asked Armie.

Going beet red and scowling, Rissy snatched it away from him. "It's mine."

Mac looked at Armie. "You always were a lucky fuck."

Even knowing Armie's language usually included profanities, Cannon told Mac, "You'll watch your mouth in front of my sister."

"Sister?"

With a deadly stare that held clear warning, Cannon nodded. "That's right."

"Damn, boy." He barked another laugh at Armie. "Scratching that itch a little close to home, aren't you?"

Armie made a move, and Cannon clasped his shoulder. "This is on me, remember?"

Ignoring that, Armie shoved into Mac's space, every muscle knotted tight. "Insult her again and I'll take you apart and there's not a goddamn thing Cannon will do about it."

Mac held up both hands. "Jesus, boy. It was just an observation." He stepped back, and then took a seat, his gaze darting everywhere. "Don't suppose I could get a cup of that coffee, too?"

Rissy refilled her and Armie's cups and handed Cannon his before setting one before Mac. She took the seat across from him, and Armie stood at her side—which meant Cannon had to stand, too, because he didn't trust Armie's mood. He looked ready to launch at Mac with any provocation at all.

"Why are you here?" Cannon asked after everyone had tasted their coffee.

"If I say that's between my boy and me, would it matter?"

Armie and Cannon said, "No," at almost the same time.

"Fine." Sitting forward, Mac put his folded arms on the table and took another shifty look around the room. "I figured we could help each other."

"No."

Exasperated, Cannon asked Armie, "Can we find out what kind of help he's talking about?"

Armie didn't look like he wanted to, but he held silent.

"I need money," Mac announced.

After staring, Armie laughed and roughly ran a hand over his head. Cannon saw Merissa touch his back.

His sister was good for Armie. Cannon hoped Armie remembered that when everything imploded for him. For too long Armie had denied his feelings—about everything. He was stoic, too strong for his own good, and more than anything else, he needed to take down some of the walls he'd built, the walls that Cannon knew he'd deny having.

"So you're broke?" Cannon asked Mac. "I'm not surprised. What does that have to do with Armie?"

"He needs an alibi." Mac held up a hand. "Or at least he needs me to say he didn't rape no girl."

"No," Merissa whispered, "he doesn't." Slowly, all but shaking with rage, she came out of her seat. "Because he didn't."

Everyone stared at her in surprise.

Mac was the first to break the spell. Frowning, he told Armie, "You managed to bury it once, but all that old shit is about to come back up again. People have already asked me about it. What I tell them is up to you."

"Tell them the truth!"

Now it was Armie restraining Rissy. "Settle down, Stretch," he told her quietly.

Instead she darted around Armie's hold. Cannon caught her before she reached Mac and kept her at his side. But he let her speak. Hell, if nothing else, it was nice to see Armie's blindsided expression.

Punctuating each word with rage, she said again, "Tell. The. Truth."

"The truth is a tricky thing, girl."

"Only to a liar."

Whoa. Silence fell around the room.

Eyebrows up, Cannon moved slightly in front of her in case Mac did the unthinkable. Stony-faced, Armie stepped up to her other side.

Mac looked from Armie to Cannon and then to Rissy. His lip curled. "Got your skirts fighting your battles now? Why doesn't that surprise me?"

Armie flattened a hand to her abdomen, keeping her still. "You have two seconds to say what you want before I toss you to the curb."

Mac shoved back his chair. "A grand."

"For what?" Cannon asked. "Spell it out."

"For me to say he never raped anyone."

"No," Armie told him flatly. "Anything else?"

Cannon wished his sister and Armie would cool down a few degrees so he could get some answers. "Who approached you?" he asked.

Mac shifted shrewd eyes in his direction, and apparently decided to deal with him while ignoring the others. "Don't know, and if you want me to find out, it'll cost you."

"What *do* you know?" Rissy demanded with palpable impatience.

"I got a call asking me about that nasty bit of business. Wanting details and such." He lifted one heavy shoulder. "Told 'em the same as I just said here—info costs money."

"And?" Cannon asked, before Rissy could tear into the bastard. "Did you come to an agreement?"

"He's supposed to call back." Mac licked his lips while sending a furtive glance at Armie. "Figured I might check with my son first, to see if he'd be interested in upping the ante."

Yeah, right. More likely the deal had fallen through

but had inspired Mac to try a scam of his own. "You don't know who called?"

"Nope." Mac worked his back teeth together and again glanced at Armie. "I saw you have that big fight comin' up. That's got to be worth something, right? I looked up paydays, and the fighters make out real nice."

Cannon almost laughed. New fighters rarely made enough to cover expenses, especially if competing meant they couldn't carry a regular day job. Armie was the exception to the rule; he really would clean up, especially after he won. But none of that was Mac's business.

"Shame to see that opportunity screwed by your past," Mac sneered. "At least that's how I see it. So what's it to be?"

Looking at Cannon, Armie asked, "Are we done here?"

"Yeah, we are."

"Now wait a damn minute," Mac said with a measure of alarm. "We can negotiate—"

"No," Cannon told him, "we can't."

"Wait here," Armie said in the general direction of Cannon and Rissy. He turned to his dad. "You leaving on your own steam, or am I putting you out?"

Mac didn't look too keen on being alone with Armie, but he went along anyway. When Rissy started to follow, Cannon caught her arm.

"No, hon, let Armie handle this his way."

Devastated, Rissy turned to him. "But, my God, Cannon," she whispered, "his father is *awful*."

"Worse than you can imagine." It worried Cannon, too, but as a man he understood Armie's need to deal with his father on his own. "I needed you to see him."

Armie had looked cold and remote, but his sister

just looked crushed. Swallowing hard, her gaze on the doorway where Armie had walked away, she whispered, *"Why?"*

"So you'd really understand who Armie is, where he came from and what he's up against."

She sank into a chair. For only a second her eyes got glassy and her lips trembled. Cannon held his breath, hoping she wouldn't cry.

He should have known better.

Rissy slowly inhaled, pulled herself together and firmed her backbone. "Armie turned out so great."

Glad his sister wasn't the weepy sort, Cannon smiled. "Yeah, despite his circumstances. But he doesn't always believe it." Angry voices came from the other room, and when Rissy started to rise again, Cannon stayed her with a hand to her shoulder. "It shames him for you to meet his father. Hell, it shames him for me to know the man."

Rissy clenched her fists. "How do you keep from flattening him?"

"Good or bad, he's Armie's father. But yeah, it's sometimes tempting." Cannon smoothed her hair. It amused him that she wore Armie's shirt but had probably forgotten. And that book… Wincing, he decided he wouldn't think about that too much. "So, hon."

She looked up at him with eyes so much like his own.

Feeling very much like the protective big brother—a role he loved—Cannon asked, "You and Armie?"

After a peek at the doorway, Rissy said, "I love him."

Nice to have it confirmed, and for her not to shy away from the truth.

"But," she added, "if you tell him, I'll disown you."

Because that was so funny, Cannon pulled her from

her chair and into a bear hug. That's how Armie found them when he stepped back in.

"Hey." Armie searched Rissy's face as she disengaged from Cannon's hold. "Everything okay?"

She nodded. "He's gone?"

"Yeah."

Probably not for good, though. Once Mac smelled an opportunity, he'd ruthlessly chase it down. "Did he tell you anything else?" Cannon asked.

"Bunch of lies. You know how he is. Don't worry about it." Clearly done with that topic, Armie folded his arms and stared at Rissy. Pretending his father had never shown up, he said, "Now, about you and whatever the hell had the cops at your house yesterday." He lifted his chin at her. "Let's hear it."

CHAPTER SIXTEEN

AFTER TELLING THEM EVERYTHING, twice, his sister stood. "I need to go get dressed for work. I'm now running late."

"Sure." Cannon caught her hand. "I don't want you to worry about anything, okay?"

She laughed. "Cannon, *everyone* worries. Allow me my turn." Bending, she kissed his cheek, and then headed off.

Armie watched her so intently that it made Cannon a little uncomfortable.

The second they heard the bedroom door close, Armie said, "Okay, out with it."

Pretending he didn't understand, Cannon finished off his coffee before asking, "What do you mean?"

More than a little wired, Armie gestured at Rissy's mug on the counter, his kitchen, then his overall apartment. "There's no way you don't know, but you haven't said a word."

"So?"

"So…" His brows snapped down. "You're seriously okay with this?"

That depended on what 'this' was, but Cannon said only, "My sister's an intelligent adult. She can make her own decisions." Cannon loved her enough that he wanted her to have the best. That was Armie.

But if Armie hurt her...

No, Cannon refused to let himself think that. He had to believe Armie would get it together, that he'd once and for all put the past where it belonged and get on with his future—with Rissy.

"There, that." Armie pointed at him. "What the fuck was that?"

Choking back a laugh, Cannon shook his head. "That was me thinking about the best way to protect her."

Stark pain shaded Armie's expression. "I—"

"Not from you, you idiot." Cannon gave him a shove that got him sitting back in his seat. "In fact, I'll need your help. Think you can convince her to stay here? To only go home when you or I are with her?"

Confusion masked the pain. "Come again?"

Cannon slid the empty mug away and braced his folded arms on the tabletop. "She's practically living here anyway, right? I know you want to keep that quiet, to keep her from being the brunt of gossip. And I appreciate that, but it's far from a secret." Ignoring Armie's deer-in-the-headlights expression, he forged on, not giving his friend a chance to react because he might possibly react the wrong way. "I believe her when she says someone was in the house."

"Yeah." Recovering, Armie shook off the unfamiliar reserve that didn't suit his usual balls-to-the-wall persona. "Rissy isn't a drama queen."

"No, she isn't. And she doesn't go hysterical—not without a damn good reason. If she says someone was in there, you and I are neither one going to ignore it."

"No, we wouldn't," Armie agreed. "If she'd told me anything about it, I'd have contacted you last night."

"It's probably a good thing you didn't. She's independent and with the cops saying they didn't find anything, she might already be second-guessing herself."

With another frown, Armie gave it some thought. Making up his mind, he glanced at Cannon. "No problem keeping her here. I mean, I think she wants to stay."

Cannon barely bit back his grin. Reticence was a weird fit for Armie. "She does. The fact that she's nuts for you also isn't a secret."

Armie said, "Uh…"

Again, Cannon pushed on, not giving him a chance to reply. "I'll probably go by her place and beef up the security, maybe change the passcode or something. I want to have a look around, too. Much as I trust the cops, no one knows that house as well as Rissy and I do."

"You grew up there." Armie scrubbed a hand over his head. "If someone's screwing around—"

"If anything's out of place, or if anyone tried sneaking in, I should be able to spot it."

Armie nodded, then looked away. "I don't like it that my dad met her."

"He could be a problem." No reason to fudge the truth; Armie, better than anyone else, knew what his father was capable of. "But we're tackling that shit head-on now, right?"

Armie glanced at him, his expression unreadable.

Cannon would have pressed him, but Rissy walked back in, refreshed, ready to go, and giving Armie heavy-duty looks of sympathy.

"Oh, hell no," Armie said, coming to his feet and lifting a hand to keep her away. "You can knock off that shit right now."

"What?" his sister asked, feigning innocence while

ignoring his preferences as she stepped up against him. Then she stroked his chest and looked at him with big eyes.

Armie dropped his head in disgust. "Jesus."

They were so damn funny together, Cannon had to laugh as he pushed back his chair. "I'm taking off. But, Rissy, no going to the house yet, okay?"

"But…" She gave Armie a sideways look. "What if I need to—"

Armie hauled her in to his side. "You're staying here, right?" Then to Cannon: "She's staying here. And if she needs to go to the house, I'll go with her." To Rissy, he emphasized, "I'll go with you."

Blinking in confusion, Rissy said, "Okay, sure. Honestly, that suits me just fine."

And that, Cannon knew, was as much proof as he or Armie needed that she really had seen or heard someone. "I'm going to check it out and change the passcode," Cannon told her. "Maybe add some wireless cameras. I don't know yet, but I'll share everything with you as soon as I'm done. In the meantime, I want to know you won't be anywhere near there without Armie or me."

"Got it." She abandoned Armie to give Cannon a tight hug. "Thank you."

After lifting her off her feet in a return hug, Cannon paused. "I almost forgot to tell you, Armie. There's a camera crew coming to the rec center today."

He froze. "For what?"

"They're doing some interviews for the Sports Talk cable show."

"Wow," Rissy said. "That's…huge."

"Who," Armie asked, "are they interviewing?"

Cannon shrugged. "They'll talk to me, to Denver and Stack, maybe do some cameos with Leese and Justice, Brand and Miles—and then they want to film you working out for a bit. They'll wrap it up with asking you some questions about your upcoming fight."

Armie dropped back against the counter with a groan. "This freaking day just keeps getting better and better." He popped his neck. "What's next? An aneurysm?"

Rissy stroked him again, Cannon grinned, and neither of them misunderstood the facetiousness of his comment. Armie was still adjusting to this new facet of his career.

Cannon was confident he'd ace it all the way.

AN ANEURYSM WOULD have been easier, Armie decided, when the camera crew spent more than two hours watching him. And since they'd interviewed everyone else already, it was nearing the end of the day.

Havoc and Simon had been around, both smug, and they seemed to enjoy seeing him under the spotlight. In fact, from what he'd gathered, Simon had arranged the whole gig.

The dick.

This business of having a manager was going to take some getting used to.

On the upside, he liked Havoc as a coach. Never had Armie shied away from workouts. The more variety, the bigger the challenge, the better he liked it. Havoc saw things Armie might not have caught on his own, and he gave a different perspective than Cannon, who had known Armie forever.

Truthfully, he knew he was in better shape, sharper

and faster, than he'd ever been. Not that he'd ever been
a slacker, but Havoc had taken him to a new level. He
liked it, and for the first time he was starting to antici-
pate the upcoming fight.

Not that he'd admit it to anyone.

With the fanfare of a camera crew, the rec center
stayed extra crowded.

He could take it—by ignoring everyone, including
the cameraman.

What he couldn't ignore was Rissy. The second she
walked in he spotted her and not once, even while going
through drills, did he lose track of her. She hung with
Leese at the desk, occasionally laughing, occasionally
leaning into Leese—

"Get your head out of your ass, man. People are film-
ing you."

Armie turned back to Cannon, dodged a jab and delivered one of his own. While he sparred, he thought
about Leese. From what he remembered, Leese was
looking for a new place to stay. Rissy had the entire
downstairs of her house that she used to rent out to
Cherry.

"Are you concentrating?" Cannon asked.

"Yeah." He threw a combo that had Cannon backing
up until he hit the cage. He caught Armie in a clench—
and down they went.

"Concentrate harder," Cannon said.

Laughing, Armie twisted fast and got Cannon's back.
Cannon exploded out of it, but Armie took him down
again.

Back and forth they went, splitting the dominant positions until Simon called time.

It was with some surprise that Armie saw Harley

Handleman step in. Harley "Hard to Handle" Handleman took life far too seriously. He was also known to be a kinky bastard—that is, before he married. But Armie knew that wasn't the sort of thing a guy just shook off.

"You and Cannon are too evenly matched," Simon said. "Harley agreed to lend a hand."

Armie felt himself grinning ear to ear. He'd followed Harley's career, knew he'd had a shit ton of bad luck when it came to getting the belt, but he'd finally done it. Armie admired him.

He held out a fist. "Nice to meet you, Handleman."

"Same," Harley said as he tapped his padded knuckles to Armie's. "Simon dragged me down for the promo—and since I've fought Carter, he wanted us to go through some series."

"I'm honored." So that was another upside to hitting the big time with the SBC—meeting the veteran fighters that he'd admired for years.

"Carter switched weight classes when he couldn't beat me," Harley said in a matter-of-fact way as they walked to the center of the cage. "Since then, he's had some success at middleweight."

"He's good." Armie swigged some water, then replaced his mouthpiece. "But then, I wouldn't want to compete with a clown."

"Carter's not a clown. I like him. And yeah, he's good."

With too many people watching, Harley took Armie through some different moves and gave him new instruction.

When Armie avoided being kicked, Harley said, "You know Carter's a leftie."

"Yup." Carter being left-handed meant he had to adjust his automatic inclinations. Most fighters found it natural to circle to the left, but for Carter, he needed to go clockwise, not counterclockwise.

"Also," Harley said, "he'll kick to the body, kick to the body, go to the liver. He might do that for two rounds, then he'll fake to the body but go upstairs to the head, so it's doubly important you circle away from his dominant leg."

"Got it."

Simon stepped in. "We'll get him sparring more with a leftie, just to bone up on it."

When they finally called it quits, the guy holding the mic was waiting for him.

And Merissa was now surrounded by Leese, Miles, Brand and Justice.

Rather than make him jealous, Armie appreciated the fact that she'd always been family to the guys. In their own ways, they each loved her—and why not? Rissy was pretty damned lovable. For years now she'd cooked for them, fed them the desserts they knew they shouldn't have, laughed with them and generally just loved them all back.

Speaking of desserts, if Simon knew that Rissy indulged him once a week—brownies, pie, cupcakes—he probably wouldn't like it. But diet or no, she was such a great baker, he couldn't resist her weekly treats.

Hell, he couldn't resist *her*—ever.

"What do you say?" the interviewer asked. "You ready to do this?"

"Sure." He let Simon open his fingerless gloves. "Here, or somewhere else?"

Looking shrewd, the guy asked, "You want privacy?"

"Doesn't matter to me. Just asking for your preference."

"Then let's do it here."

Great. Everyone was back to paying attention, gathering around for the spectacle, and damned if he didn't see a few of the women he used to know hanging around. That didn't bode well. Especially when one of them, Kizzie, wiggled her fingers at him in a teasing wave.

After drying the sweat on his face, Armie said, "Let's get to it, then."

It took just a few minutes of setup, and then the interview started with questions about his training methods, the rec center, his new coach, manager and the contract with the SBC. Some of it was the usual BS questions about whether or not he'd win—like any guy would say, "No, I'll lose for sure"—and then he was asked about his long-term plans.

"I don't make long-term plans. I mean, ideally I'll do well and advance. And to the extent that I can, I'll do my best to make that happen."

"What about your personal life? Any special ladies?"

Without faltering, Armie said, "All ladies are special, each in her own unique way."

The females in the audience wolf whistled and cheered.

The guy grinned, especially when Kizzie drew attention to herself by throwing him a kiss.

Shit. The last thing he needed was anyone interviewing her, since Kizzie's kink tended to be pretty far out there.

He'd said it to keep the focus off Merissa; his relationship with her wasn't anybody's business, and given the looming threats, he didn't want to toss her name around anyway.

When Rissy went all stiff and pissed off and the guys formed a protective barricade around her, he realized his mistake.

Should have just called her up front with him.

"Let's talk about that," the interviewer said with barely banked glee. "You're known as a ladies' man."

"Who've you been talking to—besides me?"

Loving it, the man laughed. "So you boast?"

"I don't hide from who I am." Or rather, who he'd been—because now he was a one-woman man, at least for as long as Rissy would have him.

"You've got one hell of a rep as a fighter, but an even bigger rep for—"

Letting his irritation be known, Armie cut the guy off, saying, "Look, how about we agree to keep this about the fight?"

"But your hedonist rep is so interesting."

"Yeah? To you? Sorry, dude, I'm only into chicks."

The interviewer went red-faced.

Kizzie, always outrageous, yelled, "It's the truth, because I tried." When everyone laughed, she added, "He agreed to three women, but guys were not invited."

Shit, shit, shit.

Just beyond Kizzie were the other two women, already high-fiving each other. He didn't dare look at Rissy, or hell, Cannon.

Next to him, Simon started grumbling something about idiot boys who put no limits on gluttony. Then, bless him for being a terrific manager, he stepped in and took over.

"Tell you what, Fred, you don't ask my fighter any

more personal questions, and I won't start sharing your personal business."

Armie had no idea what Simon knew about the interviewer, but that shut him up real quick. He did a wrap-up by asking Armie two more fight-related questions, then closed it down.

Thank God.

Kizzie started toward him, so he made a strategic retreat for the showers. With any luck the ladies would be gone by the time he finished and was ready to go.

When he stepped out of the shower, Leese was there, arms crossed, one shoulder propped against the lockers.

Armie eyed him as he dried off. "Okay, let's hear it."

"You embarrassed her."

"Was trying not to."

"You failed."

Armie shook his head. "You're lucky I'm not a possessive ape like Denver or I'd flatten you."

"I'd almost welcome you trying." When Armie glanced up at him in disbelief—because they both knew he'd wipe up the floor with Leese—Leese said, "I'd get in a hit or two. And that'd make me feel a whole hell of a lot better."

"Yeah, I get that." He stepped around Leese and headed for his clothes. "So you and Rissy are good friends, right?"

"Why does that feel like a loaded question?"

"Because it is." As Armie dressed, he explained about her house, the break-in, and how he knew Leese was looking for a new place to stay.

"You've got to be kidding."

"Why not?" Armie watched him. "You're not afraid to be there."

"No."

"So what's the problem?"

"For one thing," Leese said, his anger really starting to show, "if things don't work out between the two of you, she'll be moving back home. And that would be awkward as shit. Before today, I figured you'd wise up and make a go of it, but given the display you just put on, I'm now having my doubts."

"Don't," Armie said quietly. "Don't doubt me, and don't ever think there'll be an open field."

"Friends," Leese stressed again. "Only friends."

"Because you know she wants me! Otherwise you'd be all over it and you know it!"

Leese looked at him, smirked and settled himself comfortably against the lockers again.

"Admit it."

"Maybe. So? She is hung up on you. End of story."

"Damn right it's the end of the story."

"I thought you weren't a jealous ape." When Armie started to fume, Leese casually added, "And you're pissed at yourself for that idiotic reaction out front, so stop taking it out on me."

"*You*," Armie growled, "followed *me*."

"Only to tell you that Rissy wanted to storm off, but I dissuaded her. You can thank me."

Armie paused, then nodded. "Thanks."

"And also to tell you that you have a gaggle of women out front hoping to get a drop of fame thanks to their—" Leese coughed theatrically "—association with you."

Quailing, Armie asked, "They're still here?"

"Five or six of them." Leese quirked a brow. "Seems your fan club wants to intrude into the rec center now that a camera is involved."

"Shit."

With great pleasure, Leese said, "I heard one of them say you were into bondage, but another argued it was threesomes."

"Who?"

"Blonde, dark eyes. Likes to talk loud." Mocking her, Leese said, "He's totally into ménage à trois," in a ridiculously female voice. "Know her?"

"Yeah, that might be Liv."

"Might be? How many threesomes have you had?"

Armie pulled on a shirt that said: Sex Instructor. First lesson free.

"That's not going to help," Leese pointed out.

"I'll zip up my sweatshirt."

"Yeah, that'll fix everything."

Tired of being needled, Armie rounded on him. "Do you want to live in her place or not?"

Leese took his time before giving a shrug and saying, "Sure. It's nice, and if it's the same as what Cherry paid, it's plenty affordable. But isn't that Rissy's decision to make?"

"I'll talk to her about it." After he got her to cool down. Then he'd clear it with Cannon, too. With his sweatshirt zipped up to his chin and his gym bag slung over his shoulder, Armie headed out with Leese. Rissy stood across the room, arms folded tightly, eyes narrowed. Pissed. And no wonder.

The other women remained, too, and they'd obviously been watching for him. Worse, the cameraman had hung around, as had the dude with the nosy questions, no doubt hoping for some extra footage.

The second she spotted him, Kizzie pounced, cutting him off halfway to Rissy.

Walking her fingers up his chest, she purred—like *literally* purred—as she lowered the sweatshirt zipper. "You haven't answered my calls."

Normally, with Kizzie, that particular tone was invitation enough. But that was before he'd hooked up with Rissy. Now Kizzie, and pretty much every casual hookup, just felt smothering.

Armie caught her wandering hand. "Nope, I haven't."

"Love the shirt." She lowered her lashes. "I'll take a lesson."

It wasn't easy not to grin at her outrageous comment. "You've had all the lessons you're going to get." He tried to step around her, but she hugged up to his arm, so he stopped rather than drag her along. Keeping his voice low, he said, "Kizzie, honey, you're a smart girl. You know this isn't happening."

"But I already promised you."

Armie sighed. "Promised me for *what*?"

"My girlfriend had a bad breakup and I told her I knew just how to make her feel better."

The grin won out. "Me?"

"You do have a way of making a woman blissfully happy."

"Kizzie—"

Leese gave him a shove, almost knocking him off his feet since he hadn't been prepared for it. Hell, he'd forgotten Leese was even with him.

Kizzie went wide-eyed in disbelief.

Slowly, Armie turned to his friend. "I wasn't backsliding, damn it. I was just about to explain."

"I couldn't tell for sure," Leese said with a shrug. "But either way, your time is up."

Armie didn't understand until suddenly Rissy was

there glaring at him—and thanks to her height, it was a direct hit, her gaze to his. Now what? Kizzie sized her up and smirked. "Don't tell me this is the reason you're turning me down?"

Eyes mean and mouth firm, Rissy stared down at the smaller woman—specifically, the way she had her boobs all squashed up to his arm.

"Oh, uh…" Changing her tune, Kizzie rapidly disengaged, which made Leese laugh.

She pivoted her ire to him, looked him over and apparently changed her mind yet again. "Hi," she said, purring once more.

Leese grinned. "Hi, yourself."

Rissy rolled her eyes.

Not being a complete idiot, Armie slipped his arm around her and drew her into his side. "I was just coming to get you."

"Yes," she said, her voice clipped. "That's exactly how it looked."

"One second, okay?" He didn't turn her loose, but he did lean in to whisper in Leese's ear.

Kizzie smiled slyly as he did so.

"Got it?" Armie asked.

Leese's brows went up. "Seriously? You did that?"

"I'm not shy. If *you* are, run now."

Gaze glued to Kizzie, Leese said, "No, I'm far from shy."

Satisfied, Armie said, "Leese, meet Kizzie. Kizzie, meet Leese." He gestured between them, making a sign of the cross, and waved. "With my blessing."

Rissy still wasn't amused. "What in the wor—"

He kissed her. Not because the interviewer watched, even though they had the camera aimed at him and gossip would abound. He kissed her because he had to. Because after all of that, he'd needed the feel of her mouth under his.

Against her lips, he whispered, "Let's get out of here."

Appearing a little dazed, she nodded. Armie loved that, how low drama she was, how she could shift from pissed to agreeable without a lot of fuss.

There'd be speculation galore after his public display, but what did it matter? His only real regret was that Rissy, who was so very special, might get lumped in with the other women, who'd been only casual hookups content to have sex, and only sex, from him.

Crisp evening air washed over them as they left the rec center. Armie realized that now, everything he did was different because he did it with her. He wasn't just leaving the gym for the night; he was heading home with Rissy—to conversation and companionship, things he'd never really valued with a woman until now. Sex. That's all he'd wanted—all he'd taken and all he'd given.

But with Rissy, he wanted so damn much he couldn't measure it.

Rissy laced her fingers in his and snuggled closer to his side, much like Kizzie had but with an entirely different result. "Cold?"

She shook her head, too quiet, maybe even pensive.

Armie hated that they were in separate cars, but he'd follow her to ensure she got there safely.

To his apartment, instead of her house.

That was a situation they'd eventually have to resolve. Logically, it didn't make sense for them to continue sharing the minimal space of his apartment. But for now—

"So." She looked up at him, and he saw the banked annoyance still simmering in her beautiful blue eyes. "Want to tell me what that was with the girl?"

"Which part?"

She stopped cold and stared at him. "How about *all* of it?"

Why not? Without bothering to pretty it up, he said, "I used to bang Kizzie and whichever of her friends she dragged around. I don't anymore, but I guess she forgot that. Or maybe she didn't care because she wanted a chance at getting on camera. People are funny about stuff like that."

Incredulous at his outpouring, Rissy blinked at him.

"I tried to warn Leese because Kizzie has some weird preferences not suited to everyone."

Maybe more fascinated than angry, Rissy asked, "Like what?"

"She enjoys being watched, and then watching."

New ire had her doing a deep inhale. "So you *performed*?"

She made it sound bad, giving him a frown. "Pretty much, yeah."

Turning on her heel, Rissy stormed off.

Armie went after her. "You know that was before you, right?"

Her steps slowed.

"And you know you aren't surprised by any of that shit. I was an overindulging idiot and I know it. What's more, *you* knew it. Maybe not details, but I wasn't secretive about it and neither were the rest of the guys at the rec center. Hell, every man that knows me, including that dick interviewer, feels free to comment on my private business."

Arms up, she whirled around. "Because you were never private!"

He rubbed the back of his neck. "What would've been the point when the ladies all bragged?"

"Oh my God." She huffed, then dropped her head to stare at her feet. "Just...oh my God."

Armie edged in closer to her. "I don't want to fight tonight."

Head still down, she asked, "What do you want?"

"You. Alone with me." He lifted her chin, studied her eyes and then her mouth, and he knew, once again, she'd give in to him. "That's what I want Rissy. Just you."

She might not understand the significance, but she did let go of her anger.

And Armie knew—he was the luckiest guy around.

CHAPTER SEVENTEEN

NEARLY A WEEK LATER, Rissy stood in the downstairs area of her house talking to Leese as he unloaded boxes of his personal stuff.

At first he'd been really unsure about accepting the offer. It had come from Armie. Cannon approved. And Rissy claimed to love that he was moving in.

Leese again looked around, a little boggled by his good fortune. It wasn't that long ago that he'd been a total ass to Denver and Cherry. He'd screwed up bigtime and Cherry could have gotten hurt. He'd tried to correct mistakes and to get smarter about everything. Work, play, life. He'd taken a huge attitude adjustment, and hopefully he'd redeemed himself.

For sure, he felt like an insider in the pack, accepted by the guys and women alike.

It was ironic that he'd somehow become a confidant to the ladies. The other fighters might have let go of his past, but *that*, at least, he knew drove them all nuts. And being a guy himself, he loved it. No, he would never overstep, but he enjoyed rubbing it in whenever the opportunity arose.

"I'm so glad you're here."

Rissy claimed that now when she had to come by, even if he wasn't around at the time, the house wouldn't feel so empty. Knowing someone else—someone she trusted implicitly—would be coming and going made her feel safer.

Made sense to Leese. Anyone watching her house would no longer be able to count on it being empty for long stretches.

"Yeah, me, too," he told her. Between his job and working out at the rec center, plus the occasional date, his schedule could be pretty random. If anyone had been staking out the house, hoping to catch her alone, they'd now know that he might show up at any time.

"So you like it?"

He flashed her a grin as he stacked his DVDs into a shelf situated by a modest-size TV. "You're kidding, right? It's bigger than what I had, in a better part of town, for less rent and it's closer to the rec center. The furniture is great, the setup is great." He still had a hard time believing he'd been invited to move in. "What's not to like?"

Trailing her fingers along the back of the tan corduroy couch, she asked, "Me? I mean, I might end up back upstairs, so I hope that won't—"

"Rissy." Leese shook his head, slid the last DVD into place and stood. Something more was going on with her, but he wasn't sure what. "We're friends, right?"

"Definitely. Next to Cherry, you might be my best friend."

Thank God for Cherry then. He'd never hear the end of it if he was her "bestie." Biting back a smile, he explained, "I like your company. If you're here it won't be a hardship for me."

She licked her lips, thought about expounding on that and apparently couldn't. "Are you sure you don't want me to help you unload?"

Given he liked everything done a certain way, he said, "There's not that much."

She followed him as he went into the bedroom to unload clothes into the existing dresser. All of the furniture stayed with the living space. It was neutral, functional and in great shape—which suited him just fine.

Again glancing at her, Leese asked, "So how are things with you and Armie?"

He was negligent about it, tossing the question out while putting T-shirts in a drawer.

Instead of answering, she said, "You're superneat, aren't you? All your T-shirts folded precisely, the DVDs in some sort of order. And you hung up your jeans."

"I got used to hanging my jeans because I rarely had much drawer space." And since he'd grown up wearing worn-out, secondhand clothes, he now made an effort for his stuff to look fresh and wrinkle-free. "It's not like you to dodge. If you don't want to talk about Armie, we don't have to."

"It's not that." She lifted a sports magazine off the top of a box, flipped through the pages and put it back. "I think we're okay."

"You think?"

Edging closer, she sat on the side of the bed—probably having no idea how a guy's mind worked or she wouldn't do things like that. "You know how Armie was?"

"What do you mean?"

"You know—overindulging."

Leese laughed. "I'm guessing that hasn't changed much."

Her face went red-hot, making her blue eyes look brighter. "That's what I'm worried about!"

He carried a box to the closet, asking absently, "What?"

Going drama queen on him, she threw out her arms. "He's used to...*variety*. To freaking *groups*."

Glad that he now had his back to her, Leese grinned. "Yeah, so?"

"Am I enough?" She flopped back, her head on his pillow. "How is one woman going to make him happy?"

After a quick glance, Leese decided to keep his attention off her. Seeing a woman like Merissa all stretched out on his bed had the natural outcome of making him think things. "I'm guessing that depends on the woman."

"*I'm* the woman."

"I haven't forgotten, but to me, Armie seems more than satisfied."

"I don't know, but maybe." After a beat of silence, she asked, "How can I tell?"

His curiosity sparked, and he looked at her again. Had Armie given her reason to think he needed more? Or was she just being insecure, given Armie's well of experience? "As up-front as he is, I assume he'd tell you. Armie's not exactly shy."

"Brother in the room," Cannon said, announcing himself as he strode in. "And yeah, Armie's about as plainspoken as a person can be. If he wanted anything different, he'd have said so."

Rissy's face went redder than ever.

Cannon smiled at her. "Now that I'm here, I think we can agree that a topic change is in order."

"Yes." Merissa dropped an arm over her eyes. "Definitely."

Leese noticed that Cannon didn't seem bothered by finding his sister in a bedroom, on a bed, with a man who wasn't her boyfriend. But he didn't know if that was trust for him, for Rissy, or just an acceptance that they were friends and nothing more.

"The place is really something. Thanks again."

Cannon got comfortable on the other side of the bed. "I'm glad you're here."

"That's what I told him," Rissy said, finally dropping her arm. "I feel like it'll be more secure now than just sitting empty."

"I talked to Logan," Cannon told her in another topic shift. "They still don't have any clues about the bank robbery."

Rissy sat up yoga style beside her brother. "I'm starting to think they never will."

Would they both always make themselves at home in the rented space? Leese supposed that made sense, given they'd grown up here. He didn't mind. For the longest time it had felt like he was on his own. It was nice to belong to a group, to be part of an extended family of sorts.

Cannon patted his sister's knee while speaking to Leese. "Rissy's shown you how to work the keypad on the security system?"

"She did. This place is like a fortress." Finishing up, he turned to face them and leaned a hip on the dresser. "Growing up, our idea of security was to put a stick in the sliding doors."

Cannon smiled. "Whatever works."

"If you're done for the day," Rissy said, "does that mean Armie is on his way home, too?"

"If he's not already, he should be soon. And Simon is insisting he takes tomorrow as a day of recovery."

"Meaning?"

"No gym, no workouts."

Leese whistled. "He's not going to like that." Never before had he met anyone with Armie's metabolism. The guy could literally go all night and not wear out.

"He'll adjust. Havoc and Simon are determined to see that he does." Cannon nudged his sister. "Think you can keep him occupied?"

She blushed again.

Shaking his head, Cannon said, "Get your mind out of the gutter, Rissy. That's not what I meant."

A knock on the front door drew everyone's attention, saving her from having to reply.

"I'll get it." She slid off the bed but paused to say to Leese, "Just so you know, once you're all moved in, I won't just wander in. You really will have your own privacy." After saying that, she headed up the steps.

Cannon kept her in his line of sight, adding, "You should be comfortable here. But when possible, I'd prefer—"

"That I hook up elsewhere?" Leese asked.

Cannon's brows pinched down. "I wasn't going to say that. It's your place. Use it how you see fit."

Oh. Leese had been sure he was about to get lectured. Of course, Rissy spent very little time here now anyway.

"I was going to ask that you do a walk around the place every so often. Get familiar with the outside so you can recognize if anyone has been sneaking around, peeking in windows or anything."

"Sure," Leese said. "No problem."

When Rissy raised her voice, they both turned in a rush to go to her and nearly collided in the doorway. Leese lifted his hands in apology, stepped back and let Cannon take the lead.

MERISSA KNEW THE second that Cannon and Leese stepped up behind her. Mr. Jacobson lost some of his antagonism, and instead of trying to threaten, he cajoled.

She despised him. "Is that it?"

"I'm trying to help," he ground out.

"Your help isn't needed."

"What's going on?" Cannon stepped up beside her. As usual, he was calm personified. She rarely saw her brother get riled—but when he did, look out. Merissa gestured at Armie's father. "He's telling me that it's dangerous to be around Armie."

"Ah." Cannon folded his arms. "Unless, of course, she talks Armie into giving you some money?"

Mac shrugged. "Wouldn't hurt. And so you know, I did find out more info. Didn't know you were here or I'd have asked to talk to you instead."

"So you wouldn't have to bother with the *little lady*," Merissa sneered.

"Nothing little about you, now is there?" Mac gave her a dead stare. "I'd rather talk with him because he's more reasonable than you are."

"You—"

Cannon stepped slightly in front of her. "Tell me about the threats to my sister."

Mac held out a hand and rubbed his fingers together. "Pay up."

Remaining calm, Cannon said, "You have about two seconds to start talking."

Merissa felt Leese's hands on her shoulders, moving her back.

Mac said, "That's not our deal!"

"I don't deal with the likes of you." He reached for Mac.

Backstepping fast, Mac almost fell off the porch. "Now wait a damned minute!"

"Start talking."

"Fine. Jesus." He needlessly straightened his jacket, took off his hat to smooth his oily hair, then replaced it. "Understand, this isn't coming from me. But I'm told she's the way to make him suffer."

"How?"

Merissa appreciated her brother's commanding presence, but it made her nervous all the same. Mac was the kind of cretin who might carry a gun, or ambush someone when they least expected it.

"I don't know how," he argued. "I'd be willing to dig for more details if you'd pay me."

While they all ignored that, Merissa stepped forward again. "How did you find my house?"

He sneered. "You're easy to find, honey. Everyone in this damned town knows you and your brother."

"You expected to find her alone?" Cannon stepped farther out. "Or maybe you thought the house would be empty?"

Mac didn't have an answer. He scratched at his bristly chin. "What are you accusing me of?"

"Every damn thing I can think of," Merissa threw out, and she followed her brother. She heard Leese sigh, and he, too, walked out.

Mac eyed him. "I thought you were with my boy?"

"You don't need to know anything about me," Merissa said. "Except that I'm amazed Armie's so wonderful, given who fathered him."

After sucking at a tooth, Mac grinned. "You two deserve each other."

Oh God, Merissa hoped so, because she wanted Armie, now and forever.

Cannon said, "Stay here," and then he followed Mac out to a beat-up sedan. Before Mac could get in the driver's seat, Cannon caged him in, then went nose to nose with an intense conversation.

"I can't hear what they're saying," Merissa whispered to Leese.

Looping an arm around her shoulders, Leese said, "She's my sister, come near her again and you're toast."

"You can hear them?"

He shook his head. "Don't have to. I'm sure it's something along those lines."

"Probably." A shiver chased down her spine and she leaned in closer to steal some of Leese's body heat. "He gives me the creeps."

"And you gave him hell in return. Not a bad trade-off."

At the time, she'd been too furious on Armie's behalf to really think about how his father intimidated her. The man wasn't just obnoxious or mean—he had an eerie sense of immorality around him that made him feel very, very dangerous.

It was only a few seconds later, with Cannon still involved in his close talk, when Armie pulled up to the curb. He got out with a stiff neck and stiffer shoulders, then slammed his door.

Stalking forward, Armie asked, "What's going on?"

Cannon stepped back from Mac. "Your dad was just leaving."

Merissa had never seen Armie so quietly enraged and she worried about what he might do.

Mac must have been just as concerned because he was already behind the wheel. He gunned the engine and peeled out, cutting far too close to Armie as he passed.

And Armie didn't move out of his way.

Near her ear, Leese whispered, "Tell him everything." Then he went back inside.

That was the thing about Leese, why he made such a great friend. He was always willing to listen, but went out of his way not to intrude.

Armie still stood there in the street, staring after his father's car though it could no longer be seen. She looked at Cannon, but instead of going to Armie, he started for the house. When he reached her, Merissa said, "He's upset."

"And with good reason, hon. His dad somehow knows where you live, and was ballsy enough to come here."

She didn't really live at her house much anymore, but she knew that was beside the point. She was watching Armie, so she saw the second he glanced at her.

Then at his truck.

He was thinking of leaving! "Later," she said to Cannon as she took off in a jog toward Armie.

Hearing her approach, Armie turned to her, his brows down with both lingering anger and concern.

"What's wrong?" he asked when she reached him.

Merissa threw herself against him and held on tight.

"What is it, honey?" His hands went up and down her back. "You're okay?"

"Yes." She couldn't pinpoint it, but she knew things were very wrong, and it scared her even more. Tucking her face against Armie's neck, she breathed in his addictive scent and it helped her collect herself. "I'm sorry."

"For?"

"Your dad being here. Freaking out on you." Clutching his shoulders, she pressed him back so she could see his face. "You were thinking about taking off."

"Going after him," he agreed. "I probably still should." Fury reignited in his dark eyes. "He needs to understand—"

"Cannon talked to him." Taking his hand, Merissa attempted to tug him toward the house, without much success. "Why don't you see what agreement he and Cannon came to before you—" *Leave me* "—go."

"It's not Cannon's problem to deal with."

So sad that he considered his father no more than a problem. "Well, then, there are things I need to tell you. Stuff Mac said while he was here."

"All right, tell me."

With her thoughts tumbling one over the other, Merissa bit her lip, considered her options and gave it one stab. "Armie, please, come in with me. Then we'll talk."

His gaze moved over her face, first searching her eyes, then lingering on her mouth. He leaned in for a kiss.

Thinking it'd be short and sweet, Merissa accepted without reserve.

Only Armie didn't keep it easy. Nope. He turned his

head, took the kiss deeper, teased with his tongue and easily made her toes curl—and they were in the street!

Breathless, her hands still gripping his shoulders, she pulled back, licked her now-tingling lips and frowned at him. "You're impossible."

Still too solemn, he took her hand and now it was him leading her to the house.

"You want to tell me why you did that?"

"I like kissing you, that's why."

She knew it was more than that, but what? Resisting his pull, she slowed his pace and said again, "Armie."

He stopped at the closed front door, dropped his head for only a moment, then pinned her with his dark, incendiary gaze. "Before I left the rec center I got a call. Bray is missing."

"Oh no." Knowing how he felt about the boy, she ached for him. Any responsible adult would worry for Bray, but Armie felt personally attached. "I'm sorry."

"Then I show up here and my asshole father is hanging around and regardless of whatever details you tell me, I know he was here to make trouble."

Merissa swallowed. What could she say? He was right.

"So I kissed you because I can. Because it's one of the few things I can still control." He drew a breath. "And I enjoy kissing you a hell of a lot more than dealing with the rest of this shit. Now is that answer enough?"

For one of the few times in her life, Merissa felt small. "Yes."

Armie popped his neck. "Then can we get this over with?"

She understood he was angry, frustrated and worried about Bray. For those reasons only, she let him get by with taking it out on her. But she couldn't be gracious about it.

Stepping around him, she opened the door and held it for him. "I really am sorry to hear that about Bray. I hope he's okay."

Armie started to reply, but she went quickly up the steps, then down the hall and to her bedroom. Rather than slam the door, she closed it very quietly. Dropping facedown onto her mattress, she snagged one of her pillows and hugged it to her.

It wasn't like her to be tearful, but damn, she felt like having a good cry and she couldn't even say why. It wasn't Armie's soured mood; she'd been raised around Cannon and his friends and while they all treated her nicely and with respect, she'd seen her fair share of frustration and aggravation.

She felt achy and too tired and blah.

A deep breath didn't help much, but she fought off the tears all the same. She refused to be whiny and instead concentrated on ways she might be helpful. Her brother had great reach in the community, so maybe she could help organize the effort to find Bray.

When she thought of the boy out on his own, the tears threatened again. *Stop it. He'll be fine.* She had to believe that.

But on top of worrying for Bray, it brought home the resemblance to Armie's upbringing.

That awful, crude, hateful man was his father.

It was almost too terrible to bear. When she thought of how he'd been raised, and then his outrageous sexcapades as a grown man, she had to wonder: would she ever really reach him? She knew Armie trusted his friends, but would he ever trust a woman romantically?

Would he ever trust her with his heart?

Lately, he'd been amazing. Even though he spent a lot of time prepping for his fight, he remained attentive to her. He was never too tired to talk and laugh with her, to watch over her—or to have sex. Whenever they got together, which pretty much happened every day, if not twice a day, he gave it his all.

His all was pretty darned spectacular.

Her thoughts flickered around, going from one fact to the next. Armie liked her. He treated her with respect. He made time for her. He joked with her.

Flopping onto her back, Merissa groaned, because that seriously described how Armie felt about almost everyone. And as to the sex, well, she couldn't offer him anything new in that arena. So how special could their relationship be?

Turning back to her side, she again hugged her pillow and wished she knew what Armie was thinking.

But since she was pretty sure they weren't thinking the same things, maybe she was better off not knowing.

CHAPTER EIGHTEEN

AFTER GETTING ALL the deets from Cannon and seeing that Leese was settling in—and that he understood the rules—Armie decided it was time to go after Rissy. For sure she'd been peeved when she'd all but run away from him. Not that he blamed her. Lately it seemed he had so much coming down on his head that he kept a perpetual frown.

He never minded shouldering responsibility, for himself and for others. His shoulders were broad enough to carry plenty. But damn, he was starting to feel weighted down, and a lot of that had to do with worry for Rissy.

After all but begging him to stay, she'd run off and avoided him for the forty minutes he'd been at her house. It wasn't a problem; he'd put the time to good use and he was, if nothing else, at least in a better frame of mind now.

Cannon had promised to put word out about Bray. He had incredible contacts in the community, so hopefully someone would find the kid before he got into any trouble. Fifteen was too old to have to put up with seeing some abusive ass knock his mom around, and yet it was far too damn young for him to be out on his own. For a hundred different reasons, Armie felt responsible. He checked his phone again, but Bray hadn't called.

Cannon had also laid out major consequences to his

dad—or so he'd said. Somehow Armie had his doubts that it mattered. He knew his old man, knew that when cornered Mac Jacobson reacted like a rabid dog.

He went for the jugular.

Right now his dad might've acted compliant, but it wouldn't last, so on top of worrying for Bray, he now had to wait to see what his seed-donor might do. That rankled big-time, almost cranking his frustration back to the combustible level.

Then he thought about seeing Rissy, maybe talking her into some good old-fashioned physical relief, and his thoughts veered wildly from emotional frustration to sexual awareness.

With his ear to the door, Armie listened to Rissy's bedroom and heard nothing. He started to knock, changed his mind and quietly turned the knob.

When he was younger, and she'd been too young, he'd had more than one fantasy about visiting her in her ultrafeminine room. About seeing her on her frothy comforter naked. About joining her there. About the things she might do in there all alone during the years she'd been so obviously infatuated with him.

He'd have given a lot to watch her touch herself, to see her get off all hot and sweet while thinking about him.

Predictably, he was already hard as he stepped into the heavy shadows in her room. She'd drawn the drapes but he still saw her on the bed—sound asleep. His heart turned over, expanded, went soft and full. It was an odd combo to feel so tender while sporting a hard-on.

The full-size bed hadn't changed. She'd gotten the updated furniture when she was seventeen. Armie remembered helping Cannon to carry everything into the house. Back then, she'd had much girlier curtains and the fluffy bedding he remembered so well.

Now everything was classy, but still comfortable and homey—like her. She'd long ago outgrown posters on the walls and stuffed animals on her bed.

Somehow she'd never outgrown her infatuation with him.

He'd thought she would. He'd figured on her moving on, settling down with some nice guy and maybe having a kid or two. Rissy had a very big heart and mothering tendencies that everyone enjoyed. By far, she was the most domestic woman he knew. If you showed up at her place, odds were she'd want to feed you.

Unless, like now, you'd managed to piss her off.

Knowing neither Cannon nor Leese would intrude, Armie slowly stretched out behind her. With one arm around her waist, he drew her against him.

Part of a fantasy, come to life.

Now if only they were naked…

Sounding sleepy, she whispered, "I used to fantasize about this."

Huh. So he hadn't been the only one who'd thought of hanky-panky in this particular room? Fascinated, Armie nuzzled against her hair and said, "Wanna share?"

She twisted to face him. Even in the dim light he could see the softness in her blue eyes and the serious way she studied him. Her fingertips traced his mouth. "I didn't think I'd ever have the incredible Armie Jacobson in my bed."

He tucked her closer, but didn't kiss her. Not this time. It'd be in very poor taste to get carried away with her now, with her brother and Leese only a floor away. But God, she tempted him. Always did.

Always would.

He turned his head just enough that her palm settled against his jaw. "I'm sorry I was surly earlier."

"You're forgiven." She took her hand to his neck, over his shoulder, around to his chest and down, until she could slip it up under his shirt. "But only because I know so much is going on, and you have an upcoming fight."

Grateful and turned on, Armie grinned. "You don't have to protect me, Stretch. You know that, right? I can take your ire whenever you need to dish it out."

"And I would have—if you hadn't apologized."

"Mmm. One of these days, I might enjoy seeing that." He scooted closer until her breasts pressed to his chest. "But I am sorry. I shouldn't take it out on you just because I had a shitty day."

"When we get home," she whispered, her fingertips seeming to count his ab muscles, "you can show me how truly sorry you are."

Again it struck him that they needed to talk about the situation. Her calling his apartment "home" made little to no sense. But with everything up in the air, the timing didn't seem right to go into it.

Would the timing *ever* be right? He just didn't know.

"Hey." She pushed him to his back and crawled half up over his chest. "Why are you not answering?"

"I was just thinking."

Her eyes narrowed. "About what?"

"Ways to show my sincerity," he lied. Without thinking it through, his hands went down her back to her tight little ass and, with raging need, he drew her down while lifting against her.

Clearly, she didn't miss his erection. Voice faint, breath hitching, she whispered, "Armie."

So sweet. Before she could kiss him, he asked, "You ready to go, honey?"

Groaning, she went flat against him, her head to his shoulder, her breath hot against his neck. Then she said, "Yes," and rolled off the bed to flip on a light. Arms out straight, she held her fingers in a way to frame Armie in a virtual box. With one eye closed, she murmured, "Just let me take a mental picture first."

Armie laughed. "You're crazy."

"Crazy about you," she teased right back.

And damn if that didn't almost stop his heart. The words hit him, melded into him, filled him up. He stared at her, but she went about her business getting ready to leave as if she hadn't said something so profound.

Was she crazy about him?

As in *still infatuated*? Because that wasn't anything new. Or did she mean crazy as in more? Since they'd hooked up and become an item, she hadn't mentioned her feelings much. In a dozen different ways she showed she cared, but she hadn't said it.

Did he want her to?

As if she felt him watching, she glanced at him. "What?"

Catching himself, Armie rolled from the bed. "Nothing."

At least nothing he could admit to because he knew the truth; if he couldn't resolve the threats soon, he might have to put some time and space between them. Someone was gunning for him and the only way to ensure she stayed out of the line of fire was to stay away from her.

But thinking that only made him need her more, so after they each said quick goodbyes to her brother and Leese, he hustled her out the door and to her car.

"In a hurry?" she asked.

"Yeah. See, I figured we'd get to chapter two of your book."

Her eyes rounded and her face flushed.

That wasn't embarrassment coloring her cheeks. Armie smiled at her.

After clearing her throat, she asked, "Chapter two?"

"Come on." This was a conversation better made in private. After he got her in her car behind the wheel, he leaned in and fastened her seat belt. "That's the chapter where you offer yourself, quietly, staying still, so I can do anything—and everything—I want with your body."

"Oh."

"I'm thinking I'd like to start with you on your stomach."

More breathless, she asked, "My stomach?"

"I like that idea." Trailing a hand down to her hip, he murmured near her ear, "I could spend an hour on your ass." She sucked in a breath and held still. "Then an hour on your tits."

"Armie..." she whispered, sounding agonized.

"Then an hour—" He cupped his hand between her thighs and whispered, "—right here."

Her eyes sank shut.

Knowing he played with fire, Armie stepped back. "I'll be right behind you. Drive safely." She said nothing more as he closed the door and walked to his truck.

Keeping his mind focused only on Rissy, which allowed him to block out everything else, he followed her to his apartment.

Déjà vu, he thought, watching as she parked in a rush and raced for his apartment.

He'd had a lot of women. Too many, truth be told. He'd done extreme things, some that he enjoyed, and some just for the experience of it.

Now, here with Rissy, it all faded away as unimportant. Nothing and no one could compare to her, especially when she wanted him, too.

With his problems temporarily on hold, Armie jogged after her. They went straight to bed, stripping off clothes along the way.

He wouldn't—couldn't—say the words, but in the ways he touched her he tried to show her how he cared, how he needed her.

How she meant the world to him.

While it lasted, he wanted to take all that he could, then give back more—even while knowing it'd never be enough.

AFTER CALLING MERISSA TWICE, and both times being roundly rejected, Steve wasn't feeling very generous. As he walked, he worked his jaw, furious and fed up. Done playing her fucking games.

That's why he set up another meeting with Keno and Boyd.

He checked the time on his cell and quickened his step.

To keep things secretive, they agreed to meet on the street near the park. The lights at night were low, the place abandoned. He rounded the corner and immediately spotted two large bodies near a bench. Just enough light touched on them for him to recognize Boyd sitting and Keno standing off to the side.

He slid his cell back into his pocket and approached them with a casual greeting. "Thanks for coming out."

"No problem," Boyd said, looking a little drunk and a lot lazy as he sprawled on the bench. "What's up now?"

Steve looked around, saw no one, but still kept his voice low. "I need to make another run at her."

"Her," Boyd said, "meaning the banker lady?"

"Yes." Who the fuck else would he mean?

"Why?" Sitting forward, elbows on his knees, Boyd said, "I thought your PI buddy was your go-to here on out."

He should have been, but... "That's not working out how I planned."

"Why not?"

What was this? Fifty questions? He started to snap at Boyd, but Keno stood there looking suitably intimidating, so Steve sucked up his ire. "Armie Jacobson, the son of a bitch, is a damned rapist." When the two men looked surprised, Steve nodded. "You believe that shit? I figured once Merissa found out, she'd run from him as fast as she could. Not that she's a hard-core women's libber or anything, but she's damned independent and expects—"

"How do you know that?" Keno asked. "It's a hell of an accusation, and if it's true, why isn't he rotting in prison?"

"He wormed out of it somehow. I don't know the details. But I paid his old man to go tell Merissa. Only she's still with him so I think the miserable old bum failed."

"Or maybe she's into that scene," Boyd offered.

Steve huffed. "No, believe me, she's not. Hell, she borders on being a damned prude." He'd wanted to try different things, and she'd always refused. But Jacobson—that bastard had a rep that'd put a gigolo to shame. "Somehow he must've convinced her otherwise." The note he'd left with Jacobson's opponent might still sink the prick if the other guy took advantage of the info Steve had shared, but it probably wouldn't do anything to deter Merissa. "I need to know she's heard the truth. I have to drive it home to her."

Somewhere off in the darkness, a bush rustled. They all three turned to look but the inky night swallowed up everything. Six feet beyond them, even their shadows faded into the blackness. When they heard nothing else, they each dismissed it.

"You were saying?" Keno prompted.

Steve looked at both men. "You up for another job?"

Arms folded over his chest, his eyes flinty, Keno stared him down.

They were alone in a dark, abandoned park and Steve didn't like the open intimidation. He hardened his jaw and stared back. "What?"

"There's something I want to know." Lip lifted a little, Keno asked, "Why the lady? That particular lady? I get the bank robbery. There was cash to be made. But now? Hassling her for shits and giggles? What's up with that?"

"She's due a lesson—that's all you need to know."

"But you don't want her hurt."

Steve shoved away from the bench. "Because I'll be the one to hurt her."

At that, Boyd looked up. "You plan to beat her?"

"What?" God, they were awful men. Through his teeth, Steve said, "I don't beat women."

Keno looked at Boyd and together they laughed.

Affronted, Steve growled, "I'm going to hurt her in other ways."

Tipping his head, Boyd asked, "Planning a little rape of your own?"

For the love of… Two calming breaths helped to moderate his tone. "We were together until she broke things off. I'd planned to marry that bitch eventually."

Laughing again, the sound sharp, Keno sneered, "So she broke your heart?"

Steve wanted to say, *Don't be an idiot.* But any insult that bold would in fact make him the moron, so instead he took the time to explain. "I never loved her. Not even close. But that doesn't mean she gets to dump me."

Boyd looked at Keno. "Ah, she dented his pride."

They enjoyed insulting him. Steve knew that. Maybe they didn't realize it was true.

Yes, his ego had taken a hit when Merissa Colter walked away. But now was his chance to even the score. Once she let him back into her life, he'd make it hell— and then he'd be the one walking away. "Are you in or not?"

"Sure." Keno scratched at the whiskers on his chin. "We've got nothing better to be doing."

"Great." Steve felt his plans falling into place. "As I explained, we need to up the ante."

Keno shrugged. "You pay, we play."

"It's a two-step plan, and for the first step, she might recognize one of you. A woman would be a better setup."

"I know a woman," Boyd said. "She's good. Just tell us what you're thinking."

"Once we agree on the pay," Keno added, his gaze frosty, "we'll get it done. Once and for all."

FRUSTRATION BECAME HIS new best friend. All week, Armie had fought it—and lost.

And no wonder. He'd wanted to set his dad straight, to make sure he understood that when it came to Merissa, he wouldn't play. She was off-limits, period. But Mac had gone missing and Armie couldn't find him. He'd looked in all the usual places, including every nasty dive, and so far, nothing.

Worse than that, though, Bray was still gone. How the hell did a kid just disappear? It killed him, wondering if Bray had gotten hurt, taken… How did caring parents keep sane when their kids were out and about in the world?

With that thought, Armie glanced at Cannon. Soon he'd be a dad, a far better dad than Mac, and his son or daughter would be loved unconditionally in ways Bray had never been.

In ways Armie had never known, either.

"Concentrate," Simon said, always more than ready to keep Armie on task despite anything else going on. "We're working on timing more than speed."

Justice groaned and lifted a pad as Armie threw a perfectly timed series followed by a kick. Not hard. They weren't working on hard and if he got too intense, Justice would bail on him.

Even though Justice was far bigger, Armie liked working out with him. The ape amused him. And he had good instincts. Leese was good, too. But talk about intense. Sometimes it seemed Leese took himself far too seriously.

And truth? It rankled that Leese had that special relationship with Rissy. When things fell apart as they always did, would Rissy go to him?

"Get your head out of your ass," Simon barked.

Armie narrowed his focus and threw combo after combo.

Justice jokingly complained, but he handled it all.

They heard Cannon call out that he was leaving. Denver was right behind him.

More reasons he preferred Justice—he wasn't as busy as Cannon, Denver and Stack, and didn't know him as well as Miles and Brand.

"Better," Simon said.

Better his ass. He was dead-on and Simon knew it.

"Take a break. Rehydrate." Simon walked off to talk to Cannon before he left.

"Crisp," Justice said as he, too, grabbed a water jug.

"What's that?"

"The way you snap off those punches. Crisp."

Armie stretched. "A sloppy punch doesn't get you anywhere."

"You throw those bitches like bullets." Justice mimicked him, fast and straight. "Pow. Chaos is out."

"He might surprise you." But Armie hoped not. The upcoming fight—well, it was starting to matter. And that sucked. All along, he'd assumed he would win. He knew he'd do his best.

But now it actually mattered. Now he *wanted* to win, and that was different. Havoc and Simon had worn him down with their freaking confidence and enthusiasm and it made him nuts.

Simon returned and they worked for another twenty minutes or so when a hush fell over the gym. Armie looked up to see a blonde waving at Simon. She wasn't a frail woman, but Lord have mercy, she was put together nice. Dressed in worn jeans, scuffed boots and a pullover sweater, her features all bold, her manner more so—

Simon thwacked him in the back of the head.

Wincing, Armie asked, "Your wife?"

"Yeah, so put your eyeballs away."

Armie tried, but it wasn't easy. He'd heard Simon's lady was something to see and now he knew it was true. She wasn't feminine like Vanity, or overly stacked like Cherry. But she had so much energy about her, everyone in the room noticed.

Simon called out to her, saying, "Dakota, come here and let me introduce you."

She strode in but when she reached the mats, it wasn't Simon she spoke to, but Armie.

"You're Armie Jacobson."

"Guilty."

"Yeah, I just bet you are." She grinned and held out a hand.

Since he wore fingerless gloves, he enfolded her hand in both of his. "And you're Dakota Evans."

"*Love* the Evans part." Tipping her head, she gestured at the mats and asked, "Do you mind?"

Confused, Armie looked to Simon.

Simon sighed, ran a hand over his shaved head, then indicated she should go ahead. At the same time he said to Armie, "She does as she pleases. Just go with it and you might learn something."

Dakota laughed as she peeled off the lace-up boots, then jumped to the mat in front of Armie. "My hunky husband has been fine-tuning you, I know. But here's the thing. Chaos isn't a fine-tuned type of fighter."

"Thus," Armie said, "the name Chaos."

"Right. But I've been watching you. You're chaotic,

too, only in a more organized way. You're…" She turned to Simon. "What's a good word for it?"

"Slick."

"Yes! You're very slick in how you transition from one thing to the next. And that's what Chaos is counting on—you transitioning. Ready?"

Armie started to say, "For what?" but Dakota kicked out and, automatically, he blocked it. Then had to block another and another.

Simon groaned. "Just do it already."

Crazy. But whatever. Armie dived in and took her down. Carefully.

She moved, and he countered. She moved, and he countered again.

Armie half laughed. Talk about slick!

'Course, he wasn't giving it his all. For one thing, she was in street clothes, and for another, she was a woman.

Most of all, she was Simon's wife.

Wrapping her up in a rear naked choke—without applying much pressure at all—Armie looked to Simon.

"Your point, Dakota?" Simon asked.

She went limp, laughed and peeled herself away from Armie's loosened arms. "We can transition all day. *All day*, Armie. So instead, when you get him in a position you like, linger. Just a little. It'll totally throw off his game."

Armie was thinking about that as he got to his feet, and damn if she didn't attack again. Crazy lady.

He liked her.

This time, taking her advice, he shot in, pinned her down and held her there. "From here," he said, "I'd start throwing some elbows to soften you up, then go for a submission."

"Perfect," she crowed, as if he'd just passed a test of sorts.

Armie disengaged, stood and offered her a hand. "It's a good strategy, Dakota. Thanks."

It was then that they realized Justice just stood there, shocked. Dakota saw him, grinned and headed his way. Justice backed up, but Armie already knew it wouldn't do him any good.

"Every day," Simon lamented. "I deal with that every day."

"Lucky you," Armie told him with a slap to his back.

Simon shook his head, then grinned. "Yeah." He turned to help Armie remove his gloves. "She could compete, but she's not interested. She's more into her music and her work with abused women."

Armie knew Dakota performed in a band. Someday he wouldn't mind watching.

"Take tomorrow off," Simon told him. "I mean it. A full day of rest."

"Got it." Armie knew he'd still jog. Had to or he wouldn't be able to sleep that night. But now that he had Rissy around in more interesting ways, a day off sounded like a great idea.

He was more than happy to make the most of every available second with her.

When he got to the locker room, he showered, dressed and checked his phone. On the screen was a message. *Rissy was here.*

Smiling, he called her back. It took four rings before she answered.

"Armie, hi!"

"You sound busy, babe. Everything okay?" After

the robbery, he'd stopped thinking of her work environment as safe.

"Crazy busy, but yes, I'm fine. Just running late and I wanted you to know."

Checking in with him like they were a regular couple. Armie liked that a little too much. "Thanks. I was just on my way out. Want me to pick up something for dinner?" Rissy had a thing about cooking. It often seemed she cooked like he ran, to work out her frustrations, or just because she enjoyed it.

She hesitated, said something to someone at the bank, then replied to him. "Okay, sure." Distracted, she added, "Whatever you feel like having is fine by me."

He felt like having her. "Hungry?"

"I missed lunch, so yes, I'm *starved*."

Armie frowned. She hadn't had breakfast, either, and it concerned him. "You need a more regular meal routine."

She ignored that, saying, "It's crazy, but I've been hungry at the oddest times."

Stress? Armie wondered. Merissa wasn't one of those ladies on a perpetual diet, but neither was she a big eater. She ate what she wanted, cooked often and enjoyed dessert whenever the craving hit. "I'll pick out something good," he promised.

"Thanks. I should go." She made a kissing sound into the phone. "See you soon."

Even after the call ended, he stood there grinning.

"Sap," Leese said as he stepped out of a shower stall.

Armie tucked away the phone. "With good reason." He turned to Leese, then did a double take at the addition of muscle mass. "You're getting ripped."

"A sap *and* a perv."

Armie paid no mind to the insult. "Not that you didn't have a good base to start with. But all the extra time you've put in shows."

Leese gave him a look, then relented. "Maybe. But I'm still not as fast as I'd like to be. And my ground game is lacking."

True enough. Leese showed promise, but none of it came to him naturally. "Give it time."

Towel slung over his shoulders, Leese headed for the locker and drew out his boxers. "Or," he said, "I could rethink all of it."

With his shoulder propped against the block wall, Armie crossed his arms and tipped his chin at Leese. "That what you're doing?"

Leese pulled a shirt on over his head, then sat to pull on socks. "Here's how I see it. I'm good enough to have a significant edge against most yahoos on the street. But in the cage? Against guys like you or Cannon?" He met Armie's gaze. "Not a chance."

There was a dose of honesty for you. Armie silently agreed, but said nothing.

"The idea of competing and always coming up short doesn't excite me much. I love training, so I can't see ever leaving that. But I was thinking…"

When he trailed off, Armie asked, "What?"

"Just between us?"

Curiosity piqued, Armie nodded. "Sure."

"I actually wouldn't mind some input." Leese pulled on jeans, then sat again to tie up running shoes. When he finished, he stood to face Armie, tugged at his ear, then explained, "There's a security firm up north from here. They're looking to add some bodyguards who'd get hired out—personal protection type stuff."

Hadn't seen that coming! "A bodyguard? No shit?"

"No shit."

First Armie had heard of it, but damn, he liked it. "Sounds fucking awesome, dude." Grinning, he held out a fist.

Wearing his own grin, Leese bumped his fist to Armie's. "I'd have to carry a gun, along with some other equipment. And you don't get to pick your assignments so if you're thinking it'll always be some sexy lady, with me playing Kevin Costner in *The Bodyguard*, I'm pretty sure it's usually out-of-shape businessmen and visiting dignitaries that need the muscle."

"It's still totally badass."

Leese laughed. "I plan to stay in shape, and I can't see ever giving up my workouts—"

"It's in your blood."

"Yeah." Stuffing his workout clothes into his gym bag, Leese said, "It wouldn't happen for six months or so. I need to qualify, pass a background check, get in some time at the shooting range, stuff like that."

"But you'll be moving out of Rissy's house?"

"Eventually, yeah. But hey, I figure by the time I need to go, you'll have things worked out. Right?"

Six months. Who knew if he'd even be in Rissy's life at that point? So much could happen between now and then.

So much was happening *now*.

Dodging the question, Armie asked, "How do you like the house so far?"

"It's good. Lots of room." He hefted his heavy bag. "Been quiet, too, in case you're wondering."

Shrugging, Armie said, "I figured you'd mention

something otherwise." Still chatting amicably, they left the rec center together.

The night was dark earlier than usual and fat gray clouds rolled one over the other, blocking out any light from the moon.

Leese looked up at the sky. "Storm's coming in."

"Looks like." They separated, Leese heading to his truck, Armie strolling toward his across the street and in a vacant lot. He was almost to it when a shadow shifted away from a squat, squalid building. He paused, eyes searching…

"Hey."

Bray. A tidal wave of relief rushed through Armie. Caught between grabbing the kid up in a happy hug and giving him a stern lecture for scaring him, Armie stopped, his feet planted, his heart thumping heavily. He had him now, and this time he'd make sure Bray got the message.

CHAPTER NINETEEN

BRAY HUNG BACK, standing with his shoulders pulled forward against the crisp wind. He wore only a T-shirt and jeans and a million emotions clamored for Armie's attention.

He dropped his bag onto the gravel lot and reached the boy in two long strides. Clasping his shoulders, Armie went with the most pressing concern first. "You're okay?"

Looking surprised by that question, Bray muttered, "Yeah, sure."

A slight shake, and Armie demanded, "Where the hell have you been?"

If anything, that made Bray's expression more confused, as if he'd honestly thought no one would care that he was out on his own.

"I was hanging in the park."

Jesus, Joseph and Mary. The park, which was pitch-black at night and used more often than not for shady deals too corrupt for daylight. With more emphasis, Armie asked, *"Why?"*

"Doesn't matter right now. I have something to tell you."

"The hell it doesn't matter. It matters to *me*, Bray. I told you that. Damn it, I've been worried sick."

Bray tried to shrug off his hands, but Armie didn't let him go.

"Worried sick?" The kid curled his lip. "You sound like my mom when she isn't messed up."

That stole Armie's ire, because he was pretty sure Bray's mom stayed messed up. Riding the waves of conflicting emotions, he drew Bray in for a bear hug so tight it made the kid cough. "Shit." Armie held him back the length of his arms and dipped down to look him in the eyes. "I'm not your mama, boy, you got that? If I was, you could bet your ass I wouldn't let you out of my sight. Especially after this disappearing act of yours."

Uncomfortable, Bray wriggled free of Armie's hold—and Armie let him. Finally getting it together, he stripped off his hoodie and, against Bray's wishes, stuffed him into it. It fit the kid like a robe.

Armie folded his arms and said, "All right, let's hear it. What's going on?"

As if enjoying the warmth, Bray chafed his hands up and down his arms over the thick sweatshirt material. "Some people, I don't know who but they sounded bad…well, they're setting up your girlfriend. At least, I guess she's your girlfriend."

Armie stared at him, dumbfounded. "What are you talking about?"

"There were three big dudes in the park last night. I couldn't hear everything they said but I heard your name, so I tried to sneak closer to listen."

No freaking way. Armie's chest hurt. "You—"

"They didn't hear me," Bray assured him. "But they said something about getting it done once and for all."

The fact that Rissy was still at the bank gave Armie

a small measure of calm. One thing at a time, he told himself. "Getting what done? How?"

"I don't know. I was scared, so I missed a lot of what was said. But it sounded like...like maybe they're setting up a lady to help them out. She's going to be like an interviewer or something. One of the guys..." Bray hedged, his face down.

"One of the guys?" Armie encouraged him.

"He said you're a rapist."

Pain sliced into him and he stepped back.

Bray said nothing. He just stared at him as the air grew charged with the impending storm.

"It's not true," Armie finally told him. He didn't care what most people thought of him. But he wanted, *needed*, Bray to know the truth.

"I figured." Bray shoved his hands deep in the pockets of the sweatshirt. "Some of my mom's men...sometimes they make her do things."

Shit. Just...shit.

"But you're not like them." Voice strained, Bray gestured broadly toward the direction of the rec center. "None of you are."

"None of us," Armie swore. "Come on."

Bray tried to hold back, but with a hand on his elbow, Armie tugged him along anyway.

"Where are we going?"

"To check on my girlfriend." *My girlfriend.* Bray's word for Rissy, and while it sounded ridiculous, Armie enjoyed saying it all the same. "I want you with me."

"But—"

Armie opened the passenger door and more or less hoisted the kid into his seat. "You came here to tell me, right? I need all the details."

"But—"

The closing of the truck door cut off whatever Bray planned to say. Keeping an eye on him in case he bolted, Armie circled around the hood to the other side and got behind the wheel. "Seat belt on."

"This is nuts."

"Yeah it is. Crazy nuts." He speed-dialed Rissy. Unfortunately it went to voice mail. "Shit."

"No answer?"

"Not yet." Armie started the truck. "I'll keep trying while we head to her work. On the way, you can tell me everything."

"I already did."

"What'd they look like?"

"I don't know. It was dark and…and I was afraid to stick my head out and look."

Reaching over, Armie squeezed the kid's shoulder. "Thank God for small favors. Glad to know you showed some common sense." Armie sensed it when Bray smiled. He glanced at him while hitting Redial for Rissy. "What?"

"Nothing. You're just weird, that's all."

"Weird, huh? Because I don't want you to take crazy-ass risks?"

Bray turned somber. "Maybe."

Still no answer. Should he head to the apartment or to the bank? He opted for the bank. If she called him back in the meantime, then he'd change plans.

Now for Bray… "You can't go back out on your own."

"I figured you'd say that."

Armie didn't miss the note of relief. Maybe Bray

had needed a reason to come back. "I thought you liked your foster family."

He turned his face to look out the window. "I do."

"Then why run?"

Silence stretched out, the windows grew foggy and Armie tried Rissy again. Still no answer—and damn it, he was starting to get seriously pissed. Maybe he should give Cannon a call. Her brother might be closer…

"They said they want to adopt me."

Whoa. Armie felt like he'd waded into very dangerous territory; he didn't want to say or do the wrong thing. "They did, huh?" In the long run a good thing, but he could imagine Bray's internal conflict.

With his face still averted, Bray nodded. Tension built—and cracked. "Guess…" His voice went thick. "Guess my mom said okay."

Fucking son of a bitch. Armie gripped the wheel tight enough to snap it. Rage wouldn't help the kid any so he tried to tamp it down, but it wasn't easy. Damn Bray's mother for not wanting him. Damn her for not being a better mom.

Damn this all for feeling too familiar.

"She said the state won't let Russell back with me around." Bray hunkered tighter into the corner. "Says she loves me, but I guess she loves him more."

Maybe, Armie thought, it was a blessing that he'd been where Bray was at now, because it gave him a little insight.

Uncertainty hung with him, but he forged ahead anyway. "Look, I suck at this," Armie said, going with the truth. "But here's the thing, kid. Your life is what it is, and it's how you react to it that's going to matter. My mom and dad both were jellyfish."

"Jellyfish?"

"Spineless," Armie clarified. "Mom split when I was a teen, and Dad drank away the days doing a lot of the same shit Russell does. Your mom is…" So many names came to mind, but Armie passed on all of them. "She's not strong. Not like you are."

Bray laughed.

"Hey, it's true. I see it. All the guys at the rec center have seen it. You've got more backbone and character than a lot of adults. It's only words, my words, and I know they don't matter, but if you can try to focus on the upside, that a great family loves you and wants you…" God, that sounded hollow. "And you'd still get to see your mom sometimes, right?"

"I don't know."

Meaning he didn't know if she'd want to, if the foster family was smart enough to say no, or if the state would allow it. "Listen, I'm here for you—and this time you damn well better believe it. You came here to help me, so let me help you back. Trust me a little, okay? We can take it day by day. I've been where you're at now, except that crazy stuff about me being a rapist? My dad helped shore that up. He knew the truth." *Knows the truth.* Armie's eyes burned. "And still, for his own selfish reasons, he pushed the lie. I'm his son but he's willing to bury me for a few bucks."

Bray stared at him.

"It's the truth, so believe me when I say I understand that you're hurting, and *I'm here*."

Again, that strained silence stretched out, taut and uncomfortable, until finally Bray heaved a sigh and sat straighter. "Okay."

Armie released a cautious breath. "Okay?"

Bray nodded. "Okay."

A weight lifted off Armie's chest. His heart pumped easier. "Okay." There were a dozen things to do yet tonight. Hopefully Bray's foster family would forgive the delay, because first... "Let's go find my girlfriend."

DISGUSTED, MERISSA LOOKED at her dead cell. Figures. The perfect way to finish off this very imperfect day.

But then she smiled as she stuck the phone back in her purse and headed for her car. She was going home to Armie, so truthfully, it was pretty darned awesome.

"Merissa Colter?"

Looking back, she spotted the stylish woman holding a recorder and microphone. Had the woman been waiting for her? Merissa quickly scanned the area. Streetlamps countered the darkness of early evening. Off in the distance, lightning flickered against stormy skies.

Plenty of people passed around them, some driving on the street, others waiting for the bus, a few hurriedly walking by.

Uncertain, Merissa turned to face her. "Yes?"

With a coy smile, the woman said, "Rumor has it you're hooked up with Armie Jacobson, the SBC's newest rising star. If that's true, would you mind answering just a few quick questions? I promise I won't keep you."

Suspicions clamored. "Who are you with?"

The woman moved closer. "I wish I could say ESPN, but hey, we locals need love, too, right?" She held out credentials that claimed she wrote for the sports section of a community paper. "I'll keep it short and to the point, okay? Just five minutes, tops."

After the past few hectic hours, a headache pecked at Merissa's brain and her neck and shoulders ached. "It's going to storm."

"If it starts, we'll call it quits. But you know Mr. Jacobson has a lot of fans in the area. They'd love to hear about him."

Of course he did. Who could possibly meet Armie and not love him? "Wouldn't it be better to talk directly to him?" On top of the glitch at work, a disgruntled client that had to be appeased and a surprise meeting with her supervisor, Steve had called her again. He'd claimed to have heard rumors about Armie and wanted her to let him "protect" her. What a joke.

It was bizarre, but Steve was more persistent now than he'd been when they were together.

"Could you arrange that?" the reporter asked with energy. "If so, I'd *love* it!" Her expression turned pleading. "But since you're here now, can I impose for just a few questions? It would really mean a lot to me and to Quick's fans."

Given that her brother was a hometown hero, Merissa had been cornered before with questions about him. She didn't mind so much, except that she was badly off-kilter and really just wanted to collapse.

"All right. Sure. But it does need to be short." Merissa tried putting on her happy face, after all, this was Armie's career. Readjusting her purse on her shoulder, she said, "Ready when you are."

"Perfect." The reporter turned on a small recorder, holding it out so that it almost bumped Merissa's chin. "Armie Jacobson is from the area, isn't that right?"

"Yes. He and my brother, Cannon Colter, have been friends for a very long time."

"Going all the way back to high school."

"That's right," Merissa confirmed.

"I suppose that means you, too, have known him a long time. Does that make your relationship awkward?"

Such an odd question. "I don't see how that has anything to do with—"

"And now Armie helps out at the gym," the interviewer rushed to ask. "I understand that he especially enjoys working with the children?"

Okay, so that was more on track. Merissa nodded. "He's terrific with everyone, but yes, kids love Armie."

"So do the ladies."

Again, Merissa faltered. She was starting to have a bad feeling about this. "That's not much of a secret."

"His reputation doesn't bother you?"

Merissa narrowed her eyes. "I think we're all done."

"Interesting." The woman held her gaze. "Before he became an SBC fighter, Armie was accused of rape. It was never resolved, was it?"

Shoving the recorder away from her face, Merissa stepped back. "Who are you?"

The lady laughed. Not an amused laugh, but more like a "gotcha" laugh, as if a plan had just come together.

With the vague sense of a threat closing in, Merissa glanced around and realized the area now felt empty. So many things had happened lately that she didn't question her own instincts. Instead, after impaling the woman with a killing glare, she strode toward her car. The woman's hilarity followed her, but Merissa didn't give her the satisfaction of looking back.

She reached her car just as a man and woman pulled up to the curb. The woman sat in her car with two kids while the man jogged to the ATM. They looked to be in their early twenties and as nonthreatening as people could be. Buoyed by their presence, Merissa unlocked her car, climbed in and hit the lock button once more.

When she looked up, the reporter hadn't moved but she did wave to two men in a truck. As Merissa pulled away, she glanced in the rearview mirror and saw that the truck followed.

Her phone was dead. What should she do?

Daring to fumble around as she drove, Merissa found her charger and plugged in the phone.

The truck stayed right behind her.

On the off chance they didn't already know where he lived, there was no way Merissa wanted to lead them to Armie's apartment.

Instead, constantly glancing at the rearview mirror, she took a turn and headed to her brother's home. Cannon and Yvette lived closer than Denver and Cherry, and with any luck, Cannon would already be home. If these were men hoping to cause trouble for Armie, Cannon would put an end to it real fast.

But even if Cannon wasn't home, Yvette would be able to reach him. And given her awful past, Yvette lived in a very secure house with locks on every window and door.

The beep of her phone made Merissa jump. She had missed calls—but at least the cell was now charged enough that she might be able to use it. She was about to do exactly that when the skies opened up and a deluge of rain pounded her small car.

Great. Just freaking great!

Holding tight to the wheel, willing herself to pay attention to her driving and to ignore everything else, she did a hands-free call to Yvette.

"Hey, Rissy."

"Are you home?"

"Yes. Did you want to come by?"

"I do, see, people are following me. I don't want to explain it all now, but I'm almost to your house. Can you please unlock your front door and be ready for me to barrel through?"

"Ohmigod." There was a rustle of sound and Yvette said, "I think I see you."

"Yeah, I just turned onto your street." Yvette likely peeked through her front window. "Is that other car still behind me?"

"I don't see anyone else, but with this rain it's hard to tell. Come straight in when you get here. I'm going to call Cannon."

"Thanks." As soon as Merissa pulled up to the curb in front of her brother's home, she saw the curtain on the front window drop. The door opened and Yvette stood there, scanning the area and with her cell phone to her ear.

Merissa glanced around but no longer saw the truck. So why did she still feel threatened?

She unplugged her phone, snatched up her purse and ran through the downpour. She was barely in the door when Yvette slammed it and turned several locks.

"You're soaked." Yvette disappeared down the hall, returning a second later with a big towel. "Are you okay?"

"Yes." Merissa stepped out of her shoes as she dried her face and quickly peeked out the window. Nothing.

Was she overreacting again?

And why did these things keep happening to her?

Emotion welled up, fear and rage and it overwhelmed her.

"What happened?" Yvette led her to the couch. "Do you want anything?"

"You called Cannon?"

"He's on his way. He said he'd get hold of Armie."

Merissa put her head in her hands. "I feel like an idiot."

"Why?"

"Because there's no one there."

"Now," Yvette said. "But I know you, Merissa. If you say you were being followed, you were. So why don't you just tell me what happened?"

Maybe talking would help to clarify it. "I think I was set up. This lady—she said she was an interviewer but then she asked these awful questions about Armie and when I turned to leave, she laughed. Like…she was taunting me. Or maybe that she was pleased that she'd upset me because that's what she'd meant to do."

"An interviewer?" Yvette asked.

"A fake interviewer." As briefly as possible, Merissa explained. She wasn't sure if Cannon had told Yvette about the rape accusations, so she didn't dare mention them. What to do? Armie would be so upset. She folded her arms around herself and damn it, she knew she was going to cry.

Alarmed, Yvette touched her arm. "You're shaking."

"I know. I'm sorry." The first tear tracked down her cheek and she angrily slapped it away.

"It's okay." Yvette sat beside her, one hand still on her shoulder. "I've never seen you cry."

Humiliated, Merissa used the towel to scrub over her face, removing what little makeup she had left.

"Cannon will be here soon," Yvette said soothingly, as if she didn't know what else to say.

Merissa tried a breath that thankfully didn't strangle in her throat. "I never cry."

"Never?" Yvette teased, her hand now stroking Merissa's back. "You're better than me, then. Shoot, every month around my period I got so weepy, it drove me nuts. And honestly, at the beginning of my pregnancy, it was even worse."

Merissa went still. Everything seemed to slow down. Her tears, her thoughts, even her fear.

Her overblown fear.

Her overblown emotions.

She turned to stare at Yvette.

Yvette stared back. "What?"

Covering her mouth with a shaking hand, Merissa whispered, "Oh no."

"Rissy." Yvette took both her hands. "You're scaring me."

Biting her lip, Merissa tried to do some quick math. She stared at Yvette again. "Oh no."

Suddenly Yvette's eyes widened. "Do you think...?"

"I haven't had a period." How the heck had she missed that? Merissa swallowed hard and said again, "Oh no."

"So you're overdue?"

Bobbing her head, Merissa repeated, "Overdue. By at least three weeks."

"Wow." Yvette did some quick thinking. "Okay, let's don't jump to conclusions here. You've had a lot going on, right? That could mess up anyone. Are you usually regular?"

"Like clockwork."

"Your birth control doesn't inhibit your monthly—"

"No." Merissa pulled in a shuddering breath. She couldn't seem to get her brain wrapped around it. When it occurred to her, she blurted, "My boobs hurt!"

Yvette choked on a laugh.

Merissa scowled at her. "If you weren't knocked up, I'd shove you off the couch." Instead she dropped back and closed her eyes. "But I already love my niece or nephew and I don't want him or her to think I'm violent."

"I'm sorry. I didn't mean to laugh, I promise. You just surprised me." Yvette sat back, too, her head turned toward Merissa. "Being tender could be a sign. Or maybe it's just Armie's—" she arched a brow "—enthusiasm?"

"No. That is, he's definitely enthusiastic." *Very much so.* "But he's never hurt me."

"Of course he wouldn't. I didn't mean that." Yvette smoothed Merissa's hair. "Would a baby be a terrible thing?"

Armie's baby? No, never would that be terrible. Even the mere possibility had her heart ready to burst with love. But the timing… "Armie's heading into his first fight."

"If ever there was a man who could multitask, it's Armie."

True. Merissa bit her lip. "He's never said how he really feels about me."

"But you know," Yvette insisted. "Everyone knows."

God, Merissa hoped that he cared for her. "Maybe

he doesn't know. And even if he didn't already have so much on his plate, I would never want to pressure him."

Yvette considered that. "The fight isn't that far away. Would you wait to tell him?"

"I don't know." Things with Armie had been so chaotic and ever-changing that she'd forgotten all about her very regular monthly. But now that she realized she was late, she couldn't just throw that at him, not without being certain first. "Armie is…"

"Hot and complicated?"

Merissa nodded. "Yes."

"Oversexed, sexy and caring?"

Merissa eyed her. "That, too."

"Brash and loyal to a fault?"

"Yvette—"

"Funny and strong, but guarded and so, *so* deserving."

Sighing, Merissa whispered, "Yes." For her, for so many, Armie was everything. "You know him well."

"He's been such a good friend to me. To everyone." Yvette sat up and asked, "What will you do?"

"I don't even know yet if there's anything to tell him." Feeling like a complete wimp, and worse, a coward, Merissa shrugged. "I guess I need to take a test or something."

"You do and I'd love to be with you." Yvette looked a little excited. "You know, for moral support."

Yvette's kindness made her want to cry again. How had she gotten so lucky to have such an amazing sister-in-law? She sniffed, nodded. "Okay. Thank you." Much as she loved Cherry, her best friend couldn't keep a secret from Denver. And Vanity would probably insist she should shout it from the rooftops. Yvette, being the calm, deep type, would make the perfect confidante. "But you can't say anything to anyone. Not even to Cannon."

Yvette started to nod when the front door flew open, and they both jumped with a startled screech.

Merissa even snatched up her legs, curling around Yvette to protect her—until she realized it was her brother. Good Lord, she'd been so thrown by the idea of a baby, she hadn't even heard his key in the lock.

Cannon stood there in the doorway, backlit by the porch light and the fury of the storm. As soon as he saw them both the dangerous edge of rage leeched away. He opened his mouth and—

Armie plowed into his back.

They both stumbled in.

"I didn't expect you to stand there," Armie said as they righted themselves.

"I didn't even know you were behind me," Cannon countered.

There was a staring contest while everyone looked at everyone else. Lightning flashed, a crack of thunder shook the house, then Bray stepped in between the two men and smiled shyly at Merissa.

"Safe and sound," he said to Armie. "Now can I go?"

MERISSA WAS SPOOKED and it killed him.

Some asshole, maybe his dad, had set her up and scared her, and Armie really wanted to wring some necks.

But he didn't even know where to start.

They'd left her car at Cannon's with the promise Cannon would get it dropped off to her tomorrow morning. She'd ridden along in his truck, sitting between him and

Bray, while he took Bray to the foster family that, from what Armie could tell, loved him. Sally and Bill—how fucking normal was that?—hugged the kid and seemed genuinely grateful that he was safe and sound. Bray had looked shamed by how he'd scared them, but they remained understanding, even to the point of taking Armie's number and promising to keep him updated. They'd treated him like a damned hero or something.

Now he and Merissa were home and he was at loose ends, not sure what problem to tackle first, or even how to feel about it.

"Bray trusts you."

He looked over at Rissy standing in the middle of the bedroom floor, stripping off her clothes with listless disregard for where they landed. Very unlike her.

The remnants of ruined makeup remained under her eyes, and it hurt him. "How do you figure that?"

She shrugged out of a lacy bra and stood there in nothing more than panties. "I can tell."

God, she killed him. If they were together a hundred years, he'd never be able to see her like this without being affected.

But he didn't have a hundred years. After what had just happened, he didn't even have tomorrow.

On the chair by the mirror, Armie watched her as he peeled off his socks and pitched them toward the pile of Rissy's discarded clothes. "I like kids," he said, just to keep her talking.

Her gaze flashed up to his, then her bottom lip trembled before she deliberately flattened her mouth with a very phony smile. "You're good with them."

No more so than the rest of the guys at the rec center. When tears welled in her eyes, she blinked quickly and turned away.

Merissa wasn't one to cry, and seeing her fight it off now hurt something deep inside him. "Rissy." Still wearing his jeans, Armie went to her, sat on the side of the bed and pulled her into his lap. He kissed the top of her head and made sure to keep his hands on safe territory. "You're okay now."

"I know." She turned into him, holding him tight. "It wasn't that big a deal. Maybe just a prank that felt wrong." Her breasts pressed to his chest, warm and soft.

Shit, much more of that and he wouldn't be able to remain honorable. "Do you want a shower?"

She nodded. "Will you shower with me?"

He hesitated, but it wasn't like he could hide it. "Long as you don't mind me being hard."

She nuzzled into him. "I never mind that."

"Hey." He tilted her back. "You're upset."

"Mostly I'm tired. And furious. And…and…" She cuddled in again. After a stretch of quiet, she said in a small voice, "Let's go shower."

The sooner he got to it, the sooner he could tuck her into bed, cover her body and put his mind on the right track. "All right." He lifted her, very much enjoying the feel of her in his arms.

"Armie," she protested.

He headed to the shower. "Let me pamper you." He kissed the top of her breast, cursed himself and did it again. Once in the bathroom he set her on her feet and started the shower. "You sure you're not hungry?"

"Not anymore."

He'd grabbed fast food on the drive home and they'd devoured it in the car. Simon would have a fit if he knew he'd stuffed his face with burgers, but fuck Simon. He'd needed *something*, and since he couldn't beat the shit out of anyone, or screw the night away in an orgy, two all-beef patties had won out.

"In you go." He held the shower curtain aside, then held his breath, too, as Rissy skimmed off her panties.

She brushed past him—pretty deliberately, he noticed—and turned her face up to the shower spray.

Stunning.

That simple word didn't quite cover how incredibly beautiful she was to him, especially now with her long hair wet down her back, her lashes spiked.

Her nipples tight.

Forget orgies. What he wanted was Merissa Colter holding him tight enough for her nails to sting while he rode her hard.

Without looking at him, she said, "Armie?"

"Hmm?"

"Get naked, and get in."

"All right." As he stepped out of his jeans and boxers, he told his dick to behave.

His dick didn't listen.

He was trying to think about working out, the competition, hell, he even thought about Justice, anything to try to rein in his lust, but then Rissy turned to him, smiled and soaped up her hands.

"Ah, hell," he breathed, taut with anticipation.

"I love how you look," she told him while sliding those soapy hands over his shoulders.

"I'm more than a body," he said in a ridiculously offended tone that made her laugh.

"You definitely are." She slipped behind him—and now it was her soapy breasts he felt on his back. Reaching around him to wash his abs, she whispered, "You are the whole, awesome, sexy, smart, funny, endearing package."

"Endearing?" He wanted to snort, but then she wrapped a hand around his pipe and he might have gasped instead.

"Very endearing." Her lips nibbled on his shoulder. "I love how you feel."

Love.

"And I love how you taste." She licked a sizzling path from the side of his neck to his ear.

"Shit." Strung out, breathing hard, he turned suddenly and pinned her to the wall. "You like teasing now?"

"I love teasing you."

Jesus, if she didn't stop using that word, he'd lose it. All but heaving, he worked his jaw. "I can tease, too."

"Oh, believe me, I know." She touched her fingertips to his lips. "I love how you—"

Armie took her mouth, licking his tongue in, exploring her mouth, and at the same time cupping a hand between her legs, his fingers already searching.

She made a sound and went on tiptoe in surprise, but he didn't let up. So many threats against her. The danger kept getting closer. And bolder.

Someone had approached her right outside her work. Someone had followed her.

Because of him.

He'd brought this to her and now he didn't know how to keep her safe.

When she freed her mouth he kissed her neck, drawing her skin in against his teeth and deliberately marking her. He kept two fingers pressed high in her and started a slow path down her body.

"I wanted to please you," she protested, one hand already locked in his hair.

"Please me by opening your legs."

"Armie..."

He didn't wait for her to do as he asked. He put small, biting kisses on her ribs, her stomach, a hipbone, down—until he parted her lips, licked over her, then gently sucked her clitoris into his mouth.

Crying out, Rissy braced her free hand on the shower wall and parted her legs.

The water hit against his back, making his skin tingle. While he ate at her, he played with her ass. *God, he loved her ass.* And he kept his fingers in her, working her until she locked her legs and began to tremble.

His cock swelled. But it wouldn't be right to take her, not when he knew what he had planned for the morning.

"Armie," she whispered, high and thin. *"Armie..."* Her hips lifted, she pressed against his mouth and he stayed with her, rasping with his rough tongue until the climax peaked and then oh-so-gradually began to fade. Finally she eased, sated and, going by her smile, happy.

He hurt, but he deserved to hurt so what did it matter? Being sure to support her as he stood, Armie shut off the shower and pushed back the curtain. He snagged a towel and, loving her more than he'd thought possible, carefully dried her off.

CHAPTER TWENTY

ARMIE RESTED ON his back, arms folded behind his head, his expression distant and unreadable. Merissa didn't know what to make of it.

She ran the wide-tooth comb through her hair one last time and put it on the nightstand.

After that incredible encounter in the shower last night, she'd been all set to continue in bed, but Armie had put her off. He'd pulled one of his shirts over her head, insisted she eat a little soup, insisted she needed to dry her hair, and lastly, he'd insisted that they needed some sleep.

She'd tried a few moves, but he hadn't taken the bait. Thinking he might need some time, she'd let it go.

This morning, she'd opened her eyes to find him already awake and disturbingly distant. It was early still, but she wasn't sure how to proceed.

He had the day off.

She had the day off.

But he hadn't invited her to spend it with him.

So much had happened last night. Armie liked to pamper her while pretending to be immune to it all, but he was as human as anyone and had his breaking point. Inadvertently, through no fault of her own, she'd added to his concerns and she hated that.

Trying not to sound too sympathetic—something

she knew Armie would rebel against—she asked, "Are you worried about Bray?"

"The foster family cares for him."

Last night, in the dark, quiet room, he'd told her about the foster family's plans to adopt. "So right now he's in good hands. But long term?" she pressed.

"Long term, he knows his mom doesn't care enough and it hurts him, regardless of who else cares."

Given his own mother, Armie would understand that better than most. Merissa hated this distance between them. She wanted to help him feel better. She wanted to be supportive and caring—but an invisible wall surrounded him.

How could she possibly tell him she might be pregnant when he was like this? "That reporter at the bank—"

"Wasn't a reporter," he said. His dark gaze held her in place. "You know that."

"Right, I just… I didn't… You know who I mean."

"What about her?"

Merissa crawled back into the bed and got close to him. He didn't move, so she sat yoga style beside him and opened a palm over his delicious abs. His skin was warm to the touch, dusted with hair, and she badly wanted to pull off the shirt and let her own skin meld with his.

Armie usually enjoyed morning sex. But now, sex seemed to be the furthest thing from his mind.

"I think that woman and whoever hired her wanted to embarrass me." Merissa watched for his reaction. "But I don't care about any of that."

"I care," he told her firmly.

Of course he did. "I know, and I'm sorry because I don't think that'll be the only time someone tries to

bring up the old rumors. Someone is setting you up."
She wanted him to fight back.

And she wanted him to want her by his side.

"Not news." His expression hardened. "But someone used you to do it."

Now, safe with Armie, Merissa could dismiss her involvement. "I don't think I was ever in danger. I mean, I was on a street. There were other people around. It just threw me." *And I'm pregnant and my emotions seem to be on a roller-coaster ride.* "I overreacted."

He said nothing to that, but the silence felt condemning.

"It won't be easy for you," she acknowledged. "I know that. But you're strong, and you're not alone. You have my brother and Simon and the SBC—"

Armie laughed. "Is this your pep talk?"

His mood was starting to irk her. Pressing on, she added, "And you have *me*."

His eyes closed and his mouth firmed.

A terrible foreboding made her stomach churn. "Armie?"

"All of this is because of me." Again, that dark gaze pinned her. "It's either my dad hustling for an easy buck, or Lea's dad coming after me again just as he said he would. Or hell, it could be legit, could be nothing more than a few nosy-ass reporters hoping for a juicy story."

She didn't like this. "But—"

"They shouldn't have involved you." Abruptly he sat up, his back to her, his legs over the side of the bed. "Things are piling up. The robbery—"

"That wasn't related."

"Why not? Would professional robbers leave the money behind? And why did one of them isolate you?"

"I don't know," she whispered. She'd often wondered the same things.

"Then you're nearly run over, someone broke into your house, and now this."

Scared, desperate, Merissa traced the tattoo between his shoulder blades, her fingertip outlining the wings of the heart and the thorns wrapped around it. *I love you.* She inhaled to tell him.

Armie twisted to face her. "The threats started with me, and they'll stop with me." He stood, leaving her hand to drop away. "But only if you're out of the picture."

Out of the picture.

Disbelief landed a blow to her pride, and to her heart. "You're breaking up with me?"

Armie stared at her, his expression carefully blank.

An incredulous, nearly hysterical laugh bubbled up. "No, wait, we were never that set in stone anyway, were we? You wanted me to stay a convenient secret."

Dark eyes flashing, he said, "You know that's not true."

"What is true, then?"

He ran a hand over his face, cursed, turned away, turned back and started over. "We don't know how dangerous this could get and I don't want you involved."

"With you?"

"With *any* of it." He stopped, inhaled a deep breath. "Hell, Rissy, I don't even want your name dragged into it. So for your own good—"

"Oh no, you don't!" She rose up on her knees. "Don't you dare say avoiding me is for my own good."

He didn't break eye contact. After a long, very painful silence, he said, "This has all been a mistake. I should never have touched you in the first place."

Dear God, how that hurt. She reached out to him. "Armie…"

"If I hadn't," he continued evenly, "if I'd been thinking only of you instead of me, you wouldn't now be a target."

The knocking of her heavy heartbeat rocked her body. Frantically she searched his face for a way to change his mind.

Outwardly, he looked unaffected, calm. Determined.

But in his dark eyes she saw so much. *Armie cares*, she told herself. So many times she'd felt his caring.

Damn him for being a misguided martyr!

Knowing him, loving him, she understood that he wouldn't relent. Armie was the type of man who would go to any lengths to protect others. He honestly believed he'd brought the trouble to her doorstep and that by walking away, he'd take that trouble with him.

What she did next, how she handled this, might decide their future together.

She thought of how he'd protected her at the bank, literally putting himself in the path of a bullet. He would have died for her. She knew it, accepted it.

Unfortunately, he didn't realize she felt the same about him.

She'd probably never be in a position to prove it to him, but she could stop adding to his angst. She could spare him her excesses of upset and show him that what he thought, what he wanted and needed, was important to her. Instinct told her to throw herself at him, to beg him to see things her way. But Armie deserved better than that. Right now he deserved her strength.

She slipped off the bed and stood before him. When he started to speak, she put a finger to his mouth. "The

last thing I ever want to do is make things more difficult for you." She couldn't control her shaking or the
quaver in her voice.

But she didn't cry.

"So whatever you need me to do," she promised,
"I'll do it, even if it means staying away from you for
a while."

"Rissy—"

"No, don't try to convince me that this is permanent. I promise you, Armie, this whole discussion will
quickly tank if you say we're over for good."

He wisely closed his mouth. Brows gathered together, he watched her warily.

Continuing, she said, "Personally, I think I'm always safer with you than without you." She rested her
palm over his chest, slid it up to his shoulder. "I think,
together, we can handle anything."

His gaze darkened—with guilt? Pain?

She couldn't tell. "But this is your rodeo, your first
fight, your dad, your past." *And your future.* "If you
think keeping your distance is the right move, we'll
play it your way." She lifted her lashes to give him a
direct look. "For now."

"Rissy—"

"You have so much going on."

He caught her hand and held on to it. "I don't care
about any of that."

She waited, hoping he'd say it was her that he cared
about, but the words never left his mouth.

Deciding not to push him, she released a tight breath.
"You know that's not true. You care about Bray. You
care about others being hurt by past lies. And I think

you care about winning the fight, whether you'll admit it or not."

He hesitated, dropped his head for only a moment before meeting her gaze again. "It's starting to matter."

His admission lightened her heart. For so long Armie had stayed contained by a wall of resistance, as if he somehow wasn't worthy of all the love sent his way. He joked it off, teased and involved himself in sexual situations that could never possibly be intimate.

She wouldn't fool herself; Armie indulged in wild sex because he liked it. But the outrageousness of it also shored up his superficial lifestyle.

Any small crack in that wall of denial might help to crumble it for good. Everyone who met Armie cared for him. He needed to accept that. He had to know that he deserved the best of everything, and that it was okay to want it.

If it started with him making a splash in the SBC, she'd be okay with that. "I'm glad."

He put his forehead to hers. "I don't want you hurt."

Joy expanded. With Armie, that might be the closest he came to explaining his real motives in sending her away. "I know." Enveloped in the heat of his body, she kissed him. "Let's get through your fight debut, and then we'll discuss this again."

"It's not going to go away."

Neither am I. She forced a smile. "To make this easier on you, I'll go without a fuss. But you have to promise me something first." She spoke quickly before he could deny her. "If it's not me, it's no one. No other woman. You don't get to push me aside out of concern, and then drag another woman into the—"

Armie hauled her in for a hard kiss. His big hands

cradled her head; from thighs to chest, his hard body pressed to hers. His mouth moved over hers until her lips parted, then she felt the glide of his tongue and melted under the sensual onslaught.

Armie knew how to take pleasure—and how to give it. His kiss was nearly enough to make her forget everything else.

That is, until he turned her loose to ask, "You actually think I'd do that?"

His tortured voice broke her heart, and his ragged breath matched her own.

"You're used to variety, to…bulk."

He blinked at her, then his mouth twitched in unison with his eyebrows, as if he couldn't decide whether to be annoyed or amused. "Bulk?"

She flagged a hand. "Multiple women."

Gently, he reminded her, "Not since you."

She believed he hadn't, but did he miss it? "If you're tempted—"

"Are you asking me if you're enough?" He kissed her again, softer, hotter. "Because, Rissy, I can promise you, you're more than enough."

Her lips tingled. So did select body parts. To keep from grabbing him for another taste, Merissa stepped back—and he let her go. She licked her lips, watched his gaze burn brighter, and she struggled to speak normally. "I just…just wanted it on record."

"Duly noted." He watched her. "But unnecessary."

Needing to lighten the mood, Merissa smiled. "So you're telling me the infamous Armie Jacobson can keep it in his pants?"

Taking the proffered olive branch, he shrugged. "I have a hand."

Her smile slipped. "Armie!"

"Everyone does it, Stretch. You included." He stepped closer. "In fact, I wouldn't mind watching that."

A prudent time to point out the obvious. "That'd be difficult since you're sending me away."

A priceless expression fell over his face. He turned from her, saying, *"Damn it."*

So he didn't like his decision any more than she did? "Forgetting your own rules?"

"It's not a rule, it's a necessity."

"Says you."

He faced her again, and now he looked very uncertain. "Leese is at your place now."

"Yup. No reason for you to worry about me."

"I'll worry if I want to." He rubbed at the back of his neck. "You two are cozy, right?"

"As good friends, yes." Was he jealous? If so, it served him right. Or surely he didn't hope for her to hook up with Leese? Growing suspicious, she asked, "Why?"

"You're comfortable confiding in him if you need to. At night, I mean."

Merissa gave him the truth. "If I thought someone broke in, I'd have no qualms getting Leese out of bed. But if it wasn't anything dire, I'd just call my brother." She was well used to leaning on Cannon, at his insistence, for much of her life.

Armie nodded. "You won't be unprotected. Ever."

Meaning he'd help keep watch? "I know that." *You're mine, Armie.* "I'll miss you. A lot. But I'll be okay." Before she broke down, Merissa started around the room, gathering a pair of jeans, her bra, a shirt. "As soon as Cannon drops off my car, I'll be on my way." Silence met that declaration, so Merissa glanced back—and found Armie looking so lost, she almost couldn't take it. "I love you, you know."

His eyes flared.

"Always have."

Thunderstruck, he whispered, "Rissy—"

"No, don't say anything. If it's not what I want to hear, it'll just be too awful. And even if it is, right now, I'm not sure I'd believe you." She lifted one shoulder. "I just wanted you to know." Taking her clothes, she strode out of the room.

She'd be back. Soon.

She had to believe that or she'd never have the strength to walk away.

THREE LOUSY DAYS.

Armie hit the heavy bag hard enough to make Simon frown.

Three days that felt like a lifetime since Merissa had walked out of his apartment.

He threw a series, followed up with a kick, then another.

"That's enough." Simon got between him and the bag, backing him off. "You don't want an injury this close to the fight."

Simon had no real idea what he wanted. Hell, Armie was starting to wonder himself. "If I can't do this without getting hurt, how the hell do you expect me to go three rounds in the cage?"

Simon studied him. "Is there a specific reason why you're hell-bent on pushing yourself?"

Yeah. He missed Rissy, missed her so bad it was like someone had torn out a vital organ. He ached for her all day, and nights were almost unbearable. Armie turned his back on Simon and headed to the corner to get a drink.

"Ignore him," Cannon said. "He fucked up and he knows it and now he has to live with it."

Great. So Cannon was done letting it slide?

Armie snorted at himself. Cannon hadn't said much to him at all the past few days, but he'd sent him plenty of narrow-eyed stares. He'd gone from pitying Armie, worrying for him, to visibly struggling with his temper.

Armie knew he'd done the right thing, damn it.

But he'd expected—what? For Rissy to keep coming around anyway? For her to show up at the rec center and tempt him? For her to call?

For her to insist, again, that she wanted to be with him?

Yeah. That's what he'd expected. He'd figured on having to be noble, on having to resist her.

But she'd walked out and that was that.

I love you.

He closed his eyes, and again he saw her face, the stoicism, the stark honesty.

I love you. Always have.

God, how he'd wanted to say it back. The words had burned in his throat.

But he wasn't even sure he knew how to say them.

He loved Cannon as his friend, but guys didn't go around spouting their feelings to each other.

It was so long ago, he could barely remember having said the words to his mom. He knew for certain he'd never said them to his dad.

And other women…? No.

Rissy was it for him.

So how could he take chances with her? Cannon, more than anyone else, should understand that. Jesus, he should never have started this craziness with the SBC. Or maybe with Rissy.

Probably with either one.

This wasn't the life for him. He wasn't meant for the big-time career or the happily-ever-after with a nicest-of-the-nice girl.

"You taking Rissy with you to the fight?" Denver asked Cannon, making Armie's shoulders bunch so tightly that they ached.

"If she wants to go," Cannon said. "So far she hasn't said."

"Maybe Leese will give her a ride," Stack chimed in.

"I don't think she feels welcome anymore," Miles added.

And damn it, that last one hurt. Had he alienated Rissy from her family and closest friends? He'd rather lose an arm than do that.

"Don't be an ass," Brand said. "*We* all love her and she knows it."

They spoke loudly just to needle him. And fuck them all, it worked.

Simon clapped him on the back, then bent close to talk privately. "That's what's eating at you? A breakup with Cannon's sister?"

"I don't know what you're talking about."

"I'm talking about you manning up, focusing on the fight and putting other considerations on hold for now."

Armie laughed without humor. "Yeah? Were you able to do that with Dakota?"

Sighing, Simon said, "No." After raking his gaze

over Armie, he said, "That's why I decided to marry her instead."

God, he'd set himself up for that one.

"Go to her," Simon said. "Work it out so you can get your head on straight."

"My head's right where it belongs. So what next?"

Disgusted, Simon gestured for the locker room. "Go shower. Cool down. You're done here."

Hell of an idea.

"Think I'll head home to my *wife*," Cannon said as Armie passed. He probably hoped to get a rise out of him, but Armie wasn't up for playing.

He felt too damn destroyed.

"I almost feel sorry for him," Denver said.

"I always feel sorry for pathetic asses," Stack agreed.

When no one trailed him to the showers, Armie welcomed the reprieve. He showered, taking longer than necessary, soaking his head and doing his best to ignore the giant hollow pain in his soul that seemed to expand more each day.

As he was drying off, Jude called.

Naked, Armie grabbed up his cell to answer.

Before he got a single word out, Jude said, "Simon claims you're out of sorts."

Armie held the phone out and stared at it. When he put it back to his ear, he gave a bitter laugh. "You guys gossip like old women."

"Or like people who care."

He hadn't asked them to care, damn it. "You're serious?"

"Damn straight. I want to know that this fight is a priority for you."

Too much so, but Armie saw no reason to share that. "Yeah. Top priority."

"You're a miserable liar."

"I'm a terrific liar!"

Jude laughed. "Nothing makes a man surlier than woman troubles."

Growling, Armie asked, "Is that it?"

"Not quite. I wanted you to know I checked into that mystery reporter. A couple of the MMA mags said the story was turned in to them, but they passed since it was anonymous and they couldn't verify any facts."

Armie knew it couldn't be that easy. "What did you do to shut it down?"

With only a slight pause, Jude confessed, "I offered an inside scoop from you—after the fight."

"Shit."

"You can handle it. And you know it'll be good to clear the air once and for all."

"Yeah." He hated being indebted to Jude. "Thanks."

"You can thank me by wearing my sponsored gear. Now get back to following Simon's directions. Since my coach, Denny Zip, retired, he and Havoc are the best in the business. Got it?"

Since Armie felt he'd been doing that anyway, he shrugged. "Sure."

"And Armie?"

With an eye roll, he asked, "What?"

"There's a huge difference between honor and stupidity. Trust the lady."

Armie had his mouth open to reply, but he realized Jude had already disconnected.

Damn it, it wasn't about trust. Without being able to pinpoint the threat, the only sure way to keep her safe was to stay away from her. If they weren't together, no one could use her in attempts to hurt him. So he'd stick to his plan regardless of what anyone else thought about it, or how it killed him.

He pulled on jeans, then a T-shirt that said, Remember my name, you'll be screaming it later. It used to be one of his favorite shirts, but now he wondered if he needed to overhaul his wardrobe. Should he switch to—*puke*—polo shirts?

Maybe he'd have Jude send him a supply of SBC and promotional shirts, instead.

Skipping socks, he stepped into running shoes and grabbed his jacket. He finger-combed his hair, snagged his gym bag and headed out.

Since he'd finished up earlier today, he should have time to ride by Rissy's work to ensure she got out of there without a hassle.

The thought of seeing her again, even from a distance, cleared some of the storm clouds fogging up his brain. He'd done that each day, stolen little glimpses of her without her knowing.

God knew he was into all kinds of kinky shit, but he'd never considered himself a masochist.

The gym was crowded when he headed out. On one side, a group of twelve women did a self-defense class with Justice. On the other side, fifteen or so kids gathered with Brand.

When they saw Armie they called out—the women and the kids.

Armie checked the clock on the wall, saw he still had some time before Rissy would leave the bank and headed over to the kids.

It warmed his frozen heart having the younger ones

jump on him, hug him or hang on his legs. For this particular group, they were anywhere from seven to eleven years old—all of them bursting with energy, all of them pretty damned cute.

"Such a welcome," Armie said, making a point to bump fists, tousle hair or pat the shoulder of each one.

Brand folded his arms. "It's almost like you guys have missed him or something."

The resounding confirmations made Armie grin and, for only a moment, lightened his mood.

"Got a minute or two to give them some pointers?" Brand asked. And by pointers, he meant a little time to make the kids feel special.

Armie always had time for that. "Sure." He dropped his bag off to the side and after catching up on what skills they'd be working on that day, he demonstrated a few—which included some tickling and tossing and horseplay.

When they got serious, Brand said, "Anyone remember how to avoid a takedown?"

Several of the boys did, and they went through the drills with Brand and Armie watching.

Armie was about to make his excuses and go, when the front door flew open and Bray busted in.

"Damn." He walked away from Brand and met Bray near the front.

Huffing, Bray bent at the waist, his hands on his knees as he sucked in air.

"You're okay?"

Bray nodded. Coughed, drank in several more deep breaths and slowly straightened.

Armie looked beyond him through the glass front

door and out into the darkening day. "Do your foster parents know you're here?"

He shook his head. "No."

Concerned, exasperated, Armie drew him to the side where it was quieter to give them a little privacy. He stared down at the boy. "We talked about this."

"I know, but this is important." He drew a final deep breath and let it out slowly.

Justice walked up. "Everything okay?"

Armie glanced at him, then accepted the bottle of water Justice held out. "Yeah, thanks."

With a pat on Bray's back, Justice went back to the women.

Armie opened the water and handed it to Bray. "Did you run all the way here?"

"Pretty much." He chugged down some water, looked worriedly at the door, then frowned up at Armie. "I remembered something else and I had to tell you."

"It couldn't wait?"

Bray shook his head. "Those people at the park? They talked about a robbery, and how an MMA guy there screwed up their plans."

Armie's blood rushed cold. "You're sure?"

"Yeah. I forgot about it at first, but the more I thought on it, the more stuff I remembered."

If that was true, Armie needed to let Cannon know, and he needed to get hold of Logan. It might even be a good enough excuse to go see Rissy, just to update her. She'd want to know if there was proof that the incidents were all tied together, dating back to the bank robbery.

He was about to ask Bray more questions when his foster parents, Sally and Bill, showed up. He hadn't seen them since the first time they'd met under similar circumstances. This time, however, they looked plenty irritated, but even more worried.

"Oh shit," Bray muttered. "Now I'm in for it."

"And rightfully so. You could have called me." Armie cupped the back of Bray's neck, making a point before the parents reached them. "They care about you and you keep sending them into a panic. That's not fair."

"They wouldn't have let me talk to you. They...heard some things, and now they think you're a bad influence."

Well, hell. That could throw off his efforts to help. "Go over to Justice, okay? I want to talk to them first."

Bray took off without asking any questions.

The second Sally and Bill reached him, Armie explained, "He just got here."

"We know," Bill told him. "He ran off and when he didn't immediately return, we assumed he'd come here."

Sally inhaled sharply. "This is a problem, Mr. Jacobson. *Twice* he's taken off, and both times it was to *you*."

Bill put a hand on Sally's arm.

Feeling guilty when he had no reason to, Armie kept his tone calm. "You have to know I never encouraged that."

"It's happened all the same."

True enough. "He's got a mind of his own."

"He's fifteen!" Sally snapped. "Why does he keep coming to you?"

Appealing to them both, Armie stepped closer. "The way he was raised...it's made him more independent than some kids his age might be."

"He's a good kid," Bill said.

"A *great* kid," Armie agreed. "But he has a lot of anger. I understand that."

Sally, the most antagonistic, asked, "What makes you so understanding?"

"My mom threw me away, too."

She gasped. Silence swelled around them. If they thought the truth was startling to hear, they ought to know how bad it was to live it.

"Coming here, to the rec center, is important to him," Armie said. "Please don't take that from him. I swear it helps kids like him to work off anger, to belong to a group, to have that camaraderie and to talk to someone who gets it."

"*We* get it," Sally said.

"No," Armie told her respectfully. "You love him. That's altogether different. And it's great. Really great. But if you haven't been in his shoes, then you can't know." He put a fist to his chest, over his heart. "*I* know."

Sally and Bill shared a look.

Understanding their problem, Armie bit back his pride and instead of walking, he stood his ground. "Bray said you heard some of the rumors."

"Are they only rumors?" Bill asked.

"Not an ounce of truth to them." For the next few minutes Armie gave them a shortened, censored version of the old story making the rounds once more. "I don't usually explain. As you can imagine, it's a sore spot with me. But for Bray, I wanted you to understand. If too much gets said, my sponsors and I will fight it. But for now I prefer to concentrate on other things."

"Like your upcoming fight," Bill said.

That sounded as plausible as anything else, so Armie nodded. "Yes."

"And Bray?" Sally asked.

A far more important consideration. "Definitely Bray."

Bill silently deferred to his wife, and finally Sally nodded. "Can you tell me the schedule? I know he loves it, but what exactly will a boy Bray's age be doing here? What does it cost and who will be instructing him?"

Armie turned to Justice, and the big lug immediately stepped forward. "Armie has an appointment, but Bray and I can show you around, then I'll answer all your questions."

God bless good friends.

After a few more exchanges, Armie left them gawking at Justice—and with Bray smiling ear to ear.

Progress.

Now, if only the rest of his problems could be solved so expediently.

CHAPTER TWENTY-ONE

When her cell rang again, Merissa glanced at the call ID, saw it was Steve and ignored it. She had zero interest in talking to him and she'd tell him so, for the hundredth time, except that for once she wanted to get out of the bank on time.

It wasn't easy trying to stay productive while missing Armie so much.

Did he miss her, too?

From what Leese had told her, while Armie seemed gloomy and pushed himself too hard, their separation hadn't interfered with his training. She wanted him to win the fight. She wanted the whole world to take note of Armie Jacobson, to see what she saw in him, to know what an amazing man he was.

But she also wanted their relationship to matter to him.

Selfish.

Before she brought any more drama to his life, Armie needed to get through the fight, settle the issues with his father, with Bray and put the rumors to rest. Only then could she push him to settle things with her.

Unfortunately, that all felt so far away.

What if months went by and nothing got sorted out?

What if, in fact, she was pregnant?

Despite Yvette's encouragement, she hadn't yet

done the drugstore test. Truthfully, she was afraid to. If Armie didn't care enough to fight for her, why should she think he'd fight for a baby? Then again, in her heart, she knew Armie would never turn his back on her or a child of his own. But damn it, she didn't want him cornered. She wanted him to love her.

When her office landline rang, she almost welcomed the interruption to her dejected thoughts. She needed to focus on bank business, and only bank business.

Dredging up her professional voice, she said, "Thank you for calling Warfield Bank. This is Merissa speaking, how may I help you?"

"Merissa."

She dropped her head back with a silent groan.

"Merissa?"

Swiveling her chair to the door, she asked, "What do you want, Steve?"

"To talk to you." And then with accusation: "You're avoiding me."

Exactly! "If you know that, then why do you keep calling?"

He huffed out a breath. "I heard you and the rapist split up."

Glad that he'd called the bank's landline instead of her cell, Merissa slammed the phone down on him. That was something she couldn't do with a cell. A simple *click* didn't provide near the same level of satisfaction.

Of course he called right back.

Just in case it wasn't him… "Thank you for calling—"

"It's me, damn it. Don't hang up."

Sitting forward, she snapped, "You can bet I'll hang up if you insult Armie again."

"All right. Calm down."

She didn't want to be calm. For once she wished she was an MMA fighter because she'd love to beat the hell out of a heavy bag. A calming breath did nothing to help her regain her aplomb. "Without insults, what do you want, Steve?"

"You. I've always wanted you."

"No you didn't, and it's not happening now."

He growled. "Could we at least talk? Grab a coffee or something? For old time's sake?"

Merissa didn't want to, but she knew she was being surly and mean and it wasn't like her. "Steve," she complained, "there'd be no point."

"It'd make me feel better. I worry about you." He paused, then asked, "Are you and the fighter still together?"

Blast him for asking that. "It's complicated."

His chuckle grated down her spine. "That's what women always say when they're giving a guy too much leeway. He's either with you, or he isn't."

Since she feared he might be right, she said, "Fine. When and where?"

"We can get together? Really?"

The pleasure in his tone didn't fool her. Steve had never really cared about her. If he wanted her now, it was only to salve his bruised ego over her disinterest. If meeting with him now would accomplish that, if it would get him to accept the truth, then why not? "Coffee, that's all, so don't make a big deal of it."

"Tomorrow after work? I could pick you up."

No way. "I'll meet you," she said. "Where?"

After making arrangements, Merissa hung up and hurried through the rest of her work. She was determined to be out the door very soon. She wanted to get home, soak in the tub for, oh, an hour or so, and then make waffles for dinner.

Waffles usually helped everything.

Unfortunately, she knew she could eat a dozen waffles and it wouldn't matter. It required Armie himself to mend her broken heart, and he was still avoiding her "for her own good." Somehow she needed a way around his nobility.

She'd give him one week after his fight, and then she was going after him.

OUTSIDE THE BANK, on the opposite side of the street, Keno sucked on a chocolate milk shake and considered his plan. Boyd paced beside him, but Keno held still, only his thoughts churning as he went through the details over and over.

"This could backfire," Boyd said.

The chicken shit. "It's all arranged."

"What if we get caught?"

"We won't." Finishing the shake with one last long draw, Keno tossed it into a trash can. "We'll wait until she's well away from here, on one of those older streets near her house. Then we'll get her. Piece of cake."

Boyd scrubbed both hands over his face. "Steve isn't going to like it."

"Steve's a pussy. But he'll pay." Already they'd gotten good old Steve for thousands. The idiot had money to burn, an obsession with one tall, thin girl and an ego as big as his mouth. Keno saw no reason not to use the combination to his advantage.

Fretting like an old lady, Boyd asked, "What time is it?"

"We've got thirty minutes or so before she wraps it up. Should be dark enough by then."

"She noticed us last time."

"Last time, I wanted her to. Remember, Steve was hoping the truth about her dirtbag boyfriend would be enough to send her running—preferably to him. But that hasn't happened."

"Can't say as I blame her. Steve is a douche."

Keno couldn't argue that. "This time she won't have a clue we're tailing her. Just be ready to go as soon as she walks out." He smiled as he thought about it.

Finally Steve would get to be the hero, by paying to get her back.

And until then, Keno wouldn't mind getting his hands on her again—this time without her hulk of a defender around to kick his ass.

KNOWING THAT JUSTICE, despite his messy faux-hawk hair and cauliflower ears, would charm Bray's parents, Armie headed out for his truck. He had his keys in hand, the door open, when a familiar voice spoke behind him.

"It's been a long time."

He sucked in air so fast he almost strangled himself. Jerking around on high alert, he stared at the woman standing there. Her hair was darker, shorter. She'd put on a few pounds. But not in a million years would he ever forget her.

Lea Baley...all grown up.

Here.

In front of the gym where he trained.

Surprise gave way to anger, and Armie slammed the truck door hard enough to shake the entire vehicle.

He took one step forward, then stopped himself, unsure what he would—should—do.

Lea didn't smile, but neither did she look afraid. "I suggest you let me explain before you lose your temper."

"My temper shot to the moon the second you spoke."

She nodded, then said, "It's not me."

That stymied him. "What's not you?"

"Spreading the rumors. Stirring up old news that, honestly, leaves me ashamed. Probably more than you, I'd like to forget it ever happened."

Armie sucked in a longer, slower breath. "This is so fucked-up."

Now she gave a slight smile. "I had planned on never seeing you again."

He narrowed his eyes. "Would've suited me just fine."

"I know. Just as I know you have to hate me." She shifted, rearranged her purse strap, locked her hands together. "This is awkward. We both know I lied back then. I was young and dumb and you ignored me and I lashed out. I did the unthinkable. It was an awful thing to do. I wish I could redo the past, but we don't have that luxury."

Armie crossed his arms and visually dissected her. She sounded sincere enough, but hell if he'd ever trust her.

Holding out her hand, knuckles up, Lea said, "I'm married now."

After glancing at the moderate diamond on her ring finger, he asked, "Does the lucky bastard know what a conniving liar you are?"

She rolled in her lips, looked down, then again met his gaze. "Yes, I told him all about you."

"Bullshit."

She continued as if he didn't repeatedly insult her. "We have two daughters. They're two and four and I pray I'm a better, more responsible mother than I was a daughter." After tucking her hair behind her ear, she came to stand by him, then leaned on his truck. Voice lower, softer, she said, "Back then, I didn't see a way out."

"You could have told the truth."

"Yes. But after my dad believed the story and ran with it, then your dad agreed and…" She shrugged. "It's not an excuse, Armie, and it's still unforgivable. But I felt stuck with my own story. One of us was going to be shamed and I was just plain too cowardly to let it be me."

Well, hell. It took a lot of guts to make that admission.

"I called you once, years ago."

"I laughed and hung up on you." Without hearing why she'd contacted him.

"I remember. And I didn't blame you." Her shoulder bumped his. "It doesn't matter now, but I'd called to apologize."

Armie had no idea what to say. Never, not once, had he ever figured on this exact scenario. In his mind, Lea would always be the same spoiled, hateful kid he'd known back then.

But he supposed a decade could change a person. "Fine, you're all contrite and shit. Like you said, it doesn't matter now, so why are you here?"

"Because I've lived my whole life knowing the awfulness of what I'd done to you." She looked up at him. "It was a lot to bear and I didn't think I'd ever be able to redeem myself. But now, finally, I can do something to help. I know it won't change the past, but maybe it'll change the present and that has to count for something."

"Instead of the philosophical speech, why don't you get to the point?"

"All right." She stared up at him. "A man came to see me. He said he knew you were a rapist and he wanted the details."

Fucking reporters. "I bet your dad loved that."

"Dad died two years ago. It's just me now."

Damn it. He wouldn't tell her he was sorry. Her dad had made his life hell.

"I didn't understand who the guy was. But he seemed gleeful about the possibility of you being a rapist. Even after I told him he was wrong, that..." She swallowed hard. "That I'd lied. He kept insisting. So after he left I looked you up. For years I've tried *not* to think about you, about what I'd done."

"Ditto." He'd blocked Lea and the accusations the best he could—but they'd never really been far from his thoughts.

How did a man shake off the charge of rapist?

She bumped her shoulder to his again. "It's not much, but I can tell you about him. The man who came to see me, I mean. I know he thought himself anonymous, believing the lie and assuming I'd shore it up for him. He wasn't pleased when I refused. When he finally left, I watched him and got the make of his car and his license plate number. And I can describe him to you."

Excitement sparked down deep inside Armie, chasing off some of the bleak acceptance. Maybe he could still work this out.

Maybe he could get Merissa back.

He checked his watch, realized he'd miss Merissa leaving work and decided he'd just meet up with her at her house. "Got time for a ride?"

"To where?"

"There's a lady I need to check on—and since she's been threatened by supposed reporters looking for the nitty-gritty on my past, it'd be nice if I could share some good news with her."

She studied his face and agreed. "All right. I owe you at least that much."

"If we get the people threatening her, I promise, we'll call it even."

For only a second, grateful tears turned Lea's eyes liquid. But she blinked, smiled and headed for the passenger side of his truck. "You always were one of the good guys."

MERISSA DROVE SLOWLY through the old neighborhood. Each day it seemed to stay light longer. Spring would soon turn to summer. She exhaled, looking forward to more sunshine and milder weather.

Would she get to spend the summer with Armie?

Would she be noticeably pregnant?

Lost in thought, it seemed doubly startling when headlights suddenly flashed on behind her.

Close. Far, far too close.

With the memory of the last car that had trailed her, she blindly reached for her phone. She'd call her brother and—

The car rammed her, startling her so badly that she gave a short scream. The phone fell from her hand and slid off the seat to the floor. Squeezing the wheel, she frantically struggled to stay on the road. When she got rammed again, this time on the back right fender, her car jerked to the left, smashed into the curb and when she tried to correct it, she overshot to the other side of the road. She was still trying to correct her steering when the car shot around her, cut her off and stopped. Instinctively she slammed on her brakes to keep from colliding. Rubber burned and she came within inches of ramming into the other car.

Too fast for her to catch her breath, a man approached and jerked open her car door. She tried to scream but a hand clamped hard over her mouth, making her jaw ache.

He leaned in close until his hot breath washed over her face. In clear warning, he whispered, "Don't."

Oh my God. She knew the cold blue eyes staring into hers, the rough voice and the cruel attitude.

This was the man from the bank robbery.

Sheer terror narrowed her view until all she could see was his anticipatory smile. Blind with fear, Merissa struggled, striking out at him, clawing.

He released her mouth and backhanded her hard enough to nearly topple her in the seat. Dazed, she tasted her own blood as blackness closed in. Rough hands opened her seat belt and yanked her out. Her head still reeling, she half fell to the ground. The hands on her tightened, wrenching one arm as he dragged her across the rough pavement of the road toward the other idling car.

Merissa tried to get her feet under her but couldn't. She started to scream, but he knotted a hand in her hair and cursed as he shoved her forward.

No! *No, no, no.*

"Fuckers," she heard, and her mind reeled at the recognizable voice.

"Leese," she whispered, and as the flicker of hope gained life, she said again, louder, *"Leese!"*

The man shoved her from him. She collided with the front of his car, then fell to the hard, gravel-strewn ground. Her elbow cracked on something, and she felt a searing burn on her cheek, but neither injury mattered. Numbness sank in, mingling with the awful shock.

She got her head up in time to see Leese attacking the man. How he was here, she didn't know, but he threw hard, direct punches, demolishing the guy who'd grabbed her. When a second man got out of the car she scrambled toward her open door and dubious safety.

The sounds of curses and grunts, of flesh hitting flesh, assaulted her brain.

She needed to help Leese, *but how?*

Thanks to Cannon's insistence, she had pepper spray in her purse, but both it and her phone had been dumped to the floor.

Inside her car she hit the locks with shaking hands, then quickly looked through the windshield. In the chaos, with her heartbeat thundering in her ears, it was hard to tell what was happening. Leese fought hard, but just as Armie had done, he took on both men.

Knowing she had to do something, Merissa laid on the horn. The noise was deafening, but she didn't let up.

Soon the glow of nearby porch lights flickered on, two houses, then three, four, five.

Over and over, Merissa blared the horn until most of the street was awake and watching.

"I called the police," someone yelled from a house. "They're on their way!"

Leese, proving to be a maniac, held on to one man when he tried to flee. He jerked him around at the same time he threw his knee up, sending the guy back and into the side of the car. The bloodied man scrambled for the handle, screaming, "Go, go, go," to his cohort.

The driver gunned it, hit the curb, almost struck another car and sped away. Leese stared after them and Merissa, horrified by the idea of being alone, threw open her door and stumbled out. "Leese!" She knew she sounded pathetic and panicked—because she was. "Leese, *please*!"

In the middle of the street, chest heaving, blood on his face and his hands still balled into fists, Leese turned to see her.

Merissa shook so badly she couldn't stay upright and as her knees gave out, she slumped to sit on the curb just outside her car.

Oh God. She rocked, holding herself tight, watching as Leese started toward her.

He looked like walking fury, but after he crouched in front of her his expression changed. His hands were gentle as he tipped up her face, winced and smoothed her hair.

"Damn, honey, are you okay?" He stripped off his hoodie, then his T-shirt.

Merissa didn't understand. He'd never called her an endearment before—and why was he undressing? But even more important than that… "How are you *here*?"

Carefully, he used his T-shirt to clean her face. "I was following you." Chidingly, he whispered, "You should have known both Armie and Cannon would ensure you weren't alone."

"I'm so glad." She flinched as he touched a particularly tender spot. She wanted to say more, to ask him what he was doing to her, but all that came out was an awful choking sound. Shamed, she threw herself against him. Warm, strong.

Safe.

His hard arms tightened carefully around her. "I hear police sirens. I need to call them—Armie and Cannon, I mean—before things get any crazier."

She nodded. Damn it, she wanted them both...but she couldn't get herself to release Leese. Relief battled against the surge of adrenaline and emotions bubbled up. She tried to hold back the tide, but it broke free and she started sobbing uncontrollably.

Somehow Leese managed to sit and lift her into his lap. "It's okay. I've got you now."

Nodding, she burrowed close again. Her arm started thumping and her face burned, but it didn't matter. Leese was protection. She'd be safe now. If not for him, those men would have had her—and then what?

From behind Leese, an elderly man spoke. "She okay?"

Leese carefully tucked her close to his chest and half turned to the man. "You called the cops?"

"Yes, sir, I did."

"Thank you."

"Can I get either of you anything?"

"A blanket?"

The man nodded and hurried away.

Merissa knew she soaked Leese's shoulder, but she couldn't stem the tears.

He bent to her ear. "Shh, now. The police will think I'm hurting you."

"I'm so sorry."

He rubbed the middle of her back. "Take a breath," he suggested gently.

The man returned with a blanket and Leese draped it around her.

"You're the one who's naked," she whispered.

"Don't go starting rumors, Rissy. I only took off my shirt. Now, another breath."

Nodding, she inhaled shakily, then again. As the red-and-blue lights of cop cars flashed around the area, she looked up at Leese. "Don't leave me."

"I'm not going anywhere."

Cops descended on them and an ambulance pulled up. Merissa assumed it was for Leese—until they reached her.

Well, hell. She suddenly discovered that she was in worse shape than she thought.

ARMIE COULDN'T BELIEVE what Lea told him.

Yeah, he recognized the description: Steve. When he got his hands on that miserable fuck, he'd—

His phone rang, but not with the normal ringtone. It was the emergency ring, the one that meant something was wrong, the ringtone that Vanity called the "Bat signal." All of the guys worked together to help in an emergency. He'd had these calls before, knew it could mean almost anything, but tonight it sent ice through his veins.

"Wait," he told Lea, interrupting her story to grab up his cell. Caller ID showed it was Cannon. He answered with, "What's wrong?"

"Where are you?"

That only alarmed him more. "Driving toward Merissa's house."

"Pull over."

His guts twisted. "Cannon—"

"Pull over, damn it!"

He glanced in the rearview mirror, cut to the right and stopped at the curb. Chest tight, he said, "I've stopped."

"She's okay," Cannon said first, "but Rissy got jumped. Leese was following her and he got to her before they could get her into their car."

Armie tried to speak, but no words came out. *Leese got to her before they could get her into their car.* He breathed too fast and his vision narrowed. In a rasp, he asked, "Where is she?"

"I know that tone, damn it. Get it together."

"Where is she?" His heart punched so hard it hurt him, deep inside hurt.

Cannon went quiet, then whispered, "Remember, she is okay—but an ambulance took her to the hospital. I'm here with her now. I'd have called sooner, but it was a little chaotic at first."

Ambulance. Hospital.

Someone made a grab for Rissy.

And now he knew Steve was involved.

Putting his truck back in gear, Armie said, "I'm on my way."

CHAPTER TWENTY-TWO

"YOU SHOULD LIE DOWN," Cannon told her for the hundredth time.

Sitting on the side of the bed in the emergency area of the hospital, wearing a hospital gown that barely fit her tall frame and a sheet wrapped around her for modesty, Merissa shook her head. She'd been at the hospital for forty-five minutes, long enough to be somewhat cleaned up and have the cut on her face—a cut she hadn't even known about—bandaged.

She still shook from head to toe. Aches and pains had long since set in, but she had so many good friends crowded in the small room that she didn't want to upset them more than they already were.

Soon, she'd been told, her face would be stitched and her arm x-rayed. Her poor arm. She glanced at it again and saw the awful mottled bruising from her elbow halfway up her arm and midway down her forearm. It had all happened so fast, she still couldn't remember exactly how she'd gotten hurt, but she felt it now as she held her injured arm protectively against her body. Cannon stood right there beside her, holding her other hand, his thumb constantly brushing over her knuckles. Yvette stood half behind him, her cheek resting on his shoulder.

In the corner, Denver held Cherry, her back to his

chest, his massive arms looped around her. They both watched her with concern. Merissa tried smiling to reassure them, but that just made the bandages on her face pinch.

Even though Merissa had tried to protest all the attention, Stack and Vanity were on their way.

Leese, now in a clean shirt that Denver had brought him, paced in the hall while continually looking in on her. Merissa wasn't sure, but it seemed like he still had a lot of pent-up fury simmering just beneath the surface.

Even with a black eye and a bruise at the edge of his jaw, he looked dangerous.

And he'd saved her. Thinking that made her bottom lip quiver again, which of course Cannon noticed.

"Just hang on," he told her, as if her life was on the line.

And that did make her smile despite the bulky bandage. "I'm okay, just rattled. I promise."

Suddenly Leese looked up the hallway, then stepped out of view.

Merissa heard the heavy, hurried footsteps, heard Leese talking fast, and a second later Armie filled the doorway.

Their gazes clashed, and oh God, she lost it all over again. The tears welled up, her throat tightened. She tried to swallow but couldn't.

Without a word, Armie cut through everyone else and reached her.

ARMIE BARELY NOTICED the others in the room. He'd left Lea in the hallway with Leese. Cannon was talking to him. But all his focus was on Rissy.

She reached out to him and he gathered her close,

slipping one arm under her thighs, the other behind her back. Scooping her in close, using ultimate care, he moved with her to the other side of the curtain and an empty chair.

"Shh," he begged in a voice gone thick with emotion. "Baby, please don't cry."

The awful, racking sobs continued.

With his forehead to hers, he whispered, "Tell me what hurts. What can I do?" She held one arm close and when he looked at it, his heart dropped. "Your arm."

Nodding, she tried to talk and couldn't.

"I'm so sorry," he told her. "Jesus, I'm so sorry."

She took three shuddering, choking breaths, and finally spoke. "I'm… I'm okay."

Armie smoothed one hand over her back, her hip. "How bad is your arm?"

"I don't know. Something happened when he grabbed me," she whispered brokenly.

God, Armie knew he was going to kill those fucks. "Have they x-rayed it yet?"

"No." She sniffled, dried her eyes on his shoulder and lifted her ravaged face. "They're going to but I don't think it's broken."

He swallowed hard. "Okay." Being very careful, he kissed the bridge of her nose, then the bruised skin around her bandaged cheek. "What happened here?"

"He…he hit me."

He closed his eyes, swallowed.

"Then he pulled me from the car and when Leese got there, he shoved me away and I guess I hit something on the car."

That rambling explanation proved that she needed him to be strong now. "He who, honey?"

"The man from the robbery."

Armie's muscles twitched. Was Steve somehow involved in that, too? "Have you seen the cops yet?"

From the other side of the curtain, Leese said, "Some officers showed up, but when I explained, they said they'd have Detective Riske or Bareden get in touch."

Armie said, "Cannon?"

Her brother leaned around the curtain. "Logan's on his way. Should be here soon."

Armie nodded, gathered her close again and said to Cannon, "Where the hell is the doctor?"

"He's here now," Denver said.

"And," said a new voice, "he needs everyone to clear out, please. I need room to move, but I promise to take good care of her."

Rissy's uninjured arm grabbed him tighter.

Near her ear, Armie soothed, "I'm staying with you."

She went limp against him. "Thank you."

"I love you," he told her. "No way am I budging."

She shot up to look at him. Her hair was a mess, her face dirty and scraped, bruised and bandaged. Red eyes and a redder nose and she was the most beautiful, most precious sight. "God, I love you."

New tears filled her eyes. "Armie—"

He was already standing with her, carrying her back to the bed and the waiting doctor.

He and Cannon remained with her while the doctor put some very tiny stitches in the cut on her face.

When the doc first pulled off the bandage, Armie grimaced. From her cheekbone up to her hairline her flesh had been split. He'd seen worse injuries—but not on a woman he loved.

Cannon, having already seen it, still scrubbed a hand over his face.

Thank God Leese had been following her.

The doctor promised her that any scarring would fade to be almost invisible. It made Armie so damned proud that Rissy didn't look overly concerned about it.

While the doc worked on her, he talked to them, saying it was the first time he'd had a group of MMA fighters crowding the emergency room. He asked questions, not just of Cannon and Armie, but engaging Merissa, too.

Armie thought it might have been the doc's effort to put them all more at ease.

A nurse bustled around them, constantly glancing at Cannon, and then at Armie, while also being proficient at her job. When the doc finished and a guy in scrubs came with a wheelchair to get her arm x-rayed, Rissy flashed him another look of panic.

Armie helped her into the chair. "I'll go with you."

The doctor patted her shoulder. "There's a waiting area just outside the X-ray room. He'll be close."

Armie could tell Cannon didn't want to hang back, but he did it all the same. That was the thing about Cannon—he always did the right thing. Right now he knew his sister wanted Armie with her, so Cannon would wait.

More than anything else, that proved how much Cannon cared—about both of them.

There was a lot Armie needed to share with Cannon, but at the moment, reassuring Rissy took priority. He decided he'd tell Cannon everything as soon as he had the opportunity.

When they stepped out to the hallway and he saw Lea talking to Leese, reality crashed in.

He'd forgotten all about her.

Leese stepped over to them. "X-rays now?"

"Yes." Teasing, Merissa shook her head at him. Keeping her voice low, she whispered, "Even here you're hooking up? Shameless."

"What?" Blank-faced, Leese glanced back at Lea, then shook his head. "No, see…" Appearing harassed, he turned to Armie for help.

Merissa said, "You've done more than enough today. If you've made other plans, feel free to go."

Well, hell.

But it was Cannon who said, "Lea. This is a surprise."

"Lea?" As the aide tried to wheel her away, Rissy twisted around to glare at Lea with mottled fury. "Lea Baley?"

"She's here to help," Armie rushed to tell her. Then to Cannon, "Get the info from her, will you? And update Logan."

Brows up, Cannon looked at Lea again, then flagged Armie on. "Go. I'll take care of it."

Armie jogged to the elevator, sliding past the door that the aide held for him. "Sorry about that."

The aide nodded. "No problem."

Armie looked down at Merissa. *Pissed* didn't even come close to covering it. He crouched down and took her hand. "Someone went to Lea and asked her about the rumors. But she fessed up to the truth. That's why she's here. To let me know."

Incredulous, Rissy said, "And you believe her?"

The elevator dinged and the doors opened. Armie

straightened, and then kept stride with the wheelchair. "I do." He didn't want to tell her yet that it was Steve stirring up the lies. At the moment, she had enough to deal with.

When she remained irate, Armie said, "I'm not a fool, right?"

Her eyes, red from tears and a little swollen, glared at him. Grudgingly, she said, "No."

"So you'll trust me on this? Please?"

"Maybe."

At the end of a long hallway, the aide led them in to another, smaller waiting area. There were two other people there, an elderly woman glancing through a magazine and an even-older man dozing. A tall female tech gave Merissa a form to fill out. "We'll be ready for you in just a few minutes."

Armie again crouched beside her. "Lea's father passed away a few years ago. She's married now, has kids, and since she knew I wouldn't talk to her on the phone, she came to me. She was still telling me everything when Cannon called and all I could think about was getting to you."

Keeping her gaze averted, Rissy asked, "You think she can be helpful?"

"I do." Armie faltered. Damn, that had sounded like a wedding vow.

"So…" She glanced at the form, then laid it flat against her midriff. "If we get things resolved, then you and I…that is…we…"

Armie took the paper from her and laid it on the end table. As gently as he could, he cupped a hand to her face. "I love you."

Her smile wavered and her hand covered his. "Does that mean…?"

"It means I don't ever want to be away from you." He brushed her cheek with his thumb. "God, I was so stupid." Instead of protecting her from his past, he'd made her vulnerable to new threats. "Odds are I'll be stupid again at some point. When I am, please remember that I love you more than anything in life."

Fresh tears swam in her eyes. "Armie…"

He leaned in, kissed her softly on her lips. "You said you were safer with me. Well, from now on, I want that. You with me. *Always*." He kissed her again, so carefully because of her injuries. "Please tell me yes."

"Yes."

Armie searched her face, sensing some uncertainty. "I love you." Now that he'd said it, he couldn't seem to stop saying it.

She gave a laugh that sounded a little like a sob. "I love you, too. So much."

"But you're worried about something?" Was she still afraid? "I swear you'll never be hurt again. I'll keep you safe."

"You always do." After an expression of apology, Rissy looked at the form.

Armie didn't understand, but he picked it back up and turned it over.

He sensed Merissa watching him as he read.

It was just a pregnancy consent form, basically asking if there was any chance… Blood rushed to his head, making his world spin.

Even before his gaze shot back to hers, Armie knew. His entire being went blank, then burst with bright colors. "Rissy?" he whispered around hope and amazement and the utter, blinding joy.

She bit her lip and breathed faster.

Holy shit! Dropping the form, Armie searched her face. As his own eyes grew wet, he used his thumbs to brush away her tears. "Rissy?" His hands trembled. "You're pregnant?"

She bit her lip, closed her eyes and nodded. "I think so."

Staggered, Armie sat back on his heels. His attention visually pored over her body. She was so damn slim! But now that he thought about it, her breasts seemed a little fuller...

He reached out to cup one, but she shrank back. *"Armie,"* she whispered frantically. "Get up!"

Instead he leaned in and put his cheek to her belly. "A baby." *His baby.*

With Merissa Colter.

"It's not confirmed. I mean, I'm pretty sure, but I haven't taken a test yet."

"We'll do that together." He had a hard time wrapping his mind around it. It was like a dream—except that someone had tried to snatch her right off the road. He wanted to crush her close, to shout with happiness, to hide her away so nothing bad could ever again touch her.

And he wanted to bind her to him, now and forever. The knowledge of a baby sent new fear cutting into him. Overwhelmed, he held her closer and asked quietly, "Why didn't you tell me?"

Her fingers threaded through his hair. "I would have," she replied, her tone as soft as his. "The night

I realized I'd missed my period was the night before you…"

He groaned, kissed her belly and sat back to see her. "Jesus, honey, I'm sorry. I fucked up so badly."

"No." She kept touching him, soothing him when he should be doing that for her. "I wanted to let you get through the fight—"

"Screw the fight."

"Armie Jacobson, don't you dare act that way." She grabbed his ear, and though she was injured, she still had plenty of strength in that one arm. "Do you want me to feel guilty?"

Insane, but even now Rissy could make him smile. "No, never."

"Then you're going to put your all into this fight. Do you understand me?"

She'd stopped whispering, which sort of amused him. Since it started to sting, he pried her grip off his ear, kissed her palm and said with complete honesty, "Whatever you want, Stretch."

Her lips, too, twitched into a smile. "Thank you."

The technician, who was probably taller than Rissy and built like a linebacker, returned and, without blinking an eye at seeing Armie on the floor, asked, "Are we ready?"

Armie said, "She's pregnant."

The tech smiled and picked up the paper. "How far along?"

"I don't know," Rissy said. "That is, I haven't taken a test yet or anything but I'm pretty sure…"

"Just in case, we'll protect you with a lead apron." She handed Rissy the form with a pen.

"You're sure it's safe?" Armie asked, finally standing so he could meet the woman eye to eye.

"I promise it'll be fine." She patted his biceps, then nudged him toward a chair. "You can wait right there. I'll have her back to you in five minutes, tops."

Fretting, Armie watched her go. Then he sat. Then he dropped his head into his hands.

A baby!

In a rush, he stood and dug out his cell phone.

"Excuse me?" The older woman pointed to a sign on the wall. "No cell phones."

Damn. He sat down again.

"Your first child?" she asked. Then with a smile, she explained, "I couldn't help but overhear."

Dazed and somewhat dumbfounded, Armie nodded. "Yeah." Had the woman also heard him cursing? He winced. "Sorry."

She looked tickled. "I take it you're happy?"

That word didn't even begin to cover it. He nodded again. "Very."

She nodded in approval. "Our granddaughter is due in a few weeks. It's a wonderful thing. Congratulations."

His first congrats—not from his buddies or their very adorable wives, not from Rissy's brother, but from a total stranger. Some of the shock faded and he stood to approach the woman, his hand out. "Thank you."

Smiling, she stood, too, then opened her arms.

And damn, Armie hugged the old girl right off her feet.

LUCKILY HER ARM wasn't broken. The doc declared it "badly bruised"—duh—and told her to ice it often and to take it easy until it felt better.

She had scrapes on her knees, her palm and one elbow. The worst was the discoloration around her cheek from where she'd needed the stitches. Everyone assumed she'd hit something sharp on the car, like the edge of the broken bumper or maybe the license plate.

Merissa remembered how the man had backhanded her, and she assumed that had caused the worst of the bruising. Thinking about it made her shiver with dread, so she pushed it from her mind.

Armie loved her.

She had plenty to think about without dwelling on the awful thugs. Besides, they wouldn't be able to make another grab for her because she didn't plan to give them the opportunity.

She didn't want to be a wimp, but she'd had enough, so until they were caught she wouldn't be alone again. She'd already arranged some upcoming time off so she could attend Armie's fight. Well, now she'd just extend it, and her current injuries would be as good an excuse as any.

By the time the hospital finished stitching and x-raying and giving instructions, she'd been there for a little over three and a half hours. She knew all her friends were gathered in the larger waiting area at the front of the hospital, along with Lea Baley.

But she only wanted to go home, shower and crash.

With Armie.

So far, he'd barely let her out of his sight. After he'd helped her to dress, she started to zip up her jeans but he put his big hand over her bare belly and pressed his mouth to her temple.

"We're okay," she told him again, putting her hand over his. "I promise."

Armie stayed silent a moment. She heard him swallow, then felt the near-reverent kiss he teased over her neck. "When will you tell him?"

She knew he meant Cannon. Armie hadn't yet said anything to her brother, and she was glad. She didn't want to make an announcement in a hospital. "Maybe after your fight, we can get together with him and Yvette for dinner and I'll tell him then."

"The guys at the gym will want to know, too."

A thought occurred to her and, fighting a smile, she looked at Armie. "Did you want to tell them?"

He finished zipping her jeans for her, then lightly kissed her mouth. "I want to shout it to the whole world."

So he wasn't just accepting. He was happy? She licked dry lips. "Armie…" He watched her so intently that she stalled and had to try again. "I don't want to pressure you."

"Pressure me?" Far too serious, he gathered her close. "Do you know it kills me that, for even a second, you'd think that way?" He lifted her hand and pressed it to his heart. "You own me, Stretch. For better or worse. Today and forever."

That sounded so close to a proposal, Rissy lost her breath. She couldn't speak, couldn't blink. Beneath her palm, Armie's heartbeat grew heavy.

"Forget all my misguided intentions to let you find a better life with a better man."

"Armie!" That's what he'd thought? "I want *you*, and damn it, you are—"

"No one," he said, interrupting her, "could ever love you as much as I do. I swear it."

Her heart melted. That was the absolute sweetest, most wonderful thing anyone had ever said to her.

She was working up the nerve to ask him about the future when they were finally free to leave.

She and Armie reached the main waiting room to find it mostly filled with her visitors. It made her blush when everyone started greeting her at once. Sticking close beside her, Armie smiled as if proud.

Unlike the ambulance that had brought her in, her friends hadn't parked in back at the emergency entrance. There were so many of them that she was glad they hadn't remained in the small waiting area and instead had moved to the front of the hospital.

"Logan wants to talk to you more tonight," Cannon told her. "But he got a call and had to take off for an hour or so."

Biting back her groan, Merissa said, "That's fine."

"She'll be at her house," Armie told him. "With me."

"Better late than never." Cannon looked at each of them in turn, then smiled. "As long as it's never again."

"Now and always," Armie assured him.

Merissa didn't know how long it'd take her to get used to that, but she wanted to hear it for the rest of her life.

While the men clapped Armie on the back and heralded him for his good sense, Leese smiled at her, then lifted his palm for another high five. Laughing, Merissa kept her injured right arm close but slapped her left palm to his.

As a small crowd they exited the hospital. For once, Merissa didn't mind that everyone pampered her. Her poor brother especially looked ravaged with worry, so she gave him extra hugs, and accepted his hugs in return even as her thoughts skipped ahead.

Now and always. So was Armie thinking about the future? And under what terms?

"Hey." With his arm around her, Armie asked, "You okay?"

He was so attuned to her. Merissa nodded. For now, she decided to stop worrying about tomorrow so she could concentrate on the here and now.

Leese said, "I can get Lea back to her car if you want."

Armie nodded, but asked Lea, "Is that okay?"

"Of course."

Merissa turned to the woman, who, so far, had been very quiet around her. Lea didn't look like a monster, or an evil, conniving bitch. She looked like an average woman, who'd grown up.

Smiling at her, Merissa said, "Thank you."

"For finally telling the truth?" Lea returned the smile. "It's long overdue, and believe me, it's my pleasure."

Armie started to say something, but his gaze went to the far end of the parking lot.

Merissa looked but couldn't see anything.

Armie took Cannon aside and said something that clearly enraged her brother. Cannon immediately went to the other men and they, too, disliked whatever they heard.

"What in the world?"

"Stay here," Armie told her softly, then he ducked into a row of cars.

Leese showed up at her side. "Come on. Let's get you to Armie's truck."

She dug in. "No way. Tell me what's going on."

Leese took her measure, came to some decision and bent close to say, "He's here."

He who? Rather than take a chance on distracting Armie, she followed Leese to the truck and got in on the passenger side. To her consternation, Lea got in the driver's seat.

When Merissa looked through the windshield, she saw that the rest of the women had also disappeared to their respective cars. Only Leese and Cannon remained visible, but they immediately circled around the lot, going in different directions. Recognizing that they were up to something, she said to Lea, "Stack and Denver must be with the ladies."

"Fascinating." Lea held the steering wheel and looked around. "Any idea what's going on?"

She shook her head, but spotted Armie when he stepped out from between a row of vehicles.

And that's when she realized the man with his back to her, watching the emergency room exit, was Steve.

Was he waiting for her? But that didn't make any sense. Steve had no way of knowing what had happened.

"That's him," Lea told her. "The man who came to see me. He really hates Armie."

Lost in confusion, Merissa concentrated on Armie.

Unfortunately, when Steve spotted him, he turned and walked away—heading straight for the truck.

Armie shouted, "Don't make me chase you, you bastard."

Steve turned back to him and in a voice just as loud, said, "Where is she? Is she all right?"

Armie didn't slow, and when he reached Steve, he grabbed him up by the throat and pinned him—*hard*—

to a cement pier in the garage. Nose to nose, his every muscle bunching, Armie snarled, "You *dare* come here?"

Cannon and Leese showed up, flanking Armie.

Lea watched, her eyes wide.

Merissa covered her mouth. She didn't know what was going on, but she didn't like it.

"You sure about this?" Cannon asked Armie.

Lea opened the driver's door and got out. "Even after I told him it was all a lie, he tried to convince me to keep it going." Her chin lifted. "He offered me money."

"Dumbass didn't know she's rich."

"I'm not," Lea said. "Daddy left his money to my stepmother."

Surprised, Armie said, "Oh. Hey…sorry."

"It doesn't matter. I'm happier now than I've ever been." She glared at Steve. "And I definitely didn't want his money."

Merissa slowly stepped from the truck, too. She looked from her brother, to Lea, to Armie—and finally to Steve.

With both of his hands wrapped around Armie's wrist, maybe as an attempt to keep from being strangled, Steve rasped, "Merissa!"

She wasn't feeling very generous. In fact, if her arm wasn't injured, she'd have taken her own turn. "Armie?"

Negligent, he glanced her way. "Yeah, Stretch?"

"I'm glad you're finally fighting back."

He grinned while Steve redoubled his efforts to get free.

Impatient, Cannon crossed his arms. "What are you planning to do?"

"Kill him."

Knowing he wouldn't, Merissa nodded. "Sounds about right to me."

Rubbing his mouth to stifle a laugh, Cannon took charge. "As usual, I have to suggest that perhaps we ought to get some information from him before you mangle him. What do you think? It could possibly lead us to answers about other things, as well."

"You're right." Just like that, Armie opened his hand and Steve slumped while coughing.

"Asshole," he managed to gasp.

"Idiot!" Merissa shot back.

Armie glanced her way. "Honey, why don't you wait in the truck?"

Merissa arched a brow. "Why don't I not?"

Regaining his aplomb, Steve turned to her. "Jesus, you *are* hurt."

Merissa studied him.

He ran both hands through his hair, his gaze taking in her bandaged face, the bruising, the way she held her arm. "What happened? Do you know who tried to grab you?"

She was wondering how Steve knew anything about that when suddenly Armie turned an incendiary glare on him. In a voice so soft it was eerie, Armie murmured, "You son of a bitch."

Cannon, equally enraged, reached for Steve, and this time it was Armie stopping her brother.

"He's mine."

Heaving, Cannon paused and gave one small nod.

Looking every bit as enraged, Leese said, "Well, I'd fucking like a turn, too."

"Let's get those other answers Cannon mentioned, first."

The reason for their rage suddenly dawned on Merissa and she took a step forward. *"You."*

Armie nodded. "Him."

Blustering, Steve said, "I don't know what you're talking about." Apparently deciding discretion was the better part of valor, he tried to elbow his way past them. No one budged. "All of you," Steve insisted. "Get out of my way."

"Call Logan," Armie ordered while stepping Steve back.

Without taking his gaze off them, Cannon did just that. When he disconnected, he said, "He was already headed back here. He said to give him five minutes."

Armie pressed in on Steve again. "Until Detective Riske gets here, how about you tell me why?"

Gaze darting everywhere, Steve shook his head. "Why what?"

"Why target Rissy? Why hire fake reporters to hassle her?" Armie shoved him hard into the pier. "Why set her up to be kidnapped right off the fucking street?"

CHAPTER TWENTY-THREE

SEEING RISSY'S SHOCK, Armie told Cannon, "Hold him," and he reached her in two strides.

"It was *Steve*?" She clutched at his arm, her gaze baffled. "*All* of it?"

Armie led Rissy a short distance away to the front of his truck. "It appears so. I'm sorry."

In the faintest of whispers, she murmured, "Incredible," and she buckled to sit against the fender. "I never thought...never even considered..." Her gaze locked with his. "He probably knew the passcode to my house. I mean..." She flushed and glared at Steve again. "He was in my house, standing there when I reset it after we came in."

Armie bent to her ear. "Let me deal with this, okay? All I want is the truth and now might be my best shot."

Briefly, she leaned into him. "Do what you have to do."

So much faith in him. Armie smoothed her hair, then returned to Steve.

Rissy's ex was starting to look a little green.

"Let's hear it," Armie said. "You have to have a reason."

Steve gave a frantic shake of his head. "I didn't do this."

"Describe *this*."

He seemed to have trouble finding the words, but finally he gestured at Merissa. "I never wanted her hurt."

So the ramifications were starting to sink in on him? That suited Armie just fine. The bastard deserved to suffer the consequences of what he'd started—but Rissy didn't deserve *any* of it. "So tell me, Steve. What *did* you want?"

"Nothing! I..." Again he tried to maneuver away.

Armie, Leese and Cannon made that impossible.

"All this time," Armie said, his words bitter. "I thought the threats were about me."

That seemed to push Steve over the edge. "They *are* about you. You're *nothing*. Your own father admits you're a filthy rapist!"

"Shut up!" Rissy started to rise.

She stopped when Armie landed a body shot on Steve, making him double over in pain. Hitting him seemed the expedient way to end that particular accusation, and appease Rissy so she wouldn't get herself too riled.

"Thank you," Rissy said.

"Welcome." Whether Rissy or the putz realized it, Armie had pulled the punch. If he hadn't, Steve would be curled on the ground with broken ribs.

Disgusted, Lea said, "I already explained to him that I made it all up. I was a jealous brat and I told lies. End of story."

"I guess old Steve doesn't like to listen."

Arms folded around his guts, Steve wheezed. "How dare you step in behind me?"

Again Rissy rose to her feet. "He was before you, after you and *during* you, you ass!"

Leese chuckled. "Yeah, as her confidant, I can confirm that you," he said to Steve, "were just her way of passing time until Armie wised up."

Steve tried to lunge away.

Catching him by the front of his shirt, Armie slammed him to the post again.

And Steve's cell phone rang.

Looking extra panicked, Steve started fighting. Armie put him in a headlock and nodded at Cannon.

Cannon took the phone from Steve's pants pocket, glanced at the ID and put it on speaker.

Steve tried, but he couldn't speak; he barely got out a gargling noise.

Voice bland, Cannon said, "Yeah?"

"You see her yet?" Without waiting for an answer, a man laughed. "We've played it your way with the robbery and the scare tactics. Now it's going to be our way. Pay up, or next time it'll be worse for her." The call died.

His heartbeat exploding, Armie stared at Cannon.

Cannon looked just as shell-shocked as Armie felt.

With a shove, Armie released Steve—and at that moment, having his suspicions confirmed—Armie wasn't sure what he would do.

Choosing that inauspicious moment to pull in, Logan spotted them and gave a two-second flash of his lights.

Clear warning, Armie supposed, that he was *not* to kill Steve.

God, he wanted to. But as Cannon had said, Steve had more questions to answer, and he had to be alive to do it.

"Everyone take a breath," Logan ordered as he stepped from his car. Taking in the scene, he approached cautiously. His attention paused on Cannon. "Why don't you tell me what's going on?"

"They're assaulting me," Steve complained while rubbing at his throat. "That's what."

Logan lifted a brow.

Armie ignored it and gave Steve a level look that shut him up.

There was a minute of Cannon and Leese both talking, and Steve rattling off excuses, before Logan got caught up.

He cuffed Steve, sat him in the back of his car, then returned. Hands in his pockets, his gaze repeatedly going to Merissa, Logan said, "Well, this is interesting."

"If by interesting you mean totally fucked, yeah," Armie agreed. "It's interesting."

"I found your dad."

Armie did a double take.

"That's where I had to go. Cannon told us about the threats and extortion, so we picked him up for questioning, but we won't be able to hold him. Not unless we get proof that he, too, was involved. But I have an idea, a way to wrap it all up and get all our answers."

"Okay."

Cannon frowned. "You don't know what the idea is, yet."

It didn't matter. If it settled things and made Merissa safe, Armie was all for it.

Logan took a minute to explain. "What do you think?"

Seeing Merissa, her face bruised but her shoulders straight with pride, he nodded. "I'm in. On one condition."

Logan huffed a breath. "Let's hear it."

IN BED TOGETHER, Merissa's sweet tush tucked against him as he spooned her, Armie asked again, "You're comfortable?"

Sounding sleepy, she murmured, "Very," and wiggled her ass against him. She had her injured arm over a pillow. After icing it and taking her prescribed pain meds, she was already able to use it more.

Kissing her temple, Armie thought of the lengths Steve had gone to just to hurt her—all out of some ridiculous power trip because of an inflated ego, and it enraged him all over again.

"Your fight is in a few days."

"Yeah. Don't worry about it. It'll be fine." Then he thought about that and added, "You're going with me."

"Okay."

Her easy agreement took the wind from his sails. How he'd ever again let her out of his sight, he didn't yet know.

"Armie?"

He kissed her temple again. "Yeah?"

"I'm sorry."

Going still, he asked, "For what?"

She carefully turned to face him. "All this time you thought it was your past causing problems, when really it was just my stupid ex."

"That's not your doing."

"Just like ugly rumors aren't your doing?"

The quiet of the room made the conversation feel more intimate. Now that he'd admitted what he felt, he felt it in spades. There were a few moments here and there when it choked him up, others when it made him smile. "I never wanted those rumors to hurt you."

"They haven't. Steve was the only one trying to hurt me. Steve and whoever he hired."

"We'll get them," Armie promised her. With any luck, that'd happen tomorrow, early. He wanted her free from the threats.

"I know. I just want you to understand. I don't ever again want you to use it as an excuse to put space between us."

He opened a hand over her rear and snuggled her in closer. "My heart can't take it when there's space, so no worries."

She stared into his eyes. "Will you marry me?"

The smile crept up on him until he laughed. "Yeah. I'll marry you, Stretch." He stole a quick kiss. "It'd be my honor."

Finally she closed her eyes and got comfortable again. "We'll figure out details after your fight."

Armie had never really anticipated competing with the SBC. After he'd resigned himself to it, he'd ended up looking forward to it.

But now, with Rissy's proposal and the promise of a future together, he couldn't wait to get it over with.

AT THE PARK, in the shadows of predawn, he and Cannon held back. The air was cold, the ground damp and his mood heavy. He'd left Leese, Denver and Cherry at Rissy's house with her, but he wanted to be with her.

Armie watched the surrounding area.

Cannon watched him. "You sure you want to do this to your dad?"

"For your sister?" Expression hard, he nodded. "Damn right." He'd do anything for her, so setting up his old man wasn't a hardship.

They hunkered together behind a row of scrubby bushes at the perimeter of the park, both of them dressed in dark clothes to help conceal them. Armie wondered if this was where Bray had hidden. It seemed likely.

Last night, while Rissy had soaked in the tub, he'd called his dad at the motel where Logan had initially found him. Sure enough, he'd returned to the same place after he'd been released from questioning.

It had been easy to convince Mac that he was now willing to pay for information. Disgruntled that the cops had been "hassling" him, Mac was more than ready to take a payday and get out of town.

Armie had haggled with him, offering five hundred instead of the grand his father had requested. To Mac, that only made the deal more legit. If Armie had just agreed, Mac would have gotten suspicious.

He was to meet Armie at the park. Mac had complained about the ungodly hour, but he knew Armie jogged so that added to the plausibility.

Unfortunately for Mac, Steve had also been coerced to call Keno and Boyd back. They, too, would be meeting at the park, thinking Steve would pay up.

Steve hadn't acted out of any concern for Rissy's well-being. He was already caught and his options were to lend a hand, or go down for attempted murder.

Logan was none too happy that Armie had insisted on being present, and that Cannon had backed him up. If they didn't know him so well, he probably would have refused them. Luckily for Armie, Cannon was a hard man to deny—especially when he'd previously been helpful to the cops.

When Mac pulled up in his battered sedan, Armie tensed with disgust and other more anomalous feelings that he didn't want to dissect. This was the man who'd fathered him, then despised him. It wasn't natural, but he'd learned to live with it.

Cannon nudged his shoulder, his way of reminding Armie that he wasn't alone.

Mac sat in his car for the longest time before finally getting out, hands on his hips, and looking around the area. Failing to see Armie, he checked his cell phone.

He was heading back to his car when, as if on cue, Keno and Boyd arrived. Irate, they got out of their own rusted junker and approached Mac with animosity.

"What the hell are you doing here?" Mac demanded.

"I was going to ask you that," Boyd said.

Keno laughed. "If you're thinking of cutting in on our deal, the opportunity has passed."

Mac backed up a step. Voice lowered, brows bunched together, he snarled, "You miserable fucks. Did you hurt that girl?"

Armie went alert. Huh. So his dad hadn't been in on that?

"She's alive," Keno said. "The little bitch had another fighter trailing her. Guess your boy isn't the only one tappin' that."

Mac went shifty-eyed. "You made a grab for her?"

"That's how we're getting paid," Boyd bragged. "Steve wanted her hassled, but he doesn't actually want her dead."

"Guess he has a heart after all," Keno added.

Mac watched them both with disgust. "I understand losing your temper, that shit happens. But only a coward would attack a woman."

"Like your son?"

"Told you that was a bunch of lies. Armie wouldn't do that."

"Maybe he learned from his old man."

"I got drunk and out of control." Mac shrugged. "Totally different. The women were nothing, easy lays, but even then, Armie tried to defend them."

"And you were willing to use him to get your payday anyway?"

Mac shrugged. "He can afford it." And then, with what almost sounded like pride, he said, "He's done all right for himself."

"If you say so." Keno sneered. "I figure I'll like him better dead."

Eyes narrowing, Mac sucked a tooth, then hitched his chin. "That's what you're planning?"

"Smug bastard has it coming. I owe it to him for the way he botched our robbery."

Mac chuckled. "Kicked your ass good, didn't he?"

Keno wasn't amused.

"He disarmed you, right? Then whipped your ass?" Mac whistled. "Bet you wore those bruises for a while, didn't you?"

"Go fuck yourself."

"So if you can't take him head-on," Mac pressed, "what's the plan?"

Keno flashed an evil smile. "Let's just say he won't feel any pain."

"Ah. Gonna ambush him then?"

"Something like that."

Nodding, Mac seemed to consider it—then he withdrew a small black revolver from his jacket pocket. "Sorry, but I don't think I can let you do that."

"Jesus." Boyd scrambled back.

Keno stood his ground. "What do you think you're doing?"

"Takin' out the trash." Mac's arm remained steady, his finger on the trigger, his gaze unflinching. "I figure Armie was willing to pay to keep his girl safe. He'll probably double it once he knows I've gotten rid of you for good."

"I'll cut you in," Keno offered.

"That would work." Mac slowly nodded, then grinned. "Except he's my son. I might threaten and bully him every now and then, but doesn't mean I'll let you do the same."

Damn it, Armie felt Cannon grinning. Low, he said, "Not funny."

"Course not," Cannon agreed, still looking amused.

"Where the hell is Logan?"

Little by little, Boyd and Keno were spreading out. If Mac didn't get control quick, he'd lose the advantage.

"Patience," Cannon said.

"He's going to shoot that idiot."

"That's on him," Cannon argued. "Stick with the plan."

As he rose, Armie murmured, "Sorry, I can't." With as much sarcasm as he could muster, he said louder, "Hell, Dad, I didn't know you cared."

After his initial surprise and a flash of anger, Mac shrugged. "What kind of dad would I be if I didn't put him down for threatening you?"

"Thing is," Armie said, "I don't need you to. It'll be my pleasure to crush him, believe me."

"There are two of them," Mac said.

"Doesn't matter." He kept his gaze on Keno, but said to his dad, "Put the gun away."

"Think I'll wait on that." Mac shifted the gun to Boyd. "Get to it already."

Trying to get the advantage of surprise, Keno attacked.

Armie waited, then double underhooked him, catching both of his arms under Keno's. He let Keno's momentum take him off balance, and easily threw him to the ground.

He didn't wait for Keno to get up.

Instead he dropped a big hit to Keno's jaw, then started landing knees to his ribs, mixed with more punches to his face and body. He thought of Rissy and rage kept him going, each strike harder than the one before it.

A second later, with a flash of lights and sirens, Logan's men closed in. Cannon was already there beside Armie, pulling him back.

"I want to kill him," Armie growled.

Close to him, Cannon said, "I know. Me, too. But we have to let Logan do his thing."

It gave Armie great satisfaction when Boyd tried to run and subsequently got hit with a Taser. Seeing him twitching on the ground was a pleasure.

Mac, not being an idiot, put his gun on the ground with alacrity and interlocked his hands behind his head.

Deadpan, Cannon asked, "Been arrested before?"

Watching Armie, Mac just shrugged. "You set me up, son."

"Yeah," Armie said while fishing out his wallet. "I did."

As his arms were wrenched down and his wrists put in cuffs, Mac grinned. "You're fast."

"That's what they tell me." Armie took out the five

hundred he'd promised his dad and stuffed it into the breast pocket of his shirt.

Because that wasn't part of the plan, Cannon scowled over it, but he didn't say anything.

Without a word, Armie walked away.

As he was being led to a cruiser, Mac yelled to him, "Did that include a bonus for saving your ass, too?"

Armie didn't look back. Here on out, he was only looking forward.

CANNON SAW ARMIE LEAVING, knew he wouldn't go far, but figured he'd want a few moments alone. Hurting for his friend, he walked over to Mr. Jacobson. There were five cops on the scene, including Logan, who had just approached.

"Where's Armie?"

Cannon tipped his head in the direction Armie had gone.

Grim, Logan looked after him. "We got plenty, I'm sure. But I don't want him to take off yet."

"He won't." Cannon indicated Mac. "Mind if I have a word with him?"

"One minute." Logan squeezed Cannon's shoulder and went back to Keno and Boyd.

"What do you want now?" Mac asked, obnoxious to the bitter end.

Cannon stared at him, and more than anything he just felt pity. "You threw away everything."

Mac narrowed his eyes. "Pretty sure he didn't miss me."

"You never gave him anything to miss." Bracing a hand on the roof of the squad car, Cannon stared down at Mac. "Who misses abuse? Neglect?"

"I kept a roof over his head."

"Barely." If Cannon thought it would work, he'd offer Mac ten times what Armie paid him—for him to stay away. But he'd always come sniffing around if he thought there was a buck to be made.

"Feeling sorry for him?" Mac sneered.

"Armie? No." He straightened. "You're the one who's missed out on everything. I feel sorry for *you*."

As he walked away, Cannon heard Mac say, "I don't need your pity, damn you! Tell him I don't need his, either. Tell him—"

Cannon stopped listening. He couldn't tell Armie anything he didn't already know.

THERE IN THE AUDIENCE, front row, sitting with their group, Merissa stared toward him. Beside her, Bray squirreled around in his seat as he cheered.

"Not the time," Simon snarled.

Right. He bounced on the balls of his feet, his muscles warm and loose. Music blared, bright lights burned down on him and already sweat beaded out of every pore.

Again he looked at Merissa.

"Jesus," Simon said. "Now you're smiling? At least the camera loves you."

Armie glanced at the Jumbotron and sure enough, his face filled the massive screen. Hamming it up and making Simon happy, Armie put a fist in the air.

The audience roared.

Carter Fletcher walked in to a hard rock song. Some of those cheers were for him. Well deserved, Armie knew.

Cannon, Simon and Havoc were all telling him different things, doing different things.

Armie just wanted out there.

This was how he felt when fighting. Anticipation. Joy. He'd never thought to feel this at the SBC level, but other than how he felt for Rissy now, it was all the same.

This was his zone. A part of who he was.

Cannon said something to him and he nodded, his gaze glued to Carter.

They called a start to the fight. Rules were read and agreed to. He and Carter were both ready.

Armie touched fists with Chaos and they both began the dance.

They exchanged blows and a few kicks, but Armie was timing himself, waiting for an opening. When Carter threw a kick, Armie caught his leg, tucked his ankle into his armpit, and put pressure on the inside of his knee so that Carter went down.

They both scrambled, but Armie hit him once, twice, throwing all his strength behind the punches. Methodical. Fast.

When Chaos shifted, going for a submission, Armie's instinct was to stand back and let him up. But in the back of his mind he remembered what Dakota had told him. Yeah, that was probably the move Chaos expected.

Instead, Armie shifted with him. They rolled, and Armie came up in the dominant position again. He threw an elbow that caught Carter just beneath the brow bone.

A few more blows and Armie had the full mount, free to rain down heavy hits. A cut on Carter's eyelid made a slippery mess that looked a hell of a lot worse than it was. The ref hovered over them, ready to call a halt.

Carter said, "I'm okay," and rather than cover up, he

threw his own punches, leaving his face open to more punishment.

Armie landed yet another elbow, one more—

Suddenly the ref tackled him, saying, "It's over, it's over."

The arena went nuts.

Fists in the air, Armie grinned—for about two seconds before Cannon had him half lifted in the air. Havoc and Simon were there, laughing, clapping him on the back.

The audience stayed on their feet, the cheers nearly deafening.

Bloodied but far from done, Carter sat up cursing, but only for a second. Like any professional he pushed to his feet and allowed the doctors to clear away the blood.

Lights went off in a strobe effect but Armie still found Rissy in the audience. She had her uninjured arm in the air as she shouted her happiness. Bray jumped up and down like a wild monkey.

All in all, it was pretty damned great.

When things finally settled down he went over to talk to Carter, who embraced him. "We need to do this again."

Armie nodded. "Anytime." He lifted Carter's arm and the audience went crazy all over again.

Cannon dragged a shirt over his head and Armie remembered he was supposed to be touting Jude's sports gear. Showing off the shirt, he mugged for the cameras until the commentator pulled him front and center.

At first they talked about the fight—and Armie gave Dakota her due, which made Carter pretend to collapse on the mat. Everyone cracked up over that.

"Seriously," Armie said. "She knows what she's talking about."

Simon put his head in his hands, but he was laughing, too.

"Mostly, I've got great coaches and a best friend who kept me in line and got me ready. A man is only as good as his team."

There were more cheers for that sentiment.

Lastly the commentator asked, "So what's next?"

Armie grinned. "Well, I'm hoping to marry Saint's little sis."

The commentator blinked at him. "What's this? Marriage?"

"She asked and I said yes."

The camera switched to Rissy. Eyes damp and one hand over her mouth, she nodded.

Going with it, the commentator asked, "What does Saint have to say about this?"

As Cannon bounded into the cage, the audience loved it—because they loved him.

When Cannon reached Armie, he put his fists up. Laughing, Armie pretended to duck—then Cannon pulled him into a bear hug.

"So you approve?" the commentator asked him.

"Hell, yeah." His arm draped over Armie's shoulders, Cannon grinned. "I want my sister to have the best. That's Armie."

Armie smiled toward Rissy.

"He's always been my brother," Cannon said. "Now it'll finally be legit."

CURLED IN BED, which happened to be Armie's favorite location with Rissy, they talked about the exclusive he'd be giving tomorrow, which Jude had arranged. What really surprised Armie was finding out that the reporter had received testimonials from the guys at the rec center, from Bray and his parents, from Kizzie and some of the other women.

And even from Lea herself.

Half the neighborhood had wanted it known that he was a good guy. He hadn't realized his heart could hold so much love and appreciation, but damn, he liked it.

Finally, once and for all, the rumors would be destroyed.

After that, they'd segued into wedding plans. Armie couldn't wait to have her tied to him, but he wanted her to have whatever type of wedding she wanted—be it simple or elaborate, large or small.

While she went over her preferences, she seemed to inspect every inch of him, finding marks from his fight that he hadn't been aware of. He didn't complain. Rissy's attention was always a turn-on. He just wasn't sure how much more he could take before tucking her under him and making them both nuts with release.

"So you don't mind if we keep it just our family and friends?"

He didn't have family—except that the guys at the gym were all that and more, better than any blood tie could ever be. "Whatever you want is okay by me."

"So agreeable." She kissed a bruise on his cheekbone. "You looked so handsome in your tux at Cannon's wedding. Would you mind wearing one for ours?" She wrinkled her nose. "I sort of want the fancy white dress."

"You will be killer-hot in a fancy white dress and I

can rock a tux again, no problem." He'd do anything for her, except let her go.

Next she kissed his ribs. "I don't want to assume, but Cannon will be your best man?"

"He's been that since we were in high school, so yeah."

That made her happy and she smiled as she teased her lips over a spot on his abdomen. "Shouldn't we put something on this?"

Grinning, he said, "I can make a suggestion."

"Ice?"

"I was thinking of something warmer. Maybe even hot." Holding her gaze, he trailed a hand down her side to her hip, then in to her still-flat belly and down until he curled his hand over the hottest part of her.

With a sigh, she said, "You are so bad."

"Yeah, but apparently you like me that way."

"I love you—any way you want to be."

Armie carefully turned her under him. Now that a week had passed, her arm was much better and the bruising on her face had faded enough that she could cover it with makeup.

Since they were fresh from the shower, he could make out each faint mark. Her hair fell back, showing the stitches that would come out tomorrow.

Steve, Keno and Boyd were being held without bail. They wouldn't be a problem for Rissy or anyone else for a very long time. Far as Armie was concerned, they could all three rot.

Rather than dwell on that and how it made him feel, he'd rather concentrate on his future with Rissy.

She'd taken the pregnancy test and was, indeed, carrying his baby. His and Cannon's kids would be very close in age.

And they both loved it.

"I need to set an appointment with the tattoo parlor."

She smiled up at him. "For what now?"

"Gotta get the one on my back altered."

Her lips parted and her eyes went wide. "Altered how?"

He'd never explained the significance of that particular tat, but it felt like a good time for spilling the truth. "You hold my heart now, so the thorns have to go."

She blinked. "That was about me?"

"My whole life has been about you, Rissy. For so long, it seemed I could never have what I wanted most."

"Me?"

"Yeah. Hell, I love you so much, you *are* my life."

Her eyes went liquid.

He'd never get used to this weepier side of her, but she claimed it was the pregnancy and he believed her.

"I had a heart," he told her, after kissing away her tears. "But it wasn't free until you forced your way into my apartment and ignored my idiotic objections."

"And I took off my pants."

He smiled. "Yeah, that helped." His hand covered her belly. "You started talking about sex—and spanking—and you destroyed my determination to leave you be."

She softened. "I'm so glad I did."

He cupped her face. "I never knew life could be this good."

"I knew," she bragged. "Why do you think I didn't give up?"

Thank God she hadn't. Ready to tease her, he said, "So since we'll be living here in your house, can I bring over my big mirror? It'd look nice on the wall at the end of your bed."

Rissy pushed him to his back and climbed over him. "No." She took his mouth in a lusty kiss. "But the Velcro handcuffs are welcome."

* * * * *

Leese, Justice, Brand and Miles
from the Ultimate crew
will return in an all-new Body Armor series,
coming soon.

Meanwhile, read on for
an exclusive excerpt of
DON'T TEMPT ME,
a brand-new novel
from Lori Foster
and HQN Books...

HONOR BROWN WASN'T USED to eating with three men. It astounded her how fast the pizza got devoured. But then, she'd pretty much inhaled her own slice, too. Working up a hunger through unpacking all her belongings, it seemed, overshadowed other concerns—like feeling self-conscious and knowing she was an intruder despite her new neighbors' efforts to put her at ease.

They all chatted easily, except for Jason who seemed introspective. He'd gone from staring to teasing, to warning, and now quiet.

At first she'd worried that she might have offended him. But how? Not by asking that he wear a shirt, because that was a request he'd ignored.

The man was still half naked.

And it couldn't have been from accepting his help unloading her furniture, because he was the one who'd bullied his way in and insisted on…being wonderful.

She rubbed at her temples. When she'd imagined neighbors, she'd never imagined any like these.

"You okay?" Jason's nephew Colt asked.

A fast smile, meant to reassure the teen, only amplified the headache. "Yes. Just a little tired."

"She works too much." Lexie shoulder-bumped her. "I've tried to get her to play a little, too, but she's the original party pooper."

Lexie, at least, seemed right at home. But then she always did. Confident, beautiful and fun—that described her best friend.

They were polar opposites.

As if she'd known the guys forever, Lexie had heckled Hogan, teased Colt and praised Jason. Repeatedly she put her head back and drew in deep breaths, closing her eyes as she did so. Honor understood that. It was like being in a park with the scents of freshly mowed lawn, earth, flowers and trees all around them. Jason's backyard was a half acre, same as hers. But while hers was nearly impassable with weeds, his was park perfect.

A gigantic elm kept them shaded, and with the help of an occasional gentle breeze, the summer day became more comfortable. Honor glanced around at the neatly mulched flower beds, the velvet green grass and the well-maintained outdoor furniture. His garage was spectacular, matching his house. Every so often she caught the faint scent of oil, gasoline and sawdust.

She also smelled sun-warmed, hard-working male. Not at all unpleasant.

"Where do you work?" Colt asked.

"She's a stylist," Lexie offered. With a nod at Jason, she said, "Honor could do all sorts of amazing things with your hair."

Honor choked on her last sip of Coke.

Unaffected, Jason ran a hand through the dark waves. "I have a barber, but don't make it there as often as I should."

"He's always working," Colt said. "He's usually out there in the garage before Dad and I even get out of bed."

"Good thing messy looks so sexy on him, then, huh?"

Colt laughed. "If you say so."

"I do." Lexie half turned to face the garage. "You guys have a lot of vehicles."

"The blue truck is mine," Colt told her. "Dad drives the motorcycle. Or when it rains, he takes the Escort. Uncle Jason has his own truck, the red newer one, and the gray SUV. The flatbed truck he uses for deliveries."

Wow, so many vehicles. Honor glanced over and saw that the two-story garage also housed a fishing boat on a trailer, and another, older truck parked front and center.

"Who drives that one?" Lexie asked.

With something close to hero-worship, Colt said, "Uncle Jason was hired to work on it."

"Hired?"

"Yeah, that's what he does. He fixes things. He's really good, too. All these old houses? They're always needing something repaired and usually Uncle Jason can do it. Everyone around Clearbrook hires him for stuff."

"Sounds like it keeps him busy."

Colt snorted. "Yeah, sometimes too busy."

"I don't mind." Jason's gaze cut to Honor and his voice deepened. "I enjoy working with my hands."

Honor felt like he'd just stroked her. She caught her breath, shifted in her seat and tried to think of something to say.

Clearly tickled, Lexie looked back and forth between them. "So you're a handyman?"

Again, Colt bragged. "More like a contractor. He can build things from the ground up, including the plumbing and electrical. Or make stuff like custom gates or unique shutters, or repair just about anything."

"Nice," Lexie praised.

"He's a jack-of-all-trades." Hogan toasted Jason with his Coke. "Whatever's broke, Jason can fix it."

Jason gave him a long look. "Maybe not everything."

"Right. Can't fix big brothers, can you?"

Tipping his head slightly back, as if he'd taken that on the chin, Jason replied, "I only have one older brother, and far as I'm concerned, he's not broken."

Colt went silent, and God, Honor felt for him. Too many times she, too, had been caught up in the middle of squabbles.

"So with the truck," Lexie said, interrupting the heavy tension, "are you doing engine or body work?"

Before Jason could answer, Hogan said, "Why are you so curious, anyway?"

Lexie leveled him with a direct stare. "I was making conversation."

With a sound halfway between a laugh and a groan, Hogan sat forward. "We already covered that he can do anything."

"Anything is a big word. I mean, can he get the stick out of your butt? Because seriously, you're being a pill."

"He does both," Colt cut in, clearly anxious to keep things friendly. "Uncle Jason I mean. You asked about the truck?"

Lexie gave Colt a genuine smile. "So I did."

"He does body and engine work. But this time Uncle Jason's just tricking it out some."

Honor watched the back and forth conversation, noting the indulgent way Jason looked at his nephew, while also feeling the growing tension from Hogan. But why?

The quiet smothered her, especially with the palpable acrimony now flowing between Hogan and Lexie. After clearing her throat, Honor asked, "Is that what we interrupted when we first got here? You were working on the truck?"

Jason shook his head. "Tractor." He nodded toward the side of the garage. "The owner of the truck is making up his mind between two options I gave him. Today I was repairing the tractor, but it needs a part I won't have until tomorrow. I'm at a standstill on both projects so you didn't really interrupt. I was already done for the day."

Hogan ran a hand over his face, popped his neck and finally worked up a smile. "He built the garage a few years back."

"You helped," Jason reminded him.

"By *help*, he means I followed directions. No idea where Jason got the knack because our dad wasn't the handy sort. But if there's an upside to us staying with him right now, it's that he's teaching Colt."

"And Colt does appear to have the knack," Jason added.

Both Honor and Lexie looked at the garage with new eyes. Wow. Just…wow.

"It's unlike any garage I've ever seen."

"You should see the shed he did for Sullivan," Colt bragged. "And the gazebo for Nathan."

"Sullivan and Nathan?" Lexie perked up with interest.

"Other neighbors," Honor said before Lexie could get started. She pushed to her feet while saying, "This was really wonderful. Thank you again, all of you."

When she started to pick up their paper plates, Colt took over. "I got it."

Unbelievable. She'd never known such a polite young man. "Are you sure?"

He grinned, looking like a younger version of his uncle. "Positive. It all just goes to the can." He gathered up everything and walked off.

Honor turned to Hogan. "You did an amazing job with him."

"Thanks. He's always been an easy kid. Smart, friendly and self-motivated."

Again, Honor wondered about Colt's mother. Had she taken a hand in molding such an impressive young man?

Hogan said, "I need to take off now, too."

"Big date?" The way Lexie asked that, it was clear to one and all she didn't expect it to be.

"Actually," Hogan said, "yes."

In an effort to stem new hostilities, Honor stepped in front of her friend. "I hope we didn't hold you up."

"Nope. I have a few minutes yet." His frown moved past Honor to Lexie. "Guess I need to go change, though."

Laughing, Lexie asked, "Need fashion advice?"

His dark expression softened. "I think I've got it covered."

She nodded while yawning. "I need to get going, too."

"Gotta catch up on your beauty sleep?"

Honor almost groaned…until Lexie laughed again.

"Good one," she said, and then she held up her palm, leaving Hogan no choice but to high-five her. To Jason, she teased, "The differences aren't just in looks, I take it."

Jason lifted a brow. "No, they aren't."

Without comment, Hogan headed off for the house.

"Well." Honor watched everyone depart. Hogan went into the house from the back door. Lexie headed off to the rental truck. And Colt hadn't returned from taking away their trash.

She and Jason were alone and with every fiber of her being, she felt it. Hoping not to be too obvious, she took a step back, then another. "I should get going, too. I need to drop off the truck tonight so I can get my car back. After I run Lexie home, I need to stop at the grocery. It's going to take me a few hours to get back here, and I still have to get things set up for the morning."

"What kind of things?"

"Alarm clock, coffee, and I have to unpack enough clothes to get ready for work in the morning."

He had been looking down at the ground as they walked, but now his head lifted and he stared at her. "You have to work tomorrow?"

"Yes." But it wasn't a matter of having to. "I'll be taking all the hours I can get for a while. There are so many things I want to do to the house, but it all takes funds." Funds she didn't have. What money she'd saved would go to dire necessities, so overtime helped to pay for the extras she wanted.

"You have to be tired."

"A little." She rolled her aching shoulders, but resisted the long stretch. "I'm both excited and exhausted and I don't know if I'd be able to sleep anyway."

"Excited?"

There were a hundred different reasons for her excitement and one of those reasons was standing before her. Jason Guthrie was about the sexiest man she'd ever met. His careless hair, strong features, dark eyes and that body... Yup. The body definitely factored in.

But she also liked his intense focus, the way he smiled with pleasure at his nephew, and his up-front honesty. That honesty had stung a little, since he clearly felt she was out of her league. Then again, he'd pitched in and done what he could to make her move-in easier.

How could she not admire him?

Naturally she wouldn't say any of that to him, so instead she shared other thoughts. "The move, the house—now that it's officially mine and I'm here, there are a million things running through my mind. What to do first, how much money I'll need, how to do it and when to do it." She smiled up at him. "Tonight, I might just dance around and enjoy it all."

"Yeah? Well, since you don't have curtains yet, I might watch."

She laughed at his teasing. "After I get the windows covered, then I'll dance."

His smile warmed. "Spoilsport."

Their shoulders bumped, electrifying Honor. She took a step to the side, ensuring it wouldn't happen again.

"I get it," Jason told her. "First big night in your own place." Lifting a brow, he added, "And yeah, curtains might not be a bad idea. Or at least tack up a sheet or something."

Maybe, Honor thought, he didn't dislike her as a neighbor as much as she'd assumed.

Stopping in the side yard, well out of range of everyone else, Honor looked up at him. Way up because he was so much taller than her.

He stopped, too, his expression attentive.

She shouldn't ask, but she had to. "When we first met…when I hit your trash can?"

"I told you, no big deal."

"I know, but…is that why you kept staring at me?"

Those gorgeous dark eyes caressed her face. He glanced toward Colt, then over to watch Lexie climb into the passenger seat of the truck.

Finally his gaze came back to hers, and the impact took her breath.

"For one thing," he said in a low voice, "you're attractive."

Without thinking about it, Honor smoothed her ponytail and tucked a few loose tendrils behind her ears. "Um, thank you. But I'm such a mess today."

His gaze warmed even more. "Messy and a mess are two very different things."

That deep voice made her pulse race. She was such an inexperienced dweeb, she wasn't sure how to respond, so she just nodded and said, "Okay."

A fleeting smile teased his mouth before he grew somber. "I also recognize trouble when I see it."

She tucked in her chin. "Trouble?"

"You."

"Me?" The question emerged as a squeak.

"You don't fit the mold, Honor Brown. Not even close."

A rush of umbrage helped to steady her voice. "What's that supposed to mean?"

"A certain type of person moves here. Not just to the area, but to this particular block. Mostly single men who can handle themselves. Men with some contractor skills, with time and ability to do the repairs needed. Young women—"

"I'm twenty-nine!"

"—who are completely alone do not set up house here."

It hurt to know he was right, that she was alone. She had Lexie, but it wasn't the same as a significant other or family who cared. She huffed, then deflated. "Well, this sucks."

He hesitated, but finally asked, "What does?"

Putting her nose in the air, Honor stared into his beautiful brown eyes. "I haven't even finished moving in, and already I dislike my neighbor."

On that parting remark, she turned and strode away. But her heart was thumping and her hands felt clammy and her stomach hurt.

She was never that rude. *What in the world got into me?*

Right before she reached the truck she glanced over her shoulder and saw Jason still standing there, hands on his hips, that laser-like gaze boring into her.

Damn it. She turned to fully face him. "Jason?"

His chin notched up in query.

"I apologize. I didn't mean it." Immediately she felt better—even with Lexie now laughing at her.

Jason's hands fell to his sides and he dropped his head forward. She saw his shoulders moving.

Laughing? She wasn't sure.

But she smiled and started to turn away again.

"Honor."

She peeked at him and found his hands were back on his hips.

"You're still trouble, no doubt about it. But if you need anything, let me know."

Sure. When hell froze over. She smiled sweetly, waved and finally got in the truck.

Vengeful Love

by

LAURA CARTER

He's a devastatingly handsome, filthy-rich CEO.
She's a high-flying London lawyer.
All it takes is one boardroom pitch. One hostile takeover…

This darkly suspenseful, sinfully sexy white-collar romance
will be available in ebook March 2016.
Use coupon code **VLCP30** to save 30% on your purchase of
VENGEFUL LOVE at CarinaPress.com.

Offer valid March 21–April 30, 2016. One time use per customer.
Offer not valid in conjunction with any other discount or promotion.

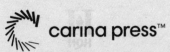

www.CarinaPress.com

CARLC427

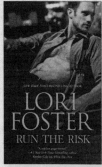

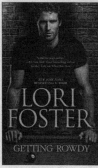
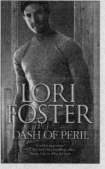

REQUEST YOUR FREE BOOKS!

2 FREE NOVELS
FROM THE SUSPENSE COLLECTION
PLUS 2 FREE GIFTS!

YES! Please send me 2 FREE novels from the Suspense Collection and my 2 FREE gifts (gifts are worth about $10). After receiving them, if I don't wish to receive any more books, I can return the shipping statement marked "cancel." If I don't cancel, I will receive 4 brand-new novels every month and be billed just $6.49 per book in the U.S. or $6.99 per book in Canada. That's a savings of at least 19% off the cover price. It's quite a bargain! Shipping and handling is just 50¢ per book in the U.S. and 75¢ per book in Canada.* I understand that accepting the 2 free books and gifts places me under no obligation to buy anything. I can always return a shipment and cancel at any time. Even if I never buy another book, the two free books and gifts are mine to keep forever.

191/391 MDN GH4Z

Name	(PLEASE PRINT)	
Address		Apt. #
City	State/Prov.	Zip/Postal Code

Signature (if under 18, a parent or guardian must sign)

Mail to the **Reader Service**:
IN U.S.A.: P.O. Box 1867, Buffalo, NY 14240-1867
IN CANADA: P.O. Box 609, Fort Erie, Ontario L2A 5X3

Want to try two free books from another line?
Call 1-800-873-8635 or visit www.ReaderService.com.

* Terms and prices subject to change without notice. Prices do not include applicable taxes. Sales tax applicable in N.Y. Canadian residents will be charged applicable taxes. Offer not valid in Quebec. This offer is limited to one order per household. Not valid for current subscribers to the Suspense Collection or the Romance/Suspense Collection. All orders subject to credit approval. Credit or debit balances in a customer's account(s) may be offset by any other outstanding balance owed by or to the customer. Please allow 4 to 6 weeks for delivery. Offer available while quantities last.

Your Privacy—The Reader Service is committed to protecting your privacy. Our Privacy Policy is available online at www.ReaderService.com or upon request from the Reader Service.

We make a portion of our mailing list available to reputable third parties that offer products we believe may interest you. If you prefer that we not exchange your name with third parties, or if you wish to clarify or modify your communication preferences, please visit us at www.ReaderService.com/consumerchoice or write to us at Reader Service Preference Service, P.O. Box 9062, Buffalo, NY 14240-9062. Include your complete name and address.

SUS15

LORI FOSTER

78905	WHEN YOU DARE	___ $7.99 U.S.	___ $8.99 CAN.
77816	HOT IN HERE	___ $7.99 U.S.	___ $8.99 CAN.
77761	BARE IT ALL	___ $7.99 U.S.	___ $9.99 CAN.
77708	THE BUCKHORN LEGACY	___ $7.99 U.S.	___ $9.99 CAN.
77695	RUN THE RISK	___ $7.99 U.S.	___ $9.99 CAN.
77656	A PERFECT STORM	___ $7.99 U.S.	___ $9.99 CAN.
77647	FOREVER BUCKHORN	___ $7.99 U.S.	___ $9.99 CAN.
77612	BUCKHORN BEGINNINGS	___ $7.99 U.S.	___ $9.99 CAN.
77582	SAVOR THE DANGER	___ $7.99 U.S.	___ $9.99 CAN.
77575	TRACE OF FEVER	___ $7.99 U.S.	___ $9.99 CAN.
77444	TEMPTED	___ $7.99 U.S.	___ $9.99 CAN.

(limited quantities available)

TOTAL AMOUNT	$ _____
POSTAGE & HANDLING	$ _____
($1.00 FOR 1 BOOK, 50¢ for each additional)	
APPLICABLE TAXES*	$ _____
TOTAL PAYABLE	$ _____

(check or money order—please do not send cash)

To order, complete this form and send it, along with a check or money order for the total above, payable to HQN Books, to: **In the U.S.:** 3010 Walden Avenue, P.O. Box 9077, Buffalo, NY 14269-9077; **In Canada:** P.O. Box 636, Fort Erie, Ontario, L2A 5X3.

Name: _____
Address: _____ City: _____
State/Prov.: _____ Zip/Postal Code: _____
Account Number (if applicable): _____

075 CSAS

*New York residents remit applicable sales taxes.
*Canadian residents remit applicable GST and provincial taxes.

HQN™

www.HQNBooks.com   PHLF0216BL